DEATH OF A BOOKSELLER

DEATH OF A
BOOKSELLER

ALICE SLATER

SCARLET
NEW YORK

DEATH OF A BOOKSELLER

Scarlet Press
An Imprint of Penzler Publishers
58 Warren Street
New York, N.Y. 10007

First Scarlet Press edition

Interior design by Maria Fernandez

Library of Congress Control Number: 2022917428

ISBN: 978-1-61316-377-1
eBook ISBN:978-1-61316-378-8

10 9 8 7 6 5 4 3 2 1

Printed in the United States of America
Distributed by W. W. Norton & Company

For my father, Nick

"There is an attraction to the repulsive."
—David Wilson, *A History of British Serial Killing*

PROLOGUE

Laura Bunting. Her name was garden parties and Wimbledon and royal weddings. It was chintzy tea rooms, Blitz spirit, and bric-a-brac for sale in bright church halls. It was coconut shies and bake sales and guess-the-weight-of-the-fucking-cake.

Pale skin, blonde bob, hazel eyes. Curvy, around five foot four in flats. A scatter of chocolate moles on her chest, neck, and arms. A silver stud in her left nostril, a pinprick scar from a healed piercing on the right side of her lower lip. Her upper arms and calves were inked with faded, clichéd tattoos: an anchor, a mermaid, a rose in bloom; a pair of swallows in flight, one on each shoulder, swooping towards her heart; a posy of lavender on her inner wrist.

Laura, with her vintage tea dresses, her berets, her crimson lipstick. Hand-rolled cigarettes, rose oil perfume that lingered.

Laura, with her poetry.

Laura, with her tragedy.

Oh, how the rest of the team just loved their precious Laura. There was nothing she wouldn't do, no section she couldn't wrangle. Business? A pleasure. History? Easy. Even the dullest jobs were transformed into breezy tasks when Laura did them: she cleared trolleys, she priced up boxes of pocket-money toys, she shelved the most obscure books.

She turned the Sunday morning vacuuming into a quick, light-footed waltz around the shop floor, flipping off the hoover to chat and laugh with booksellers as she passed. It seemed like she had something to say to everyone, some little in-joke or snippet of news that made her think of them. She slotted in so neatly, like she'd been away for a long time and the shop was pleased to have her back.

We had a connection, although she was too arrogant to lean into it. With me, she was just curt nods and clipped words and pursed lips, a frank look of dislike plastered over her face. She shrugged off my attempts to bond, took no interest in our shared history. In fact, she spent most of our shifts together looking straight through me, walking past the till without so much as a glance in my direction.

By Christmas, Laura Bunting was gone. And it was my fault.

SEPTEMBER 2019

ROACH

The neon lights that topped the dome of Brixton Academy glowed like the projectile vomit from *The Exorcist*. It was a little after six and the normies were already queueing, a thick vein that snaked around the corner and into the growing darkness, past overflowing industrial bins, stacks of crushed cardboard boxes, and slicks of piss that trickled into the gutter.

Clots of women chatted as they checked their lipstick in hand-mirrors and snapped cheerful, blank-eyed selfies. They were the kind of girls who felt a shiver of excitement as summer gave way to autumn, when Starbucks launched their seasonal menu, and it was time to wear scarves, tights, and leather boots. Pumpkin Spice Girls loved true crime podcasts these days. True crime was mainstream, and PSGs loved to clap their hands over anything that was quirky-but-mainstream. Drag queens, Halloween, astrology. That kind of shit.

The *Murder Girls* drew a different energy to the metal bands I usually went to see at Brixton Academy, where the crowd was rougher, tougher. I felt more at home surrounded by battered biker jackets and combat boots than I did with Zara dresses and publishing tote bags.

I joined the back of the queue behind two student types, plain girls with long limp hair dressed in ironic charity shop chic. One wore an oversized tartan shirt and ugly '80s glasses that reminded me of Jeffrey Dahmer, while the other wore a black T-shirt that said *I wonder if serial killers think about me as much as I think about them?* in girly pink calligraphy.

"If they do Ted Bundy," Dahmer Glasses said to the other, "I'll fucking die."

"They did Ted Bundy," her friend replied. "Like, two years ago."

"Yeah, but so much has happened since then."

So much had happened since *when*? I bristled. Ted Bundy was dead, executed by electric chair by the state of Florida in 1989. These fake fans had no idea what they were talking about. I made a derisive scoffing noise and, startled by the interruption, they turned to look at me. They shared matching looks of distaste as they took in my purple hair, my clothes, my whole dark vibe.

"What?" Dahmer Glasses snapped.

"Ted Bundy died," I explained slowly, like she was very stupid, "*like*, thirty years ago."

They exchanged uneasy glances, and then Dahmer Glasses said: "So?"

"So, realistically, how much more could have happened to a dead man?" I was being sarcastic, but then something occurred to me. What if there had been a development—a fresh angle, or some new information, and I'd missed it? With a flutter of excitement, I took a step towards her. "Wait, *has* something happened? Have they connected him to a cold case?"

"I was talking about the film," she said, taking a step back. Her friend brightened as I deflated.

"Ah, Zac Efron!"

"*Exactly*!"

With that established, they turned their backs on me and continued their conversation about *Extremely Wicked, Shockingly Evil and Vile* at a much lower volume. I wished I had a friend with me, a partner in crime to make the whole thing more bearable. I'd mutter something like,

"Hope they cover Zac Efron!" in a silly girly voice and we'd stifle our mean laughter.

Instead, I plugged in my headphones to listen to yesterday's episode again. I usually listened to every episode twice because I always missed stuff the first time around. The *Murder Girls* never scripted their shows, so there was always an edge of spontaneity, and each live show was unique. They only ever posted one live episode per tour, so if you weren't at every show, you'd never know what you'd missed from the others. The only way to catch everything—every joke and every anecdote, every story and every detail of every murder—was to go to as many shows as possible. I'd always wanted to follow them on tour, maybe catch them in Birmingham or Manchester as well as London, but the tickets cost a bomb and I never had the cash to book more than one at a time.

The queue shifted forward as fans started to trickle into the venue. When I reached the front, I held out my phone to the bouncer, at least six foot two with a shaved head, who scanned my e-ticket. A wiry woman with a lined face and a dyed red ponytail patted me down. She peeked into my bag in case I was trying to sneak in a bottle of Prosecco, or whatever basic crap normies drink when they're trying to have a good time.

Before I could think about trailing them, the Bundy simps vanished into the crowd. Although their vapid chat was enough to make my brain atrophy, I liked to follow people. The force consumed me, as Bundy himself said, and it gave me a sense of purpose to walk in someone else's shadow. Sometimes, I'd follow customers around the shop, just to see how long I could track them. Sometimes, I'd follow strangers in the street, just to see what they were doing, where they were going. Where they lived.

I felt conspicuously alone as I made my way through the foyer. The air smelled like Lush, sweet and cloying, a mingling of perfumes and body sprays, hair products and creams. Bubbly women clustered together, with mini bottles of pink wine and plastic cups from the bar, calling to one another, throwing their arms around each other in performative displays of affection. I caught snippets of conversation as I squeezed between cliques. They name-dropped high-profile serial killers like friends, like influencers, like pop stars.

"Nilsen? I'm sick of him."

"Everyone's done Manson this year."

"If they do Jack the Ripper, I swear to God I'll kill myself."

"We're due a good Gein."

Over at the merch stand, a huge display of T-shirts had attracted a hum of fans, buzzing like bluebottles over a shallow grave. I joined the scrum, used my elbows, trod on feet, twisted between friends, and forced my way to the front. I came away with two *Murder Girls* T-shirts, an enamel pin badge, a postcard set and a beanie hat—a good score. The merch always sold out before the end of the show. The total came to over seventy quid, but this was an early Christmas present to myself and, for once, I had the money ready to spend. I pressed through the crowd to the auditorium, showed my e-ticket to a young woman with an undercut on the door and was pointed to the right-hand side of the stalls. At the bar, I stopped for a couple cans of Dark Fruits and then found my seat, wedged between two women who both took one look and turned away to chat to their friends. Fuck those bitches. I settled in, snapped open my first can, and took a sweet sip of dark berry cider.

The *Murder Girls* came onstage a little before seven-thirty to rapturous applause. Claudia was beautiful in crushed black velvet, her long red curls shimmering copper under the spotlights. She waved both arms high above her head, and old-fashioned leg-of-mutton sleeves puffed from her shoulders like those of a Victorian widow. Sarah played the rebel in a white T-shirt with rolled-up sleeves that showed off her tattoos; she wore yellow tartan jeans and unlaced Doc Martens, black with yellow stitches. I made a mental note to look for a pair of boots just like that on eBay: black with yellow stitches, properly battered and worn in. The crowd wolf-whistled and whooped, and the noise ricocheted around the old theatre while the girls smiled and waved, blinking against the bright lights of the stage.

"Rock 'n' roll," Sarah yelled in her deep Southern drawl, extending her index and little fingers into an ironic sign of the horns. "What's up, London!"

The audience clapped, cheered, screamed. The *Murder Girls* soaked up their love, basked in it for a moment, and then settled themselves for the show, perched on high stools on either side of a table set with their notes, bottles of water, and beers.

Live shows always started the same: a breezy chat about their trip, anecdotes and in-jokes that reflected the sisterly nature of their bond. Just a little colour to summarise how the tour was going, as though their fans weren't following their every move online.

"So, listen," Sarah said, leaning forward and speaking into her microphone with a conspiratorial lilt. She paused for effect, and then asked: "Y'all ever heard of the Stow Strangler?"

The room erupted into a cascade of applause and a thrill of recognition shuddered through me, an electric current strong enough to reanimate the dead. I sat up straighter, leaned forward in my seat and fought against a desperate urge to raise my hand: *me, yes, me, I have.*

Sarah took the lead on this one. She got a few things wrong, but I forgave her because she was from New Orleans and didn't understand that London had boroughs, not districts or wards, and that we called it the Tube, not the subway. There was also some confusion about Walthamstow Village, which they seemed to think was an actual village outside of London, instead of just a particularly picturesque, residential part of Walthamstow.

But she got the meat of the story right, and that's what mattered. She told the whole thing methodically: it was June 2009, the weather dry and warm. By summer's end, five women were dead, each attacked by a stranger, strangled to death with a ligature looped around their throats.

They glossed over each of the dead women's lives, and I fidgeted in my seat, waiting for the good bit. Who they were and where they came from and how they ended up in Walthamstow Village late at night didn't really matter, it all blurred into one—but I snapped to attention as the girls detailed each death meticulously: broken fingernails, bruises, signs of a struggle.

The first was found by an early morning dog walker in Saint Mary's churchyard, laid out to rest as though she were sleeping on one of the old, cracked tombs. The second was found by late-night revellers on the patch of grass opposite the Ancient House, a timber-framed home built in the fifteenth century. The third was sprawled on the church path that snaked behind Vestry House, then another was found in the churchyard, this time propped against the church itself.

"Can we just pause to talk about how *awesome* these place names are?" Claudia said, glowing with the absurdity of it all.

"Right? Like, Vinegar Alley?" said Sarah. "What is this, plague times?"

It was all coming back to me—the quiet streets, the crack of high heels on stone, the air thick with the threat of summer rain as night crawled over the horizon. We grew up quickly that summer. At fourteen, I was learning how to move through the world as a woman, to study the shadows, to look over my shoulder, to scan the streets for strangers who might be lurking behind parked cars or hiding in bushes.

"Vulnerable women, right?" Sarah said with cold authority. "Women who'd been let down by society and let down by the state, and then they were let down by the cops who didn't give enough of a shit about their deaths to investigate them properly. They were let down by every single institution that was meant to lift them up."

"But everything changed," Claudia said, her eyes shining, "when the Stow Strangler attacked Karina Cordovan."

Karina Cordovan, the last Stow Strangler victim, was discovered slumped down Vinegar Alley, the ligature still wrapped around her throat. Karina Cordovan wasn't homeless, or an alcoholic, or an addict, or a sex worker. She was a local businesswoman, a mother, an active member of the community, out for a late-night run. The death of Karina Cordovan marked the end of the killings and the start of the investigation.

"Suddenly, it's like everyone realised maybe they should try to catch this fucker before he kills anyone else," said Sarah.

She put forward a theory about where the investigation went wrong—the stop and start of it, the lack of interest, the bumbling police and the scandal with the fumbled CCTV, the confusion about whether it was the same man behind all five murders. Claudia took the role of devil's advocate, picking holes in Sarah's argument. It was a lighthearted debate, explored from every angle, even though the conclusion was foregone—we knew it was Lee Frost, we knew he was a police officer, we knew that he got life in prison for the murder of Karina Cordovan and three of the four other victims, that he was rotting behind bars in HMP Frankland. At this, some girls clapped and cheered as though they were hearing the story for the first time—a frank display of ignorance that embarrassed me. Any true crime fan worth their salt knew this story.

"For me, it comes down to this," Sarah said in her conclusion voice—slow, deliberate, commanding. Had it already been an hour? She placed her empty beer bottle on the table and stood up to address her audience. "In 2009, a woman lost her life, and the cops didn't do shit to find the man who did it 'cause they didn't think she mattered. And by not catching that fuckin' asshole sooner, another woman lost her life, and then a third, and then a fourth, and then finally a fifth. Four more women lost their lives, four more families were torn apart."

A few boos and jeers bloomed from the braying crowd.

"That fuckin' asshole has kids," she said, her kohl-lined eyes glittering with a minor threat of tears that would never break because although she was passionate, her conviction was stronger than her sadness. "He still gets to see them grow up, he gets to have Christmases and birthdays, and, one day? He may even be free to kill again."

A tingle of pleasure shivered through my body. I leaned forward in my seat, ready to mouth along to the final words of every show.

"But listen, you piece of shit, you fuckin' asshole," she said, now repeating a variation of the mantra that concluded each episode. "So long as we live and breathe, we will never stop talking about what you did. You will *never* be free and we will *never* forget, and—" Sarah raised a hand in the air, fingers curled into the sign of the horns once more, and we all took a deep, collective breath to shout the last five words in unison: "we'll—see—you—in—*hell*!"

Applause thundered through the theatre, a storm of it, a pounding of hands, a stampede of feet. Women whooped, women jeered, women screamed, and I was there with them, whooping and jeering and screaming too, part of the crowd, united by the moment.

"We are the *Murder Girls*!" Claudia shouted into the mic, her voice knelling like a bell through the din. "And you've been gorgeous! Love you, London, thank you and goodnight!"

The applause swelled to a crescendo, and when a thatch of girls near the front jumped to their feet, I joined them in a standing ovation, smacking my hands together until my palms were hot and stinging, stamping my feet until it felt as though the entire auditorium would collapse under the weight of our love, our passion, our thirst for justice.

LAURA

I make myself a wholesome breakfast to undo some of last night's damage. Freshly squeezed orange juice, black coffee. A soft-poached egg, with half an avocado spread on sourdough, topped with plenty of cracked black pepper. A zingy squeeze of lime over the avo, and a splash of hot sauce on the egg, because I crave the sting of it, the burn.

In the shower, I turn the temperature up until the water is as hot as I can bear. A violet shampoo keeps the brassiness of my hair at bay, and a thick conditioner that smells like a vanilla milkshake keeps it soft. I exfoliate with a tropical body wash on a bath mitt, and when I step out of the spray, the steam that rises from my skin smells sweet as a smoothie, just the way I like it. It's cold, but it's too early to switch the heating on. Last year, I made it all the way to Christmas.

I dry off and smooth an almond-scented moisturiser over my arms and legs. Picturing my day unspooling, I flip through my rail of dresses and skirts, choosing an outfit with care. I need to be comfortable and flexible, but stylish too. A black and white striped Bardot top that shows off my collarbones, a scarlet skirt, sheer black tights, forest-green flats, and a green beret that's a perfect match for my shoes. Nice and neat and well put together. I blow-dry my hair, apply light makeup and dab a little rose oil behind each ear so that everyone I greet today will be met with the warming, welcoming floral scent of love.

In an ink-stained tote bag, I pack everything I need for an easy, organised day: phone and charger, purse, door keys, lipstick, lip balm, hand cream, lighter, tobacco, and Rizla rolling papers. I'm currently working on a poem, so I bring everything I need for that too: the source material, my poetry notebook, Post-it notes, and a couple pencils. I pick a can of sugar-free, locally produced cherry seltzer, and a Tupperware of orzo salad for my lunch. Sharona may want to go out for lunch, but I can always leave the salad in the fridge for tomorrow.

Before I go, I press my fingertips into the soil of my monstera, checking for moisture. It feels a little too dry for my liking, so I fill a delicate glass mister with tap water and spritz the crumbly soil. While I'm here, I water the rest of the plants that line the windowsill too. Pretty, leafy things that filter the air and make my cramped galley kitchen look and feel like a bright little greenhouse.

I set off early, making the most of the morning sun while it's still with us, before the wretched winter skies take over. Walking to work makes a nice change. I stroll through the park and listen to a retro playlist of American folk, and as Joni Mitchell sings about heading home, I think about the rhythm of my feet on the cracked path, and of Patti Smith walking through the streets of New York, and of Joan Didion in Sacramento, and how each footstep is another connection between me and my neighbourhood, the streets on which I learned to ride a bike, where I walked hand in hand with my mother, and that despite all the pain, and the loss, and the grief, I'm tethered to Walthamstow because she still exists in the fabric of it, a ghost imprinted on every familiar sight. She knew these streets, these trees, these bricks, these bollards. These paving stones remember the bounce of her running shoes. I still can't quite bring myself to walk past her old shop, even though it's changed hands at least three times in the last decade, so I take the long way round instead.

When I reach the mouth of Walthamstow Market, I stop to roll a cigarette, which I think is very French of me, and then take a meander past the fruit and veg stalls, the cries of the market sellers as they call, "Pound a bowl, pound a bowl!" punctuating every step. Women in salwar kameez, colourful dupattas draped over their heads and shoulders, browse stalls selling discount cookware, knockoff designer perfume, silver jewellery, and reams of fabric, ribbon, and lace. The morning smells like the rotisserie chickens that turn slowly on spits, their skins already a golden shade of brown.

Bookshops have always felt like home. There were two independent bookshops on the high street when I was little. My mother and I called them "the Marble Shop" and "the Grown-up Shop." The Grown-up Shop was a general bookshop specialising in adult fiction and nonfiction alike. It was very beige—popcorn-coloured walls, a light biscuit carpet. All I knew then was that it was boring, full of adult books with dull covers, and that the Marble Shop was magical, a treasure trove of joy and colour. It sold children's books and toys, and the walls were painted a Cadbury purple and the bookcases were an electric orange, the cartoony palette of Nickelodeon.

The Marble Shop was owned by a man I thought of as elderly due to his grey hair, long wiry eyebrows and tufts that sprouted from each nostril, but who was probably only in his forties. He wore loose woven shirts, the same kind the hippy music teacher at school wore, and a little gold ring in his left earlobe. He always smelled like Juicy Fruit gum, and I liked him because he was happy to let me take a marble from his display with every book I bought. As much as I liked books, I was particularly fond of the huge spinner of marbles, which were my childhood currency. As my library grew, so did my marble collection. My favourite was totally clear with an iridescent patina, like a dragonfly's wing. I still have it somewhere, although I think of it as an homage to Margaret Atwood's *Cat's Eye*—the exact kind of book I'd never imagined I'd be drawn to as a child. Like blue cheese or anchovies, literary fiction was a taste that children had to grow into.

Spines Walthamstow is right at the end of the market, a deep burgundy shopfront squeezed between a betting shop and a Costa. When I reach the bookshop, I stand for a minute and finish my cigarette, eyeing the tired window displays. Beyond the smudged glass, the books are sun-bleached and falling over, as though they haven't been updated in some time. A dead fly lies prone in the sun.

When this branch first opened, back in the late '90s, with its huge range and big windows full of discounted books, the Grown-up Shop couldn't compete and closed down within a couple years. Eventually the Marble Shop disappeared as well, although by the time it closed its doors, everything had changed. I was a different person, and I'd lost more than my interest in marbles.

ROACH

On my way to work, I listened to a podcast about an Indonesian serial killer who strangled women in a mystic ritual of his own devising. The hosts were a trio of loudmouthed men who cracked jokes and talked over one another as they pieced together the story. As a spiritual healer, women trusted Ahmad Suradji. They trusted him enough to follow him into the sugarcane fields that surrounded his home and let him bury them up to their waists. There, he strangled them, and reburied them with their faces pointing towards the place where he slept, in the hope that he could channel their energy and bolster his magical strength. Even though their final place of rest was either supine or prone, I imagined a field of skeletal dead women still buried up to the waist, their skulls turned towards him like flowers pointing to the sun.

It was chilly. Still buzzing from the live show, I'd dressed up a little in one of my new *Murder Girls* T-shirts, but if it was cold outside, it would be cold inside the bookshop too. I added a second layer in the form of a black shirt and attached a pin shaped like a bloody butcher knife to the lapel. Little details. Always make sure you're remembered for the right reasons. That's what my mum Jackie liked to say when I was little, although she usually hissed it as an admonition when I was doing something she

15

didn't like in front of the regulars, like letting snails slime their way along my bare arm or talking with authority about cholera, bubonic plague, or leprosy with their children. I went through a big bacterial infections phase when I was a kid.

I've always had a thing for death. It started with *Horrible Histories*, books full of rot and squalor, bloody executions, and archaic medical practices that delighted and revolted me in equal measure. They were well-thumbed library books, and while my classmates seemed happy to flick through them for school projects and forget about them once they had what they needed, I dreamed of the gallows, of leeches and lobotomies. All children were morbid, but I wore it better.

As a little girl, I was often left out. I was rarely invited for tea at other girls" houses, and they didn't want me at their sleepovers due to my peculiar disposition. On the other hand, birthday parties were a numbers game for seven-year-olds, and I'd often find myself trapped at prissy little princess parties on Saturday afternoons.

I was always struck by how very present other children were in their homes. Swimming certificates and artwork pinned to the fridge with magnets shaped like fried eggs, ice lollies, letters of the alphabet. They had toys scattered on the floor, little bits of plastic underfoot, Barbies and stuffed animals stashed under the sofa, Disney DVDs stacked around the TV, yellow mackintoshes and sparkly jelly shoes and wellies shaped like frogs by the front door. There wasn't much room at home in the pub for jelly shoes and alphabites, and Jackie didn't take many photos of me, or display my artwork on our fridge. In fact, she tended to sweep me and my interests under the carpet.

It was lonely, but books made good company. My favourites were the *Point Horror* series because I desperately wanted to be a teenager. I understood that that was when you really started living, and being an American teenager appeared to come with a certain glamour. When I was a kid, it seemed like everything good happened in America, like cheerleading, and yearbooks, and proms, Satanism and the Manson family. I pictured myself hanging out at the mall, at the drive-in, at the ice-skating rink, with friends with names like Stacy and Chuck, and one of them would be murdered, and I'd go on dates with a boy with dark flashing eyes who would leave sinister messages for me to discover through increasingly complicated means: photos with the eyes scratched out, lipstick threats scrawled on the bathroom mirror, a rigged showerhead that sprayed fake blood.

As I walked, the sun battled through soft grey clouds the colour of crematory ash. Across the street, Abbi was walking towards me, her head bowed as she raked through her handbag. She worked at the travel agents, and we regularly passed each other on our way to work. She always did this little dance of aversion, as if I had any interest in talking to her about her bland boyfriend or her holiday plans or whatever normie bullshit she thought would make her interesting to me. I called her name and waved anyway, and she raised her eyes and offered a brittle nod in return.

Abbi's family home was on the same side street as the pub, and when we were kids her parents were regulars, although they seemed to prefer one of the more gentrified establishments now. When the murders began to hit the news in earnest, they were anxious about Abbi's safety and our mums made us promise to walk home together. For the last few weeks of the summer term, I was finally living my *Point Horror* fantasy: the news was full of death, the neighbourhood was afraid, and I had something that resembled a friendship, even though Abbi continued to ignore me at school and often left for home without me.

Abbi's mum taught us how to walk through the world as women, with our door keys clasped between our fingers like claws. Jackie's advice was a little more to the point.

"If a man comes up to you giving it all that, kick him in the bollocks and run," she'd said, winking at Abbi's mum in a way that she didn't seem to find funny.

The Stow Strangler's modus operandi didn't include teenage girls, though, and by the time the press gave him his nickname, he'd already taken his last victim. I never felt like I was in any real danger, but the proximity to it was as addictive as it was thrilling. I learned to study passersby, took stock of their height, their clothing, the colour of their hair, their gait. Anything and everything could be relevant when the next body turned up.

I'd studied Abbi too, with the keen interest of a detective. Abbi had matched her lipstick to the weather: peaches and blossom pinks on sunny days, toffee brown when it was overcast. People seemed to like her, and while I had little interest in making normie friends, my natural desire to match my surroundings compelled me to visit Boots to find the same shades of peach and pink to wear on sunny days too. She wore strappy baby doll tops, denim skirts, footless tights, and ballet flats, so I wore strappy baby doll tops, denim skirts, footless tights, and ballet flats.

As a teenager, nestling in my resentment for normies was a simmering desperation to fit in. I had a handbag, and I carried lip balm that I never used and Wayfarer sunglasses with red plastic frames that I never wore. But fake tan and Jane Norman and headbands weren't the real me. I continued to follow my passion for murder, and graduated from *Point Horror* to Stephen King, Clive Barker, and James Herbert. I spent my time thinking about death as a dramatic, burlesque event that was entirely disconnected from the sad reality of Marks & Spencer funeral wear and stale pub sandwiches. When the other girls saw me reading books about women being kidnapped, murdered, and dismembered, they hated me for it. They knew I was different, and that my Primark dresses were all a disguise, a Halloween costume. My life really started when I gave up trying to fit in, when I settled into myself, like an alligator sinking into a swamp.

By the time I reached the bookshop, the podcast hosts were laughing over whether they would still consider a holiday in Indonesia, even though the murderer had been caught and executed a long time ago.

∽

I let myself in and locked the shop door behind me, deactivated the alarm, and flipped on the lights to illuminate the shop floor. I'd managed to duck the responsibility of being a keyholder for eight years, and now being temporarily in charge of Barbara's set of keys was an imposition that I begrudged. Keyholders were on call 24/7 to deal with the security alarm whenever it went off, and it went off a lot. Rats, wind, rain, homeless men pissing against the back door, teenagers scrambling on the roof. There was always something. Whenever the idea of promoting me to keyholder was raised in the past, I'd been sure to fuck up somehow so the idea was swiftly dropped. Leave a till drawer open, forget to set an alarm. Nothing major enough to get me sacked, but serious enough for Barbara to have a rethink about whether I could be trusted. With Barbara gone, I had no choice but to accept the spare set.

The official story was that Barbara, with her bony fingers and acrylic nails and cloud of frizzy blonde hair, had decided to step down as manager for "the sake of her mental health." We all knew this wasn't really the case, because she hadn't gone quietly: the regional manager Jim had spent over four hours with her locked away in the office, sweet-talking and cajoling her into accepting a position as joint-manager of the Loughton branch, taking care of the greetings cards. A Mickey Mouse position, as the Loughton branch already had a bookseller who specialised in related products. They just wanted to get rid of her because she spent all day in the office filing her nails and chatting on the phone, which suited me because if she was locked away in the office, she wasn't micromanaging me on the shop floor and I was free to do whatever I liked.

The shop was empty and dark and dull, and it still smelled like last week's heavy rain—damp plaster, mildewed carpet. There was a scatter of packages on the doormat, which I collected and ditched on the counter, and then I slipped upstairs to drop off my hoodie and bag. There was a handover note from Noor, who'd worked the Sunday close the night before, propped against the kettle: a request for someone to chase a stray customer order for a copy of *The Journalist and the Murderer*. My kind of customer. I made myself an instant coffee and carried it on to the shop floor, where I took a seat at the ground floor till to open the post while my coffee cooled. The customer order for *The Journalist and the Murderer* wasn't there, but a book I'd ordered in had arrived. *An A–Z of Serial Killers*.

"Morning, morning," Barry said, not so much to me but to the shop itself as he locked the door behind him and swept past me to the lift. He always wore a chocolate-coloured windbreaker and walking boots to work, as though he intended to hike across a lonely moor on his lunch break.

I turned *An A–Z of Serial Killers* over and read the back. *There is nothing more shocking or more compelling than those who kill.* Correct. I booked it into the system, and then reserved it under my name.

⁓

I knew she was a bookseller as soon as I saw her. She wore a green beret, the colour of fresh pine needles and a camel raincoat like a private detective in a film noir. Over one shoulder, the grubby straps of a shabby tote bag. It was decorated with a quote in a typewriter font, and although I couldn't quite read it, I knew what it would say: *Though she be but little, she is fierce*, or *Curiouser and curiouser*, or *Beware for I am fearless and therefore powerful.*

"Hi," she said, approaching the till with a wide smile full of straight white teeth. "I'm Laura."

"Hullo."

"I don't know if you were told to expect me . . . is Sharona in yet?"

She removed her coat and folded it over one arm. As I took in her neat little outfit, her colour-coordinated hat and shoes and her bright scarlet lipstick, I thought of all the normie girls like her that I'd worked with before. Those Pumpkin Spice Girls. Garden centre girls who filled their flats with macramé and air plants. Girls who spent their weekends reading Jane Austen, baking muffins, drinking iced oat milk lattes.

"Dunno," I replied, perhaps a little tartly. "Who's Sharona?"

"New BSM," she said, tossing out the initialism for "bookshop manager" with the kind of casual certainty that implied she'd been a bookseller for a while.

I don't know what she expected me to say, but my indifferent silence seemed to displease her and her smile stiffened. Other, more surprising details came into focus: a scar from a healed lip ring, a peep of inked skin just visible through her tights and on her inner wrist. Interesting. I wondered if she was genuinely alternative, or a poser, or just an ex-goth who'd grown up.

"I'm just going to take a look around," she said, turning away from the counter to gaze around the shop. "Sorry, what was your name?"

"Roach," I said.

"Rach? Like Rachel?"

"No. Roach, like the bug."

She laughed as she drifted away from the till, and the sickly scent of rose petals fragranced the air between us. "Roach, like the bug. I'll remember that."

How generous of you, I thought.

I'd been Roach for as long as I'd worked at Spines. When I first became a bookseller, there was another Brogan on the team. Five foot two, hair deep brown, eyes green, slender frame, a match-head mole under her left eye, a tattoo of a butterfly on her right inner wrist. Lots of distinguishing marks.

We started on the same day, so the rest of the team decided to differentiate between us by using our surnames. That meant the other Brogan was known as "Mackee" for her first—and to my knowledge, only—Christmas bookselling. She was let go in the January because of her propensity for lateness and coming into work with vodka breath and a hangover that left her docile and ugly and—at least once, but who's to say—vomiting into the wastepaper basket under the ground floor till.

When the other Brogan was out the picture, the rest of the team wasn't interested in rechristening me and I was only sixteen, too young to assert myself. That's just the way things go sometimes. Roach isn't a particularly sexy surname, but I like it. I'd rather be thought of as a roach, a creepy-crawly that could survive the apocalypse, than a dull little normie called Brogan.

The team from that first Christmas dissipated over the years; they moved on, moved away, were sent to different shops, found other jobs, found better jobs, found ladders to climb, but the name still stuck. And while traces of other long-departed staff members remained—names scratched onto lockers, photos from old Christmas parties pinned to the noticeboard, forgotten items like cardigans and water bottles that remained unclaimed year after year, tattered proofs and twisted tubes of hand cream, discoloured Tupperware and boxes of old teabags that smelled like dust and death—there wasn't any trace of the other Brogan left.

As I'd zoned out, two strangers had entered the shop: a try-hard bohemian woman dressed like she'd just wandered out of Glastonbury and a tall, slouching man in jeans and a black beanie.

The druid must be Sharona, I realised. Barbara's replacement.

LAURA

We embrace, and he smells warm, unshowered, like sleep and skin, like bedclothes on a Sunday morning. I can't help but think of the taste of him—cigarettes and something earthy and herbal, like green tea, like matcha, like incense.

"I didn't know *you* were going to be here," I say into his neck, like it is a bad thing, an imposition, a terrible disappointment. Eli chuckles as we pull apart, and I take him in: his dark curls have grown into a messy halo around his head, and he's gained a little weight since I last saw him. He carries it well. He looks softer with the hollows of his cheeks filled in. I try to think how long it's been—at least two years.

"I go wherever Sharona goes," he says.

"Best *fwends*."

"Hey, gorgeous." Sharona bounces over and leans into a hug of her own. She smells of her familiar perfume, spicy and warm, and she's glowing with the last of her summer tan, a constellation of freckles scattered across golden brown cheeks and the bridge of her nose. In the summer, she goes to music festivals with her girlfriend and comes to work with a single beaded braid plaited into her curls and a filigree of hazelnut-coloured henna on her fingers. Eli has been her right-hand man for the last few

24

years. I think his free spirit appeals to her, and they work well together, trading in trust and kindness to get the job done.

"God, we've missed you," she says, pulling away with an earnest grin. "Where've you been?"

"Bloomsbury," I reply. "What about you? I thought you were in Cambridge these days?"

"Nah, just for the refit," Sharona says. "Then we were at the Strand to help prepare for the new term."

"And now"—Eli spreads his hands and looks around the shop in mock awe—"we find ourselves here."

I take in the drab displays, chipped shelves, threadbare carpet, the unkempt tables with scuffed legs, the faded shelf-talkers with messy recommendations scrawled in mismatched biro.

"Are they up for a refit?" I ask.

Sharona grimaces and checks over her shoulder to see if the bookseller behind the till, the girl with the weird name and faded purple hair tied into a rough, unflattering ponytail, is listening. She's staring at us with a blank expression, completely checked out.

"Well, it desperately needs it," she replies, voice low. "But no, this shop isn't going to get a refit any time soon."

The carpet is a muted red, hemmed with grey dust thick enough to gather in woolly handfuls. A spot by the till has worn through completely, like the balding pate of a middle-aged man. The ceiling is spotted with old plastic hooks, some of which still play host to coils of nylon thread that dangle like cobwebs. Leftovers from old Christmas decorations.

"You're from round here, right?" Eli asks as we head towards the lift at the back of the shop. I can feel Roach's eyes on us as we disappear into the depths of the Children's section. Several overhead bulbs have blown and not been replaced. The deeper we walk into the shop, the darker and damper it feels, like descending into the mouth of a cave.

"Yeah, I'm just past Lloyd Park now, but I grew up in the Village."

We've reached the very back of the Children's section, and Sharona jabs a button to call the lift. An ominous clanking rattles up the shaft, like she's summoned a creature from the deep, a mechanical kraken stirring in the bowels of the shop.

"It's kind of spooky," I say, as the lift doors ping open. It smells metallic, coppery like old pennies. It turns my stomach, and I press my sleeve to my nose and breathe in the soft floral scent of roses.

"I'll protect you," Eli replies, and he gives me a little squeeze around the shoulders. Sharona pretends to gag as she slaps the button for the second floor. The doors close and the lift rumbles into life.

"So," I say, now that we're out of earshot. "What's the story with this branch?"

"Fucked," Eli says.

"I wouldn't say *fucked*," says Sharona, a small crease appearing between her eyes as she frowns up at him.

"Well, the sales are fucked," Eli replies, as the doors ping open. He steps to one side, inviting me to follow Sharona out of the lift first. "Terrible location, all the way down this long market. It's way too big for the footfall, and they've been understaffed for, like, two years. There were only five of them, including the BSM."

"*Five?* In a shop this big?"

"I think they've been relying on cover," Sharona explains, pushing open the door to a surprisingly bright and spacious staffroom. Big skylights illuminate three cafeteria tables, a dirty kitchenette, a row of thirty or so lockers and several messy bookshelves. "But the shops in this division are all so spread out, it's not really possible a lot of the time, so they just make do. I think that's why standards have slipped."

Men in suits, tucked away in the luxury of head office, had divided all the shops into divisions based not on geographic location, but by budget and calibre. The strategy was confusing, a plan devised by those who knew watercoolers, boardrooms, and PowerPoint, their days of stickering calendars long behind them, if they'd ever had them at all. I imagined head office as a gentlemen's club of sorts, all dark wood panelling and cigars, whiskey in expensive glasses, sombre with the masculine gravity of a war room.

"We're negotiating with the landlord," Sharona says, dropping her bag on one of the big cafeteria tables. "It's a massive unit, and he's going to struggle to fill it if we close the shop. If we can get the rent lowered, and boost sales enough over Christmas, the shop might be viable for another year or two. I think the dream is to reopen somewhere else in Walthamstow. A smaller unit in a better spot, like the shopping centre, but . . ." She spread her arms into an exaggerated shrug, then grabbed the kettle to make tea.

"Sad, really," Eli says, hopping on to another cafeteria table and rolling a preemptive cigarette. "Like, for the community and for the booksellers. They've all been here forever."

"Well, there were two indie bookshops around here before this branch opened," I say, dropping my bag and coat on to a battered old armchair and grabbing my cigarettes. "Spines wiped them out. It's just business, right?"

"Well, look at our little capitalist," he says, laughing.

ROACH

The three new booksellers spent their morning working their way around the shop floor like they owned the place, looking over each section with a critical eye and making notes. As Barry booked in the deliveries and served customers, he tracked their progress with an anxious expression, his mouth a tight line.

At twelve on the dot, I left them to it and went for lunch. In the staffroom, Laura had draped her camel-coloured trench coat and grubby tote bag on my armchair. I picked up the trench coat between finger and thumb, ostentatiously to toss it aside so I could sit down, but I dipped my other hand into each of the pockets as I went. There was just a purple plastic lighter and a few coins in one and a balled-up tissue in the other. With a glance towards the staffroom door, I turned my attention to the tote bag. It was printed with the words *"nolite te bastardes carborundorum,"* a bruise of blue ink on one corner. I fished around inside, ears straining for any sounds of movement from the corridor. She carried lots of different tubes of grease and slime, things I would never have thought to lug around with me. If my hands felt dry, I would let my palms crack before I'd think to buy hand cream. If my lips were chapped, I'd pick the skin off in wet strips and swallow it, relish the coppery tang of blood.

I turned a paperback over in my hands. With a jolt of recognition, I realised that it was a book I had read too: *I'll Be Gone in the Dark*, a detailed account of the crimes of the Golden State Killer. It was well-read, dog-eared, with sticky tabs marking particular passages, the odd phrase underlined in light pencil. I wondered what business she had doing such a close reading—some kind of research, perhaps for an essay or an article? Maybe she had a podcast. Either way, she was clearly into her true crime. I felt an immediate kinship melt the ice between us. We could lend each other books, go see the *Murder Girls* together. Maybe even email each other links to long reads we found on the internet about kidnappings, child killers, botched investigations. My Pumpkin Spice evaluation had clearly been off, and I had the wild image of us taking trips to the Kenwood Ladies" Pond in Hampstead to languish with the writers and artists, eat slices of home-baked apple pie, and talk about our favourite serial killers.

I helped myself to some of her hand cream, which left my palms coated in a film of sweet-smelling grease, like melted buttercream, and then I filched a can of posh cherry-flavoured pop, which I stuffed under the stacks of books, press releases, jiffy bags, and old paperwork in my locker. I hooked the tote bag on the coat rack with her trench coat, and settled into my armchair with a tub of taramosalata and a packet of crackers. I placed *An A–Z of Serial Killers* on my bookshelf and picked something else to read instead. Inspired by the conversation I'd had at the *Murder Girls* event, I settled on *The Stranger Beside Me*.

Just as I was getting into it, the staffroom door slammed open and Laura came in with one of the new booksellers in tow, laughing at some private joke.

"Ah! You must be . . ." the man cocked his head to look at the rota pinned to the noticeboard on the wall by the door, ". . . Brogan?"

"Roach," Laura said, in that bright plastic voice. "Like the bug, right?"

I thought of the copy of *I'll Be Gone in the Dark* in her bag and returned the light of her attention with a tentative smile.

"I'm Eli," he said, pulling a packet of rolling tobacco out of his back pocket and then dropping on the flaking leatherette sofa to roll a cigarette. His head rested against a 2009 *Breaking Dawn* window poster. It was one of Barbara's favourites, and I wondered if his unwashed hair would leave a starburst of grease, like those nebulous smudges of hair wax on bus windows from people leaning against the glass.

Laura perched on one of the tables and I was grateful when they began to talk shop. I hated small talk. Hated listening to people yammer on about their weekends, television, holidays. Minor gripes with their landlords and their boyfriends and their banks. I hated sharing the staffroom with strangers, and figuring out what I was expected to say when they asked me a banal question like "What are you reading at the moment?" or "What kind of music do you like?" as the truth was never the right answer, always killed the conversation dead.

Laura was still wearing her forest-green beret and her shoes were the same shade of leafy green. This particular detail stuck with me—the beret and the shoes, in the exact same shade of pine-needle green. I wondered if she'd got them from the same place, or if she'd spent months hunting. I later learned that Laura always coordinated: a glossy cherry clutch paired with shiny peep-toe wedges, a matte black leather satchel with neat brogues, casual Adidas shells with a vintage gym bag.

I found this contrived at first, but years later, when I was in New Orleans to see the *Murder Girls* record a live Halloween special, I felt drawn to a pair of deep amethyst peep-toe wedges in an expensive goth boutique because they were the exact same shade as the hairband I was wearing. It was only as I walked down Bourbon Street in my new shoes that pinched my toes that I realised Laura's ghost had reached through time and unknowingly informed my choice. I was still letting her into my mind, still letting her influence me. I kicked the shoes under the bed of the Airbnb and ignored the owner's earnest email asking for a forwarding address.

"Hey, Roach, d'you want a biscuit?" Eli held up a wrinkled paper bag that looked as though it had been used more than once. Inside, there were several grainy brown nuggets that resembled cat shit. "They're vegan—my girlfriend made them."

"I'm not vegan," I said.

"Well then, you and my biscuits have less in common than I thought," he said with the kind of good-natured chuckle that probably made women like him. "Laura?"

She fixed a blank gaze on to the paper bag, then shook her head with a curled lip. In a voice that was surprisingly deep, nothing like the bright voice she had spoken to me with earlier, she said: "Nah, I'm good."

Unperturbed, Eli took a bite of biscuit. A muscle ticked in his jaw as he chewed. "So, what's that you're reading, Roach?"

I held the cover towards him, and he cocked his head and smiled as he swallowed. He read each word slowly: "*The Stranger Beside Me.* Any good? What's it about?"

"Um. Ted Bundy."

He continued to smile his good-natured smile, so I decided to elaborate in the hope of catching Laura's attention. "He was an American serial killer. He killed over thirty people before he was caught, but we don't know exactly how many, and he was famously very handsome and charismatic, and he would often pretend to be injured to lure his victims into a false sense of security, and he denied his crimes for, like, a full decade, and he escaped from prison twice, and he was eventually sentenced to death by the electric chair and—"

I lost steam as I realised Eli was laughing, showing molars splattered with gun-metal-grey fillings and a cement of masticated biscuit caught between his teeth. He held up a palm in surrender. "Okay, okay—"

"—he kept their heads sometimes," I said, finishing my thought.

"Maybe I'll check it out," he said mildly, in a voice that suggested he would not be checking it out.

"Hey, can we smoke out there?"

We both turned to look at Laura, who was pointing out the window to the flat rooftop, to the picnic table and pigeons that pecked at the tarmac.

"Yes," I said, deflated. I thought perhaps she might pick up my conversational cue and chip in with her thoughts on Ted Bundy, but she wore a strangely neutral expression as she stared pointedly out the window.

"Cool," she replied. "Then that's where I'll be."

LAURA

I get to know each bookseller by their section. Barry leaves a tread of dried mud around History, and he keeps a tight handle on his face-outs. When Noor's working, there's a sweet thread of black cherries and almonds in Travel, where she daydreams of turquoise oceans lapping sugar-soft sandy shores, and when it's her day off, her neat cursive recommendation cards point customers to her favourite travelogues and guides to all the places she wishes to visit. Our Christmas temp, Kofi, is tall and slender, with a shaved head, arched brows, and elegant cheekbones. He prefers the bustle and noise of the till, only coming to life when he has an audience to flirt with, but as an English Lit student, he spends his breaks solemnly working through the canon—Dickens, Austen, Wilde—or staring at his phone.

I give Roach a wide birth. I can't explain exactly why. It's just a feeling, an instinctive repulsion. An aura of neediness radiates from her. It's written plainly all over her face every time we speak: *look at me, listen to me, pay attention to me, me, me.* She haunts the first floor till, seems to spend more time there than anywhere else, occasionally fussing with the True Crime section. It's much too big for the amount of stock they have, with way too many face-outs, and the books—strange, poorly printed crap from obscure presses—are constantly tumbling over.

"It's great to see some fresh faces around here." Martin smiles and rubs his hands together with earnest pleasure. He's softly spoken, in his early sixties, with silver hair and a faded hippy air about him. When he speaks, he narrows his eyes and smiles like he's squinting through smoke, and I can easily imagine him queuing behind Sharona for tofu curry at a world music festival.

My hopes for a comrade in the Children's section are dashed on my third day in the Walthamstow branch though. He hovers around me like a helicopter as I shelve, monitoring my every move, gently criticising and correcting my choices. He's resistant to change, used to doing things his own way, and seems to think I'm here to learn from him instead of the other way around.

On his day off, I pounce. I pull all the bulk stock from the shelves in the 9–12 section and swap the flat, desolate classics table for a full display of shiny new paperbacks, arranged into a perfect pyramid. The buggy books—little board books attached to elastic bungees, perfect for looping on to pushchairs, and durable against the grabby hands and wet mouths of toddlers—are all over the place, so I gather them together and put them in an acrylic box I find in the stockroom. There's an empty display unit in Children's Education, so I choose some pretty, illustrated nonfiction to create an appealing educational display, all cross sections of historical buildings and cartoonish dissections of the human body.

By the time I come back from lunch the following day, Martin has undone all my hard work. He's reinstated the flat children's classics table, even though there's no stock to fill it, and swapped my bright display of educational hardbacks for a random selection of backlist picture books. The buggy books are nowhere to be seen, until I find the acrylic box wedged into the gift book section. His choices don't make sense, commercially or logically.

"I know what my customers want," he keeps insisting, even though we have no customers.

ROACH

Laura and I didn't see much of each other during that first week. To my great irritation, I was sent to the Wood Green branch to cover a sick day, and then it was my day off, and then it was Laura's. I wondered how she spent her free time. I imagined her studiously tapping away on a MacBook in some hip little East London café, her annotated copy of *I'll Be Gone in the Dark* spread open in front of her as she worked. I desperately wanted to know what kind of debauched project necessitated such a close reading of that book, but when we were finally reunited on the shop floor, I couldn't find a way to bring it up without revealing that I'd been rifling through her things.

As I stood at the first floor till and watched her zip between sections, building displays, and rearranging tables, Eli tapped his name badge with a biro, jolting me out of my dark rumination. I'd zoned out again. Sometimes, it was like a switch was flipped and I was somewhere else, deep in the dungeon of my mind, lost in some depraved thought.

"You're looking a bit thin over there," Eli said, drumming a little beat on his own name tag while looking pointedly at mine. His gleamed with a full set of eight gold pins. "How long have you been bookselling for?"

"Eight years in December," I said.

He whistled in surprise. "Wow—so wait, how old were you when you started?"

"Sixteen."

"You must know a thing or two then." He winked, and to my supreme embarrassment, I felt my cheeks grow warm. "So how come you've only got one pin?"

I just looked at him and sighed like it was obvious. The pins were a meaningless way to acknowledge bookseller expertise. Only normies like Eli and Noor actually cared about them. Each section of the shop was assigned an icon, and each icon had been turned into a little gold-coloured pin that could be pushed into our name tags. There was a paintbrush for Art, Photography, and Design, an aeroplane for Travel, a magnifying glass for Crime, and so on. Of course, all it really meant was that customers familiar with the system learned to scrutinise our name badges with their beady little eyes, not really trusting a recommendation unless it came from a bookseller with the right fucking pin.

That was exactly why I'd declined every opportunity to up my pin count, even though you couldn't progress to specialist bookseller without at least six. My name tag would have remained at a stubborn zero, but Barbara said it looked unprofessional and forced the Fiction pin on to me, a cold and hard little book, pages fluttered by a ghostly hand.

In an act of secret rebellion, I'd sketched out my own pins based on serial killers. John Wayne Gacy, in his Pogo the Clown makeup, was the natural choice for the Humor section, although I painted him with the sour-faced pout of his mugshot. For Cookery, the blond, chiseled profile of Jeffrey Dahmer: sadist, serial killer, necrophiliac, and, of course, cannibal. The Children's section was represented by the dark mascaraed eyes and voluminous blonde bouffant of child-killer Myra Hindley. For Local History, it had to be the Stow Strangler.

I completed my sketches during the long hours spent manning the lonely enquiries desk in the History section on Barry's days off, where I used the internet connection to niff through Wikipedia for inspiration and Google for pictures to replicate a passable likeness. Occasionally, I found myself picking over the bones of long-abandoned message boards where bored teens and lonely divorcées exchanged facts and quips about the seedy underbelly of the Western world. Messages left in 2002, 2003. Sixteen, seventeen years later, and they were still there, like abandoned shopping trolleys at the bottom of a canal.

My obsession with true crime started in my teens. I remember watching a late-night Channel Four documentary about people who believed they were real-life vampires and went around in capes and expensive porcelain fangs committing murder. The documentary had a solemn voice-over and black and white reconstructions of the boring parts of the crimes, like when the high school girl—a normie, of course—pretty, chaste in a sweater and jeans, with good grades and a glittering future, climbed into the killer's car and you knew she was toast.

The documentary didn't go into too much detail, so I used my laptop to search for the actual factual details of each killing, to make sure I was fully informed on the subject. I don't like feeling insufficiently informed about things. I stayed up pretty late that night, googling.

"Anyway, did you know Laura Bunting writes poetry?" Eli said now, tapping a loose rhythm on my shoulder with his biro. I took a step away to break the connection between us.

"She's doing a reading tonight and I think you should come. Even if you hate poetry, it'll be fun."

"I don't know," I said. "I have to clean out my snail tank tonight."

A look of delighted surprise transformed his face. "You keep snails?"

"I have a giant African land snail called Bleep."

"Bleep! That's so cute." He looked amused. "Sucks, though. I know poetry probably isn't your thing, but if your snail can wait one more night, I'll buy you a beer? The whole team's coming." He paused, perhaps taking in the *Murder Girls* badge pinned to my shirt, or thinking of my speech earlier in the week about Ted Bundy. "Laura's work—well, it can be quite dark. I think you'll like it, actually."

My ears pricked at "quite dark," and I thought of the copy of *I'll Be Gone in the Dark* in her bag, all battered and underlined, read to death. Dennis Nilsen wrote poetry in prison. Damien Echols, one of the West Memphis Three, wrote it on death row. I loved the idea of poetry—loved the easy messiness of it, the darkness of it, the way anyone could slap words together and call it a poem—but I'd never been to a poetry reading before.

Just then, Eli spotted a customer who looked lost, a scrap of paper clutched in her hands as she frowned at the bay headers as though they were written in hieroglyphics. As he moseyed off to help her with whatever inane shit she wanted, he called over his shoulder.

"You're up for it, yeah?" he said, eyebrows raised.

I tried to hide my enthusiasm with a casual thumbs up, but my skin was crawling with excitement.

Of course I was up for it.

LAURA

An elderly woman with white hair and a gently curved back buys *Letters to a Young Poet*. A rosy-cheeked man with dimples and blond curls, like an overgrown cherub, buys *American Psycho*. A teenager with pastel pink hair and a healthy layer of blusher over the bridge of her nose buys *The Fountainhead*.

"Don't be mad," Eli says, stopping to rest a giant stack of mind, body, and spirit titles on the till point. Angels and crystals, tarot cards and auras. Smoke and mirrors to pad the pain of reality with a comfort blanket of mysticism.

"Don't give me a reason to be mad," I counter, sliding a pretty hardback called *Astro Poets* from his stack and turning it over to read the blurb.

"I've invited the rest of the team tonight," he says with an impish grin.

I lower the book and scowl at him. "Oh, you *suck*."

"Don't give me that face," he says, neatening his pile of books. "I invited Sharona, and then she invited Martin, and then Martin asked if he should text Barry and it just snowballed. Are you actually mad?"

"I thought it was just gonna be us, that's all."

He opens his mouth with a frown, and then pauses as he searches for the right words. I realise with a hot rush of embarrassment that it might have sounded like I thought we were going on a date. "I mean, I was going to invite Sharona anyway," I say quickly, placing Astro Poets back on to his pile of shelving. "But did you have to invite the *entire* team?"

"Isn't it for charity though? I thought the vibe was, like, the more the merrier?"

"Yeah, but . . ." A tug of uneasiness, and then the image of Roach, eyes shining as she talked about Ted Bundy, calcifies in my mind. "I dunno, it's fine. I just wish you'd asked me first."

I lean on the counter and inspect my fingernails. The polish has chipped away around the edges, leaving a craggy island of peach paint on each nail.

"Ah, you'll smash it," he says, earnest and sweet. "You don't hate me, do you?"

He smells like fresh sweat and nag champa, and when he smiles, his cheeks dimple.

"I don't respect you enough to hate you," I reply, and he laughs as he disappears towards the lift.

A little girl in a yellow raincoat picks a board book with a rubber duck on the cover. An elderly gent in a stained three-piece tweed suit buys *The Hundred-Year-Old Man Who Climbed Out the Window and Disappeared*. A woman with fuchsia acrylics and matching pink lips buys *The Valley of the Dolls*.

Sometimes people surprise me, and sometimes they do not.

ROACH

The poetry reading was in a bar called the Nib. A girl with curly green hair and a bull-like septum ring was sitting on a high stool by the door with a clipboard and a purple plastic charity bucket.

"Hi guys, it's entry by donation tonight," she said, shaking her bucket at us. "We're raising money for Women's Aid."

The bar was the kind of try-hard place that normies liked, desperate to recreate the careless cool of an American dive bar with carefully curated neglect. The walls were painted a scuffed black, and the bar was lined with ripped pleather stools. A guy with dreads poured drinks and nodded along to some wanky guitar noise thrumming from the speakers. I pictured him sliding whiskeys down the bar to exhausted, grey-faced detectives, drinking to forget, drinking to shrug off the last brutal crime scene, drinking so they didn't take echoes of homicide home to their wives.

High tables faced a makeshift stage that was covered in ripped stickers and pasted flyers, flanked by an old piano and a yucca plant in a terracotta pot. At Laura's insistence, the booksellers bagsied a table near the back. "Otherwise, I'm too aware of my audience," she said, shrugging out of her camel-coloured raincoat and reserving herself a seat next to Eli. "I perform best when I feel anonymous."

41

I grabbed the seat next to Laura's. I'd spent the whole day trying to start a conversation with her, and although she always smiled politely whenever I spoke to her, distraction clouded her eyes and her answers were short and vague. I hoped the atmosphere of the poetry reading would loosen her up, and I'd finally manage to squeeze out enough conversation for her to realise we had something in common.

Laura peeled off to say hi to a tall, thin man with sharp cheekbones and a scraggly beard while Sharona went to the bar and came back with a metal bucket stuffed with open bottles of Budweiser on ice, which leaked cold water all over the table and dripped onto the floor.

Eli, Noor, and Kofi accepted beers from Sharona's bucket, but after a quick exchange of words with Barry, Martin excused himself and returned from the bar with two pints of bitter. I wanted a Dark Fruits, but the others were still shuffling around and getting settled, and I didn't want to risk losing my seat next to Laura, so I accepted the last bucket beer instead.

"I'm just trying to save up some money," Noor was saying. "I want to go backpacking in 2020, but I don't know how much I'll need."

"Depends where you want to go, really," said Sharona, lifting her beer bottle and wiping water from the base of it to stop it from dripping on her top. "If you fancy the hippy trail, the biggest cost is the airfare. Once you're there, everything's pretty cheap. Europe gets cheaper the farther east you go, and the US is basically expensive all over. Backpacking somewhere like South America, on the other hand . . ."

She rambled on. Noor was small and thin, with delicate shoulders and skinny wrists. The only scenario in which I could picture her backpacking was as a missing persons story on the evening news.

"Sounds awesome, though," said Eli. "You have to do that shit while you're still young. Right, Sharona?"

"Oi, fuck off," Sharona said with a broad grin that revealed a missing canine. "I'm only *just* forty, thanks."

"Ah, I'm just messing. And anyway, you're never too old to travel," Eli said, raising his beer bottle to his lips. "I hope I'm still out there discovering new places when I'm a hundred."

"Yeah, all right, thanks for that," Sharona said, but she was still laughing and her laugh was infectious, and the rest of the team laughed at her expense too. When people laughed at me, I felt it in my bones, painful and acute as a dentist's drill, but it was something Sharona simply shrugged off, even seemed to enjoy.

The bar was filling up around us, but Laura's seat remained conspicuously empty. As the booksellers continued their mindless chatter, I watched her flit around the room, a hummingbird collecting the nectar of attention from people she knew. She carried a something-and-Coke and a slim pink volume of stapled pages, and when the tall man with the scraggly beard switched on the microphone, she turned to face the stage and clapped without spilling a drop of her drink.

Laura was first to read. When the compère announced her name, there was a smattering of polite applause. She stepped into the limelight and took her place in front of the microphone without a second glance towards her colleagues. Eli raised his beer bottle in silent salute, but she was flicking through her little pink book and paid him no attention.

"Hiya! My name's Laura, and I'm a local writer and poet." She was using her customer voice—perky, bright, and warm. "I'm gonna read a couple of found poems for you guys this evening. Just to explain what that means . . . I take snippets of prose from true crime narratives to create commemorative poetry about the lives of the women who are so often overlooked when we talk about violent crime. Some of them are a little darker than others, though, so please consider this a content warning."

She certainly had my attention now.

"This one's called 'It Was Now 5 A.M.,'" she said, and then she began to read. It sounded like she was recovering from a cold, and she spoke into

43

the microphone with a syrupy huskiness that commanded the attention of the room. The audience fell silent as she spoke: just the occasional rattle of ice cubes as someone sneaked a mouthful of their drink, and the periodic slamming of the till drawer. The booksellers were all captivated, apart from Eli. Although he seemed to be listening, his head was bowed as he scratched at the wet paper label of his beer bottle with a thumbnail, face bearing a grave expression. He was the only bookseller not looking at her.

At first, I found her poetry kind of boring—it was all pink skies and pale dawns—but the more she read, the more I found myself getting drawn into her dark world. If her goal was to remove the violence from true crime narratives, the result was the opposite. Between descriptions of the weather and women doing ordinary things—hanging laundry, returning video tapes, dropping children off at school—I could feel the spilled blood simmering underneath it all, the constant threat of murder, the occasional flashes of coldness, of menace. By removing the violence, it was all I could think about. What happened to these women? When did the ordinary humdrum of their lives become extraordinary with a final—fatal—chance encounter? I listened closely for clues that might indicate time period or location, any crumbs that could lead me to the killers between the lines.

When she finished, the room broke into rambunctious applause. I put down my drink and smacked my palms together as hard as I could. She nodded—a brief bob of her head that was close to a bow—collected her drink from the piano, and walked swiftly offstage towards our table. I braced myself to greet her, already reaching for the right words to express how much her poetry had maggotted under my skin. I wanted to ask which books had inspired each poem, find out which murderers made them tick. This was our moment to connect.

Laura didn't seem to think so, though. She breezed straight past me, straight through me, to Eli. He was brandishing a rollie and a something-and-Coke—no communal lager for Laura—like a spectator greeting a marathon runner at the finishing line.

"Gimme," she grinned, taking the cigarette in one hand and the drink in the other. As the compère began to introduce the next poet, Sharona leaned forward and patted Laura on the forearm.

"Well done," she murmured in a low voice. "That was epic, mate. You smashed it."

"Thanks," Laura whispered back, a smug smile playing on her lips, and then she gave Eli a look and he nodded. As they walked outside together, I was amazed that the crowd simply parted and let them through. I imagined she'd be swamped by admirers: other poets keen to congratulate her, perhaps even a poetry agent (if such a thing existed—it must do, I reasoned) waiting to give her a card, or a publisher ready to offer her a book deal then and there. I could only assume that everyone else, like me, was stunned into silence, her words still ricocheting around their heads. I found myself wishing that I was a smoker so that I could follow them into the smoking area and no one would think anything of it.

On stage, an elfin poet in chinos and an unzipped hoodie was adjusting the microphone as though nothing extraordinary had happened at all.

"This one's about my fear of churches," he said.

I squeezed my way to the bar and ordered a pint of Dark Fruits. Once the pint was in my hand, I felt bold. On a whim, I walked straight past my colleagues and took my fizzing glass outside to find Laura. Who needs a pack of cigarettes to grab some fresh air? It felt imperative that I speak to her then, while my head was still swimming, my heart hammering. If I tried to articulate that feeling later, at the shop, it wouldn't be the same. It would feel forced, and she might think I was just being nice, polite. She'd brush me off, look through me. I needed her to know that I knew my stuff too, that I'd grown up in the shadow of a serial killer, that I understood the power of violence.

The garden was buzzing, the air clouded with plumes of vape smoke that smelled like bubble gum and gummy bears. I spotted the gleam of Laura's bottle-blonde hair through the crowd, somewhere near the far corner of the courtyard. She was perched on the table of one of the round picnic benches, her feet on the seat, and she didn't seem to mind that the wood was stained dark with early evening rain, even though it must have been seeping through the thin fabric of her skirt. She was laughing at something Eli had said, really laughing, an unlit rollie pinched between her fingers.

"I can't just leave, that would look so shitty." She giggled, delighted with herself, and then she lifted her chin and fixed him with an impish grin. "I'm afraid you're stuck here. Got a light?"

This seemed like my moment. I took a step forward, and was abruptly jostled by a passing normie. A glug of Strongbow slopped down the front of my jacket, a sticky stain darkening the black denim.

"Oh hey, Roach." Eli glanced up and offered a polite smile as he pulled a clipper from his jeans pocket. "What can we do for you?"

I swallowed a rising sense of embarrassment. He thought I wanted something, that I'd been sent to pass on a message or ask a question, just like we were at the shop and I was interrupting a conversation about front of store. I blinked and decided to ignore him.

"I just wanted to say," I said to Laura, "that was incredible. Like, really incredible."

"Oh, thank you!" She spoke with a bright, impersonal tone and leant forward as Eli cracked the lighter. The flame kept stuttering until, with a small frown of irritation, she took the lighter and finished the job herself. They both looked at me, and I shifted my weight from one foot to the other.

"So, uh. Do you . . . do you read much true crime?"

She blew smoke politely out the corner of her mouth and looked away as though thinking.

"Not much," she said. "Just for poetry, really."

"Which books are your poems based on?" I asked, taking a sip of my cider. "I thought maybe one of them was about Richard Ramirez but—"

It might have been due to a sharp gust of wind, but I thought I saw her stiffen.

"I don't write poetry about murderers," she said with a sniff, tapping a short round of ash from the tip of her cigarette. "I write poetry to commemorate their victims."

"That's what I meant," I said quickly, but the misstep had clearly soured her mood, her expression had calcified into something more hard, more mean. I changed tack. "Anyway, I'd love to read more. Do you have a collection?"

"Yeah, I published a bunch of poems in a chapbook a few years ago," she said. "There's a little table by the cloakroom selling zines and stuff. They had a whole bunch at the beginning of the night."

"They might sell out though," Eli said, with a nod. "You should grab one now, before they're all gone."

"Okay, great." I clenched my teeth and took a step back. "I'll go grab one now, then."

"Great," Laura replied. She sucked on her cigarette and spoke through the smoke: "Thanks for coming, Roach."

"I'll see you in there?" I said, and she gave me a half-hearted thumbs up, exchanging a brief but sharp look with Eli. As I turned to leave, the bell of her laugh serenaded my retreat and my cheeks burned.

I pushed my way through the thicket of posers and their clouds of kombucha-flavoured air. The merch stand was a trestle table, scattered with handmade zines printed on colourful paper, pin badges and pamphlets, and flyers for poetry circles and protests and mutual aid groups. It was staffed by a woman around my age with electric-blue braids. She was knitting something from lilac mohair, although as I approached, both needles were in one hand and she was tapping on her phone with the other.

"Do you have Laura Bunting's chapbook?" I asked, scanning the table.

She glanced up from her phone and fixed me with a blank, uninterested stare. "Who?"

"That first poet, Laura Bunting? She said she had chapbooks for sale."

"Oh," she said. "Her." She placed her knitting to one side and began shuffling through the piles of photocopied zines and cheaply printed pamphlets. "You kind of just have to dig through. I'm not sure what they all look like."

We scanned her wares in a companionable silence until she found it hidden beneath an essay collection about prepackaged supermarket sandwiches. It was called *their inconsequential moments were beautiful*—no capitals, very breezy and cool—and the cover showed a line drawing of a woman with no face, head tilted towards a sash window. There were several candy-coloured covers to choose between—Parma violet, sherbet lemon, orange fondant. I fanned them out and picked a candy floss–pink cover to match Laura's copy. I paid for it with a two-pound coin, and then went back to my seat to read.

"Ah, is that Laura's chapbook?" Sharona asked, leaning forward to see what I was holding. "Can I take a quick look?"

"No," I said, tightening my grip on it.

Laura's work took me to cities and suburbs, beaches and backpacking trails. I was determined to unlock the mystery of each poem myself, like a puzzle or a game, but she had carefully razored out place names and temporal signifiers. The red-hot sun could be pounding down upon the streets of Los Angeles, Chicago, Boston, or anywhere in between. Women could have been shopping, driving, or walking in the '70s, '80s, or '90s. Rain could be slashing against the windows of Edinburgh, Manchester, or London. It was impossible to tell. She was a tease. I couldn't help but imagine how much better her work would be if she had the guts to spill the meat of the story, and stopped faffing around with the boring bits.

Another poet took to the stage to read, and then another. Laura and Eli came back inside, bringing the cold with them. Eli took the seat next to me, and Laura took his previous seat, next to Sharona. I barely moved. When I'd finished the last poem in Laura's collection, I looked up and was amazed to find myself right where I had been all along, in the same seat, in the same bar, on the same night, surrounded by the same people. It was like falling through a dream and landing back in reality.

I turned back to the first page and read the whole thing again, determined to comb through the facts one more time, to see if anything rang a bell, any phrase or sentence or line that might give me a clue as to which devil had constructed the narrative that Laura was so carefully dancing around. I was absorbed, completely adrift on the tide of her poetry, floating through a sea of words and images and ideas that morphed into different murderers in my mind's eye, as helpless and as insignificant as a piece of driftwood rolling on her self-made waves.

LAURA

I'm on the amaretto and Diet Cokes, which I can't really afford, but can't resist either. They are sweet and strong and drinkable, and I'm swallowing them back too quickly, the room sliding in and out of focus. With a wicked glimmer of trouble in his eyes, Eli had suggested we sneak out after my reading, and although I'd laughed it off, the very suggestion had given me a thrill.

Roach is making a big deal out of reading my old pamphlet, and her enthusiasm is embarrassing. I can't work out what someone like her sees in it. She looks like the kind of girl who'd hang around to watch the aftermath of a car accident, thirsty for a glimpse of blood. My poetry isn't written for people like her.

I sit and nurse the dregs of my drink and watch each of my colleagues respond to the poetry in turn. Barry looks politely indifferent as he sips his bitter, occasionally sending text messages on an old Nokia that he holds at arm's length as he types, frowning to make sense of the letters on the screen. Noor has both elbows on the table, chin resting in her hands as she stares at the stage with a glazed look, perhaps imagining the palm-fringed beaches of Koh Samui. Sharona, whose tastes run more literary than the rest, watches the poets with hyperfocus, occasionally leaning in to whisper a sincere "sick" or "wicked" into my ear.

My glass is empty again. Barry and Martin are doing their own rounds, and their pints are fresh and full to the brim. The rest of the booksellers are taking it in turns to buy ice buckets of cheap beer for a tenner, but the current bucket contains just melting ice and they're drinking slowly, their bottles all three quarters full. I don't want anyone to clock the rate I'm getting through my amarettos but I don't want to sit with an empty glass either, so I slide from my seat and creep over to the bar.

"Can I buy you a drink?"

Roach. Her hot breath smells rotten, like blackberries and tooth decay, and I turn my head away.

"It's cool, I'll get it," I say, but she flags down the barman and orders herself a pint of Dark Fruits and then they both turn to me. Fuck it. I ask for a double amaretto and Diet Coke.

"I've just read your collection," she says, as if she hasn't spent the last hour angling it towards me, desperately trying to catch my eye.

"Thanks so much," I reply, with a tight smile.

She's looking at me like she wants to eat me, a nervous energy emanating from her. I crane my neck to see how the barman's doing with our drinks, and I catch him sharing a laugh with one of the other poets, my empty amaretto glass in his hand like he has all the time in the world.

"I'm really into true crime," she says.

"Oh yeah?"

"I'd really love to know more about where your inspiration comes from."

"Look, I think you're missing the point if you're interested in marrying the poems to the cases that inspired them," I say, reeling off my party line. "I'm recontextualising work that profits from violence against women. So, if I told you what the source material was, you'd know the context and it would change the way you understood the work." Roach blinks at me

51

with a confused expression on her face, mouth hanging open. "It sort of ruins the point I'm making if I tell you who the victims are, because then you'll know who the perpetrators are."

"I love serial killers," she says, and I think *Of course you do* with an intense prickle of dislike. I don't dignify that with an answer, but she presses on: "I just really want to know."

"I know," I reply. "And I'm sorry but I'm not going to tell you."

The barman places our drinks in front of us and I whisk mine away with a quick, cold thank you.

◈

The other booksellers peel off, one at a time. Barry taps out first, right in the middle of a reading. He just downs the last of his bitter, stands up, puts on his coat, and leaves with a sharp nod. Martin follows soon after, with a quick squeeze of my shoulder, and then Kofi and Noor blow me kisses and take their leave too. Sharona calls it a night as soon as we've finished clapping for the final poet. I want another drink, though, and Eli is only too happy to go to the bar.

"We should get falafel after this," I say as he places another amaretto in front of me. "There's a great falafel place around here."

"We can get falafel," he says genially, putting a pint of purple cider in front of Roach. Roach. Why is Roach still here? Thin, greasy purple hair matching the purple of her pint, whiteheads clustered around the crevices of her nose. A third wheel of the worst variety.

I clutch my drink and focus on Eli. Our conversation circles around booksellers we know, books we've read, bookshops we used to work in, and it leaves no room for Roach to manoeuvre between us. She sits and listens, nothing to add. It's cruel, and petty, but I'm drunk and resentful of her presence, a dead weight between Eli and me.

The bell rings for last orders. I want another, but Eli is already pulling on his jacket.

"School night," he says.

"I'm up for another," Roach says in a hopeful voice.

"But it's my round!" I say to Eli, and he laughs and plonks my beret on my head. "Don't be such a little bitch."

"Laura, I'm up for another one," Roach says again, louder this time, but I pretend to fuss with my bag as though I haven't heard her.

Outside, the moon is swollen, a pregnant belly hanging heavy in the sky. Eli and I put cigarettes in our mouths, take turns with the lighter. The wheel is stiff and the wind is strong, but eventually a flame catches.

"Go on, Eli, one more," I wheedle, holding on to the first breath of smoke for a second, enjoying the burn of it in my lungs. "Don't be rubbish, we haven't had a drink together in *ages*."

"We've just had about ten drinks together," he says, with a laugh. Smoke uncurls from between his lips, and the potential for the rest of the night uncurls in my mind. Another drink or two, a pitta of falafel and hot, salty chips, then back to mine for a nightcap.

"The Mother Black Cap's open 'til two on a Friday," Roach pipes up. "It's only three quid a pint."

"Three quid a pint?" Interest flickers over Eli's face. "That's good, whereabouts is the Mother Black—"

"Ugh, *that* place," I sneer, tapping my cigarette. "It stinks. I'd rather die of thirst."

Roach's hand closes around my chapbook, the paper concertinaed in her bunched-up fist as the knuckles turn pale. Her eyes harden with dislike as I meet her gaze.

"Where d'you live, Roach?" Eli asks, with a small smile that tells me I'm dangerously close to getting my way.

"Uh. Fraser Road," she says, pointing towards Walthamstow Village.

"Ah, not far from me, then," he says. "But I better make sure this one gets home safe. You'll be okay on your own, yeah?"

"Uh, yeah," she says, deflated, and I wonder if she fancies him.

"Take it easy," he says, with a cheerful wave.

"See ya," I say, and I turn on my heel and start to walk, putting as much distance between us as quickly as possible, leaving her to make her own way home.

As Eli and I walk up Hoe Street, the taillights of passing cars smear together and the night feels bright and young.

"Wasn't that kind of mean?" he asks, eyeing me.

"Oh, fuck off," I say. "I'm not going to the Mother Black Cap. That place is the pits, trust me—no one goes there."

We pass a homeless man eating chicken wings from a cardboard box, a white Staffie wrapped in a dirty blanket asleep on his lap. Eli pauses to dig a coin from his pocket and drops it into the man's ragged Starbucks cup. The dog looks up and grins in that peculiar way that Staffies do. I should give the man some money too, I think, but I don't have any change in my coat pocket and before I can find my purse, the moment's passed and we're walking again.

"I didn't know you lived around here," I say to Eli, tucking my hands into my pockets to warm them up.

"Yeah, we just moved into a flat in the Village," he replies, skirting around a small crowd gathered at the bus stop.

"*We.*"

"Don't."

"What?"

"Don't be a bitch."

"*I'm* being a bitch?"

I simmer, and we walk in silence for a while. Shadows loom and men take up space on the pavement, smoking and spitting and stumbling, calling after one another. A woman in a red dress and heels passes us in the opposite direction, and I cringe as the inevitable wolf-whistle erupts from the crowd of men. A car horn honks, jeers rise over the hiss of a passing bus. I turn and watch her retreating back, shake the feeling that she isn't safe, that none of us are safe. The night presses in, no longer welcoming.

"Let's have another drink," I say. "Go on. I'll even take you to the Mother bloody Black Cap if you're that desperate to see it."

"I'm not sure that's such a good idea," he says.

"It's not even *midnight*."

"Lydia's expecting me," he says, and I think *ah*. My stomach lurches and a taste of almonds rises in the back of my throat. They say cyanide tastes of almonds.

"I've always thought we'd get along if we hung out."

Eli sighs and rubs his eyes. "It's not about that, Lau."

"What d'you mean?"

"She just gets a bit jealous."

"Jealous? Of *me*?" Lydia had a collection of short stories published a couple years ago with a major publisher, and then she travelled around Europe for three months "researching a novel," which looked a lot like documenting every latte and pastry on Instagram. Eli flew out to meet her in Rome, and they did Italy together. I was convinced he was going to propose, had braced myself for it, but he didn't. He just lounged in the background of her shots, all cheekbones in black and white, drinking espresso and smoking duty-free straights in dark Ray-Bans.

"You know why," Eli says, raising his eyebrows. "We have . . . y'know, history or whatever."

"A drunken fumble isn't history," I say, ignoring the rush of shame that comes from speaking so candidly about that night. "It's barely an anecdote. Old news. Yesterday's weather. We're just pals, right?"

My conviction won't stand up to scrutiny, but I'm bolstered by the confidence of a thousand amarettos. It was years ago, a few months before he met Lydia. Tears, the taste of gin, his hands all over me, and then a blank wall of alcohol-induced amnesia. Sometimes, after a few too many, it was like my brain simply stopped recording memories. There was nothing there but the ghost of recollection, a vague impression of residual feelings, and an overwhelming sense of disgrace.

"Of course we're pals," he says. The streetlights cast a warm glow over us, and he looks sweet and angelic and I could kiss him, I really could. "I just don't think Lydia's in a rush to be best mates. But that doesn't mean we can't hang out. She trusts me, she's just . . . a bit jealous. That's all."

"We can hang out," I agree, and we walk in step, and the night is fresh, and I feel like I can relax with Eli by my side. "We *should* hang out. Let's hang out, yeah?"

ROACH

Walthamstow was crawling with normies. The bars clustered around the station were teeming with drunks and losers all dressed up for a night of shit booze and bad company. I barged through a knot of girls with sambuca-breath waiting for cabs into town, knocking into shoulders, battling against the grain.

Laura and Eli walked slowly, because Laura was drunk and Eli was happy to indulge her. They stopped to roll more cigarettes, and I stopped to watch, and then it just felt right to follow in the dissipating trail of their smoke. I had a vague idea that Laura lived on the other side of Lloyd Park, but this seemed like a good opportunity to find out more. Did she still live at home with her parents, or perhaps in a flatshare full of late nights and laughter, a group of girls waiting for her, drinking wine and sharing a takeaway pizza in their pyjamas? Or a cosy Warner flat, a little hideaway shared with a smitten lover? I was also curious to see if they'd shaken me loose with the intention of continuing the night without me. That had happened more than once at after-work drinks.

They stopped to speak to a homeless man, and then they passed Mirth, and then the Rose and Crown, and it seemed like they really were just walking home. She took a left down Ruby Road but, to my surprise, they took a right when they reached Lloyd Park and walked along its perimeter until they met the main road again. It was a pointless detour—they could have just followed the curve of the main road and ended up in the same place. It would have been quicker. I wondered if she'd forgotten the park was locked at this hour, but that seemed unlikely.

They paused when they reached The Bell, and I took advantage of a green man to cross the street and avoid overtaking them. The pub was still open, all flashing disco lights and blaring pop music, and I thought perhaps Laura was angling for a nightcap, but Eli was shaking his head, cajoling her onwards. If you were so thirsty, Laura, why didn't you want to have another one with me?

I pretended to wait at the bus stop to let them gain some ground, and then I darted across the empty road so I could continue my pursuit from a safe distance. Eventually, they turned down a quiet residential street, and Laura stopped in front of a Warner flat, right on the edge of the park.

"This is me," she called over her shoulder, her voice carrying on the still night air. I hid behind a white van on the other side of the street and watched her fumble with her keys, and then she opened the door and turned to Eli and said something that was lost on the velvet of the night, and to my great interest, he followed her inside.

The garden path was made of split concrete, dark clumps of moss packed into the cracks. The bay windows were curtained and dark. Everything looked so ordinary, so disappointingly ordinary, I wondered if I'd ever find it again. I pulled out my phone and made note of her address, just in case I ever needed it.

A gap between the curtains shivered with a flickering light. I left the safety of my hiding place behind the white van and creeped into her front garden for a better look. Beneath the bay window was an empty flower bed, home only to a large, dead-looking plant. I snapped away the twiggy branches to make some space, and my feet sank into the damp soil as I peered inside. She was standing barefoot, holding a box of long cook's matches. Large votives burned in the fireplace, and she was lighting a half dozen tea lights that lined the mantle. The chimney breast was flanked by bookshelves, but the titles of the books were deep in shadow and indiscernible from my place on the other side of the glass.

Eli appeared in the living room door with a wine bottle and two glasses. He dropped onto a battered brown sofa and twisted off the screw cap, then poured out two glasses of piss-coloured wine. This was like watching television, a little documentary unfolding especially for me. She accepted a glass and lit a cigarette from a cream-coloured pillar candle, and I could have watched them all night through that little gap in the curtain, could have watched whatever seduction she had in mind, but a sharp cough directly behind me made me jump. I turned to see a man in a Nike hoodie and football shorts, his face and legs slick with sweat.

"You all right?" he said with a frown, chest rising and falling as he struggled to catch his breath.

"I think my boyfriend's cheating on me," I replied, and then I held his gaze, stared him down, until he turned and resumed his late-night run. He looked back once, twice, and then disappeared around the corner.

LAURA

Wine, music, soft candlelight. The shadows jump, and Eli laughs easily, smoking cigarettes, growing flush, the conversation flowing like the tobacco smoke that rolls off our tongues, and all the while, as we perform this show of friendship, the memory of his lips and the lingering looks continue and the thought that anything could happen prevails.

"I like your place," he says. "It suits you."

His left ankle is balanced on his right knee, one arm thrown against the back of the sofa. Dark, tousled hair like Robert Mapplethorpe, like Jim Morrison. Wooden beads around his wrists, a leather cord around his neck.

"What does *that* mean?"

He exhales and runs a hand through his curls. "It just suits you. Kind of mismatched and creative. It must get lonely, though. Living alone. And I don't know how you can afford it."

"I've rented this place since I was like . . . twenty-one?" I say. "My landlord lives in Australia and doesn't really give much of a shit about it. I don't think it's occurred to him that he could charge me *way* more now."

"Lucky." He reaches for the bottle and tops up our glasses.

At university, our student house was cacophonous, full of music and laughter and late nights, a revolving door of friends and classmates, boyfriends and girlfriends, lovers and strangers making themselves at home at our kitchen table, on our sofa, in the other girls" beds. The constant flow of people through the space shredded my nerves, and the unpredictability of it all left me anxious, unable to sleep without medication that knocked me out. It's better for my mental health to live alone—even in a place like this, with its perpetual damp and mould—but if my landlord ever decides to sell this flat or takes a closer look at the rental market in Walthamstow, I'll be in trouble. There's no way I can afford the going rate for a one-bed on bookseller wages. This train of thought leads to dark, vulnerable places, though, so I take a deep breath and swallow some wine that tastes like overripe peaches and an astringent hit of tannin.

"So, are you working on anything new?" he asks.

"Just reading at the moment, trying to decide what I want to write about next. I started working on another found poem, but the story's a bit . . . much for me. It's really violent, and . . ." I pause to collect my thoughts. I'm thinking about my mother, and I find myself wondering what Eli remembers from the night we kissed. I've always had this shameful feeling that we talked about my mother that night, but the details didn't stick and I've never found the right way to ask.

"I don't know. Maybe I'm done with the found poetry project," I say. "Maybe I should just trust my instincts and pack it in. Fuck poetry, and all that."

Eli raises his glass. "Yeah, fuck poetry," he says, and I raise mine and we clink them together.

"What would you write instead?" he asks.

Outside, the wild cry of an urban fox.

My mother, I think. I would write about my mother.

"A love story," I reply.

ROACH

On the way home, I stopped at an all-night corner shop and picked up a cucumber for Bleep and a pair of Dark Fruits to drink when I got home. At the cash register, with a devil-may-care shrug, I asked for a pack of Pall Malls, the type that came with a flavour capsule like a Rice Krispie in the filter that you could squeeze to change the flavour of the cigarette from plain to menthol. Laura, Eli, and Sharona all smoked rolling tobacco, but I didn't feel much confidence in my ability to roll. I had to walk before I could run.

The lights were low inside the Mother Black Cap, and it hummed with the late-night jokes, petty rows, and maudlin heart-to-hearts of the drunks, losers, and students who favoured cheap beer and late nights. The bar smelled like disinfectant, and Laura's words rolled around my head like a loose marble. *It stinks.* Ridiculous. She must have been thinking of another pub. She didn't seem that fussy once she had a drink in her hand.

Jackie was sitting at the bar with a vodka soda, all dolled up in a sparkly top and a full mask of makeup. She was flapping her gums at one of the regulars, a middle-aged saddo who was inching towards the door. When she saw me, she interrupted herself midsentence.

"You're back late," she said, grabbing me by the arm and kissing my cheek with greasy lipsticked lips. She was wearing too much perfume—a strong punch of Calvin Klein Obsession smacked me in the face. "I was just telling Dave here—"

"It's Frank, actually, and I—"

The man looked sheepish, like a shamefaced dog who'd shit all over the carpet and knew he was in trouble, but Jackie ploughed on regardless, with some long-winded story about her hairdresser's daughter. She kept her arm clamped around my waist the entire time, pinning me in place.

"Anyway, she got the deposit back in the end," she concluded, rattling the ice cubes in her glass with her free hand.

"Well, night," I said, trying to extricate myself from her grasp, and she blinked at me as though she'd forgotten I was standing there. The punter, Frank, saw his chance and bolted for the door with a hasty goodnight.

"Where've you been, then?" she asked, turning the full beam of her attention on to me. She had a suspicious gleam in her eye, like she was anticipating a lie.

"Just out," I said, twisting free from her grip.

"On a date?"

"A work thing."

"A work thing? What work thing?"

"It was just drinks," I said, slipping behind the bar towards the staircase before she could lock me into a proper conversation.

"Drinks? Where? Not the Rose and Crown?"

I dashed up the stairs, leaving her hanging. You had to be quick on your feet around Jackie. Keep yourself at arm's length and keep the conversation short and sharp, with as little information as possible.

Living above a pub had its perks, but it led to a lonely childhood. There was never anyone around to bathe me or put me to bed, as Jackie worked round the clock to keep the bar running. Even when she wasn't working a shift, she could usually be found in the bar choosing the music, interrupting conversations, telling stories, badgering the staff. The pub was her stage and she was the main character, the playwright, and the director all rolled into one.

I would appear in the pub at odd times, ramshackle with dried jam around my mouth, a grimy neck, hair in disarray, a smell of unwashed clothes about me, a little animal stuffed into leggings and T-shirts that never quite fit me right because I wasn't built the way little girls were meant to be built. I was big for my age, tall with broad shoulders and little oysters of breast tissue that left me feeling self-conscious. Jackie would always make a fuss of me when I appeared, give me packets of salt and vinegar crisps and glasses of post-mix Coke, and I'd tuck myself in a corner and read *Goosebumps* and *Horrible Histories* until day faded to night and I was shooed back upstairs. Sometimes, she'd take a flannel to my face and neck like an afterthought, flatten my hair with her hands, stick a padded Alice band on my crown in an attempt to make me look complete. I thought perhaps I was the problem. She wanted a little girl, but she ended up with me. There was always something missing, a hole in my heart that I filled with murder, death, and putrefaction.

Safe in my bedroom, I cracked a Dark Fruits and practised smoking out of my bedroom window, a splintered sash edged with thin metal spikes to keep the pigeons that roosted in the roof from shitting all over the front of the pub. At night the pigeons cooed to one another, a gentle, infernal symphony. I'd once heard someone call Pall Malls "virgin fags," but the menthol took the edge off, softened the burning taste to a cool chemical mint, like brushing your teeth in hell.

I grabbed my phone and pulled up Laura's social media accounts to find out more about her—how she dressed outside work, whether she liked to post pictures of her meals or the weather or if she was into vapid selfies. But no: her entire feed was just a catalogue of paperbacks held up against different backdrops: a brick wall painted eggshell blue, a field of grass, the coarse grit of a beach. Boring.

Bleep looked on, incurious about my new smoking habit. He oozed against the glass of his vivarium, a silent witness, his glistening body the colour of a ripe Conference pear. I reached a finger into his tank and stroked his smooth shell, chocolate brown marbled with white. Most people don't think of snails when they think of loving pets, but I'd always drawn a sense of calm from their timid, docile presence. The warm glow of a heat lamp in a snail vivarium was my night light as a child and snails were my most reliable source of comfort. My first giant African land snail was called Slimer. One of the regulars wanted to get rid of him, and as soon as I heard he was free to a good home, I set my heart on becoming a snail mother.

"A bloody snail," Jackie said, rolling her eyes. "Why can't she want a hamster or a kitten or something normal?"

I didn't care for hamsters or kittens. What I really wanted was a snake, but beggars can't be choosers and a giant African land snail turned out to be just as good. Slimer lived to the ripe old age of nine before he ended up on the wrong side of the grass, so to speak. After Slimer came Bleep. Bleep was still going strong. He lived a modest life on a diet of grapes, cucumber, and lettuce leaves, with the occasional scoop of calcium powder to keep his shell strong. He needed his tank cleaned weekly, and I took great pleasure in crushing the clutches of his pearly eggs under the weight of a pint glass. Aside from that, it was just regular mistings all day every day, and we lived in harmony side by side.

As I sipped cider between drags, I grew to like the contrast between smoky and sweet, hot and cold, dry and wet, dead and alive. I felt light-headed. I put on a murder podcast to ground me, and watched night buses from the city glide past, occasionally belching out a clot of staggering drunks, normies on their way home from a night out in Shoreditch or Dalston. Careless, carefree, with kebabs, clutch bags, and even their high heels in their hands, bare feet on the spit-spattered pavement, like the dark city streets were just an extension of their kitchens, and nothing awful could happen to them there.

Laura's poetry rolled around my head, the way the ordinary could so easily become extraordinary, the way you never knew what was waiting for you around the next corner. I smoked and watched the world pass by underneath me, and nothing extraordinary happened to anyone outside my window. I wondered what I would do if something did. Would my weapon of choice be my phone, to call for help, our biggest kitchen knife, in an act of vigilante justice, or my silence? Would I do anything at all, or would I just sit back and watch it all happen beneath me, a spectator with a front-row seat?

LAURA

The poetry reading hangs over me, the anxiety of another drunken night casting a shadow over my day off. I wake up to the bacchanalian detritus of the night before: the stinking ashtray, the empty wine bottle, a trail of crisp packets, a hummus pot scraped clean with a drunken finger. I cringe for being too much, too full on, too obvious, shamefaced at the memory of Eli cutting our hug goodbye short as he made his way out the door.

With a thick headache, I drag myself to the bathroom to clean my teeth and wash my face. Something on the carpet catches the light by the back door—a sparkling loop-de-loop. It looks like a dropped necklace, or a coil of silver thread, but on closer inspection I realise it's a twisted rope of slug or snail mucus. Horrified, I search in vain for the culprit but I can't find any invertebrates in the bathroom or kitchen. I clean up the mess with a square of dry kitchen roll, but as I potter around, watering my plants and tidying up, I keep expecting to feel the squelch of slug under my bare foot and I'm on edge all morning.

Once I've finished cleaning, I make myself a cup of tea and curl up on the sofa with my books, but the case is horrendous, and I can't focus on it. An uneasiness settles over me, and I realise it's because my thoughts keep returning to my conversation with Roach at the bar. *I love serial killers.* I shudder at the memory of her hot rotten breath, her uncomfortably close proximity, her fixed attention. She was practically salivating. I've met people like her before. The kind of people who have a favorite serial killer, who buy true crime merch and watch documentaries about death over dinner, who visit places where terrible things have happened like they're going to Disneyland: Chernobyl. Alcatraz. Fukushima.

Combing through stories of murder, violence, grief, and loss can be harrowing, but creating new narratives felt empowering, like I'm doing something with my grief, saying something with my anger, making a point. Now, it feels flat. Perhaps it hits differently with someone like Roach in the audience, enjoying it for all the wrong reasons.

Poetry used to come to me like summer rain—long droughts, and then a storm of inspiration that lasted a week, two weeks, a shower of words filling notebook after notebook until I had nothing left and it was back to dry skies for another month. Notebooks, so many notebooks, full of poetry and prose, notes and diary entries. When I have money, I buy hardback Moleskines for the Hemingway clout, and when I don't, I go for cheap exercise books, studious with their echoes of secondary school. I love the lure of a clean page, fresh and untouched, like a hotel bed, a blanket of virgin snow, an empty plate waiting to be filled.

I worry about what to do with them all, all the notebooks that I've already filled up. They feel important and they feel stupid. Significant, and embarrassing. There's a striking red and white mural near my house that quotes William Morris: *Have nothing in your house that you do not know to be useful or believe to be beautiful*. I can't work out where my old notebooks and diaries sit on that particular spectrum, and I'm worried about leaving a legacy of trash for my future children to deal with after my death.

When someone dies, everything becomes sacred. Greetings cards marked with their handwriting, their winter scarf, their half-used cosmetics. Everything. I'm not sure who sorted through my mother's things when she died, or what happened to them. It's all a bit of a blur—I was only sixteen, a child really—but I guess my grandmother must have dealt with it all. My father certainly didn't lift a finger.

They were long divorced, separated since I was a baby. There wasn't room for me and my grief in his new family. His second wife, Margot, had expensive taste, and I didn't really fit into her world of Waitrose, expensive holidays, and private education. All I got from my Dad was his kitschy surname and the occasional tense dinner around Christmas and birthdays during which he cheerfully dismissed bookselling as a legitimate career and instead tried to push me into getting his estimation of "a real job."

My mother was reduced to a small wooden box of trinkets and keepsakes that my grandmother had kept for me. A coral Revlon lipstick. A chunk of amethyst on a black cord that I couldn't bear to wear in case I lost it. A shopping list, perhaps for a cake—*eggs, milk, flour, vanilla*—written in rushed blue biro. A birthday card, from me to her—a blue and pink crayon scribble of flowers on green cartridge paper. A few pieces of costume jewellery—red plastic beads, silver bangles, fake pearls. A Mason Pearson hairbrush, black plastic with boar bristles set into a red rubber base, which was an eighteenth birthday present from her parents. The one thing I do remember keeping myself was a handsome monstera. I took special care of it, learned to propagate its stems and grow babies from cuttings to keep the spirit of the plant alive long after the parent plant had died.

I mourned the things I lost for a while. Her glass perfume bottles, her dresses, her trinkets. I mourned her library. She loved books—I remembered a big shelf of paperbacks in my childhood home—but teenagers aren't interested in adult things and I never thought to ask for any to keep. I wonder if she folded the corners and cracked the spines like me, or if she was fussy, kept them neat.

I found a photo of me as a toddler once, plump and happy, with elastic cuff marks around my elbows and knees. I'm holding a stuffed blue elephant and standing in front of a bookshelf. Whoever took the picture was a slapdash photographer, because the books were in focus and I was not, and although I'm sure it was a disappointment at the time, I value the photo because it's a window into my mother's library. I collected those books for a while, the ones I could see. Jilly Cooper and Jackie Collins, Jacqueline Susann, Shirley Conran. I read *Riders*, and *Lucky*, and *Valley of the Dolls*, and *Lace*, and then my attention waned, and I discovered the first glimmer of my own taste: Sylvia Plath, J. D. Salinger, Stephen Chbosky, Jeffrey Eugenides. I drifted towards narratives about forlorn teenagers, young people finding themselves, young people losing themselves.

I never got around to reading the rest of my mother's books, but the bitterness of losing her library faded when I understood the real power of reading. It's not the physical books, books as artefacts, as objets, that actually matter. The pages that my mother touched, turned, folded, read, don't hold the same reverence as her winter scarf, her handwriting. The books themselves are no more meaningful than the streets she walked on, the mugs she drank from, the sheets she slept in. It's the words that have power. Somewhere between the ink that's printed on each page and my understanding of the content is a plain across which my mother's mind has also wandered, and that landscape exists in every single edition, whether or not it has been touched by my mother's hand. That's the power of reading.

I started feeling much less precious about books after that. Now, I fold the pages, bend the covers, stuff them in my handbag, cover them in greasy fingerprints, in coffee, in wine, in bathwater. I lose them, lend them out, give them away. It's not that I mean to be careless, but the reverence I have for books only extends to the words on the page, the magic between the lines. I think that's why I'm such a good bookseller. I'm selling things, artefacts, objets, yes. But that's not all. I'm also selling magic.

∽

Hangovers always leave me hollowed out, overly analytical and anxious, but a day of moping, a long hot shower, and an early night is all I need to wash away all lingering thoughts of the poetry reading, of getting too drunk, of being too much with Eli. When I leave for work the following morning, the sky is an optimistic blue with a chilly promise of October in the air.

Over the road, a woman in pink sheepskin slippers and a grey cardigan drops a bin bag into her wheelie bin. A fat ginger cat watches her from beneath a white van, and as she turns towards her front door, he darts through the gate and into the house, mewing for breakfast.

Breakfast. My stomach aches and I remember the Tupperware of black bean salad that I've left sitting on the kitchen counter. As I turn back to the front door, raking through my tote bag for my door keys, I notice that the fuchsia beneath my living room window is bent and broken, the dormant autumn stems crooked where they have been snapped.

I swallow a rising swell of panic. Beneath the broken plant, there's the perfect outline of two boots pressed into the soil beneath my living room window, as though someone had stood in the dirt and peered at me through the glass.

OCTOBER 2019

ROACH

In the days that followed Laura's poetry reading, I felt a seismic shift between us. Despite her dismissive attitude towards me at the end of the night, something had changed. The universe had flexed, the stars had aligned, and two kindred spirits had crossed paths.

I reread her words like a prayer, like a psalm, like a letter from a lover at war. I woke up with her words in my head, I showered with them in my head, I niveli off, I got dressed, I walked to work with them in my head. I did everything as normal, but it wasn't the same because I was looking at the world through Laura's lens. The promise of violence was everywhere, the air was singing with it.

Our newfound connection was lost on Laura, though. Working with her was like this: wherever she was in the shop, she emitted a constant stream of chatter and mindless questions, a rally of nonsense aimed at whichever bookseller or customer happened to be nearest—although she never turned her attention to me. I'd hear her in Fiction (have you ever read *The Virgin Suicides*? Have you ever read *My Year of Rest and Relaxation*? Have you ever read *The Secret History*?) to YA (have you ever read *Junk*? Have you ever read *Looking for Alaska*? Have you ever read *Noughts and Crosses*?) to Poetry (have you ever read *Ariel*? Have you ever read *Let Them Eat Chaos*? Have you ever read *Night Sky with Exit Wounds*?) to

Biography (have you ever read *The Outrun?* Have you ever read *I Am, I Am, I Am?* Have you ever read *I Know Why the Caged Bird Sings?*) to Graphic Novels (have you ever read *Maus?* Have you ever read *Fun Home?* Have you ever read *Ghost World?*).

If the answer was yes, she held the book to her chest and sighed with pleasure, and if the answer was no, she held the book to her chest and sighed with pain. She held it to her heart, and closed her eyes and tilted her chin, and the look on her face was that of a woman in love, or heartbroken, or both at the same time. Laura was in love with the very pages, the ink, the actual glue, of every cheap mass-produced paperback she had ever read. She pined for them, she cradled them like precious children, like they were babies.

When it came to me, however, it was a different story. She didn't speak to me unless she had to. She was polite when I spoke to her, but she never struck up conversation with me in the same way she did with the rest of the team, and she avoided my eye on the shop floor like I was an annoying customer that she didn't want to serve. I tried everything to grab her attention—I wore my *Murder Girls* T-shirts to work, I angled *their inconsequential moments were beautiful* towards her in the staffroom, and whenever I found myself reading *The Stranger Beside Me* in her presence, I embarked on a theatrical performance of gasps and barks of laughter to pique her interest. In return, she gave me nothing, and I began to wonder if it was personal.

For example, she liked to play games on the shop floor when it was quiet. Icebreakers, like Desert Island Books or Would You Rather. One afternoon, she asked each member of staff to describe themselves in just five words.

"But that only tells you what *I* think of me, not what I'm really like," said Eli, enunciating his words by tapping her on the shoulder with a biro.

"Isn't that in itself rather telling?" she replied, her eyes sparkling with pleasure.

"Okay, I'm . . . chill, kind . . . peaceful . . . philosophical and . . . curious."

"Curious is one of mine too!" Laura replied, giddy. "I'm curious, tidy—well, mostly tidy—adventurous, stylish, and creative."

I was standing right there the whole time, but she didn't ask me how I would describe myself and I spent the rest of my shift wondering why. What had I done to you, Laura? Why was I so uninteresting to you, if curiosity was such a fundamental part of your personality?

If Laura had deigned to turn her head and ask me to describe myself in five words, I'd probably have picked curious too. I loved to do research and read nonfiction, and I was always praised for that at school, although not so much for my illustrations, which leaned into a degree of bloody realism that left my classmates unsettled and my teachers concerned.

Morbid, macabre, ghoulish, ghastly. Those were all words Jackie liked to call me, but they were synonyms really. Perhaps "creative" was more appropriate. My mind was capable of conjuring dark thoughts, and I'd always had a knack for transforming my darkest ones into poetry or drawings.

It started when I realised there were so many different ways to die. Like cancer and heart disease and brain aneurysms, sure, and car crashes and house fires and drowning. But then there's all the other ways, the ways that you didn't even think about because you were too busy eating kale and checking your breasts for lumps. Like being crushed by falling masonry, or swallowed by a sinkhole, or stung to death by bees. Ever think of that? I did.

When most normies hear about a freak accident, like a sudden fog that causes a motorway pileup or a roller coaster breaking down, they think sad thoughts for the dead, about how unlucky they were, how they were in the wrong place at the wrong time. Maybe they vow to quit smoking or start cycling to work, to book that cruise or call their parents more often.

Those are the clichéd ways in which we're meant to dream of bettering ourselves. But that revised appreciation for life doesn't last. Soon they'll be back to smoking when they're pissed and avoiding their mother's calls when they're hungover.

No one thinks they'll die in a freak accident because they're so rare. That's why they're called "freak" accidents and not lumped in with all the regular accidents—falling off ladders, being hit by buses. I started to think, though, that if we calculated how many "freak" accidents there were per year, you're probably more likely to die in one than you thought. And it's the same with serial killers. It sounds rare, but it must happen all the time. We just don't hear about it unless it's a good story.

∽

It was a quiet evening with terrible weather, the kind of weather that kept people indoors and left the pub empty. I took a seat by the fruit machines with a pint of cider, a brand-new notebook and Laura's chapbook, *their inconsequential moments were beautiful*. I had to admit, "chapbook" was a bit of a stretch. More of a homemade zine than a chapbook, held together with wonky staples, probably made by Laura herself, alone in her bedroom. The thought of it made me ache, although whether out of pity or irritation, I couldn't tell.

My copy was trashed, crumpled, the corners bent, the ink on the cover smudged and stained by my fingers. I smoothed it against the scarred table with the palm of my hand, pressed it flat.

Rain turned the windows to static. Jackie switched on the big sports TV and flipped between channels until she found an *EastEnders* omnibus to watch with the subtitles switched on, like a silent film. A couple regulars sat at the bar with pints of Guinness, sharing a packet of peanuts and talking in a low murmur.

I felt like writing something, but I didn't have anything much to say. With a black biro, I underlined the first three lines from the first poem I'd heard Laura read at the Nib.

> *It was now 5 A.M., and dawn,*
> *a hot, fiery dawn,*
> *was slowly filling a sad, tranquil sky.*

I copied the lines into my notebook, and I liked the way the pen felt as it rolled against the page. I liked the way the words looked. Neat and permanent, a tattoo. I decided to copy out the whole thing, the whole poem, like an exercise.

Poetry had been my artistic expression of choice for quite a while. It started when I was a Columbiner, although that all belongs to a different version of me, an earlier draft that occurred somewhere between scrapping the girlie-girl version of myself, the version that carried a handbag, and the creep that I am today.

I was drawn into an online community of girls who followed school shooters like rock stars. Fucked up, I know, but the heart is a lonely hunter. These girls wrote poetry, and posted drawings of the shooters, and shared impossible fantasies with all the love and dedication of starry-eyed fans. That's when I found my voice as a poet. I wrote poetry inspired by the sad, shy boy with the short blond curtains and the 12-gauge double-barrelled shotgun. I used to wear a black fingerless glove on my left hand to show my affinity with Dylan; a private homage that meant nothing to the average passerby but everything to me.

I didn't have a favourite poet, didn't read much poetry. I didn't think that mattered—you didn't have to read poetry to be a poet. I'm not sure if I'd even read a whole collection from beginning to end, cover to cover. That didn't matter, either. You don't have to read *Gray's Anatomy* to take a razor to your forearm and cut yourself, make yourself bleed. Poetry was a release, a healthy, therapeutic expression.

When I reached my late teens, I recognised that the Columbine community was much more politically hateful than I'd previously understood it to be and I no longer felt confident that I knew where the ironic misanthropy ended and the earnest fascism began. The angsty teens who posted their high-angled, heavily edited selfies, all sweeping emo fringes over thick flicky eyeliner and long striped sleeves covering self-harm scars, were growing into young adults who posed for photos with handguns and hunting knives, who wore NATURAL SELECTION and WRATH T-shirts and swapped poetry for cryptic Nazi references. It was dragging me in the wrong direction, and I pulled back.

Jackie had been relieved. "No one wants to go down the local and see the bloody trench-coat mafia," she'd said.

"They do in all them rocker pubs in Camden," one of the regulars had said.

"I'm not trying to run a bloody rocker pub in Camden, though, am I?" Jackie replied, hands on her hips, which was a bit rich coming from her as she loved to talk about rubbing shoulders with Shane MacGowan and Spider Stacy in the Devonshire Arms in the '80s.

After Columbine, it felt right to repent and pivot to something more righteous, and I got really into the West Memphis Three. I continued to write poetry, but my interests manifested around Damien Echols. He was beautiful, with his long dark hair and soulful eyes. I thought that my attraction to Damien would make me seem like a better person because he wasn't a murderer: in fact, I studied the case carefully and was convinced of his innocence. I wrote the kind of poetry I imagined he was writing from his prison cell: spiritual and folkloric, magical, patient, and wise, full of spells and incantations, inspired by nature and death. I filled notebooks with free-form verse about God and the devil, Catholicism and Satanism, although I knew nothing about any of those things. I wore black sunglasses all the time, and a homemade "Free the West Memphis Three" T-shirt.

I finished copying out Laura's poem and I read over it. I desperately wished to know which book Laura had "found" her lines in. Something about the repetition of hot weather made me think of California. *Helter Skelter*, maybe? Was it Charles Manson who lurked between Laura's lines, and his merry band of murderous followers? Or *In Cold Blood*, perhaps? Was Truman Capote thinking of Holcomb, Kansas, as he wrote such delicate lines of prose about hot, fiery dawns and sad, tranquil skies?

I had to know. There was no way Laura had sourced her prose from a book I hadn't read myself, and I was desperate to connect the dots, to reread those works through Laura's eyes. I dreamed of asking her again, dreamed of her being receptive to the question, of finally opening up. Perhaps I'd be able to recommend some titles, perhaps she'd be pleased. It felt like the only way I'd ever get an answer would be if I was somehow able to infiltrate her home, take a look at her bookshelves, and find out for myself, but that was about as likely to happen as her simply telling me.

"What's that you've got there, then?" Jackie asked, picking up my empty pint glass and craning her neck to peer at my notebook. Her pink lipstick had feathered around her mouth, faded from the centre of her bottom lip, and she had tiny beetles of mascara in the corner of each eye.

"Just some poetry," I said, covering my journal with my hand.

"*Poetry?*" she said. "Christ. What you need is to get out a bit, meet someone. When I was your age, I had a different man on my arm every night of the week."

She prattled on about how she spent her wild youth necking Pernod and black in miniskirts at punk gigs. In her stories, she always had the sharpest tongue, always had the last laugh, always had some minor connection to a major celebrity, the details of which shifted depending on how much she'd had to drink, her audience, and what kind of mood she was in. She once claimed to have snogged a young David Bowie, and then later denied all knowledge of the lie.

"I don't want to *meet someone.*" I tried to say it with a cool and breezy indifference, but it came out as a thin and childish whine. *I don't wanna.*

LAURA

I report the footprints outside my living room window to the police. The woman I speak to plays along, gives me a crime reference number and tells me to keep my front door locked, but I can tell she isn't particularly concerned, and by the time I hang up, I'm too agitated to read or write.

I've been working on a poem. It's about women and their partners, murdered by a police officer who broke into their homes in the middle of the night. I never *enjoy* reading these narratives, but I can hardly get through this one at all. It's too much for me, too close to home. I skim-read to find what I'm looking for—descriptions of the women as they were: their routines, their neighbourhoods, the weather—but each time I pick up the book, I'm haunted by the image of a stranger peering into my living room window and I feel light-headed, sick to my stomach, and have to put it down.

At least work keeps me busy. A huge drop of children's education came through just before half-term: cheap, glossy workbooks for verbal reasoning, maths, comprehension, science. I dutifully label them all with Buy One Get One Free stickers for the October half-term sale, but when the week comes, it's a total washout. Fierce winds and sheet rain plaster fallen leaves to the pavements and force all but our staunchest regulars to retreat into the shopping centre, leaving the market a wasteland of rain-battered loners walking with their heads down, striding with purpose.

We're overstaffed. Sharona, used to the buzzing pace of sales in central London, anticipated a busy week full of early Christmas shoppers, over-bearing parents stocking up on schoolbooks, and families out shopping for the day. Instead, hours stretch by with no customers in sight, and we rattle around the empty shop, finding odd jobs to busy ourselves with.

When half-term draws to a close, I dutifully de-sticker all the unsold revision guides. My fingernails catch on the stubborn glue, weaken and split and peel. It takes hours, and there's a Sisyphean futility to de-stickering books that had taken me hours to sticker in the first place, but I'm glad to have something to do.

Roach's eyes burn into me as I try my best to ignore her. She always seems to be on the brink of saying something to me but, thankfully, is prone to losing her nerve. Instead, she brings her copy of my chapbook into work every day, and I watch with embarrassed dismay as the pages get increasingly battered and worn as she rereads it to death. Even when I get a moment to myself, I can smell her strangely sweet, rancid smell in the staffroom on my breaks. Even when she isn't there, the room regurgitates a memory of her, like she's a ghost baked into the foundations of the shop.

Sharona locks herself away in the office, sorting through decades of misfiled paperwork. It's strange to see so little of her; she's usually a hands-on boss, the kind of bookshop manager who prefers to lead by example on the shop floor. She emerges periodically to smoke and brew tea, a battle-weary expression of resignation on her face. Whenever I poke my head into the dusty office to get change for the tills or offer her a drink, Sharona's incense-smell of cigarettes and essential oils makes me think of the stalls of silver rings and trinkets in Camden Market.

"It's not good," she says, nodding at the piles of brittle papers and curling receipts. "We might need to get Jim in, do a full audit."

Sometimes, between all the endless paperwork and tidying up, lines of poetry or scraps of prose come to me, and I scrawl them on strips of blank till roll and stuff them into my pockets. While I'm still struggling to get my head back into the found poetry project, I'm determined not to be derailed creatively. On my days off, when I do laundry, I find these little pieces of paper marked with meaningless words, their inspiration, their context, their significance, lost forever.

"What happened to 'fuck poetry'?" Eli says, catching me scribbling behind the till.

"I say a lot of things I don't mean after a drink," I reply, my eyes glued to the scrap of paper in my hand. I've lost my train of thought, so I write a random list of fruit to disguise how much of a distraction he is to me. *Apple, peach, watermelon, rhubarb, pear.*

"Well, I've got a present for you," he says, all pleased with himself. His hands are clasped behind his back, and he's grinning. "Close your eyes and hold out your hands."

I oblige with a nervous giggle, half expecting a spider or a slug, like some flirty playground prank, but instead he places a fabric-bound book into my outstretched hands. I open my eyes and see a child's diary, a hard-back lilac notebook protected with a tiny heart-shaped padlock. "Found it in a tote of random crap. Probably write-offs from the last stocktake. There's no barcode or anything, but it still has its little key so . . . do you want it? I thought you could use it to write your love story."

"Thank you." It comes out as a croaky whisper because my mouth has gone completely dry. I turn the book over in my hands. The cover is warm to the touch from his hands. "When I was little," I say, putting on a brighter and less earnest voice, "I wanted one of these so badly, even though I was, like, nine years old and didn't have any secrets."

He smiles an indulgent smile. "Kids love the idea of secrets, though, don't they?"

"I still do."

The shop floor is totally dead, so, emboldened by the gift, I step forward and wrap my arms around him in a hug of thanks.

"Nice to have the band back together again, isn't it?" he says, pulling away.

"Dream team," I reply, slapping a sticker on his shoulder. It's lost its stickiness, and it curls in on itself and then drops on to the carpet between us.

⁓

It's one of those gorgeous evenings, the October sun bright gold and just on the brink of setting. Outside the shop, Eli and Sharona crack jokes and roll cigarettes. They're both on the late shift tomorrow, and there's a spirit of rascality in the air.

"Drink tonight?" Eli says. "We thought we'd check out that cat pub in Walthamstow Village—the Nags Head?"

"Can't," I say, with a burn of regret. "I have a thing tonight."

"Sure you can't come for a cheeky one?" Sharona twists her key in the lock and then tugs on the door handle to check it's closed properly.

"I really can't," I reply.

"Laura Bunting, turning down a drink?" Eli grins, stretching to pull down the stiff shutters. "Should we call an exorcist?"

"Ha ha."

"Which way are you going?" Sharona asks me, lighting a cigarette and wrinkling her eyes against the smoke.

"Just gonna text my friends and find out where they are," I say. "Don't wait for me; you guys go ahead."

I wave them off and watch them mosey up the market towards the Village. When their retreating backs are lost in the bustle and thrum of stallholders packing up for the day, I follow in their footsteps. I think of the casual, easy evening ahead of them: cold rosé, piping hot pizza, and good gossipy conversation as day gives way to night. As smokers, they'll find a table in the garden under one of the heated lamps, and cats will thread between their chair legs and beg for scraps, and the air will smell like garlic and oregano wafting from the kitchen.

In contrast, the community hall is chilly, and reeks of disinfectant, the smell of my teenage years, of police stations and family liaison offices, waiting rooms and group therapy sessions. Hannah and Charity are talking in muted tones, adding sugar and UHT milk to cups of instant coffee as Des arranges the last of the chairs into a rough circle. There's a couple new faces, and a few semi-regulars whose names I can't recall. People come and go. Sometimes they say goodbye, but often they just stop showing up. Sometimes they come back, but mostly they do not.

A stout woman with unruly grey hair and baggy eyes wipes her nose with a handkerchief and a man with tight silver curls and stooped shoulders turns a flat cap in his hands. I drop my bag and coat on a chair and offer them both drinks. New people are often a little guarded and they don't always like to help themselves. The woman, perhaps a little over-whelmed by the situation, says no, thank you, but the man says yes to a tea with milk and sugar.

"Bless you," he says in a gentle Caribbean accent. As he accepts the paper cup from my outstretched hand, he gives me an awkward pat on the arm and introduces himself as John. His eyes are already sparkling with sadness. I give his shoulder a little squeeze.

I pour myself a cup of tea that I don't particularly want. The warmth of the cup is comforting between my palms, and it gives me something to do to distract myself from the nicotine itch that's already creeping over me.

"We'll make a start then, will we?" Des says, rubbing his hands together as though we're about to do something fun, like light a barbecue or watch a film. I sip my tea and wish it was wine as I listen to the woman with the frizzy grey hair introduce herself.

"It's been twenty years," she says, dabbing tears from her eyes before they have the chance to fall. "She's still the first thing I think of in the morning and the last thing I think of at night. I talk to her. I dream about her. She was my world and without her, I . . ." Her fragile composure dissolves, and she presses her handkerchief over her face. "It feels like everyone else has moved on, but I don't . . . I don't see how I can."

I feel completely detached from the moment, like I'm watching the conversation unfold from the other side of a television screen. The sadness, the pain, the gentle conversation, the hopelessness. I've seen it all before, once a week for the last five or so years.

"It can be very difficult," Des says in the nivel voice of an undertaker, his face etched with compassion. "Other people can find it difficult to understand."

"It's a different kind of loss," Charity says, nodding. "And if the talking helps, there's no need to stop. I talk to my daughter every day, like she's still with me."

"She is still with you, my dear," John says, and Charity reaches over to take his hand, and they share a moment of tender, mutual comfort.

My mother isn't still with me. She came to me once, though, when I was sixteen, right after it had happened. She was lost, trapped in the memory of her final moments. She didn't recognise me—or perhaps she couldn't see me as she ran, perhaps we were tuned into different channels. I was stuck behind glass as I watched her jog, the soles of her running shoes thudding against the pavement. Coral lips, face glowing with sweat, always so well put together. A ribbon of blood rolled from her hairline, and the skin around her neck was inflamed, swollen, mottled with a noose of bruises. A thin, milky light from the streetlights, the roads empty. It didn't feel the way that dreams do—half remembered and distorted with dream logic. It felt real. When I blinked awake, I could still smell her—a faint thread of sweat, fresh soil and Shalimar, tethering me to the dream. That lingering scent was a gift from my mother to me. A gift, a reminder, a lesson. There's a veil that hangs between the living and the dead, and dreamers have the power to pull it back and look beyond the land of the living, if only for a second.

"Sometimes it's comforting to think that she's still with me," Charity is saying to the group, her fingers worrying at a small gold crucifix that hangs from a chain looped around her throat. "But sometimes it isn't, because she should still be here. Her murder tested my faith more than anything else, before or since."

Hannah talks about her sister, murdered by an abusive boyfriend, and then another woman speaks up about her mother, murdered by her father. We all have a different story to tell, but we all share the same dreadful burden.

As I tune in and out of the conversation, I try to remember the last time I talked about my mother. I don't share her story very often. When it happened, I didn't have to: everyone knew. At school, classrooms fell silent when I stepped into them, and lunch tables grew subdued when I sat down. A trail of frantic whispers followed me wherever I went. Even the teachers spoke to me differently, looked at me with eyes that reflected the cloud of sadness that hung over me. I felt tainted, stained with grief.

At university, the anonymity was a breath of fresh air. My friends all knew my mother had passed away—*passed away* was the right term to use because it sounded so gentle, so natural, so passive—but I kept the exact details obscure. That didn't take much effort on my part. Young people aren't comfortable with death. They don't know what they're allowed to say, and they don't know if they're allowed to ask questions, so they don't mention it at all.

My mind wanders to Roach. She's the type to pry. Unwashed hair, ratty face. *I love serial killers.* She would ask graphic questions with unashamed curiosity, I have no doubt about it. I wonder if she's ever been confronted with the reality of death. I wonder if she's ever met the raw, unfiltered grief of people like Hannah, Charity, and John.

I've never felt comfortable sharing the exact circumstances of my mother's death with the group, even though I've shared more here than I have with anyone else—apart from Eli, perhaps, but it's hard to know for sure. I glance around the room, at all the sadness, the drawn faces, the sloping shoulders. If I can't be honest here, why do I bother coming? I take a deep breath, my mind made up, and when there's a natural gap in the conversation, I clear my throat.

"Hi everyone, I'm Laura. I've been coming to this group on and off for around five years now. I'm always the baby in the room." A nervous laugh escapes my lips, and Des offers a sad smile at my little joke.

"I lost my mother ten years ago." I swallow a mouthful of tea to buy myself some time while I figure out how to phrase what I want to say next. Hannah reaches over and gives my shoulder a squeeze with a small pale hand. She presses her lips together, and the delicate skin at the corners of her eyes concertinas into laughter lines as she offers an encouraging half smile.

"I've realised I don't feel as comfortable talking about her as I used to. We all have our own stories, but mine is a little different. She was killed by a stranger, as many of you know."

Des nods slowly, expression solemn as he gently tugs at a curl in his white beard.

"But I don't think I've shared this detail before . . ."

The group is quiet, poised on the precipice of new information. I learned early on that sharing this particular detail often led to unwelcome questions, even in a support group like this, so I tend to keep the story vague. So few people know, it feels almost taboo to say it out loud. I take a deep breath.

"The man who murdered her was a serial killer."

I drop my gaze to the watery cup of tea in my hands. There's a shift around the circle as the others lean forward, sit up straighter, listen with a fresh intensity, and I resent them for their inevitable interest. Des respectfully bows his head, one hand wrapped around the other, and I realise that over the years he may have gathered enough information to stitch the story together by himself.

"It was a high-profile case and . . . I just hate that my trauma is tied to this horrible story, and I can't talk about one without talking about the other. I hate that her name will forever be associated with the man who killed her, and I hate that the world only remembers her as a chapter in the story of his life."

A long silence follows, and I wonder which of them is burning to ask the inevitable question: *But which one? Which serial killer?*

Hannah squeezes my hand. "I can't imagine."

A chorus of consolation rises from the group. As I nod and accept their fresh condolences, I'm already aware of a faint kernel of regret. Words spoken can't be unsaid, after all.

"It's important to keep talking about her," Des says to me, his brows knitted into a thoughtful expression. He glances around the circle, and then continues talking to the wider group: "And I just want to say that while you're here with us in this room, you're free to share as little or as much as you like. In this group, we'll never push for details. We'll never pry. You're safe to talk freely, or not at all. It's completely up to you."

Des catches my eye and gives me a small thumbs up, eyebrows raised as though he's asking me a question. I offer a small nod in return, and he refocuses his attention on Hannah, who's picked up where he left off. The conversation moves on, and I tune out as I think of all the ways in which my self-preservation has given way to secrecy. I need to find a healthy balance between honoring her life while opening up and speaking authentically about the nature of her death. At the moment, the only time I really talk about her outside the support group is when I'm hammered, and it all comes tumbling out in a flood of melancholy that I later regret.

Through the window, the golden light of a streetlight hits the dead leaves on the trees that line the street. Anxiety curdles in my belly. I don't know what I expected, but it's as though in lieu of more information, the group had no choice but to gloss over my revelation. It's understandable, I suppose. The truth is that serial killers are rare, and even in a support group like this—one that's tailored to suit those who've lost loved ones at the hands of others—no one ever has a story quite like mine.

⁂

When I step out into the evening, the sun has set and the shadows loom. A fox slinks into the churchyard, its red coat giving way to mange, and the autumnal air carries the gentle hum of conversation, a few notes of light jazz, and riotous peals of laughter from the pub across the street.

"You off out, then?" Des says, locking the front door of the centre. He wears his kindness all over, the way some men wear aftershave. I force a sad little smile.

"Might just go home," I reply.

"Look, you did really well today," he says. "It's never easy to open up and—well, keep it up. You did really well."

"Thanks, Des."

"Until next time?"

"Until next time. Ciao."

As Des disappears into the night, I pull out my phone to check the time and see a message from Eli. He's sent me a photo of their drinks, a pair of pints under the pink fairy lights of the beer garden, the curl of a cat's tail just edging into the frame. I'd promised myself that I was going to go straight home after group—I'd been nurturing a fantasy of pyjamas, a glass of wine, a comforting bowl of pasta, and then settling down with the lilac diary to write something, anything—but the desire to write is rapidly fading. I feel the tug of the pub, think of Sharona and Eli sipping their drinks and smoking their cigarettes, surrounded by warmth and laughter, and then I remember the insidious footprints left by an anonymous creep in the soil outside my living room window and that clinches it. I can't go home yet; I'm not ready to be alone. The lure of a good time beckons.

ROACH

Laura was burrowing herself into the shop with the stubborn determination of a tick, and while she continued to treat me with cool indifference, constant reminders of her presence meant it was impossible for me to ignore her in return. A chunky knitted cardigan, the colour of old blood, appeared in one of the cupboards under the ground floor till. A metal water bottle, a peach lip balm, and a tube of slime—a clementine hand cream that I liked to use whenever she wasn't around, even though it left greasy fingerprints all over the till screen.

One rainy Wednesday, I came up for lunch and found her making herself at home in the staffroom, curled like a docile cat on the battered sofa. She'd kicked off her shoes—raspberry flats that matched her cardigan—and she was using a small lilac notebook as a makeshift desk. I hoped she was writing poetry, but to my immense disappointment I spotted a fan of recommendation cards spread around her. Her lunch was balanced on the arm of the sofa, a Tupperware box of salad that filled the room with the sharp, acidic smell of vinegar. She glanced up when she heard my footsteps.

"Hey, do you know where I might find another Sharpie? This one's a bit dried up." Her voice was bright and brittle, and lacked the warm tones of camaraderie she used with the other booksellers. It was more like the forced cheer she switched on to charm customers.

"Dunno," I said, jamming the key into my locker. "There's a cup of biros in the office, though."

"We're meant to use black Sharpie for recommendation cards. It pops more against the white, and it looks so much neater if they all match."

"We just use whatever."

"I know," she replied, with an edge of irritation. "But we're meant to use black Sharpie."

I was actually pleased Laura was there. I settled into my favourite chair and took my lunch out of my bag—a cheese sandwich wrapped in foil and the can of cherry seltzer I'd filched from her tote bag all those weeks ago. I'd kept it on my bedside table, a lone sentinel watching over my pack of Pall Malls, but something in the air had changed that day, and I'd decided that the time was ripe: I was going to drink it, and now luck had struck as Laura was there to bear witness. It was perfect. I snapped open the can and took a long, noisy draught. I expected it to taste like Dark Fruits, dark and cloying, like the juicy rot of late summer cherries, but instead it had that bitter tang of soda water and only a faint thread of berry.

"Oooh, where'd you get that?" she asked, taking the bait. I glowed as she leaned forward and pointed at the can in my hand. For the first time in my presence, a look of earnest, animated curiosity had crossed her face. "I *love* that stuff, but I always have to order it online."

"My local corner shop sells it," I improvised, grabbing hold of a potential connection with both hands. "I'll bring you one."

"Oh no, don't worry," she said quickly. "You don't have to do that."

"It's no big deal," I replied, pleased with myself. I wondered how much this shit cost—it looked bougie—and if I could order it online by the can or if I'd have to commit to an entire crate. What if she expected one tomorrow? I'd have to make up an excuse.

She picked up her fork and jammed it into her salad, spearing a mouthful of wet leaves. Every bite of my sandwich felt dense, claggy in my throat, heavy in the pit of my stomach. I craved the lightness of Laura's lunches. I was going to ask her about her salads, keep the conversation going, but as I ran a finger along the spines of my books to find *The Stranger Beside Me*, she interrupted my train of thought with a question of her own.

"Are those all proofs?" she asked, nodding at my bookshelf.

"Some. Like, a publisher sent me this one recently," I said, tugging at the spine of *An A–Z of Serial Killers* to show her a corner of the cover. "But most of these are just on reserve."

I had around thirty or so books reserved under my name. I kept them all in the staffroom and read them at my leisure. It was a good system: I didn't have to pay for them if they never left the shop.

She narrowed her eyes, like a cat watching a robin, then she returned her attention to her recommendation cards without further comment.

"You can borrow one, if you like," I said, trying to keep this newfound spirit of amity going. "There's some really good stuff here."

"Thanks," she said, her head bowed as she resumed her writing. Surely this was the moment she'd realise that we were on the same page, that we had loads in common. We both wrote poetry, loved true crime. We even drank the same hipster brand of seltzer. We weren't Bundy simps like the PSGs at the *Murder Girls* recording—we were passionate, but we were also informed. Educated. We knew our shit.

"Have you read *I'll Be Gone in the Dark*?" I tried again.

"I really don't read that kind of thing," she said, clicking the lid on to her dry Sharpie and refusing to meet my eye.

"But what about your poetry?" I pressed on.

She glanced up then, her lip curled into a sneer.

"What about my poetry?" she snapped, and I flinched. It seemed as though whatever connection I'd sparked with the seltzer was fading as she glared at me with an expression of genuine dislike. She exhaled sharply and began to gather her scatter of recommendation cards into a neat stack.

Where had I gone wrong? It was impossible to know. Laura was fickle, and her moods changed like the weather. One minute, she was on stage performing her poetry for an entire room full of strangers, then the next, it was too personal to discuss with a colleague, someone she saw every day.

"I'm going for a smoke," she muttered, slipping on her shoes and jacket. With that, she disappeared through the back door and onto the roof.

Whatever force inspired me to bring the seltzer into work that day had let me down by not urging me to bring in my cigarettes too. If I'd had my cigarettes with me, I'd have had a legitimate reason to step outside and join her, smooth things over, keep the conversation going. Smokers were always thick as thieves. I supposed there were only so many cigarettes smokers could share with one another before they developed a natural affinity.

While she was out of sight, I conducted a quick investigation and peeped under the lid of her Tupperware. It looked like snail eggs and leaf mould, wet foliage that had wilted under the astringent stink of vinegar. I snapped a picture on my phone and then turned my attention to the pale purple notebook beneath her stack of recommendation cards. I didn't recognise it from previous inspections of the contents of her tote bag. Maybe it was new. Whatever sordid secrets it contained were protected by a prissy little padlock in the shape of a heart.

Fuming at the audacity of having a locked diary at her big age, I quickly rearranged the lilac notebook and the recommendation cards as they were and returned to my chair. I tried to lose myself in Bundy's Seattle, where college girls were going missing at a rate of one per month or more, an endless carousel of young women with long dark hair, but my mind kept straying to the lilac diary.

I took another swig of Laura's precious seltzer and choked it down. It really did taste like shit.

After work I went to Tesco. Examining the pillowy plastic packets of salad leaves, I couldn't quite figure out what plant Laura had used to make her lunch—was it spinach, watercress, or rocket? They all looked the same, and I couldn't decide which one was right. I didn't eat in fancy restaurants, didn't watch cookery shows. My knowledge of food was limited to interpreting the cooking instructions on the back of frozen pizza boxes. I showed my picture to a girl restocking bananas and she looked at me like I was an alien.

"Er, salads are just behind you," she said, unwilling to get too involved.

"It smelled kind of like vinegar," I prompted.

"Salad dressings, aisle six," she replied, turning back to her bananas.

In the end, I picked out a bag of bistro salad and an orange pepper. There wasn't a member of staff in aisle six, but I found the vinegars and picked a bottle of malt vinegar that looked like flat Coca Cola because it was the only one I recognised. I couldn't work out what the snail eggs were, so I picked out a packet of microwaveable yellow rice in the flavor "golden vegetable." I couldn't think of a single vegetable that was gold.

The next morning, I woke up late and didn't have a second to think about making a fucking salad. I woke up late the following morning, and the morning after that, and so on, until the bistro salad went dark green and slimy in the bag and the taut skin of the pepper went soft and changed color.

I promised myself to ask Laura for tips—what were the snail eggs? What vinegars did she prefer in her dressings?—but the next time we were in the staffroom together, and I presented her with a can of her precious cherry seltzer that I'd found in the posh Spar in the Village, she gave me nothing but a tight thank you followed by a frigid silence. I disappeared behind *The Stranger Beside Me*, cheeks burning with humiliation. It was clear that she was all take, take, take, and my efforts to form a bond with her were in vain.

Laura was a matryoshka doll, she had so many faces. I watched her shimmy around the shop, neatening stacks of books and shelving strays, changing masks to suit her audience. With Noor and Sharona, she was a sister, a confidante, a friend. With Barry and Martin, a colleague, a collaborator. With Kofi, a mentor, an instructor. With Eli, a concubine, a flirt. With customers, an angel. And with me? A blank sheet of paper. A marble statue. A brick wall.

LAURA

On my lunch breaks, in lieu of working on poetry, I fill pages of the lilac diary with scraps and notes and memories about my mother. I write little and often, whenever her spirit moves me. I write about the way she loved autumn, how the first drizzly weekend in late August was her cue to fill our house with cosy blankets and candles to welcome in the cooler months. I write about the warming smell of cinnamon in the air as she baked apple crumbles, flapjacks, and banana bread. Her penchant for lavender. I remember her hands, the way the skin was red and cracked between her fingers with eczema. I make note of all the things she taught me: always keep nail varnish in the fridge, take good care of your shoes, wear sun cream every day, give books as gifts, buy yourself flowers.

It's another deathly quiet day in the shop, so when I run out of steam with my writing, I use the office phone to ring down to the ground floor to tell Noor I'm going to spend the rest of my shift cleaning up the staffroom.

Two skylights fill the room with late October sunshine. The kitchen counter is grubby, kissed by a thousand coffee-stained teaspoons, scattered with crumbs, coffee granules, and the grit of spilled sugar. An overfull bin bag spills crumpled McDonald's bags, food wrappers, and fizzy drink cans on to the floor, including several crushed cans of Stokey

Cherry Seltzer. I'm reminded of the can Roach gave me, presented with the earnest enthusiasm of a cat offering her owner a dead mouse. For some reason, the whole encounter really put me off the drink, and the can remains untouched in my locker.

I play music on my phone, roll up my sleeves, and rummage around in the cupboards, gathering supplies. A dusty bottle of multipurpose cleaning spray, blue roll, a sad grey J-cloth, furniture polish. I use a square of dry blue roll to brush the crumbs from the kitchen counter into the bin, then tie the rancid bin bag and place it by the door. I spray down the counters and scrub away the sepia spills of tea and coffee with the J-cloth until they gleam.

I phone downstairs to Eli, who's meant to be tackling the unruly stockroom so it's neat and tidy for Christmas. "I'm in the staffroom. Could you bring me up some empty totes?"

"Copy that," he says, and hangs up.

I throw out all the expired herbal teas and gather the stray bottles of soy sauce and sweet chilli and Marmite and honey, and put them together on one shelf. I collect stacks of scarred, mismatched Tupperware, much of it stained orange or warped from too many rounds in the microwave. I can't imagine anyone would miss it if I just tipped it all into the bin, but I need to keep everyone sweet, so I use one of the new Sharpies I'd ordered for the shop to write a note—*Unclaimed Tupperware will be recycled on Friday! Love, Laura xox*—and pile it all on one of the canteen tables.

The fridge is horrendous, a stinking tomb of rotten food. I check the use-by dates and throw out everything that's no longer fit for human consumption, and then I stick a second Post-it on the fridge door: *Fridge will be emptied on Friday, please label your food—everything else is going in the bin! Love, Laura xox*

I hoover the carpet and then pull off the main attachment so I can stick the skinny mouth of the hoover into the cracks of the sofa and armchair, and then I sweep each of the bathrooms, tip bleach into the limescale-crusted toilet bowls. I write a final Post-it note and stick it on the weekly rota: *Please label your locker! All unclaimed lockers will be emptied on Friday! Love, Laura xox*

Eli appears with a trolley of blue plastic totes, the kind we receive book deliveries in, and I sweet-talk him into helping me fill them with the shop's abundance of unread proofs.

"Only if I can DJ," he says, nodding at my phone. He swaps Fleetwood Mac for Nick Cave, and I compliment his taste even though the song is mean and cold and violent, and I don't particularly like it.

Proofs are one of the best perks of bookselling, and one girl's meat is another girl's poison so it's always worth rummaging through another shop's stash for unclaimed gems. Publishers send us books en masse: big boxes of proofs to whet our appetites for the new year, and beautiful finished copies wrapped in tissue paper, tied with synthetic satin ribbon, and packaged with postcards and bookmarks and badges, chocolate coins, individually wrapped biscuits, little miniatures of alcohol, all to try and win us over, to woo us, to make us fall in love.

As a bookseller, you quickly learn the tastes of your colleagues because all we ever talk about is books, the shop, and customers. And I like to ask questions. Sharona is strictly literary and, with limited time and energy to dedicate to reading, she tends towards Booker Prize winners, experimental books from independent presses, and works in translation. Eli is more philosophical, drawn to experimental fiction and existentialism, but he reads slowly: Camus, Sartre, Brautigan, a one-hundred-fifty-page paperback in his back pocket for weeks at a time until the cover softens and the pages dirty. You can tell a lot about a team based on what proofs they leave untouched.

Eli and I work together in a comfortable silence, separating out the proofs from the finished copies, removing old, brittle press releases as we go, checking finished copies for any signs of damage. Every so often, he stops to sing a line or two, a quick performance that I like to think is for my benefit.

"Oh hey," I say, pointing to Roach's shelf. "If you have a spare tote, do you wanna take all that true crime down too?"

"Ah," he says, glancing at the shelves. "Those are Roach's. Maybe I'll ask her to take them home."

"She hasn't paid for them, though."

"Huh?"

"She orders them in and just leaves them on reserve."

He pushes his hair back with a frown. "Well, we should give her the chance to buy them before we put them onto the shop floor, right?"

There are about thirty paperbacks on her vile shelf, with titles like *Talking with Serial Killers* and *The Murder Room* and *Forty Years of Murder* and *Britain's Most Notorious Serial Killers* and *Serial Killers of Britain and Ireland*. I recognise a couple. One or two of the more literary titles were books I'd used for my found poetry project.

"Nah, let's just stick them back into the section. I can practically *feel* their negative energy," I say.

"Bit mean, though," he says, avoiding my eye as he lifts the heavy totes back on to the trolley.

"Well, I'll leave the one she's actually reading. Mainly 'cause it's in a bit of a state. But still, I've cleaned this entire staffroom from top to bottom. She should *thank* me."

"Fine," he says. "You can shelve them, though."

"Fine."

"I'm not here to do your dirty work," he says, with a twinkle of mischief in his eye.

"I said *fine.*"

"Quick smoke before I take these down?"

"Gorge."

We sit on the table of the picnic bench, feet on the seats, and look out towards the hazy city in the distance. The Shard catches the sun, reflects the pastel blue of the sky. It's chilly but I don't mind.

Eli drums a little beat on his knees, cigarette hanging out of the corner of his mouth. Sometimes I think he forgets himself, gets lost in his head, and sometimes I think it's performative indifference. I like these little moments between us, these little moments of comfortable silence. It's a strange intimacy. You get to know people differently when you work together, especially in retail. Even in the busiest shops there are fallow periods. Long, quiet mornings, with nothing much to do but pass the time with idle conversation. You spend all day every day together, tripping over each other, swapping stories, cracking jokes, and then you go out together several nights a week just because.

I'm thinking of his words, though. *Bit mean.* Is it mean? I can't decide.

"If she has a problem, she can take it to Sharona," I say, picking up where we left off. "Or she can just eff off. It's not a big deal."

"*Eff* off," he says, laughing as he exhales. He pinches the stub of his cigarette until the cherry falls out. I take a last drag and then do the same, and he stamps on our embers. "You're too nice to say fuck, now?"

"Force of habit," I reply, hopping down from the bench and stretching. "I wish someone would crack every bone in my back like bubble wrap."

"That sounds like an act of violence."

Eli ambles over to the staffroom door and holds it open for me to go through first. As he whisks away the totes of books, I get back to work. I swap Nick Cave for Taylor Swift, and I wipe down the empty bookshelves with blue roll and furniture polish, and then nivelin the remaining 2019–20 proofs on the shelves in chronological order of release, from

October through to spring next year. By the time I finish, the sun has set and there's only one job left on my list.

On the first floor, an old man in a flat cap, shopping bags at his feet, snoozes on one of the chairs by the lift with his chin on his chest. A trio of high-spirited schoolgirls with milky, melted niveli have claimed the sofa in the Travel section, much to the annoyance of a woman in a red coat who's trying to browse the *Lonely Planet*s and *Rough Guide*s in peace.

Eli has stacked Roach's books on the till point. I tap a few ISBNs into the system, and my resolve hardens when I see that I was right: she's curated a personal library on the shop's dime and she hasn't paid for a single one.

Bookshops are oceans, and sections are like tides: they grow and they shrink, they grow and they shrink. It depends on the season, and what's selling, and what new trends are emerging. Scandi noir. Dystopian YA. Adult colouring-in. Hygge. It only takes one bestseller to start a tsunami of copycats, but just as you think the swell is here to stay, sales start to taper off and the bookshop breathes and contracts and swallows whatever stock didn't sell, reabsorbs it back into the master section, back into Crime or YA or Crafts, and we rearrange everything to fill the gap until the next trend gains momentum.

A good bookseller can sense when the tides are turning, when sales are starting to wane. A bad bookseller doesn't adapt to change, will cling to those declining sales instead of embracing the next big thing. A really bad bookseller will favour their personal taste over customer interest. Roach strikes me as that kind of bookseller, with her sad-sack selection of lurid, salacious crap. I shelve her books quickly, double-checking each one for signs of wear and tear or annotation, although I can't imagine what kind of depraved marginalia Roach would see fit to inscribe in any of these books.

Between the standard tomes on Jack the Ripper, drug cartels, and literary anomalies like *In Cold Blood* and *The Fact of a Body*, there's a dozen trashy-looking paperbacks by an author called Cynthia de la Roche. They all appear to be about violent crimes in London, and with a sinking feeling I pull a title called *Murders of East London* from the shelf. Glossy cover, cheap paper. It almost looks self-published, but as a general rule, we don't stock self-published titles. I check the index, and sure enough, there he is: the man who killed my mother. He is well represented, with a whole section on his family, his childhood, his life before his crimes. Well liked, a bit of a loner growing up. Kept to himself. Pillar of the community, a man of the law. Sure.

Cynthia de la Roche details each woman's death methodically: where she had been, where she was going, what she was wearing, what she was carrying, what the autopsy could piece together about her last few hours on Earth. Entire biographies reduced to the way they spent their last evenings, the contents of their handbags, the contents of their stomachs. I'm unsurprised to see my mother's life boiled down to her final hours, her death and the aftermath, but it stings and I hate myself for looking. *The body belonging to Karina Cordovan, forty-three, a mother from Walthamstow, was found dead by strangulation in Vinegar Alley by . . .*

I swallow a swell of sadness, close the book, and return it to the shelf. This isn't the first time I've come across my mother's name in print. It's always like this though—a tiny paragraph, a brief mention. They usually end up going out of print, and for that I'm glad. The truth is that, in the grand scheme of things, it probably isn't a very interesting story to people like Roach, people who relish in the goriest of details. When I think of the longevity of some of those cases, the famous ones with an air of mystery or an element of reasonable doubt, the stories that get picked over, that end up being made into films and podcasts and TV shows, fictionalised and retold and reimagined, I'm grateful. The chances of Roach being interested in my mother's murderer are low. It's not much, but it's something to be thankful for.

ROACH

Sharona sent me to Ilford to cover a shift one Friday—a tearful temp had locked herself out and left the bath running, and she needed to wait for an emergency locksmith, or so she said. An elaborate excuse, but I respected her bullshit. I was often sent to cover shifts as I was expendable, experienced, and would go without a fuss. The Essex branches had decent True Crime sections, although they did tend more towards the carceral: prison memoirs, East End gangsters, drug dealers, always a thick face-out stack of *Mr. Nice*.

The shop was dead and the shift dawdled along, painfully slow. I stood at the till all day and browsed books on Amazon, read the Wikipedia pages for horror films I'd already seen, and served more families buying cheap study guides for the 11+ than anything else.

On my way home, the trains were delayed. Someone on the line at Romford. My ears pricked at that. If someone was dead, I was listening. I shoved my hands deep into my pockets and stamped my feet to keep the blood circulating. The cold air smelled sweet and rotten with the creeping scent of marijuana. I craned my neck to look for the culprit. The platform was quiet—it was too early for the steady stream of partygoers that headed into London every Friday night, their astringent smell of aftershave, Lynx, and fake tan permeating the carriages.

About halfway down the platform, I spotted a metalhead smoking a joint, his breath thick with it. He glanced my way and I held his gaze. He was short at around five foot six, with pale skin and dark wavy hair that frizzed into clouds just past his shoulder blades. I expected him to turn away, but instead he walked down the platform towards me and offered me the joint. It rolled like a cigarette, but the paper was stained a darker yellow.

"Nah," I said, shaking my head. "You're all right."

He shrugged and then he just stood there, smoking next to me in silence, like we were friends. I didn't know whether I was supposed to move away or introduce myself or what, so I just stood there, and he just stood there. Stalemate.

Up close, he had the high cheekbones, protruding teeth, and dark eyes of Richard Ramirez, the serial killer who terrorised Los Angeles in the 1980s. Tattered leather jacket, a collection of rust-spotted badges pinned to the lapels. I recognised some of the band names, like Slayer and Cradle of Filth and Megadeath. Others were a complete mystery though, their names like dark incantations: Dimmu Borgir, Belphegor, Gorgoroth. I wished I could snap a photo, look them up online later.

"You look like Richard Ramirez," I said.

"Yeah?"

"Yeah."

"Funny, 'cause I'm called Richard."

"Yeah?"

"Nah." He laughed. "I'm Sam."

Two could play at that game. "I'm Brodie," I said, trying something new. Laura had a thousand different faces depending on her mood, so why couldn't I be someone else for a change too?

"Like Brody Dalle?"

"Nah, I spell it differently," I said, letting my mouth take the wheel. Where did that come from? My quick-witted ability to talk shit simply amazed me. I stood up a little straighter, drew my shoulders back.

Sam tucked his hair behind his left ear. "Sucks about the trains."

"Yeah."

"One time," he said, sucking on his joint and squinting against a curl of smoke, "someone jumped under a train and the line was out for the entire afternoon."

"That's long."

"Yeah. It's 'cause they have to clean up." He grimaced, and the knot of his Adam's apple bobbed as he swallowed. "It can take hours 'cause they have to—you know."

"They have to *what*?" I asked, licking my lips.

"It's grim," he said, staring down the tracks into the distance.

"Tell me."

"You really wanna know?"

I nodded. My palms felt sweaty and I wiped them surreptitiously on my jeans.

"Wait, I'm just gonna kill this." He pinched the joint between his lips and took a deep drag that made the tip glow with a bright fire.

With a crackle from the Tannoy, an announcement reverberated around the quiet platform: the service had been suspended "indefinitely due to an ongoing customer incident" and, in a regretful voice, a conductor recommended we looked for an alternative route into London.

Sam flicked his spent joint on to the fruitless tracks. "Wanna come for a drink and I'll tell you all about it or what?"

I followed him to a pub on the high street that had dark varnished furniture and a proper pub smell—stale booze, hot oil from a well-used deep fat fryer, commercial cleaning products. The kind of place that really went for it during the World Cup, that always had a St. George's Day party, a box of poppies for sale on the bar as soon as they could.

They didn't have Dark Fruits, so we ordered pints of cider and black-currant cordial, which he paid for with cash. A fistful of grubby notes.

It was cold, but we sat in the garden so he could chain-smoke. I pulled out my Pall Malls and lit one, and he didn't say anything. I don't know what I expected—an accusation of fraud, perhaps, or an acknowledgement that I didn't know how to hold a cigarette properly.

It turned out Sam's dad was a train manager, and so he grew up hearing his father's stories about what he called "one-unders."

"That's what they call them," he grinned.

Falling under an oncoming train had always been a great interest of mine. I was hooked on the violence of it, the mess of it, the blood. When I was a teenager, there was an urban legend about a serial killer who pushed women under trains, and even though I knew it wasn't true—he was a ghost, formed from the wind that slammed through the tunnels, from the tension of bodies crammed on the platform—I thought about witnessing someone fall onto the tracks every time I travelled.

Sam asked what I did, and I said I worked in a bookshop, and he nodded with approval. "That's a nice job," he said. "I like that for you."

"Do you like books?" I asked.

"Nah, not really. I read the first *Game of Thrones*, and the Mötley Crüe biography. That's really good, you should read that. And I like a bit of true crime."

"Me too," I said, a little bud of interest unfurling. "I *love* serial killers."

"What's your favourite murder?" he asked, and I told him about the West Memphis Three and he told me about H. H. Holmes, and eventually talk turned to the Stow Strangler and he was buzzing because he remembered the Stow Strangler too.

"It was mad. I remember my dad bought my mum knuckle-dusters even though it was all kicking off miles away. She went fucking nuts. *What am I meant to do with them?*" He laughed at the memory, and I liked how easily he laughed. He swallowed the last of his pint and pointed at my empty glass. "Another, Brodie?"

"All right," I said.

We stayed out until the sky turned black and the chill in the air numbed the tips of my toes, made my nose run. He swapped from pints of cider to Jack Daniel's and Coke, and so I swapped to Jack Daniel's and Coke too, and the whiskey warmed my core, stoked a fire in my belly that the frosty night couldn't touch. When we'd exhausted talk of serial killers, we moved on to horror films, and we agreed the bloodier and more creative the gore, the better.

Eventually, when the table was littered with empty glasses and the ashtray between us was overflowing with pinched and crushed dog-ends, he checked the status of the trains on his phone and said the line was up and running again.

"Will we ever find out what happened?" I asked. "Like if the person died?"

"You won't," he said. "But I can ask my dad. If you give me your number, I can tell you what I find out."

I typed my number into his phone and remembered at the last minute to save it as Brodie instead of Brogan. He drop-called me straight away so I could save his number too. I saved it as Sam Ramirez.

We left the pub and the alcohol made me feel bold and unsteady. I turned towards the train station, but he hung back.

"I, er . . . I live that way," he said, pointing in the opposite direction.

"If you live round here, why were you waiting for a train earlier?"

"Well, I was going to a gig in Camden."

"So why didn't you just get the bus to Stratford, and pick up the Tube from there?" I asked.

111

"Because you seemed cool," he replied, and then he was there, his teeth biting against my lips as we mashed our mouths together in a slippery kiss that was almost too much.

He tasted delicious, like sweet ash.

LAURA

Slug trails continue to appear in spirals on my kitchen floor overnight, as mysterious as crop circles. I read an article that says you have to create a barrier by placing pennies along the threshold of your back door to keep them out. The witchiness of the ritual appeals to me, and I trade a pound coin for a bag of pennies at work to place a protective line of coins on the bottom of the doorframe. An hour later, I find a pale-yellow slug oozing across the lino.

I'd emailed my landlord ages ago, and after a few weeks of radio silence, he finally replies with an offer to send his brother round to take a look. A chubby man with grey stubbly hair and a kind face turns up in a small white van.

"D'you mind if I ask how much you're paying my brother for this place?" he says, peering into each room with great interest. "Must be worth a few bob these days."

"Oh," I say, scrambling for a way to wriggle out of this one. "I'm—oh, well, my dad pays for it, actually. So I don't know."

He narrows his eyes but doesn't push it. Instead, he gets on to his knees and pokes about under the kitchen sink and around the pipes in the bathroom, but he can't work out where the slugs are getting in either.

"Once one finds its way in, they all bloody follow it," he says, heaving himself up and wiping his hands on his jeans. "You have to clean up the mucus straight away, stop more coming."

While I have him here, I tell him about the footprints I'd found outside my living room window, and ask if there's anything he can do to reinforce my locks. He talks at length about a local break-in he'd heard about down the pub and I listen in an almost catatonic state of panic, my hands gripping my phone until the knuckles turn the colour of bone. My home is my sanctuary, the place where I feel safest. The thought of someone breaking into my flat, infiltrating my space, touching my things, perhaps even waiting for me in the shadows, is enough to inspire a full panic attack. I take deep, measured breaths.

"TV, laptops—even the chargers. Took the lot," he says amiably, oblivious to my anxious state. He offers to attach a chain to my front door, and when he comes back from the hardware shop, he has a frosted sheet of sticky-back plastic to attach to the lower panes of the living room window.

"That'll keep them from looking in again," he says. "Stick the chain on at night, and always double-lock the door when you go out. They're looking for an easy target, so make it difficult for them, yeah?"

∽

On my days off, I keep the chain on the front door and watch lifestyle vlogs while I clean. Eli always hated my addiction to lifestyle vlogs—peachy-skinned women with ring lights, who drink matcha lattes one year and activated charcoal lattes the next. They all speak the same language, these women who make their millions with snappy lip gloss tutorials and guided tours of their makeup collections, their thrift store hauls, detailed inventories of the contents of their handbags and their fridges. They post pictures advertising online classes and teeth-whitening kits and vitamin-infused gummy bears that promise to make your hair grow thicker and faster, all marked with the ubiquitous #ad. Their carefully positioned, triple-filtered world is a balm to me, white noise while I fold T-shirts, hang dresses, polish shoes.

When Eli spots the paused video on my laptop screen, he's quick to comment.

"Self-edited, narcissistic bullshit. It's not real. I can't believe you buy into that crap," he says. "It's just the next generation of advertising, dressed up as entertainment. You're watching advertorials for fun."

We're sitting at an old garden table in the kitchen of my flat, drinking beers, and he's in the middle of rolling a cigarette for me because I always used to smoke straights and hated to roll my own, and he remembers that about me, even though I've been on the Amber Leaf for a while now. The table, a pretty powder blue with matching chairs, is spotted with rust where the paint has started to bubble and peel.

"These internet personalities—these *influencers*'—he pauses the rolling process to make a quick one-handed air quotes to show that he doesn't take the word seriously—'they make you feel bad, so you buy their crap to make yourself feel better, so they can afford more lip fillers and facial peels to make you feel worse. Tale as old as time."

"I don't think they're intentionally trying to make people feel bad," I say, accepting the rollie. "They're just trying to make themselves feel good. It's . . . y'know. The *fame game* or whatever." I make bunny ears around the words "fame game" to show him that I don't take any of it seriously either.

"But it's all totally curated!" He laughs, exasperated, as he licks the gum of a second cigarette.

"Look," I say. "After you texted me this afternoon, I folded the laundry that's been on the drying rack all week, and I did some washing up, and I put away the jar of coffee and the peanut butter."

"So?"

"So . . . isn't that a form of self-editing too? Wouldn't all the crap—the laundry and the peanut butter—be more real?"

"No, that's just being an adult," he replies, picking a tiny flake of tobacco from his bottom lip.

I stand up and use a wooden spoon to knock the latch of the window above the kitchen sink and crack open the window. The sky is swirled with raspberry-ripple clouds as the sun sets, and the smoky curtain between us curls out into the evening.

"Do you want another beer?" I ask, shaking my empty bottle at him.

"One more," he says. "Then I need to bounce. Lydia will be wondering where I am."

"So text her," I say, closing the fridge with my hip and popping the caps of two more craft lagers. I'd walked to the fancy beer shop on Hoe Street to stock my fridge with the kind of beer I know he likes to drink. Somehow, I'd still got it wrong. I chose novelty flavours that appealed to me rather than picking based on brewery or hop. Crème brûlée porters and blood orange IPAs and something that claims to taste of cherries and dark chocolate but still just tastes like beer and still does not impress him.

"So, how are you finding the new shop, now that the dust has settled?" he asks, tipping the bottle back and swallowing. "Like, *really*."

"It's so quiet," I say. "I miss being properly busy, you know? And the team seem quite set in their ways."

"Noor's cool," he says thoughtfully, his eyes drawn to the window as he thinks. "I can see her in a trendier branch. Shoreditch, maybe. Same with Kofi, if he'd just focus more on hand-selling."

"And Roach?" I say, with a sly smile.

He returns my smile with a laugh, pointing an accusatory finger in my direction. "This feels like a leading question. What's your angle?"

I pause and take a swig of beer. Eli has a pious streak that makes it difficult to be irrationally critical of others in front of him, but I weigh up the reality of Roach and decide it's probably a safe bet to assume he'll sympathise with me.

"Honestly? Bad vibes."

"She seems a bit lonely," he says, dropping ash into the Gü jar I use as an ashtray.

"She makes me feel really fucking uncomfortable, if I'm perfectly honest with you."

Eli frowns, and he looks so earnest in his concern that I melt a little. "How so?"

"Well, the whole serial killer thing bothers me. Liking true crime isn't a replacement for a personality."

"Yeah, I get that," he says. He leans back in his chair, face inscrutable. I'm struck by the memory of swigging gin from the bottle, the tonic long gone, and a botanical, niveli kiss, salted with grief. I open my mouth to speak, then think better of it.

As afternoon bleeds into night, we drink the rest of the beers and smoke more of my tobacco, and it's just like old times. When it's time for him to leave, he puts his arms around my waist and gives me a long, sincere hug. I breathe in the nostalgic smell of his detergent.

"Now that I live locally, we should do this more often," he says, gently pulling away. "Really. I've really missed you, dude."

"Like a hole in the head," I say, opening the front door and standing aside.

"See you tomorrow," he says, stepping out into the night.

"Another day in paradise, right?"

As soon as I shut the door, I slide the chain into place. The flat feels cold and empty without him. I open the cheap bottle of white wine I'd hidden in the vegetable crisper and count up how much the artisanal beers cost me and how much of my tobacco Eli smoked and, over a YouTube video of a woman testing a seventy-five-dollar blusher—"Okay, you guys, we're going to Trader Joe's and there will be check-ins!"—try to work out how much money I have left before payday.

ROACH

The man on the other side of the counter smelled like flame grilled steak, McCoy's crisps, and Red Bull. The syrupy, meaty blend made me think of rot, of bloated corpses on a hot summer's day. He was looking at the book of the month—some sappy literary memoir about grief and wine tasting.

He tapped the cover to get my attention. "What's it about then?"

I was skimming through a long read about one-unders so I'd be ready to discuss the subject again if Sam asked me out on another date, so I sighed heavily, to really hammer home the inconvenience of the interruption.

"It's about a guy who goes on a journey, but it's an emotional journey as well as a physical journey."

He continued to study the cover in silence, scratching at his neckbeard with bitten fingernails, and I returned my attention to the computer screen in front of me.

"Yeah?" he said after a few beats, sceptical. "Any good?"

"Best book I've ever read," I said without looking up.

"You're just saying that," he said, with a scowl. "Bet you get paid commission."

"I get paid the same whether you buy it or not."

"You're just saying that," he said again, pulling his phone from his pocket. He was growing agitated, jabbing at his phone with rigid fingers.

Noor was tidying front of store, but I noticed her hands were resting on the shelf in front of her, head cocked to one side as though she was listening.

"*And* it's cheaper on your website." He tilted his phone towards me so I could see his smudged screen. "How come?"

"Dunno," I said. "Just is."

"We have different offers online and in-store," Noor said in a smooth sales voice, an apprehensive glance in my direction. "It's cheaper online, but it's actually free in-store with any other book with the matching sticker."

"Well, that's fucking bullshit," the man snapped at her. "What if I don't want two books? What if I only want *this* book?" He stabbed the paperback with his index finger, which left a perfect fingerprint on the matte cover. If I was a crime scene investigator and suspected him of a crime, it would be the perfect piece of evidence to catch him with.

"Order it online, then," I said, returning my attention to my article about one-unders.

"Right, get me your manager." His arms were folded across his chest like a bouncer standing outside a nightclub, and he was growing increasingly red.

"There isn't a manager available at the moment," I replied.

"You're a fucking bitch," he spat, turning towards the door. He left without buying the stupid dead dad wine book.

"Why did you do that?" Noor hissed. She looked shaken by the exchange, and her hands trembled with adrenaline. "We're meant to price match."

"He wasn't going to buy it," I said. "He just wanted a fight."

She disappeared into the depths of the shop to catch her breath, leaving me to my research. Sparring with customers was all in a day's work. She would never last if she didn't grow a thicker skin.

Eli scooted behind the counter with a fresh box of till roll and several packages of paper carrier bags. There was a mousy-grey streak of dirt down the front of his shirt.

"Hey Roach, I've been meaning to talk to you," he said, stacking his wares on the counter. "We've had a bit of a clear-out in the staffroom. Sharona doesn't want us to keep any stock in there so . . . well, we've put most of your books back into the section. All the proofs are still there, and I've stashed some in the customer order cupboard, but Sharona's gunning for us to clear that out as well."

"*What?*" I gasped, a flare of outrage burning my throat.

"We can't have stock in the staffroom, Roach. You know that. Everything needs to be either on the shop floor or in the customer order cupboard."

A gust of wind blew through the doors and sent the covers of the paperbacks front of store flapping like the wings of grounded birds.

"Okay, so I'll move them all into the customer order cupboard," I said. He frowned, then shook his head.

"No," he said, "that's not gonna work. There's way too many of them. Sharona wants the customer order cupboard nice and clear, ready for Christmas. You can pay for them and keep them in the staffroom, or they need to go on the shop floor to sell through. You can't have it both ways."

"But I can't afford them all at once!"

"Well, if they do sell, you can just reorder them when you can afford them."

"But some of those took months to arrive," I wheedled. "Some of them are from America, and some came from really obscure presses."

"Hey," he said, raising his hands in surrender as he backed away from the till. "Don't shoot the messenger. Laura tidied them away, I'm just letting you know."

Laura.

I glared at his retreating back as he disappeared into the bowels of the shop. Our old manager Barbara had never given a shit about my orders. She barely stepped foot in the staffroom.

The afternoon dragged on, and I remained at a hot simmer. I served a family who wanted to buy revision guides, but they changed their mind about buying them when they realised the half-term sale was over, and left the whole stack at the till. I couldn't be bothered to shelve them, so I stuffed them on to a trolley of kids" books. Let Little Miss Laura Bunting deal with them, since she loved cleaning up other people's shit so much.

LAURA

It's one of those rare and beautiful shifts where it's just Eli, Sharona, and me on the close and we can almost pretend we're somewhere else.

"Can't wait for a drink," Eli says.

"We still have an hour to go," I reply.

"An hour?" He drops his head on to my shoulder and groans. "Kill me."

I let him rest there for a beat, his face warm against the shoulder of my shirt, then swat him away.

At the end of the day, Eli prints the till reports and gathers the floats to slide into the safe, and I nip to the bathroom to get ready. I dab a matte raspberry lipstick on to my lips, and blot it to a barely-there pink. My lips but better. I don't have anything else with me, so I dab the same colour on to my fingertips and blend a sunset streak on to the apples of my cheeks. The effect is pleasing—I look flushed, post-coital, with just-bitten, freshly kissed lips. I gaze at myself in the mirror, fluff my hair with both hands, and the girl in the mirror pouts back.

I'm meant to be elsewhere tonight. I think of group therapy, of their pained expressions masking intrigue as I'd talked about my mother last week. Des, and his kind face, proud of me for speaking her truth. A bone-deep uncertainty dissolves into the taste of that first sip of wine. Fuck it. I give myself a final once-over before strutting out of the bathroom. I don't owe anyone my time, my heart, or my soul. Or my secrets. Plus, I'm in the mood for a drink.

⁂

We go to a quiet high street pub, the kind that's part of a chain but pretends it isn't, and Sharona orders a bottle of house red and bags of crisps and dry-roasted peanuts that we split open so they lie flat on the table between us. We drink quickly, letting the rich wine work its magic, flooding into our veins and loosening us up.

Whenever Sharona comes out for a drink, the conversation circles around the shop, the company, sales, customers. Sometimes this is a good thing and sometimes it's not. Sometimes, it's exactly what I need to let off steam, and Sharona is both an excellent listener and a reliable purveyor of juicy company gossip, but tonight I'm in no mood to talk shop. I want to switch off and get on it, share jokes, and exist beyond my till number.

I let them talk for a while, happy to just drink my wine and people-watch, half listening to their conversation. Across the bar, a middle-aged woman in a silver-sequinned top drinks a gin and tonic, or maybe a vodka soda, on her own. No phone, no book. Just her and her drink and her thoughts. I admire that.

"She's a funny one," Sharona says, a honeyed fondness to her voice.

"She *is* a funny one," Eli says. "I can't work her out."

I tune into their conversation, thinking for a wild moment that they're talking about the woman in the nivelin top. "Huh?"

"Roach," Eli says.

"Ugh."

Sharona raises her eyebrows, a questioning smile on her lips.

"She's the worst bookseller I've ever worked with," I explain. "The other day, a customer asked for *Walden* and she had no idea what they were on about. I think she thought *Walden* was the author's name."

"Everyone's got gaps in their knowledge," Sharona says, in a fair, mild voice. "You weren't born with the correct pronunciation of Goethe on the tip of your tongue either."

"Yes, I was," I say, and she throws her head back and laughs.

"Okay, maybe *you* were," she replies. "But I certainly wasn't."

"Yeah, but she's been a bookseller for her *entire* adult life."

Sharona finishes her wine and shares the rest of the bottle equally between our three glasses. "She loves you, though," she says with a mischievous smile, sliding my glass towards me.

"She's a ghoul." It comes out a little more sharply than I'd intended, and Sharona raises her eyebrows again, this time in a muted display of surprise.

On the other side of the room, a young woman with a stringy fringe like a barcode squeals as a server places a small bowl of chips in front of her with the flourish of a waiter in a Michelin-starred restaurant. My stomach clenches around a rumble.

"What do you think of true crime, as a genre?" Sharona asks with a thoughtful look, and I wonder if she knows about my mother or if she's just making conversation.

"As a feminist, I don't like it," I say. "I don't like the idea of men profiting from the abuse, torture, and murder of women."

"I feel that," she replies, turning her glass in her hands.

"Women write true crime as well, though," Eli says in a cautious tone, avoiding my eye. Instead, he swirls his drink and watches the wine, the rich red of it, stain the inside of the glass. He looks like he wants to disagree with me but knows he needs to tread carefully.

"And they certainly read it," Sharona muses.

"I wonder what that's all about. Why are women drawn to these, like, super violent narratives?" Eli says, settling into the debate.

"Oh yeah!" Sharona laughs and raises an accusatory finger in his direction. "I thought girls only liked books about ponies?"

"Oh, *fuck off.* You know what I mean." He tosses a peanut at her.

I swallow some wine and wrestle with my point. Sharona's right, of course: women do read true crime, and they write about it, and they produce podcasts and documentaries about it. *I* read it, *I* write about it. That's different, though. My original point feels a little flat, but the hard knot of dislike for Roach holds true in my heart and I'm not prepared to acquiesce.

"I think a lot of women are drawn to true crime because it concerns them directly," I say. "It's like a form of self-preservation, and a way of feeling empathy for the victims."

"But more men are murdered than women per year in the UK," Eli says, leaning forward, his face a mask of intensity that suggests he's keen to have this out but knows he's skating on thin ice, knows that he can't win this round, because I have the wild card of experience up my sleeve and he does not.

"Bullshit," Sharona scoffs. "That has *got* to be bullshit."

"I swear," he says, grabbing his phone. "Look, here's a report from—"

"You sound like a men's rights activist," I snap. "I've never heard you talk about murder rates before."

"Woah, woah, it's not like that," he says, holding up both hands in surrender. "I just think it's more complicated than men profiting from violence against women. *My Favorite Murder, RedHanded* . . . all these podcasts were created by women."

"And that Netflix show, *Making a Murderer*? Wasn't that a woman too?" says Sharona, reaching for her jacket. "It's interesting. We don't have to have the answers to ask the questions. Anyway, I'm going to make a move. Stay out of trouble, you two."

She pulls on her jacket and says goodnight, but it's only nine and the night is young. I still feel a little prickly towards Eli, but with Sharona gone, the conversation moves on and we settle into ourselves. Eli orders a second bottle of house red, and then when it's my round, I'm overcome by a loose, generous feeling and treat us to an icy-cold bottle of Prosecco that I can't afford. When the barman calls last orders at eleven, the night opens like a flower.

We weave down the high street to another bar that closes at twelve and Eli gets us a round of spiced rum and Cokes, and then I get us a round of spiced rum and Cokes, and then we go to the Goose, which closes at one, and Eli orders us pints of fruity cider and shots the colour of cartoon slime that smell like apple-flavoured boiled sweets and he forgets himself and puts his hand on my thigh and then removes it, embarrassed.

"I feel like I should apologise," he says, his words thick with alcohol. "I shouldn't have pushed the whole true crime thing earlier."

"It's fine," I say quickly. "It doesn't matter."

"It does matter," he says, and he puts his hand on my thigh again and this time it stays there as we hold eye contact. His eyes are glassy and earnest, and I swallow. *Please don't,* I think. *Please don't bring her into this.*

"Eli—"

He blinks, lips loose, and then he breaks the spell by removing his hand and picking up his glass to drain it.

"Anyway, let's have another drink," he says. "Isn't that pub you hate, the Mother Black Cap, open until two?"

I excuse myself and go to the bathroom. In the privacy of a toilet stall, I cry until I throw up. My sick is fizzy and purple like Vimto. Did I drink Vimto? No. Dark Fruits, it's the Dark Fruits cider, the one that Roach likes. Roach—is she here? Did she buy me this? I flush the loo and lower the lid and plonk myself on the toilet seat to wipe my face. A hammering on the door and a girl calls, "You all right in there, babe?" and someone else says, "I think she's being sick." Roach, was that Roach's voice?

A wave of intense panic crests within me as I realise I'm not safe. I need to leave. I book a taxi, forgetting or not caring that I'm only a fifteen-minute walk from my flat. I squeeze one eye shut so I can make out the blurring letters on my phone screen, but they shift and shimmy in and out of focus. I think I've managed it, but I could be heading anywhere. Fine, I think. Anywhere will do.

Eli catches me staggering from the pub, dragging my coat across the sticky carpet. He follows me out to the car that waits for me on the corner.

"Hey, what's happening?" he says, bleary-eyed, wet lips, a rough-looking drunk. "Can I come?"

"No," I say, slamming the door shut as the driver pulls away from the kerb. Walthamstow flashes past the window as the cabbie whisks me towards home.

It's not that I don't want to sleep with him, and it's not because of Lydia, but because of this: I never want the nights to end—I'll always suggest another bar, always know where to go next, what stays open later, which stepping-stone to hop on to next, to bring us closer to dawn—but I need to wake up in my flat alone. No stragglers sleeping it off on my sofa, no strange presence in my bed. No postmortems, no awkward breakfasts. If I wake up alone, I can draw a line under the whole thing and start again, like it never happened.

∞

I wake up with the night before hanging over me, an ominous cloud. A thick head, a splitting headache. I retrace my steps, circle the blackouts, examine the anxiety that lingers. Have I done anything wrong, anything bad? Have I said anything I shouldn't, have I kissed anyone, have I fucked up?

I check my phone. It's still early; I have some time before I have to get going. There's a typo-filled message waiting for me from Eli: *Thank for te heart-warning goodbye mate!* It's time-stamped half past two in the morning.

I reply now: *Still mad?*

And he texts back immediately: *No! Not mad, never mad. Prob best we called it a night or I'd have ended up on your sofa haha*

We both know you wouldn't have ended up on the sofa, I type, then delete, retype, and then delete.

ROACH

Sam the metalhead who looked like a white Richard Ramirez liked to text, and since our date, he texted me most days. With him, I was Brodie and I slipped into a different skin. Brodie was a writer, and she was chatty and friendly and fun, and she asked lots of questions, and he seemed to like the attention because he asked lots back. *What's your favourite scary movie? What's your favourite death metal band? What's your favourite method of execution?*

If you had to describe yourself in just five words, what would you pick? I texted him, late one night.

I watched him type for a while, and then finally:

morbid

idk what else

morbid. Metal. Cider. Fags. Jäger.

It was love.

He invited me over on a Friday night and for once I spent my shift thinking about something other than death. I wondered if he'd make dinner. Light candles. I wondered if we'd watch a horror film and if he'd put an arm around my shoulders, or if we'd just go straight to bed and fuck like animals. I projected a series of increasingly improbable pornographic scenarios in my mind's eye while I scanned the purchases of interchangeable and indifferent customers through the till.

After work I rushed home to feed Bleep some grapes and mist the glass walls of his vivarium. He seemed fine—a little withdrawn, perhaps, but when it came to affection, snails offered a limited return on investment.

With Bleep sated, I transformed into Brodie with an oversized Metallica T-shirt belted over black velvet leggings and my second-hand Doc Martens—black with yellow stitches, just like Sarah from the *Murder Girls*. Brodie wore smudgy black eye pencil around her eyes and enough mascara to turn her lashes into spider legs. I fastened a bunch of silver chains around my neck and pushed cheap silver rings—a pentagram, a moon, and a coffin—on my fingers. My hair didn't look right on Brodie, though. The purple had faded to a patchy pink, and sooner or later I was going to have to deal with it. Would I choose a Roach shade, or a Brodie shade? Roach would pick amethyst or moss green, but perhaps Brodie would deviate. Maybe she'd dye it jet-black? I couldn't decide.

Downstairs, the evening was warming up. The lights were low and the heating was on full blast, boiling the drunks in their skins. Jackie was at the jukebox, sipping on a vodka soda as she picked tracks to get the evening started. She knew the numbers for all her favourite songs by heart and I watched her quick fingers tap at the keypad for a few seconds: 401, 402, 409, 509, 611. The Stranglers, The Clash, Killing Joke. She looked small beneath the bright light of the jukebox, dressed in a cold-shoulder T-shirt and faded jeans.

"Where are you sneaking off to, then?" she said, catching me as I tried to creep past her to reach the side door. She turned to a regular at the bar. "She's always sneaking off," she said to him, and then to me: "You're not going to another pub, are you? Not the Duke?"

"No."

131

"Not the Coach and Horses?" she said, her eyes narrowed into slits of suspicion, and then her face fell. "Oh God, tell me you aren't going to the Lord bloody Raglan."

Jackie had nurtured beef with every publican in Walthamstow, was ferociously territorial and expected nothing but full solidarity from me. Most pubs were off-limits.

"I'm *not*. I'm just going . . . out," I said with a little shrug of my shoulder, which felt like a very Brodie thing to do.

"Out? What d'you mean, *out*?" she said. She looked me up and down, taking in my makeup, my clothes, my boots. "Where's *out* if it's not a pub?"

"Just *out*," I said, sacrificing some of my Brodie cool to whine.

"She's got a fancy man," said the regular, taking a sip of his bitter. I imagined slamming the glass into his face, breaking the skin.

"You haven't, have you?" Jackie said, one hand on her hip, hungry for details. I clammed up, wary of her interest. If I gave her an inch of information, she'd turn it into a mile of conversation and make me late.

Instead, I pulled on my hoodie and headed out without giving her an answer.

Let her wonder.

⁂

Sam's flatmate had the worst skin I'd ever seen. His face was red and swollen with cystic acne, and his cheeks were pockmarked with deep amethyst scars. His lips were cracked and flaking and his chin and jowls were covered in a fine spray of stubble where it looked too painful to shave.

"Brodie, yeah?" he said, stepping aside to let me in. Their hallway was dingy and smelled like weed and mildew. It was carpeted with junk mail, local newspapers, takeaway flyers, and petrified autumn leaves. I stepped over the mess, careful not to add to the tapestry of footprints covering the top layer of envelopes.

"Yeah."

"Sound. Sam's just having a shit," he said with a snort.

"Oh," I said. "Right."

I followed him into the living room. Woodchip wallpaper, curtains half closed. Empty beer cans, discarded jumpers, and stacks of PlayStation games and horror DVDs were scattered over a carpet thick with crumbs, pen lids, hairbands, stray Rizla, bottle caps, odd socks. The flatmate dropped onto an incongruous, chintzy sofa and picked up a controller to resume some kind of zombie shooting game on a large flatscreen TV.

"Oh hey!" Sam appeared in the doorway, grinning and wiping wet hands on his T-shirt. His hair was pulled back into a lank wet ponytail, and he looked freshly showered. "I didn't hear you come in."

"I told her you were taking a shit," the flatmate said, tickled by his own crudity.

"Thanks, man. I was actually washing up, which I recommend you try some time."

"Oh yeah? How about I try your mum sometime?" the flatmate replied, with a frantic flurry of taps on his controller. A pixelated wash of blood flooded the screen, and I couldn't tell if that meant he was winning or losing.

"Do you want a drink?" Sam asked, turning to me. "I've got cider or Jack Daniel's."

"Cider sounds good," I said.

"Johno?"

"Yeah, cheers, mate."

He disappeared to get the drinks and, not sure what to do with myself, I just stood there and pretended to be interested in the rows of video games on the bookcase by the sofa. They all had names like bad horror films.

"Take a seat if you want," Sam said, handing me a can of Dark Fruits. Dark Fruits. A sign, a message from the universe.

I perched on a chunky armchair and gripped my can with both hands. Sam took the seat on the sofa next to Johno. We all drank and watched as computer-generated blood spattered and splashed over the screen. I kept stealing glances of Sam, wondering if this was going to be it. A whole night of this. He was so handsome, with his strong nose and high cheekbones, his dark eyes fixed on the TV, that I didn't even mind. There was something oddly soothing about watching someone play a violent video game. It was kind of like watching a film but you didn't have to pay attention or keep track of who was who. I slipped into a kind of trance. I liked not having to think about what I was watching.

When I finished my can, I glanced at Sam, and this time he met my eye. He cocked his head towards the living room door with raised eyebrows. I nodded and when he stood up, I followed him.

His bedroom walls were bare and most of his clothes seemed to be on the floor, creating a thick black carpet of mixed fabric. The bed was spread with unwashed black satin sheets. I liked the way they smelled, all rotten and sweaty.

Before the bedroom door was closed, he was on me, kissing me with hard dry lips, his tongue forcing a bunch of sweet, berry-flavoured spit into my mouth. It was rougher than last time. Hungrier. One hand clawed at my breasts, kneading and squeezing my flesh, while the other tugged urgently at my clothes. His sheets felt cool and luxurious under my bare skin, like the lining of a coffin.

"You're really sick, aren't you," he grunted, parting my legs and thrusting into me without a condom. I gasped at the sharp sting of it. I wondered if I should say something, but decided it might out me as a virgin if I stopped things now. "Are you into kink?"

"Yes," I improvised. I'd never really thought about it before but it sounded like the right kind of thing to say in the moment.

"I knew it, you dirty fucking slut." He began to pound harder, grinding me into the bed sheets. Everything hurt. "You sick fucking cunt, you—you dirty fucking raggedy bitch—" His face broke into a rapturous expression of exquisite pain, and then he came inside me, a sudden hot rush of it, again, and again. Then he relaxed, dropped his full body weight onto me so that it was painful to breathe. The whole thing had lasted less than a minute.

"Raggedy?" I said, and he burst into laughter.

"I'm sorry, man, I was just riffing." He rolled off me and stood up. "You all right, yeah?"

"Yeah."

"Did you come?"

"Yeah."

"Sick."

He pulled on a pair of black jeans and a hoodie, and left the room. The sound of running water—or possibly piss hitting the toilet bowl—echoed around the bedroom. While he was in the bathroom, I pulled on my knickers and bra, my Metallica T-shirt, my velvet leggings, one sock caught in the leg, the other lost in the soup of material beneath my feet. I shoved my boots on anyway, and the cold leather felt rough and uncomfortable against my bare foot.

Sam returned with two cans of Dark Fruits, his ponytail askew.

"You got dressed," he said, disappointed.

"I have to get back in a bit," I said.

"Aren't you gonna stay over?"

"Nah. Work tomorrow."

I accepted a can from his outstretched hand, and we went back to the living room, where Johno was still firing shots into the undead, their rotten corpses bucking and spasming with every bullet. Between my legs, I felt a vague stinging sensation and then an unexpected flood of warmth. I excused myself and went into the bathroom to clean myself up. The toilet bowl was streaked with shit, and the white vinyl flooring was speckled with drops of piss and little black commas of curly hair. There was no loo roll in sight, so I took off my knickers, wiped myself with them and threw them in the bin.

Back in the living room, I retied my ponytail and then chugged the rest of my Dark Fruits.

"I should get going," I said. On the television, a zombie groaned and Johno fired a shot straight into its putrefied face. Pixelated gore made the room glow haemoglobin red.

Sam followed me to the front door, and kissed me chastely on the lips as though those same lips hadn't just called me a *dirty fucking raggedy bitch*. "Do you want me to walk you to the station?"

"Do I look like a fucking pussy?" I asked, walking out into the night with a wave over my shoulder. He laughed and slammed the door behind me.

Animals aren't repulsed by their own stink, by the stench of their own nests, and I liked the reek of Sam's sweat and spunk that anointed my skin. On the bus home, I listened to the heavy thrum of AC/DC's "Night Prowler," and thought of Bon Scott, dead in the back of a car outside a house in East Dulwich, and then the bus pulled into my stop and I forgot all about him again.

In the morning, I went to Boots on my lunch break for the morning-after pill and a box of Durex. I had bruises in strange places that were tender to the touch.

LAURA

While I'm in the shop, I dream of all the things I could be doing if I were at home. Cleaning my flat, reading the stack of unread books by my bed, cracking on with the poem I'd started back in September. But when my days off come around, I waste them in bed on my phone, scrolling and scrolling and scrolling and stalking Eli's girlfriend.

I'd planned to start writing something that I'd been thinking about for a while, something about my mother, but everything feels soupy, my body a great weight I have to drag through my flat. I never have the energy when I have the time, and I never have the time when I have the energy. On my days off, the inspiration leaves me and I write nothing. My lilac diary goes untouched for weeks, a symbol of my failure to commit any time to my writing.

Instead, when I'm not doomscrolling, I lie on my bed and try on every shade of lipstick I own. I take photos of myself so I can get a better idea of what my collection is missing. For example, I have several matte pinks but no sheer pinks, and three different berry shades that look almost identical in the tubes, but one swatches much redder than the others, another pulls more purplish, and one has a bricky undertone.

My mother loved her lipstick. She wore the same sheer coral every day to work, but she had a whole collection for special occasions. She was a florist by trade, but the shop specialised in houseplants. Succulents and cacti, ferns and monsteras. She loved to garden, so her hands often smelled like soil, but the scent of Revlon lipstick is what really brings her memory to me. I unscrew a tube of my signature poppy red and take a sniff.

I think about writing something about my mother and lipstick, perhaps a poem threading together lipstick and nostalgia, but instead I watch a video about the history of gothic fashion, narrated by a gothic girl who has positioned herself as an expert by watching someone else's carefully researched video and filming her reaction to the various high street renditions of the subculture. Her face, with her dramatic white skin, overdrawn eyebrows, and Siouxsie liquid liner, is oddly static and her voice oddly flat, and I find her solid and unmoving presence so soothing that I fall asleep and waste the rest of my afternoon dreaming of the perfect matte black lipstick.

It's dark when I wake up, and there's a small yellow slug sliding across the moon-licked lino of my kitchen floor. I shriek and pad around it in a panic, before gathering myself together and fishing a toilet roll tube from the recycling bin. I scoop it up and flick it out the bathroom window, and then on my hands and knees, I try to follow the path of mucus to the source of the break-in, but it disappears under the fridge and the whole task proves to be quite impossible.

∽

Once he recovers from the shock of it, Eli thinks it's charming that I've never listened to *Dark Side of the Moon*.

"You're like a newborn baby," he says, handing me a couple glasses from a kitchen cupboard. "Aren't you even slightly curious about the world around you?"

"Oh, fuck off."

He laughs as I splash a generous measure of spiced rum into each glass. The Coke is room temperature, and he doesn't have any ice in his over-frozen freezer. I find an ice cube tray, fill it with tap water, and slide it into the top drawer of the freezer for later.

"You won't care about ice later," he says, taking his drink and walking through to the living room. It's lit with the cosy glimmer of fairy lights.

His place is a big, bohemian flat in Walthamstow Village, filled with luxury candles, expensive art books, and plants that hang from the ceiling in ceramic pots. I've seen plenty of photos of the space on Lydia's Instagram, but being inside is a different story.

I pull a cushion from the sofa and settle myself on the floor in front of the coffee table while he slides a liquorice disc from its battered cardboard sleeve and drops the needle on to the record. It pops and skitters and then it's a bit of a let-down because nothing much happens. Eli grabs a cushion and sits next to me on the floor, and as he reaches for his tobacco, the room fills with the beating of a heart, the ticking of a metronome, the tocking of a clock, a manic laugh and then the song breaks into a gentle wave of sound.

"I feel like we should wait until we're high to listen to this," says Eli, licking the gum strip of a Rizla, rolling it with a quick flick of his fingers and passing it to me. "But once I'm in the mood to listen to this record, I literally have to listen to it. I can't *not* listen to it. It's like a compulsion, I'm powerless to resist."

I light my cigarette with the flame of a Diptyque candle and blow sour smoke into the air between us. Breathe.

"Stop calling it a record," I say.

"But it *is* a record."

"Just call it an album, you pretentious wanker."

The candles flicker in their jam jars. The room smells like clean laundry, stale weed, and melting wax. He closes his eyes, legs crossed, hands loose in his lap. I think about his body beneath his clothes, the snatches of it I've seen, and how sometimes it's the most desirable thing I can imagine and sometimes it's just there, skin and dark hair and the faint outline of bones and blood vessels.

"Lau . . ." he says, opening his eyes. He pokes my ankle with a toe. His sock is grey and bobbled from too many spins in the washing machine, which seems ridiculous because I can't imagine either him or Lydia washing socks.

"What?"

"I can tell you're not listening. Listen to this bit," he says. "Listen properly. I really want this to be special." It takes me a second to realise he's not talking about the evening, or the proximity of our bodies, but of my experience listening to *Dark Side of the Moon*.

I want to know where Lydia is, but I don't want to break the spell by bringing her into the moment, even though I'm in her space and she's everywhere—in the shoes by the door (black leather Jeffrey Campbell boots), in the photos on the mantlepiece (Lydia and Eli in Florence, Lydia and a bunch of girls holding steins in a beer garden, Lydia posing with a writer I vaguely recognise but can't place), in the books on the shelves (midcentury novels written by women with neat hair and striking clothes).

"Listen, wait—" He twists the volume dial, and the song swells to fill the room. A gentle piano melody, and then a woman's soulful voice, a wail that crashes and breaks against the growing refrain.

Eli has tears in his eyes. He's overcome by his own moment. He starts to tell me some titbit about the woman who shrieks her way through the track, but I can't marry what he's saying to the song we've just listened to because I wasn't in the room, I was elsewhere: I was in the memory of that time after Lounge Bar, when he stripped off his T-shirt and gave it to me to wear so that my silk blouse wouldn't be ruined by the rain. I'd placed my palm on his chest, over a tattoo of a bluebird, and felt the beating of the muscle beneath his breastbone.

"Isn't that just the best song you've ever heard?" he whispers.

"Yes," I say.

His phone buzzes and he reaches for it and I think this is another moment I will return to for the rest of my life. All this—the bougie candles and the awful record that I'll grow to love. His solid presence, and the details that I'll inevitably forget to remember: the cut of his jeans (loose, stonewashed), the breadth of his hands (surprisingly small, slender fingers), the stupid tempo of his stoner drawl (low, slow), his taste in music and films and books (predictable, pseudo-intellectual, macho, melancholy).

"C'mon, you're a poet. Doesn't it resonate with you?"

I take a deep breath and start to roll a cigarette to distract myself.

"I'm not much of a poet," I reply.

"What? Of *course* you are," he says, leaning back with a surprised expression on his face. "You're so talented, and your work is really . . . well, it really gets under people's skin." He laughs. "Look at Roach, she can't get enough of it."

"Well, exactly," I say. A long sigh escapes my lips. "I know this might sound stupid, but . . . Roach has really made me question my poetry, actually."

"How the fuck has Roach made you question your poetry?" he asks, sitting up a little straighter and almost—but not quite—laughing.

"I told you it might sound stupid," I say, watching the candle flame flicker. "It's just . . . she seems to *really* love it, and she keeps asking me about my process and my influences . . ."

"Well, that's kind of cool, right?"

"Nah." I shake my head and wrap my arms around my legs, cigarette still pinched between my index and middle fingers. "It feels . . . icky."

"Icky?"

"I know that sounds bad," I say. "But the whole point of my poetry was to commemorate the people who are often forgotten by true crime narratives, and then I have this true crime nut all over it, desperate to know who the murderers are, like it's a fun puzzle to piece together."

I finally light my cigarette, take a drag, and sit it to rest in the ashtray. A thread of smoke rolls to the ceiling like a trail of incense.

"You haven't failed," he says, resting a comforting hand on my arm. "Just because one weirdo misses the point doesn't mean the point is lost entirely."

"It's not just that," I say. "I feel like she's circling me. She's always there, always watching me, always trying to get my attention. All this true crime stuff is wearing me down. I'd pay a fucking fortune to never hear the words *serial killer* again."

There's a pause.

"Laura, can I ask a question? About your mum?" He speaks softly, his face a picture of gentle concern, and my heart sinks because there's only one question left to ask.

"Yeah," I say. "It was a man called Lee Frost."

He winces. "Oh God, sorry—no, I know that. You told me that. I mean, that's not what—I was just going to ask if you've ever written anything about her?"

I blink, and place my hand on the floor between us.

"Eli—"

His phone buzzes, and he glances at the screen.

"It's my dealer. He won't stop by the flat, he needs me to go out and meet him."

"Sure, let's go," I say, brushing tobacco fronds from my lap and getting ready to stand up.

"You don't need to come with me," he says, pulling on a pair of dank trainers. "It's late. And you absolutely cannot stop listening to this record.

It's bad enough that I have to stop listening to this record. We don't both need to suffer."

"It'll only be on pause," I say, searching for my shoes. "A thirty-minute pause, to digest everything I've heard so far."

He shakes his head, counting the notes in his wallet. "Fuck no. I'll be right back. Trust me, it'll be worth it. Just enjoy the ambience, let it reframe your mood. Maybe it'll inspire you!"

He slams the door behind him.

Alone in Eli's flat, I smoke the rest of my cigarette, pour myself another rum. Side B finishes and the air is filled with the endless, itchy snap and crackle of the needle looping round and round. I switch the record player off, but I feel intensely bothered by the situation. His fucking candles are high-end and pretentious, and his stupid Jack Kerouac poster pisses me off because I know he's never read *On the Road*, and his guitar is dusty because he neither plays it nor puts it away.

My eyes are drawn to the dark corridor and I think, fuck it. I follow my feet, refusing to think too much about what I'm doing. In his bedroom, the duvet is thick and white and rumpled. I sink my hands into it, feel the luxurious sheets, the weight of the duvet. The bed is flanked by midcentury modern bedside tables, and I sit on Lydia's side and touch her things: a copy of *Bad Behavior* by Mary Gaitskill, a green glass dish of earrings, a bottle of Jo Malone perfume, a wicker basket of millennial pink and white cosmetics—expensive, barely there makeup for women who don't really need to wear it. I try on a gold ring, steal a squirt of perfume, dab on a little sheer pink lipstick in the colour "Cake."

A shudder of self-loathing. What the fuck is wrong with me? I feel vile, disgusted with myself. When he gets back to the flat, Eli will roll a joint and ask what I thought of the record, and I won't have anything meaningful to say. The truth is that I barely listened to a single note because I was so preoccupied with thinking of clever things to say that would prove I had listened to it.

I find my other shoe under the sofa, pull on my coat, and do a French exit. When I'm halfway home, I send him a rubbishy text about feeling shit and then ignore his calls. At home, I put the chain on the door and draw the curtains closed. A thick, dark night. A siren, foxes crying, the loose vowels of a drunk singing "Don't Look Back in Anger." Late, it's late, and so dark. I hate the dark, hate the night. It's thick and heavy and cloying and suffocating. My mouth tastes like Lydia's lipstick.

The footprints outside my living room window have long since been eroded by the weather, but I still think of them often. Had they ever returned? Had they ever tried to break in? Was I safe?

ROACH

On Halloween, I usually liked to shotgun horror films—one after the other, the bloodier, the more horrific, the better—but Sam was more of a social creature. He insisted we go out drinking in Camden, where men in Halloween masks prowled through the crowd, sniffing after devils in black dresses, and the shadowy corners of rock bars were thick with copulation and simmering aggression, waiting to be pounded out one way or another to the frantic drums and bone-rattling reverb of thrashed guitars.

From our favourite table in The Black Heart, we listened to the music and people-watched the normies walking by, playing dress-up. Next to us, a girl in a red velvet dress kissed a vampire, her lipstick staining his chin like smeared blood, his plastic fangs lying forgotten next to his pint. Sam caught me watching them, threw an arm around my shoulder and kissed me sloppily on the corner of my mouth, and I turned to him and kissed him back, delighted to be included in the carnage of the night. The leather of his jacket was cold and stiff, and he pushed his face into the warm crook of my neck. He smelled like outside, like fresh air and cigarettes and sour beer.

"Would you like me to strangle you?" he whispered, hot breath in my ear.

"Like, now?" I said, jerking my head away from him so I could look him in the eye and gauge the seriousness of his offer. He laughed affectionately at my response and pulled me back.

"Like, while we fuck," he said, raising his voice over the pounding music.

"Maybe," I lied, taking a sip of cider. The cold fizz of it made my molars ache.

"Would you ever have a threesome?" he asked.

I thought about this. My options felt limited. On the next table, the kissing couple seemed to be disappearing into one another, all spit and red lips and groping hands. They were attractive, but I couldn't imagine them asking me to join them. I tried to picture a viable alternative, but sex still seemed like something that belonged to other people. I pictured Sam's flatmate Johno, with his crooked teeth and pockmarked cheeks, then Eli with his cigarette breath, and then Laura. Rose oil, peachy skin, the gaping wet yawn of a spread vagina. I felt absolutely nothing, no whisper of arousal. Ambivalence wasn't what Sam was looking for in this conversation, though, so I smiled.

"Yeah," I said, and he beamed and leaned in and kissed me again. He liked this line of questioning, as though we were these super kinky people who had wild, adventurous sex instead of our routine sixty seconds of quick, dry rutting.

∽

After the bar, Sam was in the mood for a bit of violence. Back at his place, we dragged the satiny duvet on to the sofa in the living room. He grabbed us ciders, a half bottle of Jäger, and a bag of cheese Doritos while I wormed my way under the cover like a maggot digging into a corpse.

"Do you want a little bit nasty or bloody disgusting?" he asked, popping a stray DVD back into its case.

"Bloody disgusting," I said, settling down with my notebook to read. "But something I've seen before, so I don't have to watch it properly."

He put on *Martyrs*, the American remake of the French film, because neither of us liked movies we had to read unless we were really in the mood. Sam rocked from his knees on to his haunches and stood up, then settled on the sofa and cracked open the Jäger. An apothecarian smell filled the room as he took three big swallows, then there was a sharp *psssst* as he cracked a cider.

I flipped through my notebook, glancing through the strange mix of Laura's words and my own. In my tiredness, my tipsiness, our words blurred together until I didn't know where she ended and I began. Our styles were seamless. It was uncanny how she was able to capture on the page exactly how I wanted to write, and how I was able to pick up where she left off to create something new, something rounder and more whole. I had the stomach to write about the parts that she didn't dare go near: violence, cruelty, pain.

"Did I ever tell you about Laura?" I asked. Without looking up from his phone, he offered me the bottle. I took it and held it in my lap.

"Dunno. Is she fit?"

"She's this girl at work. We have so much in common, but she fucking hates me. It's so unfair."

The weight of injustice ached in my throat, but it wasn't very Brodie of me to whine. Sam's indifferent thumb rolled rhythmically over the glass screen of his phone.

"Well, she sounds like a bitch," he said, scrolling.

"She *is* a bitch," I replied. That was more like it, that was more Brodie. "She's a stuck-up snob," I continued. "She thinks she's better than me. We have so much in common, loads and loads, but she doesn't give a shit."

After a few seconds, Sam turned to me. "Shall we kill her?"

He reached for the Jäger bottle, so I took a pharmaceutical swallow and handed it to him.

"Okay," I said with a snort, wiping my mouth. "Let's do it."

I focused on the film for a bit, then picked up my phone and scrolled for a while. Brunch, Prosecco, sunsets. Babies, birthdays, holidays. Everything was boring. It was like everyone else was living an approximation of the same life, sharing endless snapshots of the same cocktails and the same poached eggs and the same trendy paperbacks, the same peachy sunset reposted a thousand times.

"How should we do it?" he asked, lips wet with liquor.

"We'll push her under an oncoming train and tell everyone she fell."

"Sick."

On-screen, an insidious theatre of brutality played out in real time, until the body was finally, fatally purified and the soul of the dead girl was free to ascend. The blood, the screams. I watched with blank indifference. I'd seen it before.

"Or we could cut her throat," Sam said. "Do it properly."

A blow to the head. A boating accident. Apparent food poisoning. While I considered the various ways in which we could kill Laura, I browsed the internet. It was payday and I found myself on a normie fashion website. It was the kind of place Laura would shop, and sure enough, they had berets in stock. I ordered a black beret and matching black brogues and a vial of rose essential oil to wear as perfume.

"*It was now 5* A.M.," said Sam, in a theatrical voice. I turned in surprise, and saw he was holding my notebook open, reading from a random page with a devilish smirk on his face.

"Hey!" I sat up and tried to grab it from him, but he leaned as far away from me as he could without upsetting the cider can balanced on the sofa between his thighs.

"*And dawn, a hot—*"

"Stop it, give it back!"

"*—fiery dawn—*"

I reared up and snatched the book from his outstretched hand. We tussled until he let it go with a bark of laughter.

"All right, chill out," he said, settling back into the sofa. After a pause, he nudged me with his foot. "I'm only having a laugh. Read me something."

"Nah," I said, embarrassed, smoothing the bent cover with the palm of my hand.

"So, what, you don't think I'll get it?"

"It's not that."

"You don't think I'm smart enough."

"Shut up, it's *not* that."

"Stop being tight and read me something, then."

"It's not finished," I said. "It's all a work in progress."

He leaned forward with a hard expression on his face, and I reared back, suddenly frightened by the spark of hatred in his dark eyes.

"What are you even here for?"

"It's Halloween," I said in a small voice, confused.

"Yeah, but what are you here for if you don't even like me enough to read me something?"

I felt myself relax as he laughed and swigged from the dark green Jäger bottle in his hands. He loved to joke like this, as though the idea of me not liking him was unthinkable.

I opened the journal. "I'll read you one thing, and then can we drop it?"

"Yes," he said, pleased with himself.

I read him my favorite Laura piece, the darkest one, the one that I had embellished with explicit gore, and when I finished reading, Sam was staring at me as though he wanted to eat me alive.

"You wrote that?"

"Yeah." I closed the notebook and snuggled back into the sofa.

"Fuck," he said, lips wet. "Fuck, Brodie. That's so dark. That's dark as fuck."

"Sorry," I said, a creep of embarrassment heating my cheeks.

"Nah, I loved it," he said, standing up and pulling me to him. "I loved it," he said, leading me into his bedroom, spreading me over his satin sheets. "I loved it," he said, working his hands under my Napalm Death T-shirt.

"I love you," I whispered, as he wrapped his hands around my throat.

It was only when I left for work the next morning that I realised I'd left my notebook on the sofa, forgotten in the moment.

NOVEMBER 2019

LAURA

November starts with a sharp headache and sambuca-breath that leaves me feeling sick to my stomach. I'd spent Halloween with my friend Maggie, a bookseller from the Bloomsbury branch, in a bar decorated with plastic bats and pumpkin-shaped fairy lights. In a scandalously low-cut Elvira dress, I'd knocked back lethal shots called Black Jacks and danced to cheesy Halloween music until I was no longer capable of retaining fresh information. I think Maggie booked me a taxi, but the end of the night is frayed.

It's the kind of hangover that can only be cured with a takeaway pizza and one of those saccharine, cookie-cutter Christmas films in which a brassy city girl returns to her hometown and falls in love with a charismatic yet mysterious local. The gentle predictability of it all soothes me.

Christmas has always been my favourite time of year. When I was a little girl, the festive season was a whirlwind. My mother worked long hours at the shop, and although she was in a constant state of exhaustion, she'd bring home velvet-leafed poinsettias, sprigs of holly and mistletoe, a real fir wreath for the front door so the house smelled like fresh pine needles. In the evenings we'd eat pesto pasta and watch corny Christmas films under twinkling lights, with hot chocolate, sweet and smooth, studded with marshmallows and spiked with a warming hit of cinnamon.

By the time she died, I thought I was too grown up to enjoy Christmas, too grown up for hot chocolate and childhood nostalgia. I was a teenager who slept late and tried to hide my joy at every turn. I wish I could step through a doorway into Christmas morning as a child and experience it all again for one last time.

Lilac diary spread open on the arm of the sofa, I write all this down, all her beautiful, inconsequential moments, and as I write, an idea starts to take shape. I like the idea of writing about my mother, a memoir celebrating her life instead of ruminating on her death, but I know enough about publishing to know that the two have to come hand in hand. No one wants to read about her life when her death is so much more interesting, I think bitterly.

But what if it was something more—a grief memoir, and a polemic about true crime? I could write both narratives side by side—the story of my mother and the story of the case, eventually weaving them together until one bleeds into the other. I tap my pen against my teeth. It's one thing to write about her life, but quite another to write about her death, though, and I'm not sure if I have the strength to do it.

⚬

Christmas is transformative: wine is transformed with spices, butter with a wicked splash of brandy, orange juice with champagne. We have to transform the shop into a winter wonderland, so as soon as October gives way to November, Eli and I begin the long and laborious task of doing it ourselves. We spend a whole morning in the stockroom listening to *Songs for Christmas* by Sufjan Stevens and carefully threading cardboard snowflakes on to nylon string. We pin them to the ceiling front of store where they drift in a paper blizzard, gently turning on their lengths of thread. We hang twinkling white fairy lights from bay to bay, and cardboard icicles dangle from the bay headers.

The window displays are still dominated by study guides and sticker books from half-term, but that won't do for the festive season. The Christmas windows have to be opulent and inviting, a cornucopia of treasures to tempt passersby into coming in and spending their hard-earned money with us. I gather toys and books, choose new titles from familiar authors to build an eye-catching display. Martin follows me around the shop, offering a running commentary on my selection, until finally he gets agitated by a stack of middle-grade titles written by celebrities and dumps them on a trolley in the stockroom.

"But they're bestsellers," I argue, picking them back up again. "We sell, like, ten a day."

"So, if they're selling anyway, then they don't *need* to be in the Christmas window," he says, triumphant. "Wouldn't you rather support authors who write their own books?"

"But it isn't about what *we* want," I reply, losing my patience. "It's about what our customers want."

"They only want this trash because it's what you're telling them to want," he snaps back.

"But . . . kids like them too. And the Christmas windows are all about bestsellers. You *know* that, Martin."

"I've been bookselling for longer than you've been alive." His cheeks are flushed, and he jabs an angry finger in my direction. "Don't tell me what I know."

"Don't yell at me," I say, a little flame of shame burning in my belly.

He marches off, and I fill the window with stacks and stacks of Christmas paperbacks from the big brand authors, the authors whose books are ghostwritten and sell by the truckload as long as you remind customers that they exist. When I finish, I'm red-faced and sweating, and my muscles hurt from all the stooping, stretching, and contorting it takes to fill a tight window display with carefully balanced books, but it looks incredible.

I call Eli and Sharona over to admire my hard work, and to my surprise, Martin begrudgingly follows them. We all step outside into the cold. It's dark already, and drizzling. Golden light spills through the windows and gilds the wet pavement. It looks like a postcard.

"Excellent work." Sharona throws an arm around my shoulders and gives me a little squeeze.

"Perfect," Eli says, nodding. He's holding a price gun, and he twirls it around his index finger like a pistol.

"Fine," sniffs Martin. He heads back into the warmth of the shop, and Sharona follows him, grinning at me and rolling her eyes at his expense.

"Drink tonight?" asks Eli.

"Do you ever feel like all we do is drink and work?" I say, wrinkling my nose. I'm tired, and my head feels thick and my face aches from smiling. That's not why I'm hesitating, though, not really. It's group tonight, and I'd promised myself I'd go as tomorrow marks a painful day in my calendar and I could use the emotional support. I think of that cold community hall with its miserable instant coffee and posters for jumble sales and flu jabs, and then I think of a fun night out with Eli by my side, of cheap beers and silly jokes and good times.

"What's wrong with drinking and working?" Eli says with a grin.

⁂

Martin and Sharona are on the midshift and, eyeing the heavy clouds, they decide to head straight to the pub to avoid the rain. By the time Eli and I finish closing up, the drizzle has turned into a heavy downpour that lashes against the windows.

Wind whips my hair, and I have to hold a palm to my crown to keep my beret in place. Within a few minutes, I'm soaked. Sodden clothes cling to bone, and water seeps into my shoes so they rub against my heels. London rain falls quick and clean, but it mingles with the scum that coats everything, the pollution and dirt that felts the brick buildings, the roads, the cars.

I follow Eli to the far end of the market, where a scarlet and gold smear of neon brightens the night. A red plastic lantern hangs over the doorway, and golden letters spell HAPPY VALLEY in a mock calligraphy.

"Are you taking me to dinner first?" I joke.

"Oh yeah," Eli says, laughing. "Cosy little dinner for two, fuck everyone else. Nah, this place sells big cans of lager for a quid."

"So?"

"So, are we made of money? Besides, it's the happiest place in Walthamstow!"

A jolly little bell jangles as he pushes the restaurant door open and lets me step inside first. The warm air smells like hot toasted sesame oil and roasted meat. My saliva glands ache and my stomach rolls with hunger.

A lone waitress is standing at the service station, refilling soy sauce bottles. Her hair is a dark curtain that parts to reveal a soft face that tips towards us at the sound of the bell.

"Two?" she calls, flashing an incidental peace sign and grabbing a pair of oversized plastic menus.

"Nah, our friends are out back," Eli says, offering a dimpled grin. She meets his warmth with a tentative smile and waves us inside. He ambles confidently through the empty restaurant—he knows exactly where to go, swinging his hips between empty chairs like he's done this a thousand times before.

The booksellers are gathered around a large circular table spread with a white tablecloth, underneath a flat screen television. An American football match plays out in the lurid technicolour of a poorly adjusted set, solemn in its silence. The lights are low, and the table is strewn with beer cans, baskets of prawn crackers, plates of spring rolls, and little saucers of orange dipping sauce.

Roach is there, sullen in an all-black ensemble, between Kofi and Barry. Her greasy roots catch the light, and her dark eyes and pink-purple oil-spill hair make her look like a beetle. I choose a seat as far away from her as possible. Eli slides into the seat next to her, on the other side of the table.

"This beer reminds me of Beijing," Sharona says, tipping the last of her can into her mouth. She catches the waitress's eye and orders another round for the table.

"Tell me about Beijing!" Noor swoons, warming her hands on a speckled stoneware cup of green tea. I grab a spring roll and take a happy bite. It's cold and has lost its crunch, but it's delicious.

Kofi turns to me and sighs with the air of someone whose patience for travel stories is starting to wear thin. "Thank God you're here," he says, reaching over and clanking his can against mine. "It's been like a bloody Lonely Planet editorial meeting."

I laugh and pop the second half of my spring roll into my mouth.

"Better than being at work, though," he says. "Today I was on the early, and I was, like, oh my God, will someone just come and murder me? Just take me into the stockroom and put me out of my misery."

"Do you not like bookselling?" I ask, and there's a crisp note to my voice.

"No, oh my God, I *love* it," he says, rushing to cover his indiscretion. "Sorry, yeah. Of course, I love it. I would just love it so much more if it weren't for the customers." He laughs, but I remain stony-faced.

"The customers keep you in a job," I say. He throws me a sour look and shifts his focus back to Noor, Sharona, and Eli. Our waitress reappears with emerald-green cans of Tsingtao. I take a long swallow of beer to wash down my spring roll, find myself draining half of it in one go. I order another before the waitress has finished handing out beers to the rest of the team. When I return my gaze to the table, Eli is staring at me.

"That was quick," he says, with a nod to my can.

"I'm a thirsty girl," I reply, but he doesn't look amused.

It doesn't matter, though. It's the kind of night where the drinks keep coming and no one cares about the bill. Sharona tries to keep things grounded by ordering side dishes to soak up the booze—little plates of prawn toast, wontons that kiss our lips with oil—but the alcohol stacks up inside me until I'm glowing with it.

At around nine, when the rain slows to a patter, Eli, Sharona, and I walk to the newsagents to pick up more cigarettes. Walthamstow is a blur of streetlights staining the sky yellow and cars speeding through puddles. I feel light and nimble, bubbly and fun and funny and bright. This was the right decision, I think. Better than spending another evening drinking tea and thinking about other people's grief in a cold community hall.

"Listen," says Sharona, gesturing towards Eli and me with her cigarette as we walked. "Are you guys up for Brighton in the new year?"

"Like a trip?" I ask. I blink hard, but everything in the world around me is duplicated.

"No, like a job," she says, with a sweet laugh. "Just for a few weeks. They're having a refit and I've been asked to assemble a crack team to oversee it."

"You know I'm down," Eli says, cigarette hanging from the corner of his mouth. He raises his hand and Sharona meets it with a high five.

"Laura?" she says, and they look at me.

"I can't afford to commute from Walthamstow to Brighton every day," I say, disappointed. I've always loved the seaside. When I was a little girl, my mother used to take me to Brighton on day trips. We'd eat chips and scan the shingles for pretty stones. I loved the old penny arcade, with its vintage mechanical puppet shows and fortune-telling booths, loved the pier with its garish rides, doughnuts, and candy floss.

"Oh, don't worry about that," Sharona says with a dismissive flap of her hand. "Spines will cover it while we do the refit. Or maybe we'll get a hotel, if the commute really kills us. We'll only be down there for a couple of weeks either way."

When we get back to Happy Valley, Eli drops the end of his rollie on to the damp pavement and steps on it to extinguish the cherry.

"Please say you'll come," he says with a grin, pushing open the restaurant door and holding it ajar.

"I'm in," I say, with a rush of excitement as I follow Sharona back into the warmth of the restaurant.

"You drunk?" he asks.

"No," I reply as the room gently spins.

I go straight to the bathroom to throw up. Strings of bean sprout stick in my throat, and I rinse the bile from my mouth with water from the tap and then return to my seat like nothing happened. The perfect crime.

Roach is hypnotised by Eli as he rhapsodises about the politics of shelving. I know this speech, I've heard it a thousand times before, but Roach is on the edge of her seat, completely enraptured. She wants to fuck him, I think. Let her try. I grab a limp spring roll and stuff it into my mouth.

"Shelving is a political act," Eli says, concentrating on rolling a cigarette that tapers in that telltale way marijuana smokers roll when they've had a few drinks. "Do you splinter Fiction into subsections for LGBT Fiction and so on, or do you keep everything together in General Fiction? How about *The Handmaid's Tale*? Does it go in Fiction or Sci-Fi?"

"I mean, it's dystopian," says Kofi, uncertain, answering the rhetoricals like a rube.

"There's no sci-fi element to *The Handmaid's Tale*," Barry interrupts in his nasal voice. "Everything in there has actually happened. The real question is: Where do you shelve the *Oryx and Crake* trilogy? Do you shelve them separately from the rest of Atwood's work, or do you keep them all together?"

"Can't you just put it in both places?" asks Kofi.

Eli tucks his cigarette behind his ear and rolls his clipper between the palms of his hands, nodding thoughtfully. "Where does it end, though? Do you stock multiple copies of every book that could sit in more than one section? Two copies of *Beloved*? Two copies of *The Alchemist*, two copies of *1984*, two copies of . . . I dunno, man, two copies of *Gone Girl*? Do you double up on everything, on every genre title, because they all go into Fiction too?"

"Well, with Toni Morrison, you do," says Sharona. "You shelve Toni Morrison in as many places as humanly possible."

"We're straying from my original point. Shelving is political," Eli says, with an emphatic hand slapped on to the table. "Think about it. What about books on the Holocaust? Where do you shelve them? Noor?"

Sharona holds up a finger as she swallows a mouthful of beer. "This is good, I want to hear this."

Noor looks thoughtful as she fingers an earring, a silver teardrop that dangles from her lobe. "Well . . . you put them in with the Second World War."

"Barry?" Eli says. "As our resident history expert, what d'you say to that?"

"You could do," Barry says mildly, with a pause that implies that Noor isn't necessarily wrong. "The problem with that is that victims of the Holocaust weren't victims of military action. The context of it predates the beginning of World War Two, and many schools of thought treat it as an entirely separate thing."

The rest of the table grows quiet as each bookseller waits for someone else to make the next suggestion.

"Um . . . what about Jewish History?" Noor says, wrinkling her nose like she already knows it's the wrong answer. All the more experienced booksellers groan or shake their heads and she covers her face with her hands in mock embarrassment.

"Think about it," says Eli. "Do you want to shelve your books about the Nazis next to your books about the history of Jewish cooking? It's totally inappropriate. Customers would complain."

"Well, books about the history of Jewish cooking would go into Food Writing anyway," Barry says.

"Plus, we have to be mindful of books about other groups who were persecuted during the Holocaust," says Sharona.

"German History, then," says Kofi, with a shrug.

"Auschwitz was in Poland," Barry says, his voice grave. "It didn't all happen in Germany."

I pick up my can of Tsingtao and take a long lukewarm draught until it's empty. I crane my neck for the waitress and everyone slowly turns to look at me.

"Where would you shelve them, Ms. Laura Bunting?" asks Eli. "Really. Be serious. I know you know the answer."

"Well, the Holocaust can't fit into any one section," I say. "It's too big, too broad, too much of a muchness. It has to go into its own section in General History, regardless of how many books you have, regardless of the size of the shop. And it should be the same with books about colonialism, and slavery too. Shelving them under one country or continent will inevitably result in the erasure of another, and that's a political choice."

"Exactly," says Eli. "Exactly. *That's a political choice.* Where you choose to shelve a book creates context, whether you intend it to or not."

"This is why I don't believe we should have a True Crime section," I say, finding my sea legs, getting into my stride. "It's disgusting to see heartfelt literary memoirs shelved next to all that exploitative, voyeuristic shit."

Sharona nods and says, "Yes, exactly."

"It isn't shit," Roach cuts in quickly, her voice dangerous. She's gripping her can of lager with both hands, the metal indenting beneath her fingers.

"Oh please," I say, swatting the air. I'm drunk. Words tumble from my mouth like the scatter of dried seaweed across the tablecloth. "It's men profiting from violence against women."

"White women," Noor says quickly. "They never write bestsellers about brown or black women."

"Sorry," I say, placing a hand on the table in the space between us. "You're totally right. I just get kind of sensitive about this stuff." And then, without really meaning to, I find the Tsingtao taking over and a rush of words spill from my mouth: "My mother was murdered when I was a teenager."

There's a shocked pause. *This is fine*, I think. *I'm being open.* I catch a glance between Sharona and Eli, as though she's looking to him for con- firmation. He blinks at her and then drops his gaze, and then she reaches over and gives my forearm a squeeze.

"You poor thing," she whispers, empathy written all over her face.

"I'm really sorry," says Noor, biting her lower lip and looking uncomfortable.

Roach leans forward. Her countenance turns my stomach. She looks hungry and hopeful, like a dog that's just heard the rustle of a bag of treats.

"What happened?" she asks, unable to disguise the lilt of enthusiasm in her voice.

"Well, I don't really want to talk about it," I say, nipping this in the bud. "I was just saying."

"Yes, of course," says Sharona, rubbing my arm and then reaching for her beer can. "Let's change the subject—let's get another round."

She sits up and waves a hand to catch the waitress's attention, silver bangles rattling. Eli catches my eye and mouths, "You good?" and I nod.

The conversation moves on, and the table contracts and relaxes, but Roach's eyes drill into me, and the prickle of her curiosity creeps over the back of my neck. I knock back beers and ignore her, drinking to pad the raw embarrassment of my outburst until the waitress kicks us out and we spill onto the wet street. It's bitterly cold, and the moon is rising high above us.

Once they're out, the other booksellers seem to feel the thirst of the night rising inside them. I want another drink too, but I wish Roach would just leave, would just go home. I can feel her eyes on me, and regret curdles in my stomach. It feels different this time, nothing like the uncomfortable but cathartic divulgence at my support group. My resentment towards Roach simmers and I walk briskly ahead of the others, head down as I smoke.

ROACH

I was buzzing as we walked from one bar to the next. Laura's mother, murdered! This was juicy information. I wondered when. I wondered how. I wondered who. Who had done it, what was the story? Perhaps I already knew it. The thought made me tingle. I hadn't planned on staying out for much longer, but I wasn't going to walk away from Laura while she was feeling so confessional.

It was cold and the air was damp, so—shyly—I reached into my bag and pulled on my new beret. It was the first time I'd worn it in front of the other booksellers, and it took me a moment to get it to sit right on my head without a mirror. I wondered if anyone would notice or comment on it, but—aside from Laura, who was striding ahead—everyone had paired off and I was walking by myself at the back of the group.

Laura's proximity to murder made absolute sense to me. However bright her smile and however loud her laugh, however perfect her lipstick and however full her wine glass, a dark cloud hung over her, a cloud that only I could see. The big question rolled around my head, possibilities unfurling: which dark devil had taken her mother, and changed the path of her life forever?

It's disgusting, she'd said, *to see heartfelt literary memoirs shelved next to all that exploitative, voyeuristic shit.* Everyone had looked at me, and

I'd tried to think of something to say, something cutting, something that would articulate exactly why true crime mattered. The path to understanding the human condition was soaked in blood and guts, it was stalked by serial killers and sadists and mass shooters, and it was laced with upsetting stories, stories of violence and death, of neglect and abuse. If we really wanted to better ourselves as a society, we had to be prepared to deal with the unsavoury parts as well as the nicey-nice parts. Life couldn't always be a fairy tale, Laura. The bad man couldn't always be caught. But then she'd said her piece about her mother, and suddenly it all clicked into place. Avoiding my eye, side-stepping my questions, resisting my offer of friendship. Laura was a matryoshka doll, all right, and at her core was an obsession with murder, an obsession with death. But unlike me, she couldn't bring herself to admit it.

LAURA

At the wine bar, we start strong with two bottles for the table, which Sharona pays for. It's fun, everyone out together. I try to stay in the present and focus on the wine in my glass, the laughter around me. Even Martin's in a good mood. He buys me a little glass of port that tastes like chocolate, dark cherries and spices—an olive branch, perhaps, to make up for our little tiff earlier. He really knows his port, and he tilts the glass and talks me through the different layers of flavour, and I'm just happy to be there in the moment, enjoying my drink and feeling like I'm part of something.

"So, what's your story, Martin?" I ask him. There's a slight slur to my words, a softening around the edges. "You're so great with kids—do you have any? Are you married?"

"No, no kids. I've been with Frank for twenty years. I had a go at teaching, and then I opened my own little bookshop around here. Closed down in the noughties, though. First Spines, then Amazon. Couldn't compete."

Juicy Fruit gum, a little gold ring in his ear.

"You ran the Marble Shop?" I say, my face a picture of surprise.

"Is that how you remember it?" he asks with a sad smile.

"That's how I knew it," I say. "There were two bookshops, right? Yours and another?"

"Yes, there was mine, and then there was Clements" Books too. I focused on the kids" books, and they focused on adults."

"Your shop was magical to me," I say. "I loved it. I think it's the reason I became a bookseller. I want to recreate that feeling for little kids, that excitement of walking into a bookshop. In fact, I still have some of my marbles."

"Well, that makes one of us at least," he says with a laugh, and then, after a pause, he pats me on the back. "Thank you for saying that. You can't know what it means to me."

I finish my port, then dabble between reds. The window is hemmed with hanging plants, the glass running with condensation, and our table is wet with spilled drinks. I reach for my glass and misjudge the distance, knock red wine everywhere.

"Maybe you've had enough," Eli says, with a serious look on his face as he rights my upturned glass and places his hand over it as Kofi tops everyone up.

"I'm fine," I say, as the floor tilts beneath my feet.

"Another glass!" Kofi says, accidentally pouring wine over Eli's splayed fingers. Messy loves company, and Eli's half-hearted attempts to retain order are overruled by the collective desire to keep going.

"You're drunk, little friend," Eli says, in a quiet voice meant only for me. His eyes are shining.

"And you're Eli," I say, tapping him on the nose with an imprecise finger, mimicking his habit.

"And tomorrow you'll still be drunk and I'll still be Eli," he says. "No, wait . . ."

"Tomorrow I'll be Laura," I say.

"And I'll—"

". . . be in my bed?" I say, leaning into him and laughing. "Kidding, just kidding. Don't freak out."

Eli looks uncomfortable, but when Kofi tops up my glass again, he doesn't say a word.

ROACH

The stuck-up wine bar was too good for Strongbow, so they didn't have Dark Fruits. They poured me a bottle of flat scrumpy, topped it up with an artisanal blackcurrant and elderflower cordial and charged me seven quid for the pleasure. It tasted brambly, like rotten apples.

The conversation swelled around me, and I watched Laura swallow wine, glass after glass of it, her pallor pinkening, her hair frizzing into a golden halo in the humidity of the bar. She became exaggerated as she drank, her voice louder and bolder, and she laughed harder for longer. She punctuated her words with sweeping hand gestures that knocked over drinks and bumped against strangers.

I turned to Eli. "So, do you know what happened to Laura's mum?"

He looked revolted, his face a death mask of surprise. "Mate, you can't ask me that."

"Do you, though?"

"She doesn't like to talk about it, and you shouldn't bloody well ask."

"If she doesn't like to talk about it, why did she bring it up?"

He didn't have an answer to that, just shook his head and turned away to talk to someone else.

I saw no reason not to conduct a quick bit of research then and there. I typed *Bunting murder London* into Google but nothing came up. I tried

Laura Bunting murder and *Bunting mother murder* but no dice. Maybe it didn't happen in London. I tried *Bunting murder England* and then just *Bunting murder victim*. Maybe she was lying, maybe it didn't happen at all. That seemed unlikely.

When the smokers stood up in unison, in that unspoken way that smokers always fell into step, their need for nicotine in sync, I followed with my pack of Pall Malls.

In the smoking area out front, a pack of menthols was a pathway to connection, a honeytrap for conversation. Eli, Kofi, and Laura sat huddled on a low brick wall, laughing and joking, passing a lighter between them, but Sharona hung back, eyeing my cigarettes.

"Are those the ones with the little . . . ?" she asked, doing a pinching motion with her finger and thumb. She looked smaller outside the shop, petite in her Thai fisherman's trousers and black woven hoodie. I nodded and offered them to her.

"I haven't had a menthol in years," she said, sliding one from the pack and placing it between her lips. This was my cue to offer her a lighter. Smoking was a dance and I had finally learned the choreography thanks to smoking regularly with Sam. She leaned forward to light the cigarette and then closed her eyes and exhaled slowly, like she'd been holding her breath for a long time. She tipped her head back, stretching the muscles in her neck.

"I swear, every bone in my body aches," she said. "And it's only November."

Across the patio, a glass smashed, and there was an eruption of cheers from the trio perched on the wall. In the distance, a dog barked.

"Do you know what happened to Laura's mum?" I asked.

Sharona stopped her gentle stretching and gave me a reproachful look. "That's not cool," she said. "You can't ask me that."

"I'm just curious," I said. "Curiosity isn't a crime."

"I think you know you're crossing a line." She expelled a lungful of smoke by scrunching her mouth and blowing it over her shoulder.

"Hey, Sharona," Eli called from across the patio. "Come here a sec!"

"Don't ask anyone else that, okay?" she hissed over her shoulder in a scolding manner that reminded me of Jackie. "And Christ, promise me you won't ask Laura."

I followed her towards Eli, Laura, and Kofi.

"Oh, for God's sake," muttered Laura, too drunk to hide her open disdain at the sight of me approaching.

"We're gonna play Never Have I Ever," Eli said as we niveli with them. "You in?"

"Absolutely not!" Sharona laughed and took a sharp drag on her cigarette, then flicked it, only half smoked, into the bushes. "Cheers for the menthol, Roach. I owe you one."

As Sharona ambled back into the bar, I lit another cigarette—my backstage pass, in case anyone wondered why I was out there.

"Since when has she smoked?" Laura said to no one in particular.

"Right, Never Have I Ever," Eli said, clapping his hands together. "Roach, you down?"

"I don't know," I said. "I've never played it before."

"Everyone on the fucking planet has played Never Have I Ever," said Laura. "Didn't you go to uni?"

"No," I said.

Laura rolled her eyes and slumped forward, elbows on her knees, head resting on her hands. "Hate Never Have I Ever," she whined. "It's just an excuse to trick women into talking about sex."

"Well, it's not my fault you've only ever played with Oxbridge perverts," Eli said.

"You know I didn't go to Oxbridge," she replied.

"Ah no, it was Durham, right?"

"Fuck *off.*"

"Okay, darling, you start," Kofi said to Eli, his legs crossed neatly at the knee.

"Never have I ever . . . gone skinny-dipping," Eli replied.

"See?" said Laura, triumphant. "Sex!"

"Nudity isn't sex, and sex isn't nudity," Eli said. "You're so repressed."

No one drank, so Eli had to swallow a finger of red wine. He winced and held his glass up. "This is not good wine."

Kofi went next. "Never have I ever . . . had sex at work."

Laura shrieked. "*That's* about sex."

"That *is* about sex," Eli agreed.

"*I* never said I had a problem with sex," Kofi said, shrugging his shoulders with a sly smirk. And then Eli laughed, and with a sheepish look, he took a mouthful of his drink.

"You've had sex in a shop?" Laura said, incredulous. "With who?"

"Never you mind," he said.

"Which shop?!"

"Never you mind! That's not part of the game."

It was my turn. I took a sip of my drink and extinguished my cigarette to buy some time, but all I could think about was death.

Never have I ever been out walking my dog on a lonely windswept moor and stumbled upon human remains. Never have I ever seen a suspicious suitcase and discovered a dead body inside it. Never have I ever smelled a strange smell emanating from my neighbour's drainpipe that turned out to be rotting human flesh. Never have I ever lost my mum to murder.

"Never have I ever had sex with a stranger," I said.

"Oh, for God's sake," said Laura.

First Kofi, and then Eli, and then, eventually—laughing at herself—Laura, all raised their glasses to their lips and drank.

"You have to do a forfeit," Eli said. "'Cause we all drank."

"What's my forfeit?"

"Shots! You have to buy us all shots!" Laura said. "Shots of chartreuse."

"But it's your turn," Kofi said to Laura. "You have to go first, to complete the round."

"Never have I ever . . . read *Ulysses*," she said, triumphant, her bell of a laugh ringing around the empty patio. "See? Everything doesn't always have to be about sex."

"No one drank, though," Eli said. "Because no one has actually read *Ulysses*. So, you have to do a forfeit too."

"What's my forfeit? We can't all buy shots."

"We'll see," he replied, tapping her on the nose with one finger and making her squeal like a stuck pig.

"I'll buy the shots," I said.

Inside, the bar was busy and there was a warm crush of normies queuing for drinks. When it was my turn, I bought four shots of chartreuse—a light green liqueur that smelled herbal, like sage and vanilla—but when I turned away from the bar, I saw the others had come inside and taken their seats around the table. It felt like the game was over.

I took a seat next to Noor, who was deep in conversation with Martin, Barry, and Sharona, who all seemed happy to ignore me. I drank one of the shots and offered another to Noor, who wrinkled her nose and turned away.

The chartreuse sat forgotten in front of me. They had cost over four pounds each. Laura tipped her head back, turned her wine glass upside down, and a bloody pink trail ran from the corner of her mouth down her chin, a vampiric smear that she wiped away with the back of her hand.

The atmosphere in the bar changed as the clock approached midnight. The booksellers were still going strong, but the lights were on and the woman behind the bar was stacking glasses, wiping tables, gathering up the dripping plastic bar mats to run through the dishwasher.

"We'll go to the Victoria, it's open until three," said Noor.

"I'm off," said Sharona.

"Same," said Barry, and Martin agreed.

"Mother Black Cap?" Kofi said, and Noor turned towards him to make a case for her pub of choice.

"Shall I take you home?" Eli said quietly to Laura. Her eyes were half closed, elbows on the table, her face resting in her hands, distorting her cheeks.

"I think Laura can take herself home," Sharona said, pulling on her jacket, and she locked eyes with Eli and then looked away.

"She really can't," Eli said, with a look of concern aimed at Laura.

"I don't live far," I said. "I can walk her home."

"I don't needa be walked home," Laura snapped, but it came out in a way that told the room that she definitely needed to be walked home.

"That's kind of you, Roach," Sharona said, although she was frowning, clearly torn over the best course of action. Eli held her gaze for a few beats and then, finally, gave the smallest shrug and looked away.

LAURA

A cold walk. A heavy blanketed sky. A creamy half-baked moon, a moon the colour of marzipan. The streetlamps and headlights haloed with fog. Living room windows jump with blue, with the cosy glare of late-night television. Fireworks pop. Crackle. Bonfire night, sky scattered with stars.

Eli looks to me, all sincere and wide-eyed. "Are you sure you don't want me to take you home?"

"Are you sure you don't want me to take you home?" I say it back to him in a mean singsong voice, ask for a cigarette, drop it, shrug it off. Whatever.

"Fine," he says, taking off towards Walthamstow Village.

"Fine," I say, tripping a little on the rolling tide of the pavement.

Sharona peels off at the station, then Noor and Kofi towards the Goose, and then Barry and Martin turn right and I turn left up Hoe Street.

"Shall we get another drink?"

Roach. Roach, tagging along. Is she wearing my beret? I snatch for it and she pulls back, a hand on her crown to hold it in place. She smells sickly and familiar, like roses on the turn, when the stems have been in a vase of water for too long.

"Shall we get another drink?" I parrot. "God, why are you even here?"

"It's late," she says. "I'm just walking you home."

"I don't *need* to be walked home."

A flare of bright light. A cyclist whizzes past, nearly clips my arm. He yells something and I yell back, call him a bitch, a cunt, a fucking murderer on wheels. I stagger with surprise, and the ground rushes to meet me as I lose my balance and fall.

ROACH

A pungent smell of roses and fresh sweat lifted from her underarms as she scrambled to her feet. She walked slowly, like a somnambulist, trailing her fingers along the brickwork, pausing to look at her phone or pick leaves from the hedges that lined the street, or even just to orientate herself, blinking as though she'd woken from a deep slumber and found herself in an unexpected location, a sleeping princess in a fairy tale.

"Did you grow up around here?" I asked, but she didn't seem to be processing new information, just sighed like it was all a great inconvenience.

I wondered if we should nip inside one of the many late-night off-licences and buy something for us to drink when we got back to Laura's place. However drunk she was, she always seemed to have one more drink in her. A bottle of chilled Prosecco, a four pack of Dark Fruits, or perhaps a bottle of bourbon? Jack Daniel's would fit the bill, I decided. In my mind's eye, we were already letting ourselves in. Laura was kicking off her shoes, lighting incense and candles, picking a playlist for us to listen to on her phone. I'd head straight to the kitchen, fill two heavy-bottomed glasses with ice. We'd sit on the sofa, spill our guts. She'd tell me about her mother, the whole messy sorry story, and I'd say something like, "And that fuckin' asshole may even be free to kill again one day." I'd say, "So long as we live and breathe, we will never stop talking about what he did. He will *never* be free and we will *never* forget, and—"

Just then, Laura's foot slapped hard against the pavement. I thought she'd tripped again, clumsy and uncoordinated with all the wine, but as she lifted her foot, I saw the crushed shell and phlegmy yellow smear of a dead snail, murdered under Laura's spiteful step.

"Little bitch," she said, inexplicably, to the mashed snail. "You little fuck."

I stared at the crime scene in muted silence, and she drifted on without me. With her inhibitions lowered, the true depth of Laura's cruelty revealed itself. Under a streetlight, her orange skirt glowed like a flame. She's the devil, I thought, taking one last glance at the oozing shards of snail shell.

"This is me," she said, turning down her dark garden path and trudging towards her navy-blue front door. She stabbed her key in the lock and I hovered, breath held in anticipation, as she pushed open the front door. The air in the flat smelled funereal, of dust, dried flowers and spent matches.

She tripped and stumbled into her hallway. "Whoops!" she said brightly. I was about to ask her if I could come in, maybe have one more drink, but before I could open my mouth again she'd called an indifferent, "Bye then!" and slammed the door in my face.

Her keys dangled from the lock and before I could process the weight of my decision, they were in my hand. I went to take a look through the living room window, but to my great annoyance, she'd installed some kind of matte sheath over the glass—presumably to prevent peeping Toms. How incredibly presumptuous, I thought.

I adjusted my beret, lit a cigarette, and smoked it as I walked home. I had a vague plan to dump her keys somewhere out of spite—a bin or a skip, a drain, somewhere irretrievable, just for the sake of inconveniencing her but I quite liked knowing that I had them. I felt like I'd scored a point over her, and I decided to keep hold of them for a little while.

Never have I fucking ever. Never have I fucking ever read *The Virgin Suicides*, Laura. Never have I fucking ever read *My Year of Rest and Relaxation* never have I fucking ever read *The Secret History* never have I fucking ever read *Junk* never have I fucking ever read *Looking for Alaska* never have I fucking ever read *Noughts and Crosses* never have I fucking ever read *Ariel* never have I fucking ever read *Let Them Eat Chaos* never have I fucking ever read *Night Sky with Exit Wounds* never have I fucking ever read *The Outrun* never have I fucking ever read *I Am, I Am, I Am* never have I fucking ever read *I Know Why the Caged Bird Sings* never have I fucking ever read *Maus* never have I fucking ever read *Fun Home* never have I fucking ever read *Ghost World*, Laura, never have I ever got a tattoo, never have I ever kissed Eli, or worn lipstick to work, or read my poetry at an open mic night. Never have I ever been loved, been cherished, been celebrated, like you have, Laura. Never have I ever had everything I ever wanted, at the drop of a hat, a hat that perfectly matched my shoes.

～

When I got home, I lay on my bed and googled murdered women in London, speculating over which one could have been Laura's mother. The possibilities were limited, but at the same time they felt endless. I didn't know for sure where Laura had grown up, after all, and besides, even if she had grown up in Walthamstow, her mother may not have been murdered in the area in which she lived. She may not have been killed in London. She may not have been killed in England. And of course, "mother" could mean stepmother, or adoptive mother, or estranged biological mother, all of which could have an impact on whether they shared the same surname, looked alike, or lived in the same place. With the information I had, it was impossible to draw any conclusions. I couldn't rule anyone out. If I was going to get to the bottom of this, I needed more information, and if Laura wasn't willing to give it to me, I was going to have to take it.

I fell asleep and dreamed of all the possibilities, of lonely moors and barren wastelands, of mirror-still lakes and the murky depths of undredged canals.

LAURA

In bed, alone and drunk, so drunk I travel the world with Lydia. I work my way through the Europe tour first. Custard tarts in Lisbon and bookshops in Paris, a bowl of fat queen olives in Barcelona, a cluster of heart-shaped padlocks in Florence. And then I keep going. I look at vegan currywurst in Berlin in spring 2016, and clinking champagne flutes at the top of the Eiffel Tower in winter 2015. I look at a hotel brunch in Edinburgh in summer 2014 and I watch the sun set over the Golden Gate Bridge the previous spring. I look at the milky waters of the Blue Lagoon in 2013, and the creamy head of a Dublin Guinness in 2012, and over-filtered cocktails on Thai beaches in 2011, and grainy Mardi Gras in New Orleans in 2010, where she laughed with strings and strings of plastic beads around her neck, and then I accidentally hit the heart-shaped like button and although I unlike it immediately, my cheeks are red-hot and I know I've fucked up.

∽

I wake up early, way before my alarm, to the sound of a neighbour's baby crying, a bold and throaty wail of anguish. I lie in bed and stare at the ceiling. Shame creeps over me as fractured pieces of the night before float to the surface of my hangover. Flirting with Eli, spilling drinks. *And you'll . . . be in my bed?* Everything feels muggy and fuggy and foggy. Ugly.

The bedroom curtains are open—I forgot to close them last night and I feel sick, sick to my stomach, at the thought of being so exposed. Exposed. *My mother was murdered when I was a teenager.* My stomach churns with the memory of my words, of Roach leaning across the table, so transparently desperate for the details.

It's another clear and bright morning, the sky cross-hatched with scars from passing planes. I imagine I'm on one, heading to New York or Tokyo or Bali, and the thought of travel takes me to Lydia, and to my stupid fumbling thumbs. She might see the notification, curse me out to Eli. Laugh at me. Then again, it might not matter. She might not care at all.

A collection of empty wine glasses and jam jars line the windowsill, etched with fingerprints and smeared with different shades of lipstick. A different lipstick for every day of the week. *My mother was murdered when I was a teenager.*

I close my eyes, scrunch my face against a growing swell of sorrow. It's November sixth today. An internal latch unfastens somewhere inside me, and my eyes brim with tears. Flat on my back, staring up at the lace of mould that stretches from the window like a shadow, I let myself break apart. I cry because the mould that blossoms from every corner of my flat has the mottled quality of dead skin. I cry because when I take a deep breath, my lungs push against my rib cage as though they haven't enough room to manoeuvre, all the spare space instead filled with smoke. I cry because my kitchen floor will be looped with the tracks of a slug infestation that I cannot seem to control, and my vegetable rack stinks of mouse piss, and I will still have to wash those shrunken carrots and eat them. I cry because I can't afford better.

My mother was murdered when I was a teenager. I cry for my mother. I cry because she should be turning fifty, and instead she's just an imprint, an echo, a line in someone else's story. And, like the rest of the dead, she's being submerged by the tides of time, and each day that passes is another day further from her last, and she's already been gone for ten years. I cry because eventually I'll have spent more time on this Earth without her than I did with her, and one day I'll be older than her. I cry because we'll all end up dead, just a string of memories so utterly devastating, so painful, tender as an open wound, that we'll hardly be spoken about at all, and then the people who remember us will die too, and so on, and so on, until there's nothing left of any of us.

On the floor, on top of a pile of books, sits the lilac diary Eli gave me all those weeks ago. I can't be bothered to find my door keys to open the stupid little lock. This makes me laugh out loud, a wild incongruous sound. What a stupid obstacle to have to overcome. I shove it under my pillow and, determined not to be derailed, I use the notes app on my phone to write it all down, fill three pages with rambling, emotional metaphors about imprints and tides and open wounds, and the act of writing is like a cool slick of aloe vera smoothed over a sunburn.

When my thumbs feel cramped and I have nothing left in me, I wipe my face on the duvet. I'm calm, focused. With a fresh mindset, I climb out of bed and gather the empty glasses from the windowsill. I wash up, make myself some buttered cinnamon toast and then shower, washing my sadness away. I pick out a midnight-blue dress, thick black tights and step into matching blue flats. I make up my face to hide the sallow skin of my hangover, and spray rose perfume over my clavicles, and then I feel ready to go to work, ready for another day of bright smiles and forced laughs and absolutely impeccable customer service.

I don't have time to make lunch, but it doesn't matter. I check my tote bag for everything I need: phone, battery almost flat as I forgot to plug it in to charge, and charger. Purse, water bottle—no time to fill it, I'll have to remember to fill it at work—lipstick, hand cream. Lighter, almost out of gas. I crack the wheel and the flame stutters and dies. An empty Rizla packet. Tobacco, almost empty, and a midnight-blue beret. I go through my bag once again, raking through my things, but no: I can't find my door keys, they aren't there, and they aren't in the pocket of my coat, either. I try to think what dress I was wearing yesterday—did it have pockets? Unlikely.

I'm inside the flat, so they must be inside with me, otherwise how else would I have let myself in? I look under the sofa, feel between the cushions, check all the strange and unusual places a careless drunk might discard her keys, like inside the fridge, among my cosmetics in the bathroom, in the fruit bowl. I try to retrace my steps, but the end of the evening is a bit of a blur. Did someone walk me home? I have a vague, squicky memory. Was it Eli? Was it *Roach*? I can't think. I'm running late now, getting stressed, losing my cool. I can't face the expense of a locksmith, can't bear the thought of calling my father and asking if I can borrow some money.

"If you can't afford to live alone, don't live alone," he'd say.

Finally, I have to give up and tip the contents of my kitchen junk drawer over the floor to riffle through the scattered playing cards, sachets of ketchup and ramen seasoning, incense sticks and dead plastic lighters. I scrabble through the detritus until I find the spare set of keys, hooked on to a lustrous tiger's eye key ring. I'd always meant to give them to a neighbour in case of emergencies, but my neighbours were a revolving door of strangers and I'd never bothered to introduce myself to any of them.

By the time I get to work, I'm only a few minutes late. I lock myself in the loo and kneel on the cold tiles, head hanging over the shit-streaked bowl. My stomach convulses and I regurgitate a mouthful of bitter bile that marbles the water, thick as phlegm. In the mirror, my eyes are threaded with red. I splash my face with cold water and dab it dry on those green paper towels that smell of school. A little dab of lipstick and I'm ready to face the day.

In the staffroom, Eli is sitting on one of the cafeteria tables, waiting for me.

ROACH

It was my day off, and I listened to a murder podcast about death row brides as I walked through the park. A fussy little spaniel in a pink jacket and a scrappy, bow-legged mutt darted after one another on the muddy grass, occasionally succeeding in their quest to insert their noses into each other's rectums. Their owners chatted at a distance on the cracked, leaf-strewn path.

I'd always fancied myself as a death row bride. I'd rock up in black lace, a leather jacket, sunglasses. I liked the idea of writing to a serial killer in jail, striking up a friendship, finding out what made them tick. It was difficult to find cool serial killers to write to in the UK, though. They lacked the glamour of the Californian devils of the 1970s, the wry smiles and sarcastic waves to the press, the rock-star swagger, the achingly cool indifference to it all. There were loads of them in the '70s. It was like the Satanic American dream: girls with bare shoulders hitchhiked and climbed happily into the cars of strangers, housewives left their back doors unlocked, slept with their windows wide open and welcoming. But that was then. The golden age of serial killing was over, and the chances of me finding one to marry were slim. Sam, with his nivelin echoes of Ramirez, would have to do.

Richard Ramirez got married on death row, had groupies. They turned up to court every day during the trial, and sent him letters, flashed their knickers and their bare breasts, sent erotic photographs of themselves, and detailed their most private, most morbid fantasies for his pleasure. He didn't want any of that, though. His bride wasn't like the other groupies. She was a normie, a Christian drawn to the idea of saving his soul. She wore white lace on her wedding day and divorced him when DNA evidence linked him to something that was too much even for her strong stomach to digest. I thought about that a lot. It was almost like having honour among thieves. We all had a line, I supposed.

Laura's keys were cold and light in the palm of my hand. She had two standard door keys looped on to a rose quartz key ring, along with a tiny thumbnail-sized key. They were just ordinary keys, but the doors they could unlock! A doorway into Laura's mind, her past, her present. Her inner self, her sanctuary, her history. The story of her mother. She was impenetrable, but I had found a way in. I felt excited as I walked to my destination. I was just going to go in, take a look around, and leave the keys somewhere stupid but plausible, like stuffed between the sofa cushions or kicked underneath the fridge. She'd never know I'd been there. A perfect, victimless crime.

When I reached Laura's flat, I knocked on the door as a precautionary measure, but the living room window was dark and I knew she was working that day because the night before, in the wine bar, Eli had ribbed her about whether she'd turn up to work with a hangover. A tingle of pleasure shivered through my body as I plunged the Chubb into the lock and felt the mechanism catch. Her door sighed with relief as I let myself in, as though the flat had been waiting for me to come home.

As I prowled through each room, I felt underwhelmed. It was a one-bed with a pokey living room, a galley kitchen and small bathroom with a cracked tub. She kept everything nice and neat but there was a faint, cloying smell of mildew in the air.

In the living room, she had four cheap bookcases stuffed with paperbacks. The books were arranged in alphabetical order by author surname. I couldn't help but laugh. You could take the girl out of the bookshop . . . I scanned the shelves, rows and rows of normie shit, mass-market paperbacks from mainstream presses, all bestsellers, all predictable and familiar, the occasional cool-girl romance or indie short story collection. Boring. Whichever true crime books Laura had sourced—stolen—her words from, she clearly hadn't kept hold of them.

I couldn't let myself get distracted. What I really wanted to find was a cache of old diaries, a box of keepsakes, a scrapbook. Anything that might provide me with enough clues to begin my investigation.

Abandoning the bookshelves, I slipped into her bedroom. Her bed was made, and the curtains were open to reveal an overgrown garden. I could just see her rising at dawn and making her bed like a little chambermaid. The bedroom smelled like clean sheets and cosmetics, but underneath the powdery scent of flowers, there was that sour thread of mildew again, stronger than anywhere else in the flat. It turned my stomach, and I had to open the window to stop myself from gagging.

Disappointment permeated the air around me. I flopped on to Laura's bed, just to lie there and feel nothing. Her sheets smelled like sheets. Boring. Fabric softener that faded to skin. I hadn't been as drunk as Laura last night, but my late night was catching up on me. There, I fell asleep.

LAURA

Eli makes me a coffee, rolls us both cigarettes, and we take them on to the roof. Bundled in our winter coats, we smoke and look across the city shrouded in a light morning fog. There's a mean bite in the air, and a column of steam rushes from my cup towards the sky. I take a drag of my cigarette and swallow the fresh urge to vomit.

"You don't look so good," he says.

"I don't feel so good."

A V of geese flies overhead in perfect formation. We watch the birds disappear into the distance, and I keep my eyes on the horizon. Somewhere down below, an accordion player begins to play a melancholy tune.

"Have you been sick?"

I close my eyes and nod, take a deep breath of cool air in through my nose and out through my mouth. The taste of stale alcohol stirs at the back of my throat and I press a hand to my lips to control the rising tide of nausea.

"Look, you can't be on the shop floor in this state."

A thin tear rolls down my cheek and I smudge it away.

"It's my mother's birthday today," I say sadly. There's a pause, and then in lieu of platitudes, he scooches over and takes my hand. I lower my head on to his shoulder and we sit like that for a minute in silence, just smoking and exhaling thick winter breath.

"There's five of us in today," he says in a gentle voice. "I'll check with Sharona but I don't think we need you. Maybe she'll let you go home. Have a bath, eat some toast, watch a film. Take a day out. Come back tomorrow swinging."

"Yeah?"

"Of course."

"Thanks," I say, surreptitiously wiping my nose with the fingers of my free hand. "I won't let it happen again."

"I'll believe that when I see it," he says with an affectionate smile, letting go of my other hand.

∞

It's cold but fresh, and the unexpected time off unspools ahead of me. I start to walk home, thinking of the lure of fresh pyjamas and the chance to sleep off the dying embers of my hangover, but the pull of the pavement feels good under my feet, distracts me from my hangover, so I just keep going. Everything will be okay if I just keep walking.

Instead of walking home to a long, lonely afternoon in my sad and empty flat, I take a bus to Leytonstone. Even though I'm hungover, the rhythm of the bus as it winds its way through the leafy borough takes my mind off the anxiety churning in the pit of my stomach.

I go for a stroll around the neighbourhood, and it feels good to do something for myself. My walk takes me over the railway bridge, and from the caged overpass, London shimmers, the skyscrapers of the city just visible on the seam of the horizon. Next, I walk through a council estate where I'm greeted by several chubby cats that welcome chin scratches, then over a big grassy roundabout and around the edge of the Catholic cemetery, where jackdaws peck at the earth and the pockmarked graves lean at jaunty angles. I end up on a street lined with cute little shops: several cafés, a florist, an Italian deli, a wine bar, a bookshop, a bakery. Maybe I'll stop for a treat. A can of elderflower pop, a chocolate muffin, a bunch of gypsophila, or just a browse in the little community bookshop to see if they have anything interesting in stock.

It's a calm day, a sunny day, the kind of weather that reminds me of spring even though we're still on the wrong side of Christmas. It makes me feel like good days are coming, like winter will be quick and easy and summer is already waiting patiently in the wings for her turn to shine. I walk slowly, taking in the rich palette of the falling leaves. I really do feel better.

The bookshop smells of fresh espresso. They serve pay-what-you-can oat milk lattes and vegan snacks, and the shelves are stacked with indie books and zines—lots of underground stuff, small print runs from micro presses, as well as the more esoteric titles from the Big Five. There are little woven baskets full of political pin badges and patches by the till.

I wander around, taking in the posters, mentally replanning the shop: I would tidy the racks of zines and move the flyers so customers don't get confused between what they can take for free and what they have to pay for. I'd refresh the tables, order in a little more stock to make them look fuller, make it all look more appealing. Their Fiction is splintered into too many subgenres, some of which only have one or two titles. Silly. I would alphabetise y the whole section, and then you could lose the busyness of all those unnecessary shelf-talkers. The whole shop would look a little neater, and it would be easier for customers to find specific titles. That would also solve the problem of where to put books that fit into multiple categories—Carmen Maria Machado's *Her Body and Other Parties* could sit comfortably in M, instead of being torn between Short Stories, Queer Fiction, and Horror. But then again, it would be a different shop if it was organised alphabetically. Maybe all the signage and overcomplicated subsections are part of its charm.

The Red Parts by Maggie Nelson, a deeply personal memoir about the murder of the author's aunt and the subsequent trial thirty-five years later, is shelved alongside copies of *Bluets* and *The Argonauts*. I like that. I like that it's with her other work; that first and foremost, it's hers. Her story, her writing, her auntie, her trauma. I don't own a copy of *Bluets*, so I take it to the till in an act of reckless solidarity with the bookshop, even though it means paying double what it would cost if I bought it from work.

"I can't help but notice something," I say to the person behind the till. They have round cheeks, a short crop of bleached hair, and an enamel they/them button badge pinned to their shirt pocket. "You don't have a True Crime section, but you do sell true crime."

"Uh," the bookseller says, scanning *Bluets* and putting it into a neat paper bag stamped with the shop's logo. "Yeah, some. Not a lot. Like, as a section, it doesn't really fit with our ethics."

"How so?" I say, tapping my card on the card reader. It makes a jolly little beep.

They scratch their head and squint, searching for the right words. "I guess it's just . . . it's mostly about violence against women? And it tends to be written by men? And it's, uh, it's quite anti-sex work, a lot of the time. And, like, we are an anti-carceral collective, so we don't, uh, we don't stock work that's explicitly pro-police, or overtly pro–capital punishment."

They tap an ACAB pin on their lapel, and I notice bitten fingernails with chipped blue polish. "We have a whole section on police abolition, actually. But, uh. We can order anything in for you. Like, it's not a problem, we don't believe in gatekeeping literature, either. Like, it's all there if you want it, you just have to ask."

"It's fine," I say, accepting the paper bag from their outstretched hand. "I don't want it, I totally agree."

My nausea has dissipated, and I take my new book to one of the cafés down the street and order a rose latte and a white chocolate and cranberry muffin. In a window seat, I sip at the frothy pink foam and nibble my muffin and read my book, and while I still feel fragile, I no longer feel sorry for myself.

Outside, a child rides a sweet yellow bicycle in a figure of eight. A woman walks a fat little pug with a face like a crumpled paper bag. Inspired by my surroundings, I reach into my bag for the lilac diary, but it isn't there. I must have left it at home. My heart sinks when I remember that without my main set of keys, I can't unlock the heart-shaped padlock anyway.

Determined not to lose my train of thought, I ask the guy behind the counter for a pen, and I start to make little notes in the back of my copy of *Bluets*, just jotting down whatever I can see out the window. The pen on the page feels comforting.

By the time I leave the café, the sky is streaked with pinks and purples and I'm ready to go home.

ROACH

With a start, I opened my eyes to darkness, the thick blue of a winter's evening. A strange bed. I reached for Sam, only to find cool sheets that smelled like an alien brand of detergent. My searching fingers found the cold, hard spine of my notebook, lost beneath the pillows. No. Laura's bed, I was in Laura's bed, and I had fallen asleep, and now it was late, and it was dark, and I was on the brink of getting caught because the noise that had disturbed my peaceful sleep was the sound of a key twisting in a lock.

Frozen, I listened with mounting horror as the front door slammed shut. The flat shook in response. I pictured Laura in the hallway, hanging up her coat and tote bag, slipping off her shoes, padding barefoot into the bedroom to change out of her work clothes, her shock at finding me, an intruder, curled up for a catnap in her bed. Would she call the police, or would she give me the chance to explain myself—and if she did, what on earth could I say to explain this?

Footsteps, heavy footsteps—not the dainty steps of Laura in her size-six ballet flats, but the substantial tread of an unknown neighbour ascending the stairs to the flat above. I listened carefully to make sure I wasn't mistaken, but the gap underneath the bedroom door remained dark, the hallway beyond it silent, and the footsteps passed over my head.

Relief flooded me with an almost euphoric high, and then I realised that of course it wasn't Laura: I still had her keys.

In stealth mode, I slipped out of Laura's bed and closed the bedroom window. As I gathered my things, I realised with a jolt of excitement that the notebook I'd found under the pillow was the lilac diary, the one with the fussy little heart-shaped padlock.

I creeped to the bedroom door and peeked into the hallway. Silence, stillness. Fuck it. I shoved the diary into my bag and let myself out the front door like I owned the place. My heart was hammering, and I broke into a run.

At the bus stop, an old woman in a thick mulberry coat watched me catch my breath, her eyes reflecting an air of judgement. A deluge of paranoia: did I leave everything as I'd found it? Was the bed made before I climbed into it? Did I leave a light on, did I close the window, did I leave anything behind? My brow prickled with sweat. I felt sick, an intrusive image of Laura catching me in her bed playing on repeat in the dark theatre of my imagination.

Across the street, I caught sight of a woman in a camel-coloured raincoat and a midnight-blue beret that matched her shoes. Laura. I had missed her—she had missed me—by minutes. The bed would still be warm. With her keys still in my bag, I wondered if she even knew they were missing yet. I felt powerful, watching her stroll unknowingly towards a locked front door. Did she have a spare set of keys, I wondered, or was she locked out?

A bus pulled into the bus stop, and as I glanced up to check its destination, I was humbled by the familiar presence of the moon. Under her watchful white eye, a cataract in the blanket of night, I could finally breathe. The moon kept me tethered; I'd always felt a real affinity with her. She was of the night, just as I was of the night.

I climbed on to the bus, grateful to make a quick escape.

If I'd left anything behind in Laura's flat, there was no reason it couldn't have been from the night before. Laura was drunk, perhaps too drunk to remember exactly how the evening had ended. Maybe she'd let me in to use her loo. Maybe she'd invited me in for a drink. She wouldn't remember. It would be her word against mine. She wouldn't remember. All was well.

I checked my phone, and saw a message from Sam. He wanted to meet in Camden, in the Devonshire Arms. A busy bar, a cold pint. An alibi. I fired off a quick message to say I was on my way, then fumbled with my headphones. The chatty babble of the *Murder Girls* filled my ears, and as I listened to Sarah describe the mercilessness of another killer, the cruel psychological games he played, I felt a sense of tranquillity wash over me.

I turned my attention to the lilac diary. The heart-shaped padlock and the little fairy key were a match, and I opened the diary to reveal several pages of Laura's girlie bubble-writing. She wrote in short bursts, little scraps of recollection, random phrases. *I think about the rhythm of my feet . . . where I walked hand in hand with my mother . . . despite all the pain, and the loss, and the grief . . . tethered to Walthamstow . . . she knew these streets, these trees . . . gone for ten years this summer.*

As the bus shuddered to a stop at a set of traffic lights, I felt a soft flutter of excitement in the pit of my stomach. *Ten years this summer* had certainly caught my eye. Summer 2009 was the Summer of Frost. That's what the papers called it. It was a summer of death—both for me and for Laura too, it seemed. For me, it was a summer of strappy baby doll tops and pink lipstick, of walking home from school with Abbi and studying passersby, learning to look for the face of a killer on every street corner. How many women were murdered in Walthamstow in 2009? I knew of at least five—not by name but by killer. It had to be Lee, it had to be. I could feel it in my blood, in the marrow of my bones, like a premonition. A detective's hunch.

The bus pulled into my stop then, and in an almost catatonic state of euphoria, I disembarked. I felt itchy all over as I headed towards the Tube station. Excited, like I could quite easily peel my skin off in pink leathery strips. I'd assumed Laura's mother had met her maker at the hands of a husband or boyfriend. A marital spat turned deadly, as they so often do. A woman is more likely to be murdered by her partner than a stranger. That's just a fact. But, if my instincts were correct, I was on the brink of an incredible discovery.

I gave myself a little shake. I was getting ahead of myself, needed to do my research. But the net had narrowed considerably—there was no denying that. I just had to dig into the history of each of the Stow Strangler victims, and figure out if any of them had a daughter called Laura.

By the time I reached Camden, I felt serene. Laura had so very nearly found me in her flat, but dark forces had brought us together for a reason, and they were keeping us apart for a reason too.

*

The pub was tucked down Kentish Town Road, all darkly varnished wood, stickers plastered over the bathroom doors, a neon orange Jägermeister sign behind the bar. The ceiling was papered with nicotine-stained posters of goth bands and rock stars and vampire movies, stuck down with wallpaper paste twenty years ago or more. I thought of Jackie, strutting under these posters a decade before I was born, smoking cigs and showing off her legs in a leather miniskirt. Embarrassing.

A couple guys, soft around the waist with thinning ponytails, in Motörhead and Metallica hoodies and combats, propped up the bar. A dude with a bridge piercing and an illegible tattoo above his left eyebrow leaned on the beer taps and joined their conversation.

Sam had snagged my favourite table, the one under the Ville Valo poster in the farthest corner of the room. A pint of cider and black, already half finished, sat on the table in front of him, and he was fiddling with his phone.

"All right," he said by way of greeting, accepting my kiss by offering a bristly cheek. "I'll get a round."

He lifted his glass to his lips, and his pale, stubble-speckled throat constricted with each swallow as he downed the last half of his pint. A drop of pink cider rolled from the corner of his mouth and left a dark stain the size of a thumbprint on his Slayer T-shirt.

He moved across the bar with a broad-shouldered swagger. While he ordered us drinks, I pulled out my phone and searched the internet for Lee Frost. The details of the case were so familiar, but the names of his five victims blurred together. At first glance, most of them looked old enough to have a teenage daughter: Meadows, Gamble, and Cordovan for sure, and Matthams couldn't be ruled out either.

Sam placed a tray of purple pints and two neon orange shot glasses filled with a syrupy black on the table and planted a kiss on my cheek. I picked up one of the shots—Jäger, herbal like an old-fashioned tincture for a sore throat. The sickly smell rose into the air between us.

"Shots 'cause we're celebrating," he said with a triumphant grin.

"What are we celebrating?" I asked, lowering my phone.

"Aha." He smiled a broad, toothy smile, and he was so handsome then, all flushed and excited. He stuck a hand into his back pocket and pulled out a folded piece of paper. He handed it to me, and I began to unfold it, flattening the creases on the sticky table. It was a printout from a website, with all the banners and ads reproduced in pixelated black and white printer ink. He raised his fingers to his lips and pretended to bite his nails.

"What's this?" I said, even though, clear as night, I could see there was one of my reworked Laura poems typed on the page. My mouth felt dry, the room hot and loud.

"What does it look like?" Sam asked. "I found this poetry website, and I sent them one of your poems, and they liked it, and they published it."

Vertiginous, the room skewed out of focus. A jolt in my stomach, the heat of the Jäger rising, burning the back of my throat as I read the first stanza.

> *It was now 5 A.M., and dawn,*
> *a hot, fiery dawn,*
> *was slowly filling a sad, tranquil sky.*

"Are you psyched?" he said, putting his arm around me and pressing his nose into my cheek. "Or did I fuck up?" He sounded unsure now, worried that he'd made a mistake.

"I'm speechless," I said, alcohol and panic fizzing through my veins. "Absolutely fucking speechless."

"Phew," he said, relieved. "I panicked for a second, there."

It wasn't Laura's work, I told myself. It was a found poem to begin with. I had just repurposed it again. It was a hybrid. It was inspired by. It was an after. It was an homage. It was a response, an answer. It was a continuation of the conversation. Laura's work raised questions and my work offered a fresh perspective, a new angle, another way of looking at it, examining it. Poets and writers were always doing that, weren't they? Referencing each other and circling back to one another? It's how you created steam, how you created a moment, a movement. And it wasn't a big publication anyway, just some website that my boyfriend—my boyfriend!—had found because he wanted to be a good boyfriend, wanted to show me how to be bold, how to take life by the throat and squeeze.

LAURA

I smell a rat when six customer orders come through for six tacky true crime books. I shuffle the paperwork with a frown. These names feel familiar; there's something about them that rings a bell. Atkins. Fromme. Kasabian. Krenwinkel. Van Houten. Watson.

A low-carb diet, a rock band I used to like, Sherlock's sidekick. No pattern, no connection, but something makes my stomach roil, and so I google the most unusual name—Patricia Krenwinkel—and I'm faced with a 1960s passport photo of a plain young woman, and a picture of an old woman in a courtroom, and a snap of three girls with pale skin and long dark hair, all in matching light blue dresses and dark blue cardigans, smiling like schoolgirls.

> Patricia Dianne Krenwinkel is an American murderer and a former member of Charles Manson's "family."

Susan Atkins, Leslie Van Houten, and Patricia Krenwinkel. Manson girls.

I open the customer order cupboard and scan the spines. Every time I see a true crime title, I grab it, until I have a stack of around nine or ten. The first is a book called *Twisted Tales of True Crime: Murders, Disappearances, and Serial Killers* and it's reserved for a Nannie Doss, who chose not to leave a phone number. I google the name.

> Known as the Giggling Granny, the Lonely Hearts Killer, the Black Widow and Lady Blue Beard, Nannie Doss was an American serial killer responsible for the deaths of eleven people between the 1920s and 1954.

The next is a book called *Cold Cases: SOLVED*, reserved for a Jane Toppan.

> Nicknamed Jolly Jane, Jane Toppan confessed to thirty-one murders after her arrest in 1901. And another: Aileen Wuornos. An American serial killer and sex worker who murdered seven men in Florida in 1989 and 1990 by shooting them at point-blank range.

Lydia Sherman. Florencio Fernández. Eric Edgar Cooke. Sachiko Eto. All of them, every single one of them, is the name of a killer.

Eli appears at my elbow and logs into the other till, chatting brightly to a customer as he starts to scan several walking guides and a couple of garish romance paperbacks.

"Reading and walking," he says with a wistful expression on his face, slipping the books into a plastic bag. "Taking care of your mind and your body. You're going to live forever!"

"Chance would be a fine thing!" The customer, a robust middle-aged woman in a quilted green gilet, laughs as she taps her card and accepts her bag of books from Eli's outstretched hand.

Eli watches her leave the shop, then turns to me. "Okay, I can feel your energy," he says. "Did you think that was a weird thing to say?"

"No. I mean, yes, but that's not what I'm annoyed about." I slap the stack of true crime on the counter and he eyes it warily.

"I don't like where this is going."

"She's still ordering in fucking books without paying for them," I hiss. "Look at these! Every single one was ordered under a fake name. I can't find a single one that looks legit."

"Oh, for—"

"I've googled every single one of them and they're all convicted serial killers."

Eli bursts into laughter. "You googled every name here?" He picks a reservation slip at random and squints at my biro annotations, and then looks at me and cocks a sardonic brow. He nods towards the shop floor. "Busy, is it?"

"Shut up." I drum my fingers on the counter, itching for a cigarette. "Even if we take them off reservation, they won't sell. They'll just take up space and end up on a return."

"You have to admire her ingenuity," he says, amused.

"No, I don't."

I stand at the till, working my way through Roach's orders and taking them off reservation one by one. It's dull but satisfying work, and each one feels cathartic, like a little *fuck you*.

∾

Eli and I have the same lunch break for once, so I insist we walk to the café over the road for sausage sandwiches, chips, and mugs of tea.

We take a table right in the farthest corner, tucked beneath a photograph of the neon art deco signage of the old dog track, Walthamstow Stadium.

"So kitsch," I say happily, picking up a tomato-shaped ketchup bottle and weighing it in my hands.

"And yet so earnest," he replies, settling into his chair. I like the way he's content to just sit there and gaze around the café, study the other diners, wait for conversation to happen naturally. I keep myself busy and fiddle with my phone.

When our food arrives, I squirt a heart of ketchup on to my plate from the tomato-shaped bottle.

"Lydia's really keen for me to go fully vegan," Eli says, holding his sandwich in two hands and taking a massive half-moon bite. "She's bought all dairy-free stuff like coconut cream cheese and oat milk yoghurt."

"How vile," I say. I break my ketchup heart with a chip.

"I know. I'm going to have to have an affair with sausage sandwiches."

He takes another big bite, and a lick of ketchup runs down his chin. He looks happy as a clam.

"She'll smell the sausage meat on your breath," I say. "Like lipstick on your collar."

"The smell of bacon fat in my hair, like another woman's perfume."

We both laugh, and I try to think of another one to keep the joke going, but fall short because nothing else fits the sausage theme. Sexy text messages? Another woman's dirty knickers? I shake my head. We chew in a comfortable silence for a while. The sausages are cheap and salty, the kind that melt in your mouth.

"So, y'know that indie in Leytonstone—All You Read Is Love?" He nods, mouth full, and I continue. "I got chatting to a bookseller in there about true crime the other day, and I thought this was really interesting: they just don't have a section."

He swallows and takes a sip of his tea. "That's not that surprising," he says. "It's such a tiny shop."

"Yeah, but it's like a political stance."

"Isn't that kind of like censorship?"

"Hardly," I say. "Is it censorship if we don't stock Bukowski? Or Hemingway, or Nabokov?"

"No, it would be business suicide not to stock Bukowski, Hemingway, or Nabokov," he says, swallowing the last bite of his sandwich. He reaches for the napkin dispenser and grabs a handful of tissues to wipe his mouth and hands, then starts on his chips.

"It's not an act of *censorship* though." I use my last piece of crust to wipe a smear of ketchup from my plate. "Are we obligated to stock every single book that's ever been published because if we don't, it's *censorship*?"

He pulls out his tobacco and starts to roll us a pair of cigarettes. An itch of irritation shivers over me as he fails to take the bait, won't be drawn into another conversation about true crime. Instead, he hands me a cigarette and places the other behind his ear.

"True crime packages up other people's trauma and sells it for profit. Isn't that fucked up?" I try again, shrugging into my coat and picking up my tote bag, rollie pinched between my lips.

"I just don't believe all true crime fans are like Roach," Eli says, pushing the café door open and letting me step out into the bracing November wind first. "There are loads of different reasons someone might be buying and reading true crime. Professional reasons, personal reasons. You're imagining one type of reader that *you* find unsavoury, but that reader isn't necessarily representative of the whole readership."

The market is quiet, with very few people out shopping. Somewhere in the distance, the accordionist plays a bright, repetitive waltz. A man in a stained coat sits on a bench with an empty glass bottle in his hands, his head bowed as though in prayer.

"You don't get it," I say, lighting my cigarette and exhaling a stream of sour smoke.

"Well, whatcha gonna do?" he says with a shrug. "As long as people keep writing it, people will keep buying it."

I suck on my cigarette and scowl. I imagine a future in which I've written a book about losing my mother, that all my sprawling grief and spiralling pain is distilled into a narrative and packaged up by a publisher. Who would read it, and where would it be shelved? Picturing my pain for sale next to serial killer colouring books, murder trivia, and the kind of tacky, exploitative crap that Roach seems to read is unthinkable.

"Sorry," he says, catching sight of my expression. "Am I being a dick? I wasn't really thinking. I do get it. Or like, I get that I don't get it. Are we still pals? Are you mad at me?"

"I'm not mad at you," I say, checking the time on my phone. I have a message from my friend Stuart, the guy who runs the poetry readings at the Nib. I flick open the message.

> *Hey Laura—do you know Ambient Ambulance? Thought you should see this—maybe you already know about it? Looks familiar, no? Anyway, hope you're good x*

A link to a website follows. Eli is absorbed in his phone now, smoking his cigarette and sliding his thumb down the screen in a well-practised scroll. I return my attention to Stuart's message and click on his link.

Ambient Ambulance looks like an online poetry journal, although it's not one I've heard of before. The poem does look familiar, though.

> *It was now 5 A.M., and dawn,*
> *a hot, fiery dawn,*
> *was slowly filling a sad, tranquil sky.*

He's sent me a link to one of my poems, published by a random journal, without my permission. I take a deep breath and scan the poem properly, but it isn't quite mine. My gentle, mournful found poem has been stitched with crude violence, with bloodshed and gore. Someone has lifted my work and fucked with it. A tingling sensation, red-hot rage. Through my anger, I'm about to tap the homepage to find the editor's contact details, and then I clock the byline, I see the fucking byline in bold black and white:

by Brodie Roach.

ROACH

Laura and Eli were having a cosy lunch for two at the café over the road. They were ten minutes late back to the shop, making me late for my break. Every minute was pure psychological torture. I was desperate to get off the shop floor, to get away from the humdrum of my colleagues" chatter, the customers and their stupid questions.

When Laura finally marched into the shop, she looked flushed, as though she'd been slapped. Eli trailed behind her looking completely baffled. I wondered if they'd had a fight, a little lover's tiff. Whatever. I turned to Sharona and nodded in their direction. "Can I go? They're back."

"Can you wait to be tagged?" Sharona replied, meaning can I wait at least another five agonising minutes for them to go all the way upstairs, drop off their things and return to the shop floor. "I don't really want us to get into bad habits before Christmas."

Laura stormed up to the till and fixed me with a furious gaze, her eyes hard and glassy, shining with hate. She was almost shaking with it.

"All right, Roach," she said, and it came out like a snarl, like she was possessed.

"Hullo," I said, uneasy.

Eli inched closer to her and put a hand on her shoulder. The proximity of their bodies was intimate, and I wondered if he could feel the heat of her anger as it lifted from her skin, if she felt hot to touch, if she was burning with it.

"What's happened?" he said, looking between us, a look of pure bewilderment on his face.

I swallowed, and then swallowed again. The door keys, hooked on their rose quartz key chain, and the lilac diary were both in my bag. Incriminating evidence. Stupid of me to bring them into work, but I hadn't thought to take them out my bag.

"Go on," she said tartly. "Tell them. It's your good news, after all."

"I don't know what you're talking about," I said, and I meant it. All thoughts of the stolen hour I spent prowling around her flat, and my parasitic nap in her bed, faded. Good news? My mind was racing to catch up.

"Oh, shall I do it, then? Shall I tell everyone what you've done?" She turned to Sharona and Eli, and her anger was so frank and so naked and so out of control, it was almost exciting to witness. "Roach stole my fucking poem," Laura said, and a little missile of saliva flew from her mouth and landed on the desk between us.

Sharona frowned and opened her mouth to respond, but Laura wasn't about to be interrupted. This was her moment. "She added a bunch of mindless violence, and then she submitted it to some shitty journal under her fucking ugly name, and they *published* it."

"What the fuck?" Eli said, looking from me to her in shocked confusion.

"Is this true?" said Sharona, an expression of frank horror on her face. I felt a flare of fear and excitement in the pit of my stomach. Everyone was furious, and it was because of me. Like an alarm ringing, the words *deny, deny, deny* were on a loop in my head.

"No!" I said. "I'd never—"

Laura pulled out her phone and handed it to Sharona, whose eyes narrowed and then widened in surprise as she processed the words on the screen.

"You read this at the Nib," Sharona said, looking at the phone and then looking at Laura, who was now trying not to cry. Her upturned nose leaked a snail trail of clear snot, which she wiped on the sleeve of her neat cherry-red cardigan.

"Do you have any idea how fucked up this is?" Eli said, taking the phone from Sharona to see for himself. I caught a glimpse of the byline. *Brodie Roach.* It was as though a cloud had shifted, and a ray of sunlight had illuminated my way out. I burst into a bark of laughter.

"That isn't even my name, you stupid cunts."

I knew immediately that it was too much, that I'd taken things too far. Laura gasped, and Eli flinched and glanced over his shoulder at the empty shop floor for customers. It felt good, though—kind of great, actually—to say something so crude, to make them recoil in shock.

"Upstairs," Sharona hissed at me. "Right now."

"I need to leave," Laura said, as though something inside her had snapped. She held up both hands, showing palms of surrender. "I can't . . . I actually can't work with her right now. I can't even look at her."

"Don't—just—listen, go and have a cigarette," Eli said.

I opened my mouth to argue, but Sharona held up a finger in my direction. Her cheeks were flushed, and there was a fire behind her eyes.

"No," she said to me, and then to Laura: "You go upstairs and catch your breath. We'll go out for a second."

"Can I at least get my coat?" I asked.

"No," Sharona snapped. "No, you can't."

⁓

Noor and Eli covered the shop floor while Laura ran upstairs, presumably to smoke and cry on the roof. Sharona took me out to buy a round of coffees. The windows of the coffee shop were already steamed up as Christmas shoppers gathered for an afternoon caffeine fix. Big, silly drinks topped with cinnamon foam, Christmassy sprinkles, and mini gingerbread men. Frappés in plastic cups, mounds of whipped cream drizzled with syrup. Very normie, very PSG. Very fucking Laura. Little Miss Laura Bunting who couldn't even get my name right, who thought my name was Brodie.

Sharona ordered a black Americano so I ordered a black Americano, and then she ordered hazelnut hot chocolates for Laura and Noor, and an oat milk latte for Eli. We waited at the other end of the counter in silence, listening to the bustle of the coffee shop, the baristas foaming milk, whizzing ice in an industrial blender, squirting peaks of cream, calling out orders and customer names. I kept stealing glances at her, trying to work out her mood.

"Listen," she said at last. "I don't really care to know the ins and outs of it."

"But—" I began.

"Are you serious? Be quiet." She caught herself, and softened her tone. "It's just . . . it's too much, Roach. Do you have any idea how serious this is?"

Before I could reply, a barista called her name, and she broke off to collect our drinks from the counter. Four were fitted snug into a cardboard tray, and she handed the spare to me. The odd one out. The paper cup was almost too hot to hold, but I didn't want to ask her for a cardboard sleeve to protect my hand. She was focused on stirring agave syrup into her drink and looked like she was gearing up to say something. It was best just to shut down, let it flow over me. It was a forgone conclusion: she was going to side with Laura anyway, so what was the point in fighting back? I wondered if I was going to get fired, and realised I didn't care either way.

"Laura's a sensitive soul," she began, walking towards the café door and pushing it open. We stepped into the cold and, without my coat, I braced myself against the drop in temperature and traipsed in her wake, head bowed in a pantomime of humility.

Sharona took pause, her eyes thoughtful as she watched a brass band setting up beneath the Christmas tree. They were drinking cups of steaming coffee, adjusting music stands, tuning their instruments, all stuffy and formal in their matching black overcoats with shining gold buttons. Try-hards. Do-gooders.

"I'm only going to ask this once," Sharona said at last, returning her focus to me. "Did you do it?"

"No! It's not even my name," I whined. "I'm *Brogan*. She can't even remember my name. She just saw Roach and thought the worst 'cause she fucking hates me."

"She doesn't hate you," Sharona said automatically, and I could see a shade of impatience shining through her otherwise diplomatic expression.

"She's always ignoring me, acting like she's better than me."

"Look, I don't know what's going on. If this is all a misunderstanding, then I'm sorry, I really am. But you have to see this from Laura's perspective. You have to admit, it's pretty incriminating, right? I've never met another Roach before."

"But it wasn't me," I sulked. I couldn't let this happen, couldn't let this slip-up force a wedge between Laura and me.

Sharona bit her lower lip and exhaled. "Look: we have four weeks left before Christmas. Let's just do our best to get through it without any more bullshit."

"I don't understand, though," I said, with a pathetic voice that betrayed me, thickened with the threat of tears.

"What do you mean?"

"Why does she get special treatment?" It came out as a bleat.

Sharona shook her head, confused. "What do you mean, special treatment?"

211

"Why is everyone automatically on her side? It's not even my name, and everyone's just automatically on her side."

"It's not about taking sides, Roach!" she said. "If you say this has nothing to do with you, then I trust you. I *want* to trust you. But Laura has been through a lot, and she's sensitive."

I remembered the way Laura had crushed that snail, that innocent little beast, and wondered if Sharona had ever seen that side of her, ever witnessed her inclination for murder firsthand.

"Her work is personal," Sharona continued. "Far more personal than you or I could ever understand."

"'Cause of her mum?"

A dark look flashed across Sharona's face. "That's none of our business. And this whole situation—whether you were involved or not—is still a massive violation, and you have to understand that." She paused, and then she softened. "I think the best thing to do is to put some distance between you both."

And that's when she swapped me to night shifts. She said it had nothing to do with my situation with Laura, that she was going to ask me anyway as I lived so close to the shop.

"We all live close to the shop," I said, but Sharona ignored the remark.

"Just for a couple of weeks," she said, stepping back into the warmth of the bookshop. "And then we'll see how we go."

∽

I had no intention of sacrificing a single second of my lunch break to Laura's drama, so I went upstairs to the staffroom and disappeared behind *The Stranger Beside Me.* I was a slow reader at the best of times, but the font in this edition was small and the print dense, and the words were blurring on the page, refusing to make sense. My salad was bitter and unpleasant, the black coffee sharp and cruel on my tongue.

After a few minutes, the back door snapped open and Laura appeared, bringing cold air and a tense, angry energy in with her. She eyed my Tupperware of salad with a small frown, then stashed her tobacco in her jacket pocket.

"You can check my phone," I said, determined to regain some ground. "Check my inbox. Check my browser history. I've never even *heard* of that stupid website before today."

She paused, and I thought for a second that she was going to argue with me, but instead she just shook her head, her blonde hair shimmering in the light.

"Fuck you," she said, slamming the staffroom door behind her as she stormed out of the room. I listened to her stamp down the corridor, the building thrumming under the weight of her anger. Let her rage for a while, I thought. Let her burn out.

LAURA

The manager's office still doesn't feel like Sharona's office, but of course we aren't going to be in this shop for much longer. It's full of relics from the old manager, gathered by Sharona and packed into a cardboard box—several cans of hairspray and deodorant, a pink hairbrush, a stack of battered dark fantasy novels, a cardigan, a metal water bottle—but it has this beautiful Sharona smell to it, this earthy, herbal smell, perfumed with sandalwood and infused with warmth. I breathe it in, trying to calm down.

"I just want to go back to the Bloomsbury branch," I say, wrapping my fingers around my hot chocolate. "I can't work with her anymore, Sharona. She's driving me insane. This is the final straw. I'm done."

"Look," says Sharona, elbows resting on the desk between us as she cradles her coffee cup between her hands. "I'm on your side, but I honestly can't see why she'd pick a pen name that's so close to her real one. Don't you think that's a bit strange?"

"It's her. Trust me, it's her. You've seen what she's like, the way she's been all over my chapbook."

I remember the weeks she spent thumbing through *their inconsequential moments were beautiful*, the way she always seemed to have it with her.

Poring over it in the staffroom, asking me tedious questions. I'd misread the situation, dismissed it as attention-seeking. But no, she was a thief, a leech, a parasite. A vulture. Picking over the bones of my work, stealing whatever took her fancy, and then regurgitating it with her own sick spin.

"She's a strange girl," Sharona says, nodding. "Just a bit lonely, I think. Desperate to find someone to cling to, however inappropriate."

I look to the ceiling, try to breathe through the growing flare of anger burning in my belly. I don't understand why Sharona isn't taking this more seriously. I want to shake her, scream, cause a scene. I want Roach sacked, and instead we're sipping our drinks and talking about her like she's just a silly little girl who doesn't know any better.

"Inappropriate? That's an understatement," I say bitterly. "She's stealing my work, adding in all this horrible misogynistic violence, and putting it online, and the worst thing is that she won't even admit it."

Sharona tips the last of her coffee into her mouth and swallows, then tosses the empty cup into the bin.

"Well, look," she says, opening her desk drawer. She rummages until she finds a hemp lip balm in a metal tube, which she dabs on to her lips. "I've spoken to Roach, and she *knows* it's not okay. And obviously I'm not going to keep you here at gunpoint. If you really want to move shops, I can speak to Jim and see what we can do. But you're doing an amazing job." She breaks out into a warm, encouraging smile, and places both hands on the desk between us as though reaching for me. "I'd really like to see you rise above whatever this situation is with Roach. In the new year, we'll head off into the sunset and all this will just be another anecdote we'll tell each other down the pub."

On the CCTV screen, I see that Roach is back on the shop floor. She's standing behind the till, perfectly still, with her dark purple hair hanging over her face. There's something unsettling about the image, like she's not really there.

"Right," I say. I feel exhausted, defeated by the whole situation. Roach is going to get away with it, simply because she held her nerve and abdicated herself of responsibility. I pop the plastic lid from my empty hot chocolate cup, then click it back into place.

"And hey: you'll get a break from each other while she's on night shifts, and then we'll be rushed off our feet with Christmas. How does that sound? Bearable?"

"Okay," I say, eyes downcast. I pop the lid, click it back into place. Pop and click, pop and click.

"Fab," she says, checking her watch. "You're on the early today, right?"

"Right."

"Well, look. It's gone four now. Knock off early, take it easy, and come in tomorrow feeling restored. Okay?"

"Yeah? For real?" I glance up, catch the warmth of her freckled smile. "Thanks, Sharona."

"No problem," she says, and I force my face to return her smile. I don't want to work with Roach again, not even after her night shifts are over, but I'm in no position to negotiate. Sharona's doing me a favour—she knows that bringing me to Brighton in the new year will be a good career move for me. I need to show off my skills, show the higher-ups what I'm made of, what kind of bookseller I really am.

∞

It's already dark outside. A car honks gaily as it sails past, thumping bass blaring from powerful speakers. I jump out of my skin, and a peal of laughter rolls from the window. The driver continues to blast the horn long after he's passed me, way into the distance, and I have this familiar, disquieting sense of fragmentation, like I exist only in the context of other people, like I no longer belong to myself, like I'm public property for other people to consume. I used to feel this way a lot when I was a teenager, when my mother's story was all that anyone wanted from me. A sob story, a tragedy. A warning. A lesson.

I pick up the pace, on high alert but with my head down.

People were always trying to pin down what she did wrong. *Well, she shouldn't have been jogging alone,* or *She shouldn't have jogged at that hour,* or *She shouldn't have worn headphones,* or *She shouldn't have taken a shortcut,* or *She shouldn't have stopped running.* Different versions of my mother dance before my eyes. There's the version of her that jogged along the main road and didn't cut through Vinegar Alley. There's the version of her that ran without music, and heard the footsteps of her attacker coming up behind her, had enough of a warning to react, to sprint from harm's way, to run without stopping. There's a thousand things she could have done differently, but I've never believed for one second that any of them would have made the slightest difference. If someone wants you dead, you're done for, and there's nothing you can do to protect yourself. It's just luck. Bad fucking luck.

The wind stirs the bare tree branches, and a man walks towards me, hood up, face hidden. Despite my bravado, my it's-just-luck bullshit, I cross the street, check over my shoulder, hold my keys between my fingers.

When I used to feel this way, paranoid and vulnerable, like nothing we did actually mattered, I'd ground myself with the sting of a tattoo needle, or the sharp pain of a piercing. Now, I prefer to float away with the burn of whiskey or the warmth of wine in the back of my throat.

When I get home, I climb into bed fully clothed and cry until I'm sick with it, the roiling heat of acid at the back of my throat. I know I should at least thank Stuart for tipping me off to the plagiarism, but the thought of unlocking my phone and typing an entire message feels impossible. When I finally catch my breath, I know only the comfort of a pen rolling against paper will really soothe my soul. I rummage around for my lilac diary, but it seems to have vanished into thin air. I can't find it anywhere.

ROACH

A snivelling Laura left work early, so I didn't get the chance to make things right. I knew that if I could just show her my squeaky-clean search history, the contents of my inbox and outbox, I'd be able to prove that I had never submitted my work to that stupid poetry magazine and things could easily be smoothed over.

Cabs sailed down the street and there was a chill in the air. It was too late to cut through the park, and as I followed the curve of the main road towards Laura's flat, I remembered the strange route she had taken home after the poetry reading, the night I had followed her and Eli back to her flat. As I walked along the main road, I passed late-night hairdressers, and parents pushing prams of sleeping children, and Turkish men gathered outside cafés to smoke and drink strong black coffee. It was busy and ordinary.

Potential outcomes played over and over again in my mind's eye. I'd show her my outbox, prove that I hadn't submitted the poem, that I was not Brodie Roach. She'd invite me in, we'd talk. She'd cry, and the conversation would swing to her mother, and then I'd say, "It was Lee Frost, wasn't it?" and she would nod, and then I'd say all the right things, and she would reach over and touch my hand. "You really get it, don't you?" she'd say. Or perhaps she'd be outraged, and we'd come together over the injustice of it all. Me, innocent. Her, the victim of a terrible crime. The situation was salvageable, I could feel it. We had a dark connection, and I wasn't prepared to give up on it so easily.

The door opened, and Laura peeked out with a world-weary look that curdled to hate as soon as she saw me. She couldn't even be bothered to give me her blank customer service face any more. She should be grateful: with her keys in my bag, I could have walked straight in if I wanted to, but I was respectful of her boundaries.

"Sharona told you to leave me alone," she said. Her breath smelled boozy, and she looked a little unfocused behind the eyes.

"I'm just here to talk," I said.

"As opposed to what?" she said, with a bitchy little sneer. "Cocktails?"

A gust of wind sent a chill through us both. She shivered, but I did not. Somewhere in the distance, a man shouted, and Laura's eyes darted over my shoulder, scanning the dark street.

"If you aren't going to admit you stole my poetry, I don't have anything to say to you. Do you know how personal poetry is? Do you even understand the poem you stole? Do you even *get* it?"

I just stood there. She was always more open to conversation in my head, always more interested in hearing what I had to say when I imagined her. In my head, I'd pictured a thousand different possibilities, but now that we were face to face, my courage was failing me and I couldn't find the words to make it right.

"Do you even know what it's like to lose someone? The fucking burn of it?" She was standing too close to me now, her hot brandy breath fanning my face.

"At school, a boy was knocked off his bike—" I began, taking a step back.

"So no," she said, with an ugly sneer. "The answer is no, you don't."

"Laura—"

"It's like blood," she said, eyes shining like polished glass. "And you have to carry it around inside you, all the time. And suddenly, it's like everything's made of broken fucking glass. You'll hear a song in a bar or smell perfume on a stranger and it cuts you deeper than anything has ever cut you before. And when you bleed, everyone fucking knows about it, everyone can see it, and everyone knows why."

Ugly crying, snotty philtrum, crumpled, crunchy face.

"There was a freak mist, and he was hit by a Royal Mail van that didn't see him."

"Jesus fucking Christ," she said, raising her fists and pressing them against her temples.

"I could never get it out of my head," I said, persisting, determined to connect with her. "He was alive and then he was dead. Everyone talked about it for years afterwards. He was a legend."

"That still isn't your story to tell," she shouted, throwing her hands up in the air. "That *still* isn't your story!"

"Your poetry," I explained, "makes sense to me in a way that nothing else has ever made sense to me."

I thought of my journey as a true crime fan, from Columbine to the West Memphis Three. I had always circled the killer, always imagined myself in his shoes, imagined the world through his lens. Laura's poetry introduced me to a fresh angle, a new way of thinking about murder. The victim. It was like, for the first time, I understood the finality of death. I understood that the power of a killer lies not in their actions, but in what they choose to destroy.

"I don't give a fuck how my poetry makes you feel. I don't give a *fuck*, Roach. I don't give a fuck. I'm sorry that boy died, but it doesn't actually explain anything at all. And I don't actually care. You're a fucking cockroach, a thief, a liar. You stole my words, you butchered them, and you passed them off as your own."

"*It—wasn't—me!*"

She slammed the door in my face, and her cheap shitty wreath dropped from the hook and bounced on to her front doorstep. I kicked it, stamped on it, and stamped on it again, until it was a shredded mess of broken foliage.

I walked in the cold, toe-punted empty Coke cans, scattered a band of pigeons pecking at fallen chips outside a takeaway. A bus rolled past, windows steamed up, stifling. I walked past Tesco, past all the hairdressers and cafés, all the cosy pubs that cast piss-yellow light on the pavement, to the cheap corner shop. I bought a four-pack of Dark Fruits and a cucumber for Bleep, and the plastic bag sliced into my fingers as I trudged back to the Mother Black Cap.

"Not out with your fancy man tonight, then?" Jackie called from the bar. She was sitting with a drink, watching her bar manager Connie wipe down the taps. Only one or two tables were occupied by customers. Pathetic.

"Piss off!" I yelled back, stamping up to the flat.

"Oi!" She chased me to the foot of the stairs. "You don't speak to me like that in front of customers!"

"There are no fucking customers!" I shouted over my shoulder.

Upstairs, I slammed my bedroom door as hard as I could because she hated it when I did that and I was feeling bitter and spiteful. I opened the door and slammed it again. The room was murky and dark, aside from the glow of Bleep's vivarium. His gentle warmth was the only light I needed to calm myself down.

I popped open a warm can of Dark Fruits and opened YouTube. I watched a video called "Reacting to Your True Crime Unpopular Opinions" and a video called "Chatty Get Ready with Me: Smoky Eye, Red Lips, and JonBenét Ramsey" and a video called STOP ROMANTICISING SERIAL KILLERS and a video called "Everything WRONG with Making a Murderer" and then "SOLVED: My Thoughts on the Stow Strangler'. Calmness rolled over me in gentle waves as I forgot about Laura and the shop and poetry and plagiarism and focused on the crimes instead. Law and order, crime and chaos.

By the time I drained the last can, I was feeling drunk and lucid. I'd had a message from Sam—Laura must have snitched, because the editor had removed my poem from the website, sent Sam a bitchy little email, all ruffled, puffed-up feathers and grand sentiments about the sanctity of poetry. Sam thought the whole thing was hilarious.

I don't get why u didn't tell me tho, his message said. *U should just find ur own thing to write about.*

I opened my bedroom window and lit a cigarette. On the street below, a black cat darted beneath the dark underbellies of parked cars. The hollow clack of heels on paving stones preceded a woman who walked quickly with her head down. I watched her until she was out of sight, the sound of her footsteps fading into the night.

That still isn't your story to tell.

I mulled Laura's words over. She was selfish, a hypocrite. She was furious with me for borrowing lines of her poetry, but wasn't the very nature of her work exactly that? Found poetry from an uncredited source was just pretentious theft.

Sam's words. *U should just find ur own thing to write about.*

As I smoked, a project of my own unfolded. No more poetry, no more plagiarism. I did have a story to tell, a story that would bring Laura and I together irreversibly, in a way that she could never reject or reclaim or control, our names for ever linked in black ink.

Somewhere in the rafters, a pigeon cooed.

DECEMBER 2019

ROACH

The evening before my first night shift, I decided to stay up late rewatching *Making a Murderer* on Netflix to recalibrate my sleeping pattern for my new nocturnal schedule. I assumed transferring my energy from day to night would be easy for me, as I had always been one with the night. Not so much nocturnal, but crepuscular: most active at dusk and dawn.

I put the first episode on at seven and cracked into a can of Dark Fruits. By 4 a.m., I was groggy, and the haunting folky theme and gentle montage of desolate, snow-covered Wisconsin soothed me into a gentle sleep. I dreamed I was on death row for a murder I did not remember committing. It wasn't an anxiety dream; the situation simply left me feeling curious about what I had done, and sad that I couldn't remember it.

When I woke up, it was past lunchtime and the day was overcast. I slapped the space bar to revive my idle laptop, and replayed the last episode of series one while I ate a breakfast of cold pizza, then I snapped open a can of Monster and switched to series two. The room grew dark around me as afternoon turned to evening. I kept my eyes on the screen as I tugged on yesterday's jeans and sniffed my armpits, which smelled grassy and sulphuric. A dab of rose oil in strategic places would do to cover the smell of sweat. It was in a small brown glass vial, like an apothecary's tincture, and I liked the feeling of the bottle in my hand.

I couldn't find clean socks, so I pulled on a dirty pair from the soup of clothes on the floor, then stepped into my boots. I wrapped an extra-long scarf around my throat until most of my face was covered, and pulled a black beret over my unwashed hair.

The night was already dense and dark, and heavy with it: no stars or even a shy sliver of moon interrupted the weighted blanket of sky. As I trudged through the Village, braced against the bitter evening chill, it began to sleet. My breath collected in the folded knit layers of the scarf and my eyes began to water against the cold. A creeping damp seeped through my hoodie, through my hat. In my boots, my feet felt clammy.

The shop floor lights were on but I couldn't see anyone on the other side of the glass. I'd long since given Barbara's keys to Sharona, so I was trapped outside in the cold, ringing the staff bell.

Across the way, a Christmas tree seller was piling his stock into the back of a white van. I imagined him beckoning me over, asking for a hand. How vulnerable I'd look from a bird's-eye view, trotting across the dark street, how easily I could climb into the back of the van to help reposition a fallen tree, and how sharply the door would slam, how quickly it would happen, how the smell of pine sap would rise with the bile in my throat, the metallic sting of fear.

The shop door opened, and I jumped, and the Christmas tree seller was just a man again, and not an E17 Ted Bundy. Eli greeted me with a grave expression and ushered me into the shop.

"You were meant to get here at nine," he said gruffly, locking the door behind me. He already looked a bit rough—tired around the eyes, his usual sparkling charm tarnished by a bad mood. Of course, I was the devil now, wasn't I? Can't have his precious little Laura upset by the big bad Roach.

"I thought we were doing ten 'til six-thirty," I replied.

"Well, yeah, but Sharona wanted to do a handover—she was going to stay late and we were going to arrive early on the first night."

"Oh, hey, *Brodie*," Kofi said pointedly, wheeling a trolley of hardback celebrity biographies towards the front of the shop. "How's it going?"

"My name's not Brodie," I said.

Eli shot him a warning look—perhaps afraid of a confrontation that would further sour the mood—and picked up a takeaway coffee cup from the till point. He had a habit of swirling his coffee as though trying to mix it by sloshing the liquid from side to side. I could tell by the swiftness and lightness of his movements that his coffee was almost done.

"Can you start in Kids'?" Eli said to me, scanning a list pinned to his clipboard. "Just a bit of recovery while we finish unpacking the stock on to trollies."

"Fine," I said.

The bookshop was bright against the backdrop of night pressing at the windows. Someone must have replaced all the dead light bulbs, because walking through the shop felt like walking on to a brightly lit stage.

In the Children's section, I set a can of Monster, a packet of crisps, a notebook, a biro, my phone and headphones on to the Lemony Snicket shelf. I kicked off my boots, peeled off my stagnant-smelling socks and walked barefoot on the threadbare carpet.

Laura had worked the day shift, her claws firmly hooked into Martin's section, so of course the displays were all perfect, not a page out of place. The shelves were freshly dusted and the tables, though depleted, were perfectly pyramided with no gaps. With nothing else to do while I waited for Eli to bring me my stock—because I certainly wasn't going to go out of my way to busy myself—I sat on the floor, my back against the bookshelves, and continued my research.

Three of the five Stow Strangler victims were mothers, but there wasn't much information available online about their children. Elsie Meadows had four children according to one article, five according to another. Safa Gamble had two. Karina Cordovan was a mother of one. She had a bigger paper trail than any of the other victims, but that was because she was the hinge that opened the case. A florist, she was pretty and looked well put together. My spidey sense was tingling, and I thought of the rose tattoo on Laura's bicep, the lavender posy on her inner wrist, and something she'd written in her lilac notebook about flowers.

Eli rounded the corner with a trolley packed with stacks of children's paperbacks and a thick wedge of price stickers. He eyed me sitting on the floor with no shoes on, fiddling with my phone, but said nothing.

I scrolled for a podcast, eventually settling on one about the Stow Strangler. I still didn't know for sure if my hunch was correct, but it felt like a sensible avenue to explore and potentially easy to rule out. Whenever the hosts dropped a nugget of information about one of the victims, I paused to jot it down, slowly putting together a skeleton from the jumbled bones of the case.

I didn't shelve with quite as much care as Laura would have liked. I slapped stickers on haphazardly, dumped stacks on to tables any which way. I drank my can of Monster, listened to my murder podcasts, and ate prawn cocktail crisps as I shelved, leaving greasy fingerprints on the shiny covers. There were no customers to get in my way, to bother me, to ask me questions. It was kind of perfect.

⌀

Richard Ramirez said that the best time to break into a target's house was between two and four o'clock in the morning, because those were the dead hours when people were most likely to be in the deepest of sleeps, tucked up safe in their beds. This is because most people's diurnal minds have a natural affinity with the daylight and prefer to switch off when the night is at its thickest and most impenetrable.

Eli and Kofi were normies, so they flagged during the dead hours, withered without the light of the sun. They were made for daylight, for sunshine and fresh air. Despite frequent jokes about their stamina for late nights, they both seemed to wane after two A.M., perhaps struggling without the illegal stimulants they were used to swallowing and snorting to carry them through to dawn. Their eyes became unfocused, their movements less coordinated. At half two, Eli came to find me and told me they were taking their first proper break, for coffee and cigarettes and something to eat to get their energy back up.

I didn't flag, though. I was of the night, and I felt energised, like the power of the unseen but ever-present moon had recharged my batteries. Three o'clock in the morning was devil's hour—the hour in which the veil between our world and the next fluttered, and all manner of insidious things could pass through. Black magic burned at its brightest, ghosts became more solid, witches more powerful. In the sixteenth century, the Catholic Church banned people from doing things between three and four A.M. in an attempt to curb the rising deluge of witchcraft. It made sense that I felt most alive as the clock struck three.

Buzzing, I went for a creepy-crawl around the shop. Barry had told me once that the shop was built on the approximate site of an old coaching inn, a place for weary travellers to rest on their way into London. Several pubs claimed the same illustrious past and one even hung a framed illustration of the old inn in the corridor outside the bathrooms to add credibility to their story, but Barry had studied historical maps and was sure their claim was incorrect.

I'd always thought devil's hour would be a good opportunity to see if I could tune into the same psychic channel of any lingering ghosts in the shop. I stood in the stockroom and tried to transform the smell of dust and paper and damp into the warmth of hay and horseshit and oak barrels of rum and ale, but the smell of dust and paper and damp prevailed.

✑

At four A.M., we ate lunch together in the staffroom. There was nowhere else for me to go, no coffee shops or cafés open for me to hide in, so I was stuck with them. Eli ate hummus with carrot batons, a glazed look on his face, and a thick tiger bread sandwich wrapped in tinfoil. He took frequent, solitary cigarette breaks on the roof with a battered paperback copy of *The Electric Kool-Aid Acid Test*. I could see no benefit in joining him and wasting my conversation cigarettes, which I kept on me at all times now, so I left him to it. Kofi ate a pungent beef and tomato Pot Noodle, then spread himself across the sofa and remained engrossed in his phone. I couldn't imagine what was happening on his phone in the middle of the night and had no desire to find out. I kept myself to myself, ate taramosalata and crackers, and read *The Stranger Beside Me*. I still had over one hundred pages to go.

Eli came in from the roof, bringing the cold and the scent of London at night with him.

"Hey, what's this I'm hearing about a party?" Kofi called out, pointing to the staff noticeboard. Eli shrugged off his coat, a flannel shirt lined with a cheap, synthetic-looking sheepskin, and peered at the sheet of paper Kofi was pointing at.

"Ah, the Christmas party. There's one every year in central London. All the shops go, it's a massive deal."

"We don't usually go," I said. "We usually go for dinner at Route 66."

Every December, we had to endure a staff meal at the same American-themed chain restaurant on the high road. It was my idea of hell in red, white, and blue. The servers wore baseball caps and Converse, and flashed blank-eyed, uncanny smiles while children ran between the tables and screamed in a collective sugar-induced mania. They served a disjointed mix of international dishes and it was impossible to place an order that reflected only one continent: vegetable spring rolls, seafood jambalaya and tiramisu, calamari, chicken fajitas, and New York cheesecake. We were meant to tick off our order to be sent to the restaurant in advance, although it didn't really matter what you ordered, as every dish tasted like a microwaved sanitary towel smothered in regurgitated mozzarella.

"Is it any good?" Eli asked me, with a doubtful grimace.

"No."

He laughed and hung up his coat.

"Well, that was never going to happen this year. Sharona's idea of a good meal is a vegan thali at the Hare Krishna temple in Soho. You were never going to get her into a restaurant that sold cheeseburgers and milkshakes without a fight."

The thought of the Strand party did not spark joy. It was infamous: every central London shop was invited, along with a guest list of stuck-up literati—writers, literary agents, and editors that the company liked to keep sweet. Apparently, Helena Bonham Carter turned up one year, with her elderly mother holding on to her arm, both dressed in layers and layers of lacy shawls that gave them the air of Victorian strawberry sellers.

"Hope you've got something fancy to wear," Eli said, more to Kofi than to me, who raised his arms in an elegant pose, as though he'd reached the end of a catwalk.

I wondered what Laura would wear. A dress—velvet, satin, lace? Something understated and glamorous, something that made her look effortlessly cool and beautiful.

At 6:30 A.M., the stockroom was stark, gutted of the tower blocks of totes that had stood on the scarred concrete floor the night before. That day's delivery was probably already making its way to us, a fresh city of plastic boxes to be processed and unpacked.

As the sun came up, the shadows shrank, and my energy sank with them, but my day was not yet done.

LAURA

It's a frosty, pink-nosed kind of morning with an ombré pastel sky. An apricot glow warms the chimney tops. When I get to the shop, I don't have a knot in my stomach, I don't feel tense or nervous. With Roach gone, I can breathe, and I find that with Eli gone, I can focus.

The pace on the shop floor always picks up as Christmas appears on the horizon, and while the shop is busier than usual, I'm light on my feet and energised. Even though we're three booksellers down while Eli, Kofi, and Roach work nights, the team is a well-oiled machine and we don't suffer from being short-staffed. We skirt between tables and straighten colourful stacks of hardbacks, neaten piles of paperbacks, fix book pyramids, and plug gaps where books have sold. We find titles and answer questions and hand-sell extra books to push the average transaction price up a little higher. It's like a dance, the choreography so well baked into my brain that I can perform it without even thinking about it. Barry cashes up, a jazzy playlist crooning from the digital radio while he makes quick work of the stacks of cash, the piles of receipts, the long strings of numbers. On Barry's days off, Martin reassures us that he's happy to step in, unflustered by the ancient computer system, happy to do the long calculations by hand with a sharp pencil and clean sheet of scrap paper instead of using the calculator on his phone like everyone else.

"Thank God things are finally picking up," Noor mutters to me, slamming the till drawer on another sale. "I thought I was going to die of boredom."

Personally, I rather like bookshops when they're quiet. I like the neat stacks and the clean carpet, the milquetoast playlist of Joni Mitchell, Fleetwood Mac, Belle and Sebastian. I like watching the rain lash against the windows. But it's undeniable that busier is better. Busy means money in the till. It means our jobs are safe, it means the ebb and flow of books through the shop is working as it should.

"You're wasted here," I tell her. "You should transfer. Sharona'll put in a good word for you."

"You think?" She looked surprised, perhaps even a little flattered.

"Definitely. She loves you."

"Sharona loves everyone," Noor says, calling over the next customer by raising her hand, but she says it with a smile because it isn't strictly true. Sharona values kindness and hard work. We both know she does not value all booksellers equally.

ROACH

Shoe polish, leather, the whining grind of machinery. A man in a burgundy apron was only too happy to turn two keys into four, no questions asked. He whistled along to Aerosmith while he worked, and I noticed a feathered ace of spades tattoo under his right earlobe.

When he was finished, he simply handed the new set of keys to me with a carefree smile. It was amazing to think about how much trust there was in society, I thought. I could be anyone, and these keys could belong to any lock.

The shopping centre was busy and claustrophobic, the shops all blasting the same five Christmas songs on repeat with their central heating cranked up high. Shoppers, bundled into their winter coats and weighed down with plastic Christmas trees and bulky shopping bags, wiped sweat from their brows and grew irritable. My skin was crawling, and I made a beeline for the exit, ploughing through families and packs of feral children with rough determination.

Outside, it was a bitter day, the bracing air stinging like a slap to the face. Tiredness itched, the weak winter sun draining me of my juices. I snapped open a can of Monster and the sweet caffeine carried me towards Laura's place.

By the time I reached the park, it was a little past eight. Laura was on the early, which meant she wouldn't be leaving for work for at least another half hour by my reckoning. I found a bench and sat in the morning light to finish my drink. It was cold and the park was dead, but I switched on a podcast about the Vampire of Sacramento and listened to the soothing voices of the hosts as they explained the Macdonald triad theory, which links animal cruelty, arson, and bed-wetting with a propensity for violent psychopathy.

I had never been much of a bed-wetter, aside from the usual childhood accidents. I liked animals too much to be interested in inflicting pain on them, and the thought of harming Bleep made me feel physically sick. I'd been a little pyromaniac when I was a kid, though. I was always finding lighters and packs of lost matches in the pub. I liked candlelight best, not because it felt magical or romantic, but because there was something almost Satanic in the act of nurturing a lick of fire. I loved to pick off strips of dribbling wax and feed them into the flickering teardrop flame. I'd lose myself in the act, spend entire family dinners entertaining myself by digging and poking at the candle, the dribble of red wax on my fingertips providing me with a thick, horror-film rendition of blood.

Eventually, Laura appeared on the path, about two hundred yards away. She was wearing her camel mackintosh and smoking a cigarette as she walked. She only had to turn her head a fraction to the left and she'd have seen me sitting there watching her, but she was too self-absorbed, focused on her destination, and didn't take in her surroundings at all. I took her lack of awareness as a sign that our connection was weakening, as we were spending less time physically in the same space, breathing the same air. For a moment she looked so fragile, so alone as she walked, that I almost felt bad. Almost, but not quite.

When she was out of sight, I waited for another few minutes in case she'd forgotten something and turned back. When I felt sure she had gone, I made my way to her flat. The cold bench had numbed my legs, and for the first few steps I staggered with a rigor mortis stiffness, until blood returned to my limbs and loosened my muscles.

I held my breath as I slipped the new key into the door, and exhaled when the mechanism caught and the key turned smoothly in the lock. So, she hadn't bothered to change the locks, obviously wasn't too concerned about the missing set. She must have had a spare set after all. I stood for a second on the doormat, breathing in the smell of fresh coffee and toast and the sharp acidity of recently sprayed perfume.

The living room wasn't as tidy as it had been the last time I'd been there. The floor was scattered with discarded shoes and jumpers, and there was an empty glass marbled with a smear of dried berry smoothie on the table by the sofa. I picked up an open bottle of Pinot Noir from the mantle and sniffed it, took a tentative sip. The wine tasted like pennies fished from the bottom of a well. A tiny particle caught between my teeth and I picked it from my tongue with a probing finger: a fruit fly, which I wiped on to the right thigh of my leggings.

She'd eaten a mango some days earlier and left the skin, now curled and dried into a gnawed-looking piece of leather, on a plate in the middle of the living room floor. It was next to a green velvet scatter cushion and a paperback, which I poked with my toe: *Julie & Julia*. Of course. Cosy, but decadent. I could just see her reclining, propped up on the cushion, fingers of one hand splaying the pages, the other sticky with mango juice, sucking the pulp, sweetness running down her chin, as she dreamed of Paris, of dishes rich with butter, of two women unknowingly linked, a connection that stretched through time.

Last time, I'd combed through her bookshelves for true crime, looked for a scrapbook or a diary, but she didn't seem to have anything like that lying around. This time, I planned to probe some of the darker corners of the flat. In cupboards, under furniture. The hidden places where someone like Laura might squirrel away their secrets.

The mildew smell in the bedroom had grown worse, developed a heavier and more pungent presence. I couldn't stand it, and I had to wrench open the bedroom window to let some fresh air circulate.

Underneath her clothes rail was a rack holding three fabric boxes. One contained a cacophony of shoes, all tossed together. Another held pyjamas, and the last contained her underwear. Little lace knickers and gauzy tights, like shedded snakeskins.

Under her bed, behind an empty suitcase and a white oscillating fan, I came across a wooden crate full of battered, ink-stained notebooks. Jackpot. With shaking hands, I opened a pocket-sized Moleskine and found scraps of half-finished poetry and lists—lists of songs, lists of words, lists of books. I picked another one at random, and found it was an old diary from her student days. She talked at length about a flatmate she didn't seem to get along with, a film she hadn't liked, a date that flopped. Another entry lamented the failure of a class she'd struggled with, a lecturer she felt looked down on her. I revelled in all her hidden depths of negativity and sat there for a while, hunched over the crate, reading. She didn't seem to write about her mother—there was no mention in any of the notebooks I dipped into, but there were too many to review them all in one go. I decided to move on, with a plan to return my attention to them later.

I reached under the bed again, and my fingers brushed against a small wooden box. This time, the contents leaned towards the sentimental: a child's scribble, a dried-out lipstick, a gold wedding band, a craggy chunk of amethyst on a black cord. Mostly garbage, fragments of a mediocre life, although I quite liked the necklace. There was something almost witchy about it. At the bottom of the box was an unsealed envelope, the paper flap tucked into itself. With a lurch of excitement, I opened it, half expecting to find newspaper clippings inside, but it only played host to a selection of faded, '90s-looking photos. They were all of a glamourous woman with blonde hair. She looked familiar as she stared out a train window, stood in front of a church in the white froth of a wedding dress, sat on a beach, her tanned arms looped around the belly of a laughing toddler. And then there she was, posing with a champagne glass in front of a flower shop. I recognised that photo, I recognised that woman. I recognised the building—it was on the main road, the strip of Hoe Street that Laura seemed to avoid. With an electric prickle of anticipation, I pulled out my phone and searched for Karina Cordovan.

Blonde hair, hazel eyes, a bright smile.

Not Bunting, but Cordovan.

I knew that name, of course. It wasn't garden parties, or Wimbledon, or royal weddings. It was blood, trauma, and darkness.

My fingertips felt numb with adrenaline. I put everything—aside from the last photograph—back into the box and slipped it under the bed. A bone tiredness was lapping against my concentration, eroding my productivity. I needed to sleep before my next night shift, so I packed the scattered notebooks back into their wooden crate and interred the whole thing under the bed, returning the empty suitcase and oscillating fan to their rightful place so there was no evidence of my snooping. I closed the bedroom window, surveyed the scene. There was no trace of me left.

Before I slipped out the front door, I tucked Laura's original set of keys between the sofa cushions. There. Proof I could be extremely kind, when it suited me, and now I could come and go as I pleased, without worrying about her ever thinking to change the locks.

LAURA

At the end of my shift, when I start to flag and my bright smile turns brittle, Sharona keeps me motivated by painting a picture of our next shop, working in Brighton together in the new year.

"Just think: fish and chips for lunch," she says, resting her head on my shoulder. "Sea air in your lungs. Pints after work on the beach."

"We'll walk down the pier," I say, imagining the smell of candy floss, the brine of the sea whipping through my hair. "And watch the sun sink under the horizon."

"Ugh, you're such a poet!" She laughs, giving me a playful shove.

⁂

When I get home, I pour myself a glass of Pinot Noir and collapse into my unmade bed with my laptop. The air in the flat feels cold, like I've left the back door open, but all is as it should be. I pull on a sweater and watch a time-lapse of a girl in Yorkshire reading *A Little Life*. In the sped-up footage, her chest rises and falls in staccato like the nervous, shallow breaths of a panic attack. Her eyes flick periodically to the camera and then back to the page, as though she can't ignore the feeling of being watched. It makes me feel anxious, like I'm spying on her, and I can't relax.

An intrusive image of footprints pressed into soil looms in my mind's eye, and I have to get up and check I've put the chain on the front door.

I wish I could shake this sense of vulnerability. It's always been there, but it feels like it's getting worse. A thread of fear was stitched into my soul the day my mother died and I've been frightened ever since: men frighten me, and police officers frighten me, and strangers frighten me, and darkness frightens me. Living alone frightens me, but living with other people frightens me more. At least by living alone, I'm in total control. No one comes in without my say-so.

The video of the girl, cheeks now streaked with tears as she read the final chapters of *A Little Life*, comes to an end. The evening feels like it's stretching ahead of me, a long and lonely road to nowhere. I feel like maybe I should write something, but the lilac diary still hasn't turned up, and without it, my motivation to pick up where I left off wanes. My solitude is both a comfort blanket and a weight. I send Eli a message. *Miss you, bud.*

I pick another video to watch, and this time the same girl embarks on a twenty-four-hour read-a-thon. Her hourly updates become increasingly less chipper, until she falls asleep at hour twenty and the screen fills with a stretch of her living room wall, dappled with an ever-changing light, just above the sofa where she lies. This is soothing, and I watch the splashes of yellow and gold light shimmer on the wallpaper until, finally, she cut the footage.

When I see a notification flash up on my phone, I expect it to be Eli replying to my message, but no. It's my father. My fragile mood sours completely and I swallow the rest of my wine. It must be that time of year.

ROACH

Thanks to my affinity with the moon, I experienced a smooth adjustment to night shifts. Sam worked in a rock bar in Soho, so he was most active on his phone from dusk 'til dawn anyway, often getting home around four A.M. and sleeping well into the afternoon. Bleep was nocturnal too, and while I felt bad about missing his prime social hours, I liked to think of us as creatures of the night, perfectly in sync.

During night shifts, Eli and Kofi preferred to work together, like children afraid of the dark. Their music and laughter would drift through the quiet of the night, like a distant party to which I was not invited. I didn't mind—I was delighted to prowl around on my own.

I listened to my murder podcasts while I shelved, and I travelled the world with serial killers: as the hours ticked by, John Wayne Gacy murdered at least thirty-three young men and boys in a ranch house near Chicago, Illinois, and Roshu Kha murdered eleven garment workers in the Chandpur District of Bangladesh, and Leonarda Cianciulli murdered three women in Correggio, Italy, and rendered their body fat into soap, which she gave to her neighbours. I imagined washing my skin with the soap of women, the way it would feel smooth and slippery between my hands.

I got a lot done during those long and lonely hours in the shop. I combed through the True Crime section, looking for references to Lee Frost. There wasn't much about him in print, but he did get a mention in a few true crime compendiums, and there was a whole chapter about him in a book of East London murderers by Cynthia de la Roche. It looked like the most detailed account I'd found about the case so far, and skim-reading it at two o'clock in the morning wasn't going to be sufficient. Alone in the True Crime section, I made the executive decision to steal it. While I had every right to read about the Stow Strangler if the spirit moved me, it would upset the normies to learn I was sniffing around Laura's past, even though it was my past too: I'd been there, lived under death's shadow. She just had a bigger role to play in the theatre of cruelty designed and directed by Lee Frost.

⁓

I started creepy-crawling rather brazenly during those few weeks of night shifts. I kept a photo of the shop rota on my phone, and when I felt like it, I walked to Laura's house in the morning after work, past the normies with their briefcases and their rucksacks heading in for another flavour-less day at the office. I'd wait to see her walk through the park, and then stroll to her house and let myself in without a care in the world. If any of her neighbours saw me, they'd probably assume she'd hired a cleaner and I was in there picking up after her, hoovering her crumby carpets and washing her tights. After all, what kind of thief breaks in at nine o'clock in the morning with a key?

Laura's flat was a productive hive for my research, my personal sanctuary in which I could gather my thoughts, recalibrate our dark connection. I spent my days reading through whatever notebooks I could find. Her handwriting was a round, inviting cursive that was easy to read, and the words flowed like wine as I read about her past loves and regrets, the minutia of her school days, her life as a student in Durham. Stories of booksellers she'd slept with, booksellers she'd fallen out with, booksellers she'd secretly fancied or secretly hated. Pages and pages analysing Eli's every move—his surreptitious looks, his comments, shared jokes and flirtations. His attention was a source of great interest to her, and she noted down every interaction with the clinical eye of a doctor tracking the progress of a rash. She mentioned her mother only in passing. *Bought tulips today—thought of Mum. The leaves are changing—Mum's birthday soon.*

Frost's other four victims weren't very well represented online. Elsie Meadows, 54, had short, grown-out red hair, grey at the roots. Homeless, four adult kids, a drink problem. Agata Matthams, 31, gaunt and pale, with thick eyeliner and raven-black hair that she wore slicked close to her scalp. She worked in a massage parlour. Safa Gamble, 39, was a probable sex worker, although her family denied it, and one newspaper claimed she was a drug addict, but they denied that too. The only picture of her was a grainy image taken from CCTV footage that showed her pink zip-up jumper and low-rise jeans, several inches of midriff on show. Lana Brown, 22, was a student and probable sex worker, although again the information was scatty and her family weren't forthcoming with information about her life in London. There was almost nothing else about them on record.

Between research sessions, I looted Laura's fridge for morsels—not just out of hunger, but an insatiable curiosity. She had expensive taste and gravitated towards posh, organic things. I nibbled punchy kalamata olives and sour goat's cheese, swigged flat Prosecco from the bottle, dragged a stale crust of sourdough through salted butter peppered with toast crumbs. I tasted a spoonful from every Tupperware in the fridge: leftover daal, wilted Greek salad, pesto pasta. Her fridge went through a cycle of fresh food that gradually turned to rot. She was careful to save leftovers, but seldom remembered to eat them, and seemed to think nothing of allowing whole bags of salad to turn to slime. It was like she had the best of intentions, and filled her fridge with beautiful things, but was never home for long enough to eat them. I thought of my attempts at making salad, and realised I hadn't been so far off the mark by letting my produce turn to algae.

She didn't seem to have a good grasp of what she already had, and it wasn't unusual to find a plastic tray of rotten plum tomatoes hidden behind a tub of fresh ones, so I began rescuing bits and pieces just before they turned and saving them for later, to eat at work: single pots of yoghurt, a handful of loose, wrinkled carrots, a bag of bagels spotted with the first furry signs of mold.

Laura's wardrobe was my fancy dress box. I tried on her dresses and shoes like a child playing with her mother's things. I flipped through hanger after hanger of vintage-style dresses, all with surprisingly dull high street labels. Topshop. Zara. H&M. Atmosphere. Not such a vintage queen, are we, Laura? Based on the fussy way she dressed for work, I'd expected a whimsical wardrobe full of outrageous things, beautiful prizes won by rummaging through piles of faded crap in vintage markets, designer dresses bought for a steal in charity shops. Clothes for every occasion. I was wrong. Her wardrobe was surprisingly pedestrian, and lacked the glamour I had expected. Strings of plastic pearls, berets in jewel colors, Swarovski brooches, ballet flats with blood stains on the inside of the heels. Nothing quite looked right on me, and I realised it was because of my washed-out purple hair. Blondes are meant to have more fun, I reasoned. Perhaps it was time for a change.

Once, I even took a bath. I filled her tub with steaming hot water and poured half a bottle of watermelon-scented bubbles under the stream. I felt like I was in a thermal spa, treating my sore muscles to a therapeutic soak. I flipped through an Emily Dickinson collection while I reclined, because that seemed like the kind of shit Laura would do. I dawdled through poems that were all "banished air" and "cunning moss" until the water turned cold and the bubbles flattened to a milky scum, and none of them spoke to me at all. When I pulled the plug, I watched the bathwater drain, stained grey-pink with my rapidly fading hair dye, and decided to leave the faint trace of soap, pink stain and lingering smell of synthetic watermelon behind as a subtle message for her to find.

Her bookshelves were my personal library, and I took great pleasure in moving single titles to random places. Yaa Gyasi next to Michelle Tea. Ferrante between Emma Cline and Rachel Cusk. I marvelled at the sheer number of them, and counted how many on average were on each shelf and how many shelves there were per bookcase and calculated an approximate total from there. Over a thousand. That wasn't all of them either. She separated out her poetry—there was a tightly packed shelf of skinny spines, chapbooks, and pamphlets in her bedroom, and her cookery was stacked along the windowsill in the kitchen: handsome matte Diana Henrys and compact little Nigel Slaters and a mix of posh baking books in gelato colors. No one needed to hoard over a thousand books, Laura. It was an obscene display of wealth, and I spent a lot of time carefully inspecting them, trying to figure out how many she had even bothered to read—an easy task, as she seemed to read books like she was making a point: bent covers, dog-eared pages, stains, and Post-it tabs, margins spidered with annotations.

I read her books like they were my own, roughly, bending them to suit my position, my light, my mood. I read pages of both poetry and prose with reckless abandon, and I left the half-read books in strange places around the flat when I grew tired of them, all folded corners and cracked spines, covers smudged by my sweaty, oily fingers: Toni Morrison shoved behind a radiator. Shirley Jackson under the sofa. Patti Smith's *Just Kids* slipped beneath the fridge.

The mould in the bedroom continued to get worse, spreading from the corners of the room like shadows, and the carpets were gritty with crumbs, hair, and fluff, and looped with the occasional stain from a slug's slithering underbelly. A fellow pilgrim, just passing through.

LAURA

An alarm ravages the morning and pulls me from a dream about preparing the shop for the day—sliding till trays into drawers, restocking carrier bags, printing a break rota and pinning it behind the till. It feels so unfair to dream about something I'm usually paid to do by the hour.

It's starting to feel like the alarm wakes me up earlier and earlier, like the long nights are gone in the blink of an eye, as soon as my head touches the pillow. I feel lead-heavy, drained, like I've had no sleep at all. Dinner with my father looms on the horizon, and a constant sense of dread over-shadows everything I do.

I often skip breakfast, fall behind on the washing-up, get dressed on autopilot, chug coffee in lieu of proper sustenance. I can't seem to keep track of what's in my fridge, forget what I've eaten, always seem to think I've got more than I do. Overnight, the silver snot-trails of my mysterious slugs continue to appear on the bathroom floor, on the hallway carpet, on the lino in the kitchen, and—perpetually running late—I scuff at them with my foot instead of cleaning them up properly. The slime traces act like semaphore, guiding more slugs to follow their sticky paths, rewilding my flat one invertebrate at a time, but I'm too exhausted to do anything about it. I have no energy; I have no time. I dream of living the kind of life where I can go to therapy, where I can go to the gym and take care of myself properly, where Christmas means winding down instead of ramping up.

The sun finishes its gentle ascent while we set up for the day, and the shop turns gold with an easterly light that flows through the windows and drenches everything in amber. The pages of the books glow with it, their covers illuminated. By the time the first customer arrives, the sun has disappeared behind the old department store, and the light is back to its usual dishwater, and no one sees its gentle fade from amber to yellow to grey but me.

The quiet autumn hasn't prepared me for the Christmas rush, and the shop is busy from the moment we open to the moment we close. Retail is like that—even shops destined for the chop pick up the pace with Christmas on the horizon.

There's still so much to do and it feels impossible to get anything done; to replenish sold-out stock, to tidy up the tables that are in a constant state of disarray. We have to juggle distributor deliveries, take expired reservations off the system, shelve them again, complete stock returns, order sundries, order change, cash up, and deal with regular visits from Rentokil and Prestige Hygiene and the Post Office. The phone rings all day every day, an endless ringing, like an alarm, but no one can ever get to it, so it rings and rings, and the sound fills my waking hours and infiltrates my dreams.

And the customers—oh, the customers. The customers are everywhere, like lice, crawling all over the shop, touching everything, knocking things over, dropping rubbish, leaving destruction in their wake. And they just keep coming, more and more every day. Customer enquiries, customer reservations, customer orders, customers lost, customers queuing, customers that need serving, customers that need the toilet, customers that want someone to yell at because their lives are spiralling out of control, because suddenly they're tired and it feels like only yesterday that they were still sleeping around and partying and couldn't care less about any-thing else, and now they're in their thirties, forties, fifties, sixties, and everything hurts and no one cares and life hasn't worked out the way they'd expected it to, so all they have left is the dizzy power of punching down at the bookseller who's ordered in the wrong book on kindness. They dawdle and moan, always in the way, always wanting something, demanding attention and servitude with an anxious impatience, their expectations high and their fuses short.

A woman in a raincoat makes Noor cry because we've sold out of *Pride and Prejudice*. A guy with the casual posture of a guitarist loses his cool when I break the news that someone ordered the wrong edition of the book he wanted, and now it won't arrive in time for Christmas. An older man who smells like shoe polish asks for someone "with half a brain" to help him when I misspell Woolf three times in a row. I'm so tired I can't even process my obvious mistake and keep retyping "Wolf" and hitting enter, over and over again.

There's an endless parade of threats to go elsewhere, to go to Amazon, to speak to the manager, to complain to head office, to go to the local papers, to take to social media. Threats to get me fired, threats to never come back.

So fucking what, I think to myself, forcing a smile as my stomach snarls. Without Eli, there's no one to go for a drink with after work, there's no reprieve, and I find myself thinking about all the friendships I've allowed to sour over the years, and I yearn for the kind of easy company that only comes from longevity.

∽

Instead, I have to meet my father for dinner in Soho. His invitations are sporadic and last minute, an afterthought whenever he discovers a blank page in his diary on a Friday night. I don't mind. I accept them with a steely determination to keep the paternal fire stoked. Family's family, and his distant approach to fatherhood is all I have left.

He's picked one of our regular spots, a sleek tapas bar that only takes walk-ins. We've shared many uncomfortable meals here, picked at many small plates of padrón peppers, sipped many glasses of dry Spanish sherry. I hate the long queue and small plates, hate perching at the counter, the close proximity to strangers. He likes the cacophonous bustle of the restaurant's open kitchen, though, and he likes surveying the other diners squeezed around the bar. Oily fingers and crumpled napkins. Animated chatter, the banging of pans, the occasional fizz of sizzling oil and cries of "Backs!" and "Sí, chef!," all reverberating against mirrored walls and steamy windows hemmed with garlands of fresh holly.

I didn't grow up eating in restaurants like this, didn't spend my childhood learning how to read French and Spanish menus. My father's relationship with my mother was over before his stock had risen, and their time together was far more modest than the indulgent lifestyle he seems to have grown accustomed to with Margot and the boys.

I find him nursing a glass of cava and scrolling on his phone, right at the end of the queue, which wraps around the interior of the restaurant. I slip between chic Soho diners who hold their winter coats and sip wine while they wait for their turn at the counter. At this time of year, the queue can be an hour or more.

"Darling," he says, offering me a stubbly cheek to kiss. A strong, astringent smell of aftershave. He hands me a glass of cava and points to a dish of fat gordal olives laced with lemon zest. We clink flutes and I take a generous swallow that fizzes in my throat, then place my glass on the dark marble ledge that lines the restaurant.

"You're looking well," he says, unbuttoning his collar and loosening his tie as he gazes around the restaurant. I glance into the mirror behind him, and the girl that meets my eye looks frayed, faded. Gaunt, with waxy skin and dark circles under her eyes.

"Thanks," I say, turning away from my reflection.

"And how's work?" He pops an olive into his mouth and offers me the dish again. I take one and hold it between my fingers.

"Fine. Good, actually."

He chews and swallows, circling the inevitable. "And are you still at the Strand? Or was it Bloomsbury? I can't keep track."

"No, I'm at the Walthamstow branch at the moment."

"Christ, do they read much up there?" he says with a sly look in his eye. *You fucking snob*, I think, gripping my glass.

A gust of wind sweeps through the restaurant, and we both glance towards the door as a woman in Louboutins and a fur coat the colour of Branston pickle steps into the evening. Outside, night brews in the shadows.

"Are you still looking for a proper job?"

I count to ten and watch the passing crowd through the window, veiled by a layer of condensation. Cigarettes, expensive coats, all braced against the cold, heading to the theatre, to dinner, to after-work drinks.

"I *have* a proper job," I reply through gritted teeth. "I like bookselling. I like books."

"You need to think about your future, though, darling," he says with faux concern. My feet burn against the hard floor, and I shift my weight from one foot to the other. My future is a hot bath with watermelon bubbles and a glass of wine to soothe every aching muscle in my body.

"And are you still in that terrible little flat?"

I bristle and feel my cheeks flush.

"It's not *terrible*," I reply tartly. I finally place the olive in my mouth, and a lemony brine floods my tongue as I crush it between my molars.

When I graduated from university, I didn't have a plan. I'd studied English literature and dreamed of becoming an English teacher or a school librarian. I had this wholesome Miss Honey image of myself dressed in cardigans and brogues, sharing the magic of reading with wide-eyed children. In reality, my final year was a blur of late nights and bad habits, and I missed the window to apply for a post-grad for the following year. I moved back to London, found a cheap flat in Walthamstow, and applied for jobs bookselling.

"You need a career," my father says, chewing another olive. "You can't just tread water forever."

When I think of the world of work beyond retail, I think of white noise. I've never worked in any other industry. I went from school to sixth form to university to bookselling. What is it that other people do? What do people do in offices? Job ads are written in a language I don't speak. *Self-starter, results-focused, proven track record.* And salaries are shrouded in code: *industry standard, highly competitive, pro rata, OTE.* How do you pick a career if you don't know what anything means?

I open my mouth to respond, but the queue surges forward again, and I take advantage of the disruption to change the subject.

"Is Margot working at the moment?" I ask.

"She's between projects," he replies in a stiff tone.

When it's our turn to be seated, we're led to a pair of high stools right at the end of the shiny bar. My father scans the menu, taking his time, crooning after our server—a neat Eastern European girl with a thick brown fringe—to ask her to repeat the specials two, three times. He settles on glasses of sherry, chilled to a crisp, with razor clams, king prawns cooked in chilli and garlic, and an onion tortilla.

"I'll just have the bravas French fries, please," I say, nauseated by the raw seafood displayed on the counter opposite us. Mottled squid with a hideous bridal froth of tentacles, king prawns with pleading eyes, clams like gnarled toenails, all on a bed of packed ice chips that drip on to the floor in a milky puddle.

"Well, it's all for sharing," my father reminds me, unfolding his napkin and placing it across his lap. The dishes are small and come at random intervals, appearing in front of us with a dramatic clatter and a cry from the chef, who announces each one in brisk Spanish.

"I do need to talk to you about something, actually, darling," he says, slicing into the rich, golden tortilla, shaped like a honey-coloured hockey puck.

I search his face for a clue to his mood, but he looks perfectly calm, if a little red from the warmth of the restaurant. He has a strong brow and downturned mouth, so his neutral expression is solemn, serious, even when he's in a good mood. I can never see any trace of family resemblance between us. My features are delicate, those of my mother.

"I've taken on a new role at work," he says. "It's a big opportunity, but it means a bit of a change of scenery."

"Oh?"

"We'll be moving to Frankfurt in the new year."

A young chef places a dish of stuffed courgette flowers between us, the butter-yellow petals cocooned in a delicate web of crispy batter.

"Buen provecho! Compliments of the chef," he says.

"Ah, gracias, gracias!" my father crows, slapping him on the back in a genial display of gratitude. He's pink with pleasure, in his element. I pick up my sherry glass, but it's empty.

"Are you okay, darling? You look a little—" He flutters his fingers around his eyes and blinks. "You're not upset, are you?"

"No," I say, twirling my empty glass, feeling nothing. "Of course not."

He soliloquises about the job, about Frankfurt, about the winter snow. Margot wants to get a cat, the boys want a dog.

"You'll visit, won't you, darling?"

"Of course," I say, with a bright blank customer-service smile.

"And listen: it's time to get serious." He raps his knuckles on the marble counter to signal a change of tone. "It's time to either match your work to your lifestyle, or your lifestyle to your work."

"I'm thinking about writing a book," I say, a tumble of words falling out of my mouth in a great defensive rush. I don't want to hear his thoughts on my *lifestyle*.

He blinks and leans back in his chair, amused.

"A novel?"

"No, a memoir. About Mum."

He opens his mouth and takes a breath, but the words die on his lips as he thinks twice about whatever he was going to say.

"Well," he says at last, and then he just lets the word hang there.

I want to ask him if he ever thinks of her, if he misses her. I want to ask him what he remembers about her, what their life together was like before they had me. I want to ask him what it was about her that made him fall in love. I want to ask him if he regrets the way things ended, if he ever regrets leaving us. I want to ask him if her death mattered to him, if it hurt him. I want to ask him if she ever came to him in his dreams the way she came to me.

I press my fork into the wilted courgette flower, the batter softening as it cools, and a little worm of congealed cheese squirts on to the plate. Our server, the pretty one with the thick fringe, appears and starts stacking empty dishes.

"Was everything good with your meal?" she asks, a perky smile plastered on her face.

"Oh, delicioso! Bien asado, muy bueno. Compliments to the chef," my father says. "And listen, sweetheart, could we grab the bill?"

I flinch at his casual sexism, his lack of please, and chirp a quick thank you to her retreating back. While we wait for the bill, he gives me a creased paper gift bag. Inside, there's two MAC lipsticks—freebies from a press pack—and a silk Karen Mabon scarf that smells of Margot's perfume.

"Oh, and here," he says, passing me a paper shopping bag from Lina Stores, the good Italian deli on Brewer Street where he insists the staff know him by name. "Just some good olive oil, white pesto, and pappardelle."

"Thanks," I say, taking the bag.

"Look darling, I'm desperate for the loo. Shall I meet you outside?" He pays the bill with a credit card and then squeezes past me to the bathroom at the back of the restaurant. While he's gone, I check the receipt. He's only tipped five per cent, the cheap bastard.

I stick a twenty-pound note under the napkin dispenser and then I slide the silk scarf and lipsticks into the Lina Stores bag and tuck it under my stool, perfectly placed to look forgotten. I imagine our kind server finding them later, perhaps trying on the lipsticks after her shift, in the bathroom of a late-night Soho cocktail bar where she drinks for free because she sometimes sleeps with the mixologist. Or perhaps one of the chefs, the young handsome one with the green eyes, will take it home and make his girlfriend pappardelle with white pesto and wind the scarf around her neck and let her kiss him with cupcake-scented lips.

The room is too hot, crowded, noisy, full of laughter that distorts into jeers in my tired mind. I gather up my coat, and push my way through the narrow gap between the stools at the bar and the queue that twists around the edges of the restaurant, towards the door, towards the rain.

My father follows soon after and frowns as I light a cigarette. "Oh, darling, no. You must quit—it's such a vile habit, really hideous."

"I like it," I say, blowing smoke straight into his face.

"Shall we go for a drink?" He squints through my smoke, flaps a hand to disperse it. "Groucho?"

"I have work tomorrow," I say.

"Oh, go on, you can have one more drink with your old dad."

"I can't, I'm on the open. I have to be up early."

"Look, are you sure you're okay? I didn't upset you back there?"

"Of course not." I cross my arms against the chilly night air. "I'm absolutely fine."

He leans forward and kisses me on each cheek. "I'll speak to Hugo at the magazine, see if there's anything coming up, if you like?"

"Fine," I say. "Great. Thanks."

"And listen, we're going to be in New York for Christmas, but perhaps we can have dinner for your birthday? Get a table somewhere fancy, one last big hurrah before we move for good in the spring?"

"Sounds perfect."

We hug, and I breathe him in, feel the shape of him, and wish—not for the first time—that our relationship existed beyond light criticism, money, dinners.

"Merry Christmas, darling."

I watch him weave his way to the Groucho, where he'll drink glasses of Sancerre and rub shoulders with all the faded luvvies and publishing ra-ras. Perhaps in another life he might have had the kind of daughter he really wants, a daughter who'd find a high-flying office job, the kind of girl who'd suggest a cocktail at the French House, who'd wear designer scarves and look chic, who'd know how to move through Soho the way he does, side-stepping the drunk tourists, the drag queens hustling for an audience, the cooks on their haunches smoking and scrolling, the girls in party dresses with their shopping bags, the teens drinking bubble tea, the artists with their stained fingers and cigarettes, the bleached blond beefcakes with Pomeranians and espresso, all of them just the supporting cast to his one-man show.

ROACH

Between shelving trolleys of stock, I continued to flick through books and make notes. There really wasn't much about Lee Frost in print. As cases went, even I had to admit it was a little dull. It lacked mystery, it lacked glamour. He was no tantalising enigma, no Jack the Ripper, whose identity was obscured by a shroud of London fog, no Axeman of New Orleans, whose real name was known only to the cobbled streets and flicking gas lanterns of the French Quarter. Lee Frost was caught, and he was found guilty, and he was sentenced to life in prison, and that was that. He spent five years in the men's high-security prison in Wakefield, where he walked in the shadow of Harold Shipman, before he was transferred to HMP Frankland where he may have rubbed shoulders with many of the modern British heavyweights.

There was no big-budget Hollywood film on the horizon, no Netflix documentary in the works, no serialised investigative podcast to pique people's interest. Murder most ordinary. He was only caught because he pivoted from low-hanging fruit to a woman who mattered in the eyes of the community. The only thing that made the case special was the simple fact that serial killers were exceptional, which made them automatically more interesting than your average run-of-the-mill murderer, and that he was a police officer, which caused quite a stir.

I moved over to the till, opened a private browser to cover my tracks, and googled him, just to see his face again. Lee Frost had the bald-headed, double-chinned, nothingy face of a customer. He was every man, any man. I could comfortably place him buying the latest Lee Child, or a last-minute birthday card, or pushing a trolley around Homebase, reading the Sunday paper, watching the football, eating a roast dinner.

There was a courtroom sketch, his slumped shoulders and downturned eyes brought to life in scribbled colouring pencils. He was not a showman in the courts, didn't thrive in that environment the way some of them did, all cocky smiles and swagger. And yes, there he was before his arrest: pressed white shirt, epaulettes, sunburned nose, squinting against the sun in a peaked black cap with the distinctive black and white diced band of a police officer's hat. I had always found it difficult to imagine those smiling eyes, flanked with crow's feet, as the eyes of a killer. He lacked the stature, the charisma of the A-listers—although by modern standards he was quite extraordinary for racking up such a number.

It was more difficult to get away with serial killing these days. We lived in an age of information, after all. There were approximately five hundred thousand CCTV cameras in London, and the average citizen was caught on camera over three hundred times per day. We all carried smartphones that continually tracked and transmitted our location, our steps, our heart rate, our habits and behaviours. Every single move we made was observed, recorded, and remembered in one way or another, and that was before we even think about the forensic capabilities of a contemporary homicide unit. Forensic anthropology; entomology; linguistics; facial recognition technology; toxicology; bloodstain pattern analysis; semen analysis; impression evidence, including ballistics, bite marks, fingerprints, footprints, and tyre tracks; and trace evidence, including fibre, soil, glass, and handwriting. It was difficult to create a crime scene without leaving a trace of yourself behind.

Serial killers were an endangered species. It wasn't so much that the world was a kinder or safer place: we were just better at catching murderers after their first kill, and we were better at recognising the signs that point towards dangerous psychopathy in children and young adults. As a society, we were also more careful, less trusting of others: we locked our doors, we feared strangers. Hitchhiking was an archaic practice, like trepanation or going to the barbers to have a rotten tooth pulled.

Spree killers were the new serial killers. One after the other, in quick succession. That's the way to do it. Rather burn out than fade away. No, to get away with serial killing, you needed several stars to align: low-profile victims, a healthy pinch of police incompetence or corruption, and a splash of sheer good luck. If these factors were a Venn diagram, Lee Frost landed right in the middle, where each circle overlapped. His luck only ran out when he targeted Karina Cordovan.

On the first floor till, I typed her name into the search bar. She was not a low-profile victim, she didn't exist on the fringes, and her death was not so easily shrugged off by the press. A florist with a flair for lush green foliage, she was a familiar face to anyone in Walthamstow who planned a wedding or planted a garden and chose to shop locally. She was well known, she was liked. She had a beautiful daughter, a wholesome business, a good name, a reputation for being kind and community-minded.

I copied and pasted news articles from digital archives into a blank Word document and emailed it to myself. She was bequeathed an obituary in the local paper, and there were dozens and dozens of articles that rehashed the same scraps of information: what she looked like (pretty, petite, blonde), what she was wearing (a loose peach T-shirt, black leggings, running shoes), where she had been (jogging through the Village), where she was going (heading home to her sleeping daughter), who found her body (an unnamed passerby), where she was found (Vinegar Alley, Walthamstow Village, London).

I searched the names of his other four victims, but apart from where they were from, how many children they had, how old they were, their occupations and their addictions, there was almost nothing else about their lives on record.

LAURA

While Eli's team focus on books, a backlog of gifts starts to build in the stockroom, and one evening Sharona and I stay late to get on top of it. We play Hole and Bikini Kill and the Yeah Yeah Yeahs and scream the lyrics as we price up letter-writing sets, posh notebooks, leather bookmarks, and water bottles decorated with flowers and constellations. The gift range has little to do with books, but it has everything to do with lifestyle. Reading is a way of life for some customers, the kind of customers who buy more than they read, who behave as though "bookworm" is as inherent as their blood type or their astrological sign. They're easy to sell to because their enthusiasm clouds their judgement, but they can be difficult too. They take up a lot of time, and they often misunderstand what the relationship is between a bookseller and a customer. They think my sales patter is an attempt to connect, and try to recommend books back to me without knowing anything about my taste.

"Wish we had wine," I say, opening a box of calendars. Wall calendars, box calendars, and diaries, the same designs every single year, a strange mix of fine art and cartoons, pop culture and dated humour. When I think of the new year, I hear the cry of gulls and smell the fresh sea air. Thoughts of Brighton keep me going.

"Your liver will thank you if you take a break once in a while," Sharona says, not unkindly.

Wrapping paper. Reams and reams of it. Decorations in every colour and material: soft wood, red velvet bows, gold bells. Ribbons in jewel colours, balls of brown string. When we uncover the third tote of 2020 diaries, we realise they won't all fit on the little freestanding unit we have by the till. There are too many, they'll take up an entire bay, and if we're going to sell through, that bay will have to be in a high-traffic area, where the most customers go.

Sharona loves to crunch the numbers, and make commercial decisions based on facts, not feelings. She stands in front of the till on the first floor, checks sales figures, clucking her tongue, deep in thought.

"If we can find something to condense up here," she says, evaluating each section in turn, "we could move the world map–themed gift range into the Travel section. That would free up a bay downstairs for diaries." She taps a finger against her lips. "True Crime looks pretty baggy."

"Roach won't like that," I say with a little shiver of pleasure, crossing the shop floor to have a look at the section. "Though we could easily condense this down to half a bay."

"We need a whole bay, though,"

"Let's just break it up," I say. "I bet a lot of it can slot into other sections."

"What, like Jack the Ripper in Biography?" she says, amused. "I feel like Barry might have some strong opinions on that one."

"Well, maybe not Biography, but what about Victorian History? Or London? Honestly, I bet we could dissolve the whole section really easily. Job done."

"All right." Sharona nods, her mind set. "It's late. Let's just do it."

"Roach is gonna hate us," I say with a nervous smile.

"Ah, she'll get over it."

"I just don't want her to break into my house and murder me in my sleep," I reply, only half joking.

"I'll tell her it was my idea." Sharona checks the time on her watch. "Y'know what, it's actually pretty late. I might just hang on and wait for the night shift. I can break the news to Roach in person and check in with Eli."

"I'm up for waiting with you on one condition," I say, with a giddy feeling at the thought of seeing Eli. "Let's go for a glass of wine afterwards. My liver can take it if yours can."

She rolls her eyes with a wry smile, but she doesn't say no.

By the time Eli arrives at nine-thirty, I'm crouched by the gift bays front of store, filling a display with a new line of scented candles in woodland aromas. Synthetic pine, cedar, and an enigmatic scent called "freshly fallen snow" cloud the air around me.

"All right, mate!" he says with obvious delight, ruffling my hair as he walks by. The cold clings to him, and I remember that he never replied to my last text message. A flush of embarrassment creeps up my neck.

"You heard about the Christmas party?" he asks, unwinding a brown scarf from his pale throat.

"No—what's the story?"

"Sharona's got the whole shop into the Strand party," he says with a dark smile that makes his eyes dance with an impish delight. We both know exactly what that means: a free bar, a mix of different shops, our best clothes, our worst behaviour.

"Oh," I say with forced neutrality. "Cool. I thought we'd be missing out this year."

"As if Sharona would let us down," he says, peeping into the nearest tote. He lifts out a canvas bag that says *Bookworm* on it in a cute typewriter font.

"Ugh. The commercialisation of our hobbies." He drops the bag back in to the tote and shakes his head. "I swear, the people who buy this shit aren't actually bookworms at all. They're just shopaholics."

"I have that exact bag," I say, even though I don't.

"You would, Laura Bunting," he replies with a dimpled grin, and he ambles towards the back of the shop to find Sharona.

ROACH

The living room had grown dark around Jackie, and the glow of the television cast her in a watery, flickering light. A lurid Christmas film was playing at full volume, music and laughter blasting, and yet she slept, her face slack, head tilted to one side. I picked up the remote control and switched off the telly, but the change in the ambience of the room—if you could call the garish colour and tooth-rattling sound ambience—made her jerk awake anyway.

"What's that?" she said, disorientated and blinking. The room was dark without the light of the television, and she groped around the base of the lamp until she found the switch.

"Just me," I said, shrinking away from the warm light. "I'm heading back out in a minute, just need to get changed."

She wiped her loose drool-slicked lips with the back of her hand, then checked her wrist for a watch that wasn't there. "What?"

"It's just me," I said again, louder.

"What's the time now?"

"Nine," I said.

"Christ." She rubbed her eyes and then blinked at me, as though seeing me for the first time. "And you're going out? Now?"

"In a minute," I said. "Still on nights, aren't I?"

"Dressed like that?" She cocked her head and eyed my outfit. I was dressed as Brodie, in a loose AC/DC T-shirt and black skinny jeans with ripped knees. I'd spent the afternoon sleeping in Sam's bed, and my skin still smelled of his bedclothes, of his sweat. I loved the feeling of carrying the memory of the day with me into the night, but I couldn't wear a Brodie outfit to work.

"No, I said I'm just gonna get changed."

She used her fists to push herself into a more upright position on the sofa.

"That reminds me," she said. "Biker Paul's daughter Emily says she saw you with some goth down in Ilford yesterday evening."

"Bollocks. I don't even know who Biker Paul is," I said, pulling a stink-face as I slipped the straps of my rucksack off my shoulders.

"You know Biker Paul." She said this with confident authority, picking up the remote and switching the television back on. Her film had come to an end, and the credits were rolling to a saccharine Christmas song that lit a match of irrational dislike within me. It took me a few beats to realise it was because it was one of the songs from the Christmas playlist at work. "He's Louisa's bloke, the fella with the—"

"Gonna be late," I said, cutting her off before she could circle back round to her original point.

"You can tell me if you've got a boyfriend, you know," she said with a sly look. She scooped her frizzy over-dyed hair into a stiff bun and fastened it with the hairband she kept looped around her wrist. The pressure of the elastic had left a deep red impression in the delicate skin, like the marks left by a ligature. "But if you do have a fella, I want to meet him."

"I *don't* have a fucking boyfriend," I snapped, making a swift exit.

The jig was up. She had eyes everywhere, a network of regulars who reported back on every scrap of gossip. If I'd been spotted with Sam once, it was only a matter of time before I'd be seen with him again.

In my room, I gave my sweet Bleep a scoop of calcium and tipped some grapes into his bowl, then changed into a more Roach-like outfit—a *Murder Girls* T-shirt, a dab of rose oil behind each ear, and a black beret—and used a makeup wipe to smear the last of the Brodie makeup away.

LAURA

In another life, Mirth was a beautiful art deco cinema, but the building sat abandoned for at least twenty years before developers cleaned it up and turned it into a ritzy, high-ceilinged bar with marble floors, dramatic sweeping staircases, and beautiful mirrors framed in gold, which still bore the echoes of graffiti etched on to the glass.

"Actually, can we make that a bottle?" Sharona says to the barman, waving her credit card. "Might as well, right?"

"That's the spirit," I say, relieved. I won't have to worry about convincing her to stay for a second drink if we have a whole bottle to get through.

Sharona and I have never had a drink together just one-on-one before, and the wine is exactly what we need to relax into the night. I keep Sharona's glass topped up, and our conversation circles the shop and the company, as it always does. It's impossible to get off the topic of work, until finally we land on Eli.

"How long have you guys actually worked together?" I ask.

"Ah man," she says, fluffing her curls with a dramatic sigh, eyes to the ceiling as she casts her mind back. "Let's see . . . we both started in 2012, I think? No, Christmas 2011."

"He thinks very highly of you," I say, improvising with a conspiratorial grin. "You must know all his secrets."

"Eli doesn't have any secrets. He's an open book," she says, with a warm fondness in her voice. She looks at me for a moment, mind working behind her eyes. "Lydia's good for him, I think."

"Yeah?"

She tips the last of her wine into her mouth and I reach for the bottle, but it's empty. I want to buy us another, to keep the night alive, but it's late and I know that if I interrupt her train of thought now, we won't come back to Eli and Lydia. I hold tight and wait for her to speak.

"He's a handsome lad," she says mildly. "He's broken a few hearts over the years, and I don't think that ever really made him happy. I think Lydia keeps him grounded."

"Are you saying Eli used to be a player?" I laugh, and she throws her head back and laughs too, and when she laughs she glows, relaxed and warm from the wine, the music, the buzz of the bar.

"Like I said, a few broken hearts," she says, side-stepping the question. "I'm glad to see him settled."

Sharona checks the time on her watch, then slides her phone into the pocket of her jeans and gathers her tobacco, her lighter, her Rizla.

"Another drink?" I say hopefully, holding up my debit card even though I'm already into my overdraft and she's clearly getting ready to leave. "It's my round."

"Nah, it's late," she says. "And I think they're closing soon anyway."

"The Victoria's open until three," I say. "One more drink, go on."

She stands up, pulling on her coat, her eyes distracted. She's already left the bar in her head, thinking about her journey home, about her girlfriend and her cats and her books, all waiting for her on the other side of London. "Another time, yeah? I've got to get all the way back to Peckham."

"Well, come back to mine and crash! I think I've got some peach schnapps and some brandy."

"Tempting as that sounds," she says, laughing, "I want to get back to Charlie. She'll be waiting up."

"Boring," I say with a hint of a sneer, yanking on my coat.

ROACH

"You're late," Eli said, stooping to pick up a fallen paperback. He returned it to its place on the table with a pathetic, almost fond little pat that made me feel sick. "Sharona wanted to talk to you."

"Sorry," I said flatly, as he locked the shop door behind me.

"Hey, listen," he said, turning away from the door to face me, his hands fiddling with the keys in his hands. He had this look of concern plastered over his face, like he was a doctor about to deliver bad news, and I swallowed. "Look, Sharona axed the True Crime section today," he said. "She wanted to tell you herself, but . . . well. Anyway. I'm really sorry, I know it was kind of your thing."

"She *what?*"

"We don't have a True Crime section anymore. It was Sharona, she—"

"Laura did it," I said quietly, venomously, looking him dead in the eye. My accusation took him by surprise and he laughed a nervous laugh and scratched the back of his head.

"What? No, no—this has nothing to do with Laura. It's just a bit of a dying trend, and Sharona needed to find some space upstairs and—"

"Bollocks," I spat. "It's not a fucking trend, everyone loves true crime. Like students and doctors and housewives and police officers . . . all walks of life."

"Maybe in general," Eli said, cocking his head to one side and narrowing his eyes. "But in this branch . . . well, that just isn't actually true, is it?"

I simmered, lost for words. I barely registered Eli's weak apology, his reassurance that Sharona was *always open for a chat*. Without a word, I scuttled off to the Children's section to stew.

True crime wasn't a trend. Not in the bookshop. *Serial* and *Making a Murderer* and *My Favorite Murder* and *The Staircase* and *RedHanded* and *I'll Be Gone in the Dark* and *The Last Podcast on the Left* and whatever else—that disastrous Instagram festival for rich idiots and the fake German heiress and the Silicon Valley fraudster—none of this manifested as a bookshop trend. My section wasn't a fad, wasn't crammed with shitty popular garbage that normies bought because everyone else was buying it, destined to be purchased, and then gifted, and then shelved, and then never read, and then eventually donated, and finally, fatally pulped.

I thought spending time in Laura's flat had strengthened our bond, but every time I took a step towards her, she was taking a step back. She had a knack for finding new ways to drive a wedge between us, an unexpected talent for malevolence. I carried the heat of her betrayal throughout my final night shifts.

Once I understood the depth of Laura's spite, random acts of destruction became my poetry. The words all but memorised anyway, I burned the lilac diary in a disquieting ritual of my own devising, but that wasn't enough. I picked books from her shelves and used a razor blade to remove the odd page at random, and I took those pages home and pinned them to my bedroom wall to create a tapestry of sacrifice, of trendy women's writing, the kind of shit that got normies like Laura excited. I poured vinegar into the soil of a particularly handsome houseplant, a leafy monstera, and imagined its leaves would wither and lose their shine. I stole every single hair elastic I found, took odd socks, dropped bobby pins between the floorboards, tipped expensive silver-tone shampoo down the sink, threw single earrings in the bin. I pissed in her toilet and didn't flush, so my urine would greet her like a frothy glass of champagne when she came home from work. I dreamed of filling her wardrobe with house moths, or infesting the place with mice or rats or roaches. Anything vile, anything cruel, to burst her bubble of safety and to say *Hi Laura, it's me, I was here while you were gone and there's nothing you can do about it.*

And yet, all the while, I never lost focus. In Laura's bed, on her sofa, in her space, I continued to read her diaries, and wrote page after page of prose. I transcribed podcasts, and copied entire sections from Wikipedia, news reports, online magazine articles, blog posts, and old, inactive message boards. I was an archaeologist digging up the story of the Stow Strangler, arranging the bones of it into chronological order.

Of course, if I was a real investigative journalist, I'd likely have some tricks up my sleeve. Chewing a biro, squinting over microfiche in some dusty library, I'd spend hours flipping through articles until I found my quarry. I wasn't sure if my local library provided that kind of service, though. I wondered if those clunky old machines were only available to police officers and journalists.

Or perhaps I could write to Lee Frost. I'd strike up a correspondence, earn his trust, become his confidante. He'd open up to me, tell me about life in prison, share intimate thoughts and ideas, eventually spilling the details of the murders, what made him do it, what depraved motivation made him tick. I needed to find a way to write to him, the way I knew fans wrote letters to their favourite serial killers on death row, but finding his information proved to be more difficult than I'd imagined. I learned that I couldn't simply address a letter to him and send it to the prison.

I needed Frost's prisoner number too. I picked over Reddit pages where people claimed to have corresponded with murderers for tips.

> *I was pen pals with one for a while—we talked about religion mostly . . .*
>
> *Don't bother writing to him, all he wants to talk about is baseball . . .*
>
> *My husband wrote to one and he wrote back . . . I feel violated knowing the hand that held the knife was the same hand that held the pen to write that letter.*

In the murky deep of a thread on some old, abandoned forum, I found someone who claimed to have written to Lee Frost. The poster had included a scan of their letter, and an earnest promise to update the message board with any response they received from the big man himself. They had never updated their thread so the letter must have gone unanswered, but that didn't matter: right there, on the top right of the page, was Lee Frost's name, address, and, written in a neat hand, his prisoner number.

I was so excited, I messaged Sam to tell him the good news.

Swear ur more into him than me, he complained. He was growing clingy, his enthusiasm for the project waning when he realised it was eating into our time together. He didn't understand what it was to be a writer, to slice open the belly of a story and perform an autopsy. I was also unsure about whether I could trust him with the truth of how I was spending my time. I couldn't articulate how essential the access to Laura's flat was to my process. The work came alive when I was in her space, reading her words, surrounded by her things. I couldn't let anything jeopardise my process.

LAURA

Something breaks the surface of my sleep. My bedroom is dark, and still, and cold, and I lie and listen to the silence. We live in close quarters around here, all terraced houses converted into flats, and it's not unusual to be disturbed in the night by windows slamming shut, or drunken fights, or glass breaking, or the distant cry of a teething baby.

I listen, and the only answer is the silence of the night outside my bedroom window. But there's a change in the air, that's the only way I can describe it. With a creeping sense of dread, I realise it could have been the gentle change in air pressure as a closed door opened, or the sound of a forced latch, or of a jimmied door being pulled shut.

Someone has entered my flat. Someone has entered my room. I can feel their presence, a thickness, an invasive heat rising from their body, carried on their breath. I can't breathe, and panic flares as I scramble for the light switch.

Nothing, there's nothing, there's no one there. Just my clothes rail and my dressing table, my books and my things. My bed smells strange, though, and the room feels wrong, tilted, fragmented. Nothing is where it is supposed to be, nothing feels right. The footprints pressed into the soil outside my living room window pop into my head, still haunting me months later.

Adrenaline washes away the last traces of sleep, and my heart beats against my breastbone. I climb out of bed and tiptoe to the front door to check that the chain is in place, then peep into the moonlit living room. All is as it should be, but in the kitchen, there are three slugs creeping across the lino, secreting silver meandering tracks. I make an involuntary, guttural noise and smash one into snot with a well-aimed ballet flat. Brimming with self-loathing, I have the repulsive realisation that I now have to wipe up mashed slug from the kitchen floor.

It's gone six. My alarm was set for seven anyway. I fill the kettle and make myself a cup of spiced apple tea. While it's brewing, I use a toilet roll tube to scoop up the remaining live slugs and toss them out the back door, and with a handful of kitchen roll I mop up their dead brother.

Outside the kitchen window, beyond my row of wilting houseplants, darkness presses against the glass, and I force myself to look and I do not cower or flinch at the reflection that stares back. I look drained, but every early morning reflection looks a little frayed around the edges. I can't find my little mist bottle, so I fill a jam jar from the tap and water my beloved monstera. An odd smell, like the acid tang of a fish and chip shop, emanates from its roots.

I feel like writing, but the lilac diary is long gone, lost on some drunken bender, no doubt. I feel like reading, but I can't find any of the books I'm in the mood for. My copy of *Bluets* seems to have vanished into thin air. I crave comfort, warmth, and creativity, so I settle on *Just Kids*, thinking of the bit where a young Patti Smith is jobless and hungry in New York— *'Even Baudelaire had to eat'*—but I can't find that either.

Despite a somewhat laissez-faire attitude towards their condition, I do keep my books organised so that I can always find them on a whim, usually late at night and with a glass in my hand, succumbing to some late-night drunken desire for the familiar.

I try to keep my life together because the state of my flat reflects my state of mind. As long as my home is organised, I know my mind is clear. If a library is a window into the soul, then the more scattered my books become, the more scattered I feel. The more scattered I feel, the more scattered they become. It's one of my first external warning signs that I'm not doing so well, along with drinking until I black out, skipping meals, and forming obsessive one-sided attachments to men I can't have.

I give up on Patti Smith. I retreat with my mug, and curl under the still-warm covers. Propped up with pillows, I read *The Year of Magical Thinking* instead, and when my alarm goes off at seven, it's still dark and I can't do it, I can't get out of bed. I read until the sun rises and bleaches the room of shadows, evaporates the ghosts.

Ghosts aren't what keep me awake at night, though. Ghosts aren't what scare me. Ghosts can't harm me, they can't break into my home, they can't rob me, they can't rape me, they can't murder me in my sleep. There's a lot to fear in this world, but when something goes bump in the night, it isn't ghosts that haunt me.

I can't afford a therapist to fix me and I can't get to a doctor easily during December when the shop needs me most. I haven't even been to my support group since October, and I'm too tired, too busy, barely making it from one day to the next, to think of going any time soon.

I read once that people who read true crime believe there's a disproportionate chance of something terrible happening to them, that serial killers are more common than they are. But what about those of us who have lived through it? My mother's murder changed my understanding of the world around me. Lee Frost may be locked away, but whatever misogynistic thirst for violence curdled inside him to make him murderous could curdle in others too. I never want to become a woman who sleeps with a bread knife under her pillow, but I know how cruel the world can be now. I can't carry on like this, living with stifling anxiety and paranoia, a constant dread lapping at the shores of my sanity, eroding my nerves and manifesting as threats that simply are not there.

I get up late and don't have time for breakfast, which is lucky because the avocados have gone rotten in the bowl and I don't seem to have any bagels left, even though I'm sure I had four on Sunday. Or was that last Sunday? I can't find anything. Odd socks, missing earrings. I'm losing control but there's no time to recentre myself. I settle on grungy loungewear—a vintage Guns N" Roses T-shirt, leggings, thick, comfy socks, and army boots, knock-off Jeffrey Campbells. I make an instant coffee, which I hate, but there's no time for a cafetière, no time for Starbucks. I do take pause in the living room, however, cradling my cup under my chin for a few moments and standing in front of my bookshelves, scanning, scanning, scanning the spines for my missing copy of *Just Kids*.

The sound of rush hour traffic swells on the thin morning air as I leave for work on the last day of Roach's night shifts, my last day of freedom.

∽

A customer comes over to the till, a woman who wants a book of baby names. She's wearing chic makeup, and expensive-smelling perfume, and her chocolate brown hair is piled in that messy style rich women sometimes favour. She reminds me of my dad's wife, Margot, and I feel a shiver of irritation. I show her the section and turn to leave, keen to get back to my task, but she keeps me there while she picks up each book in turn, examines it, puts it back, asks my opinion of every single one. They are all the same. Impatient, I decide to take a punt and grab one with a fat, naked, blue-eyed baby giggling on the cover.

"This is the bestseller," I say. "It's the definitive baby-name book."

"Oh?" She takes it from me with interest and flips through the pages.

"I know so many people who picked their babies' names from this one. Is it for yourself?"

"Yes," she says. "I'm getting a dog."

The customers are constant, relentless, an endless ream of questions. Are you open? Do you work here? Do you have this in stock? Do you have any more copies out back? Is anyone on the till? Is anyone serving? Is there anyone else that can serve me? How much is it? Where's the price? Why isn't there a price on it? Well, why isn't it on the front? Can I have a discount? Is this one in the offer? Can I have this one instead? Are you still open? Do you work here? Can you help me? Are you still open? Are you free?

I text Eli—*Reunited soon, pal!*—and he doesn't text back, and I realise he's probably dead to the world, fast asleep, all thoughts of me forgotten.

ROACH

The book of the year was *Flower Crowns of the Arctic*, like I gave a shit. Another mass-market paperback with a pseudo-smart title for book clubs full of Lauras to fawn over. It was about some girl's dead mother, and climate change. Laura had written a neat little recommendation card for it: *a sweeping novel about the way things can feel broken beyond repair, how things can feel ruined, and how we must heal before we can move on. Laura xox* Sentimental bullshit.

Eli, Kofi, and I had the weekend off to ease our transition back into day shifts but we were still expected to attend Sharona's team meeting on Sunday night to discuss strategy, which didn't seem fair to me.

In the staffroom, the booksellers slouched around with coffees, dishevelled with fatigue. Eli had bruise-coloured bags under his eyes, his skin the sallow sour-milk tint of too many days without sunlight. He was standing next to Laura, who was sitting on one of the cafeteria tables and swinging her legs, delighted to be back in the glow of his mediocre presence.

"Hi Laura," I said.

With a reproachful glare, she offered a cold hello before returning her attention to Eli. She looked sweet and small, a schoolgirl kicking her heels and flirting with a Chad. In that moment, I saw Eli as captain of the football team, and Laura as a bubble-gum-chewing cheerleader. She didn't care about me. She didn't care how much work I had put into my section, or into our friendship, or how much time I'd spent on the project that would ultimately bring us together. A rising tide of anger flooded through me, and I snapped.

"Hey Laura, I have a question for you. Why did Sharona get rid of my section?"

Her cheeks went the colour of freshly slapped skin, stinging red, hot with the embers of shame, and she laughed a hollow, exasperated laugh. "Are you serious? How should I know?"

"Hey, we've been over this," said Eli, ever the mediator, ever the voice of reason, the lone diplomat, parting a sea of hysteria to home in on the most logical conclusion. "It was nothing to do with Laura."

"I don't believe you," I said to him, although I was looking at Laura. "We've always had a True Crime section. It doesn't make any sense to get rid of it."

"No one buys it," Laura said, pulling her tobacco from her handbag. "*You* don't even buy it. You just order in the books under fake names and read them in the staffroom."

She held the plastic pouch of tobacco up to Eli, and he recognised the smoker's universal sign for an exit. He nodded and reached for his jacket.

"Don't take it personally," he said. "It's not like we've stopped selling the books, they're all still here."

"But it was *my* section," I said. "I've been taking care of it for years and years."

"Thing is," he said, "it was never actually *yours*, was it?"

He offered a smug smile, and they stepped out on to the roof together. My conversation cigarettes were in my bag, but I found I couldn't move. As the other booksellers arrived, I remained in my seat, gripping *The Stranger Beside Me* in both hands, but failing to crack it open, frozen rigid with the injustice of it all.

Sharona liked to speak, and in that meeting she spoke. She had high expectations of *Flower Crowns of the Arctic*, and even higher expectations of her team's ability to sell it. She had made a chart to track how many copies each bookseller sold each day, and there were gold star stickers and goofy prizes and all sorts of nonsense to incentivise us to sell, sell, sell.

"We're in a position to create bestsellers, okay?" she said. "We trust head office to choose good titles; our customers trust us to recommend good books. We should be able to recommend *Flower Crowns of the Arctic* to every single person who walks through those doors. We should be able to make it fly. I want everyone to focus on it."

"And—one more thing, guys." Eli leaned forward as he took command of the room. "If you haven't already, can you please RSVP for the Christmas party and let us know if you're bringing a plus one? Partners are totally welcome, and it's a really nice chance to get to know each other a little better."

I swallowed a smirk at the thought of Brodie and Sam at a poncy bookseller party. Us, with our edgy Rock 'n' roll swagger. Sam, in his cracked leather jacket, swigging from a hip flask of Jäger. We'd blow their minds.

"Well, that's all," said Sharona. "Cheers, guys. Let's smash it."

The others began to pull on their coats and check their phones, chatting and making vague noises about going for a drink. Laura slipped straight out the door, a little light-footed fox sliding between garden fences.

"Roach, hang on a sec. I'd like a word." Sharona came over and sat on the cafeteria table opposite my armchair. Over the weeks since I'd last seen her, Christmas was taking its toll. Her face looked lined, her eyes puffy, and she smelled faintly of cigarettes and tiger balm.

"Eli tells me you're upset about the True Crime section," she said, turning her cup in her hands. "I wanted to tell you myself, but you were late into work that day. I'm really sorry you didn't hear about it from me."

Violence simmered inside me and I clenched and released my fists.

"I'm giving you the chance to talk your feelings through," she said. "Don't you want to take it?"

"It's just not fair," I said, and I sounded whiny and I hated myself for it, but I couldn't help myself either. "That's all I have to say. It's not fair."

"Look. We needed the space, and it was the most logical section to break apart. And I will say, this isn't actually up for debate." Her voice was calm, but her eyes were sharp. "It's been done, and that's that. It's not something I'm interested in revisiting before Christmas. And Roach, listen. I don't know what the story is between you and Laura, but it ends here, okay? She's asked for a transfer, but I'm not going to let you push her out. The night shifts were meant to give you both some space, but if you don't simmer down, I'll have *you* removed and sent to another shop. Is that clear?"

"But it's not my fault! I've never done anything to her, she's just got it in for me. She's nice to everyone else and looks right through me like I'm not even there."

"The changes to the shop floor have nothing to do with Laura, Roach. *Nothing* to do with her. It was my call to make, not Laura's. Do you understand?"

I glared at her. She was underestimating me, underestimating my power.

"I know you're disappointed," she said, her voice softening. "But this isn't the way we do things. We're still stocking the books, we're just rethinking how we present them, the context that we put them in. Okay? It's all about context."

"Can I go now?" I asked. She held my gaze for a few seconds, and I felt like a germ under a microscope. I wondered what she was thinking.

"You can go," she said, and there was the faint trace of disappointment on her face.

⁂

Day shifts were hell once I'd grown accustomed to the gentle silence of the night. The constant stream of normies with their inane questions was like a form of psychic torture. I couldn't think, couldn't focus on anything else. A woman with spit in the corners of her mouth threatened to get me fired when I asked her to please be quiet and let me think while chasing her missing order. A man who smelled like burned hair tried to negotiate a hefty discount on an expensive coffee-table book and reacted badly when I said no.

"Your shop's a rip-off," he snapped.

"It's not *my* shop," I replied.

I thought a lot about death. Not in a misanthropic way—I didn't dream of killing customers specifically—but I did think a lot about the grace of God, so to speak, and took comfort in the thought that one day all these horrendous people would be dead, and that their cruelties wouldn't save them.

On my long and lonely walks to and from the shop, shrouded in darkness, I listened to chatty murder podcasts and felt myself relax. My jaw unclenched and the tension in my shoulders lifted. Slipping on my headphones and spending half an hour steeped in their honeyed voices was like sliding into a hot bath, and I started work each day with a funereal determination, humbled and soothed by thoughts of death. The great leveller.

If dark ruminations were carrying me through to Christmas, it was the glitter of novelty that carried Laura. She was in her element. While she looked pretty rough, her shine tarnished by the gruelling workday, she loved to strut through the crowd, wearing antlers one day, a Santa hat the next, offering a plastic tub of Quality Street or a plate of mince pies to customers. She was sparkly and sweet as she squeezed between shoppers with a cheerful indifference to their moods, wishing people a merry Christmas, cooing over babies in their prams, asking children if they had been naughty or nice with the kind of energy and enthusiasm usually reserved for primary school teachers and Blue Peter presenters. If she was in the middle of dealing with a customer enquiry and another tried to grab her attention, she asked them to follow her as she made her way from one section to the next. She weaved through the shop with a queue of customers in her wake, like Mother Goose, and she made them laugh and always managed to add something extra to their baskets: a half-price paperback for themselves, a new thriller for their mother, a Secret Santa gift for a coworker, a toy telescope or glow-in-the-dark stars for their niblings.

Laura had this way about her, an earnest and lighthearted way of carrying herself that customers just seemed to like. She was trustworthy. She was kind. She listened to what people had to say and was able to match their mood, match their energy. She found a way to recommend the book of the month to every single customer as though, out of all the many thousands of books in the bookshop, *Flower Crowns of the Arctic* just so happened to be the one that was written especially for them. The perfect fit, Cinderella's glass slipper.

"I've never seen anything like it," Sharona said as Laura sold her tenth copy of *Flower Crowns of the Arctic* that day.

"She could sell a pair of boots to a dead man," Eli replied, slapping the till drawer closed and tearing off the receipt. A puzzled expression crossed his face. "Is that the right expression?"

Customers didn't trust me in the same way they trusted Laura. When I tried to be enthusiastic, I sounded insincere, and when I tried to be myself, they recoiled. Customers were sharper with me, blunter, less forgiving. And when I tried to sell the book of the month, they listened with doubt shining in their eyes, like they could tell that I hadn't read it for myself and that I didn't really know what it was about. When I recommended it, it was always as an afterthought, along the same lines as "Would you like fries with that?"

I was so accustomed to rejection that on the rare occasion the damn thing piqued a customer's interest, I would more often than not absently replace the book on the stack instead of scanning it.

"Don't think that you don't have to try because Laura's filling our sales quota," Sharona said to us one morning during a briefing. "She's setting the precedent. You should all be trying to match her. If every single person on shift sold even half of what she sells, we'd be number one in the division."

When I finished work, I was often too tired to trek to Ilford to see Sam, and I wasn't ready for him to meet the full force of Jackie, although I knew time was running out on that front. Instead, when I got home at night, I'd switch the oven on and stand at the counter in a trance, mechanically chopping salad for Bleep while a frozen pizza baked just long enough for the cheese to melt, and then I'd take it to my room, dump Bleep's vegetables into his bowl, and crawl into bed, into stinking sheets that smelled like dirty knickers and last night's oven pizza, and I'd lie there and chew on slices of rapidly congealing pizza, listening to the distant bustle and jeers from the bar downstairs until I fell asleep, when I'd dream of a fetid summer heat, a killer on the loose, and five women walking through dark and silent streets, walking straight into the mouth of the lion.

LAURA

"It's like a margarita, but Vegas-style," I say, chopping limes into wedges and squeezing the juice into a scratched plastic Fosters jug that I'd stolen from the Walthamstow dog track the summer before it closed down.

"What does Vegas-style mean?"

"Big and cheap."

"A poor imitation of the real thing, then," Eli says as I mix a quarter bottle of tequila and three frosty bottles of Corona into the jug of lime juice. I top it up with Sprite and ice.

"It's nice, I swear," I say, stirring it with a wooden chopstick. "You're gonna love it."

He fiddles around with the Bluetooth speaker on the fridge and puts on a Spotify playlist of '90s grunge, then starts rolling a pair of cigarettes.

"Where's Lydia tonight?" I ask, light and casual, checking my reflection in the back of a spoon. I'm trying out an old liquid lipstick called Unicorn Horn. It's the kind of David Hockney blue of an LA swimming pool, and I bought it when unusual lip colours were still cool. I could tell as soon as I'd opened the front door that Eli hated it but there's no casual way to back down from a bold lip unless you're going to eat or fuck.

"Dinner with her family," he says, passing me a rollie and accepting a Mason jar of cloudy yellow cocktail in return. It spits silver bubbles into the air. I'd ordered Mason jars from Amazon in 2014, before they were everywhere. Now my glassware is as passé as my lipstick.

"Why didn't you go?"

He squints, searching for the right words. "I'd just get in the way. Her sister got engaged and . . . you know what women are like."

He lights his cigarette with a green plastic lighter and passes it to me. Although he's licked the gum strip of a thousand cigarettes that I've smoked, there's something oddly intimate about the dampness of the filter as I take a drag of mine.

"What are women like?" I ask, letting smoke drift from my mouth for a few seconds before huffing it away.

"Oh no, I'm not falling for that. I spend enough time with Sharona to recognise a trap when I see one," he replies, with a grin.

After two jugs of my Vegas-style margarita, Eli borrows my old bike and cycles to the new hipster bar on the high street for two rounds of sriracha cauliflower hot wings with vegan blue cheese dressing to go. I'm tipsy already, tipsy enough to wipe off my lipstick and repaint my lips a bitten, sheer raspberry pink. I tell people it's the perfect my-lips-but-better shade but it's actually a perfect match for my nipples.

When Eli gets back with the steaming cardboard containers, he nods towards my face. "You ditched the weird lipstick."

"Well, we're gonna eat," I say.

We sit on the living room floor, legs akimbo, the cardboard containers between us on the carpet. Eli picks up a chunk of battered cauliflower and dips it into a tub of buffalo sauce. I lean forward and reach for a piece, and our fingertips touch as he double-dips his wing.

I'm drunk already, but I need these late nights, need an artificial way to unwind. It's dark when I leave for work in the mornings, and it's dark when my shifts end. My days are spread with navy skies and a damp chill in the air that makes my knees ache. Everything aches, every bone and every muscle in my body aches. My head aches from dehydration because there's never time to drink water and I'm always hungover, and my stomach aches because I work through my lunch breaks. My arms are sore from moving totes and pushing trolleys, from carrying stacks of books, from stretching to reach the top shelves. My legs burn from running up and down the stairs because it's quicker than waiting for the lift, my feet pulse with pain, and when I close my eyes, all I can hear is the tinny refrain of Wham!, Wizzard, and Slade playing on repeat inside my head, and the incessant chorus of customers, of "Excuse me?" and "Does anyone work here?" and "Is anyone on the till?" and "Do you work here?" and "Well, you should get more staff" and so on and so on and so on.

Eli is tipsy and rambling, talking at length about Charles Bukowski, and I listen, mouth full, content to let his monologue wash over me. I'm a piece of glass, and he is the sea, and his chatter smooths my edges, makes me soft.

"It's like, he was a fucking good writer," he says, licking hot sauce from his fingertips and taking a covert look at my breasts through the thin grey cotton of my T-shirt, "but he was also an abusive alcoholic."

Grease etches the Mason jars with the loops and whorls of our fingerprints. I rotate the glass in my hands and lick the sting of chili from my lips.

"No, he wasn't," I say.

"Trust me, Lau," Eli says, chewing a piece of sticky beer-battered cauliflower with his mouth open. "He was vile. No fucking doubt."

"No, I mean he wasn't a good writer."

"*What?* Oh, fuck off. You're just saying that 'cause everyone says that. I bet you've only read *Post Office.* You really need to read *Factotum.* Or even some of his poetry. I'll lend you some—I have loads of it back at my flat."

Actually, I want to say, *I've read pretty much everything Bukowski has ever written. Even a collection of his fucking letters. Actually*, I want to say, *I went out of my way to read everything I could find by Charles Bukowski, and none of it made a difference because I never told you, and you picked Lydia instead of me anyway, and now it's too late.*

"I just don't care for Bukowski," I say, and I remember the time he'd read me a Bukowski poem about bluebirds and hearts and how much I'd hated it.

"You need to read more of his poetry," Eli says with a dull kind of authority. "I'll order the big collection into the shop tomorrow."

I pull a packet of straights from my hiding place under the sofa and light one. Eli wipes his fingers on his T-shirt and reaches greedily for the pack, but I jam it back under the sofa.

"What gives? Let me have one."

"Roll one if you're that desperate."

"Why are you being weird?"

"I'm *not* being weird."

"You're being weird," he says, forcing his hand beneath the settee to retrieve the pack of Marlboros. He puts one in his mouth, but I tuck the green lighter into my back pocket.

"I'm absolutely not being weird in any way, shape, or form," I say and then I lean forward and press my hand over his T-shirt, over the approximate spot of the bluebird tattoo, and then he looks at me, and I look at him, and I pluck the cigarette from his mouth and kiss him on the lips.

As we kiss, music swells inside my head, but it's the tinny refrains of Wham!, Wizzard, and Slade on repeat on the shop speakers. His hand cupping my breast through my T-shirt is the incessant chorus of customers shouting "Excuse me?" and "Does anyone work here?" and his breathless "God, I just can't help myself with you," is the sound of a till drawer slamming, the phone ringing, the back doorbell buzzing.

"This is just for tonight, yeah?" he says, and the sound, the sound that he makes when I press the cherry of my burning cigarette into his stubbled cheek: that is a bluebird, that is poetry.

ROACH

On Friday night, alone in my room, I sucked down a can of Dark Fruits while the bleach worked its magic. I was concerned that the strong, swimming-pool stink of ammonia would be harmful to Bleep, so I opened the window to keep the fresh winter air circulating. My scalp tingled and burned, which felt like a bad sign, but sometimes you just have to trust the process.

Absorbed in an amateur YouTube documentary about Lee Frost, I lost track of time. When I rinsed my hair under the kitchen tap, it was more of a yellow-blonde, the colour of melted vanilla ice cream, with patches still tinged a light pink where the purple dye had failed to lift. As I ran my fingers through the lengths of my hair, the ends frayed and came away in my hands. Undeterred, I took a pair of scissors and snipped off all the straw, leaving me with a blonde jaw-length bob just like Laura. Blonde suited me. I snapped a photo and sent it to Sam. *Do blondes have more fun?*

U look like Myra Hindley, he said, which I knew to be a compliment.

Work Christmas party tomorrow, I said. *U wanna come? Maybe come to the pub after, meet my mum?*

The Christmas party was to be the evening that my fractured self would become whole again. Sam's Brodie and Spines' Roach were going to come together as one. It seemed like as good a time as any to bring my third self, Jackie's daughter Brogan, into the mix too.

At the crossroads where Brodie, Brogan, and Roach met, I needed to figure out what to wear. I'd never really been the kind of girl that wore pretty things. My own wardrobe was a mix of black jeans, black leggings, black T-shirts, and black hoodies, and so of course I turned my sartorial eye to Laura and conceded to one more creepy-crawl.

I turned to look at myself in the mirror, wrinkled my nose and tried to laugh like Laura, and the girl in the glass laughed at me, and she looked like she meant it.

LAURA

Everything hurts. My eyes are gluey, stuck together at the lashes as though I've been crying in my sleep, but of course I haven't slept. Rough tongue, teeth fuzzed, throat sharp with the ghost of vomit. The pain in my head is almost unbearable, and the night before is more of a feeling than a memory.

A deep-rooted shame creeps over me as I piece things together. Margaritas. Greasy fingers. A fight with Eli—but did we kiss? Yes, the desperate kiss of a late night. Fragments of a fight surface and fade. I remember feeling absolute bone-deep disgust, both with him and with myself. The pathetic predictability of it all, from the hardness of his cock to the hunger of his lips, his clawing hands raking my body. As we kissed, the rest of it happened in my head like a premonition: our desire swelling, the inevitable hard, fast fuck, a rushed climax, then emptiness. What's the point in any of it? Lust boiled over into loathing and I pulled the brakes, lost control of the car, crashed it.

I check my phone, and my stomach sinks when I see an email from my landlord.

Laura, it says. *As I'm sure you're aware . . . loyal tenant . . . average price in Walthamstow . . . no longer tenable . . . if you can't pay the going rate . . . one month's notice . . . sure you understand . . .*

Everything blurs into a kaleidoscope of misery. His brother must have tipped him off, made him realise that Walthamstow's stock had risen. I'm too hungover to feel anything but bitter regret. I should never have reached out to my landlord, should have just ignored the footsteps in the soil like I did the mice and the damp and the mould and the slugs.

Blue dawn fills the living room and I feel like I'm floating facedown in a swimming pool. I'm shivering, still a little drunk. I listen to Sufjan Stevens and watch the light change. The ceiling turns from blue to pink, and then from pink to gold.

I check the time. I'm meant to be on my way to the shop. Christmas party tonight, big night. Can't miss it. I try to make coffee, pour cold water over the spent grinds in the cafetière by mistake. No milk left. I try to get dressed, but I can't find anything, can't get myself organised—my tights are all dirty, I can only find one winter boot, one glove. I realise I'll need to bring my evening outfit into work with me, and the thought of assembling two outfits brings me to tears. I call the shop, but no answer. I call Sharona. No answer. I call my mother, going through the motions, pretending she might answer. The phone rings because the number was reassigned years ago, and I hang up before the spell can be broken, before a stranger answers and tells me to stop calling.

Every single member of staff will be on the rota for today, one of the busiest retail days of the year. There will be too many of us. It will be claustrophobic, stifling. We'll outnumber the customers, a thick but steady stream who'll grow angrier as the day progresses, flushed from long boozy lunches, afternoons at the pub, and the begrudging realisation that they still have shopping to do. Customers with time to kill, meandering past the bookshop, drawn to its glow, its seasonal opulence. Choosing last-minute gifts, spending money for the hell of it. Staring openly at my bum, looking down my top, asking for a smile, cracking the same tired jokes that every other customer cracks—'Does that mean it's free?" when the barcode doesn't scan—expecting you to laugh, expecting you to smile, expecting, asking, demanding, forgetting that you aren't there for a laugh, you don't work for tips, you don't work for them. Stewing in misanthropic thoughts, I sound more like Roach than myself.

Roach. The memory of her makes my stomach roil and my skin burn. Roach, sallow, sullen, a vampire, a leech, taking whatever she can from me, picking over my poetry, swallowing scraps of my past like a vulture, stealing whatever takes her fancy.

And Eli. Eli will be there too, with his tousled curls and sleepy eyes and dimples, following me around, squeezing past me, fingertips on my hips, a warm flat hand on the small of my back, breath on the nape of my neck, trying to pretend he isn't smelling my hair, my perfume, taking shy peeps at my breasts, as bad as the worst of the customers, leading me on, holding me at arm's length, keeping me sweet with breadcrumbs of attention, pulling back, always on the brink, never taking things further. But not anymore, I realise. That's fucked now, too.

Outside, a pale morning sun. It snowed overnight, and a few cottony scraps cling to the conifers. This would usually delight me, but London snow never lasts long. It's fleeting, dirty, not built to last.

I stand at the bus stop. Smoke drifts from a nearby chimney, fills the air with the biting bonfire smell of burning wood. A bus sails past, and I stay where I am until I'm ten minutes late to work. When I'm half an hour late, my phone rings and I watch Sharona's name flash on the screen, but I can't do it. I can't answer.

It's calm and quiet and the buses come and go.

⌀

They are scattered. Agata Matthams was cremated, her ashes taken home to Poland. Safa Gamble was buried in Ilford Cemetery, and Lana Brown was laid to rest near the family home in Bristol. Elsie Meadows and my mother shared the same fate in more ways than one, though.

Instead of going to work, I buy two poinsettias from Tesco Metro and take the bus to Lavender Hill, where the sky is the colour of milk and crows peck at the frozen ground. It takes me a while to find her. Some graves bear flowers, plants, or cuddly toys, but not this one. This one is stark, bare, unkempt.

I set a poinsettia on Elsie's grave, and use my door key to scrape the mushroom-coloured lichen from her epitaph—OUR LOVING MOTHER in a rough, weather-worn Copperplate. A scrap of poetry comes to me then. *Do not stand at my grave and weep, I am not there, I do not sleep.* I run my hand over the pockmarked granite, and a crescendo of sorrow beats down on me with the force of an autumn storm. I hunch forward and my knees press into the cold, hard dirt, and I cry for her, for Elsie, for this woman that I have never known, that I will never know, and that I have always known, and I cry for the grieving children represented in that simple, mournful epitaph. Grown now, perhaps even with children of their own.

Gathering myself together, I take the second poinsettia to my mother, and I feel much calmer, like I've cried myself out. I sit there for quite some time, not reading, not writing, not even thinking.

ROACH

It was a cold, miserable night. Dense traffic clogged Hoe Street, and a thin mean rain speckled the paving stones as I walked to Laura's flat. She was meant to be at work that day, but I still felt compelled to look for her in the face of every stranger that passed me on the pavement, in the steamed-up windows of the crowded pubs, on buses that stuttered their way through the traffic to the station. I knew she was meant to be at work because everyone was meant to be at work that day. Not me, though. Sharona had given me the day off. An unexpected boon, perhaps orchestrated to keep Laura and me apart.

I'd promised myself I'd stop creepy-crawling once night shifts were over, but needs must. The significance of the night was threefold: I was going to the Spines Christmas party as Roach, and Sam was meeting me there as Brodie. Afterwards, he was going to come back to the Mother Black Cap, where I lived as Brogan, to meet Jackie for the first time. That meant all three versions of myself—the bookseller, the daughter, and the girlfriend—were coming together as one. Faced with such an important evening ahead of me, I couldn't resist the siren call of Laura's wardrobe one last time to guide me through.

I hadn't told Jackie about any of this. I was operating on a need-to-know basis and her input wasn't necessary. She'd only work herself up, jump to conclusions, tell all the regulars, wear something outrageous, cause a scene. It was best to take her by surprise, force her to roll with the punches.

As I walked through the drizzle, I imagined what it would be like if Laura and I were getting ready for the Christmas party together. I'd bring a bottle of wine, she'd choose the music, and she'd look me over and take some umbrage with my outfit, curl her lip, and shake her head. She'd say something like, "No, absolutely not. You cannot wear that." Glass in one hand, she'd flip through her clothes rack and pluck something gorgeous from its hanger, maybe the black floor-length dress with the slit up the thigh, and hold it up to me with an infectious smile.

"Try this," she'd say, and even though I'd protest, she'd grin and say: "Trust me."

And I would, I would trust her. I'd try it on, embracing my transformation under her expert eye. A caterpillar unfurling her wings as a butterfly, I'd turn this way and that, and we'd both agree that I was born to wear that dress.

It felt so real, I could practically taste the velvety red wine flooding my tongue, smell her cloying rose perfume, feel the soft fabric of her dress against my skin. Deep in the throes of my fantasy, I let myself in. The kitchen light cast a golden rhombus across the dark hallway, but I thought nothing of it. I didn't have much time, so I headed straight for bedroom. That awful mildewy smell of rot hits me in the face like a damp flannel, and I open the window before focusing my attention on the clothes rail. I began flipping through the florals, polka dots, and stripes, just as Laura had done in my head. I imagined my hand was hers as I parted curtains of fabric, running my fingers over lace and silk, velvet and satin, until I found the perfect stretchy black dress, the slinky one with the scoop neck and thigh-high split. Tossing my coat to one side, I pulled off my hoodie, T-shirt, and jeans, then pulled on a pair of tights and slipped the dress over my head; Turning this way and that, I studied my reflection in the mirror, glowing at the thought of Sam's reaction. My hair still surprised me—a shock of yellow-blonde that made my face look oddly pink.

There was a cluster of whiteheads on my chin; I popped them like bubble wrap and then smeared the blood away with the back of my hand. I smoothed a fleshy cream on to my cheeks to flatten the colour of my face, and then smudged on some rouge to bring them back to life. It was like finger-painting, and I enjoyed layering the different powders and creams until I looked faintly monstrous. I jabbed a scabby mascara on to my eyelashes, painted my mouth with a jammy red lipstick that smelled like a funeral home. I stashed the lipstick in the pocket of my hoodie for touch-ups later.

She had a whole shelf of dusty glass perfume bottles, and I sprayed myself with an eau de toilette the colour of whiskey that made my eyes water. The bottle said Shalimar, and it was thick with grey dust.

I knew exactly which necklace I wanted. She kept it hidden away under her bed, forgotten in a box of sentimental keepsakes. I fished around for the wooden box, and tied the raw piece of amethyst around my throat. It felt cold against my skin, like it carried a chill with it, but I liked the way it looked. A chunk of purple ice, catching the light.

While I was down there, I folded up my clothes and stashed them under the bed, then turned my attention back to the mirror to admire the finished look. Tilting my hips, I fluffed my hair and tried to think like Laura, tried to step out of myself and think the way she would think. I scrutinised my lipstick, ran my hands down my body, from shoulders to hips, smoothing the fabric. Was this right for tonight, was it right for Brodie? I couldn't tell. Time was ticking on and I needed to get going, but indecision made me linger, made me turn back to her wardrobe and scan the hangers once more.

A burgundy velvet minidress caught my eye, and I had just lifted it from its hanger when I heard an alarming sound, the cascading sound of water rolling from a raised limb. The floor tilted beneath me and my fists clenched around the velvet dress as I strained to listen—and then, yes, my worst nightmare bloomed from the silence: a lone voice swelled from the bowels of the flat, a voice that sounded like poetry. Laura, it was Laura, and she was singing to herself, unselfconscious and alone, alone in the sanctity of her bathroom.

"Jesus died for somebody's sins but not miiiine."

I jammed my feet into my unlaced boots, grabbed my coat and bag, and closed the window. Then I ran without stopping, through the flat and out of the front door, into the night.

LAURA

Lorde serenades me as I fill the bath with hot water. I'd called Sharona as I'd left the cemetery, full of apologies and excuses. *I didn't realise*, I'd said. *I didn't set my alarm. I thought it was my day off. My phone battery died. I'm being kicked out of my flat. I'm a mess, I'm sorry, please forgive me.* She didn't sound like she believed me, and I wondered if Eli said anything about last night. Anything. Everything. Nothing. It doesn't matter. There wasn't much she could say in the face of so much bullshit, and she didn't seem willing to call my bluff.

"We'll talk about it tomorrow," she said, in a steely voice that suggested it wasn't over. Then she sighed, and her tone softened. "But look, I'm glad you're okay. I was really worried—you can't just not show up."

"I know," I said, in a small whisper. "I'm just feeling quite overwhelmed."

"We'll talk tomorrow," she said again. "You're still coming to the party tonight though, right?" Sharona isn't one to play the corporate game, but she likes to be seen surrounded by her team, all smiles and good times, at events like the Christmas party. She wasn't going to let me wriggle out of it.

"Of course," I'd said through gritted teeth. "Sure, of course. See you later."

Submerged in watermelon-scented bubbles, Lorde soothes me in her husky sad-girl way until the water grows cool and I realise I need to shake off this self-indulgent malaise if I'm going to make it to the party. A deluge of bubbly pink water rolls from my limbs as I heave myself up, and I trade Lorde for Patti Smith to reset my mood. Everything is going to be okay, I think.

Wrapped in a towel, I pad through the kitchen to my bedroom. The flat feels cold again, that familiar ghostly chill as though I've left a window open. I wonder if I should report it to my landlord, and then I remember, and it hits me all over again. An ache of bitter regret for what I've lost: my flat, my home, my space. Gone. There's a faint smell in the air, a fading perfume. I breathe in deeply and catch a ribbon of scent that almost reminds me of my mother, but as I breathe in again, it's already gone.

Getting ready feels like a chore, and nothing goes right. My signature scarlet lipstick, the one that makes me feel invincible, is nowhere to be seen, and I can't find my mother's amethyst necklace. I'd planned to wear it with a clingy purple dress. I never take it out of the wooden box under my bed, but then, I can't think when I'd last seen it either. Had I worn it on Halloween? Yes. No. I can't think.

I can only find one of my good high heels, and all the clean tights that I can find are the wrong denier, the wrong colour. I turn the bedroom upside down, but things are messy and out of control and my brain feels fried, so I make a snap decision and pivot to a wine velvet minidress that's fallen off its hanger and pooled on the bedroom floor. It skims my thighs, hugs the swell of my breasts. I pour myself a glass of Prosecco, swallow it, pour another, and take a fresh look at my reflection. With a little Prosecco buzz, I look acceptable. I find a pair of super thin black tights that are laddered but clean, and I pick a different lipstick, a deep red that matches my dress and brings out the honey of my hazel eyes.

There's nothing that can be done about the missing high heel. Fuck it. I jam a pair of black Converse on to my feet instead. It will look effortlessly edgy, I think. Chic, laissez-faire.

I glance into the hallway mirror as I put on my coat, and I look half-finished, half formed, half there.

ROACH

On the Central line, I felt dizzy, giddy, running through the city, a blonde girl going on an adventure in a sexy black dress. I fingered the amethyst around my throat. There was definitely something witchy about it, and I imagined the chunk of rock held some of Laura's power.

The Strand was gauche and festive, the roads lined with industrial fairy lights that blinked and twinkled against an indigo sky. I walked east, past the buzzing chain restaurants and brightly lit theatres. Central London felt like a foreign place that belonged to other people: tourists, yes, but also the rich, old-money Londoners, who strolled through the National Gallery and went to the opera in their designer coats and expensive scarves like they owned the place.

When I reached the shop, I lit a cigarette to keep myself busy while I waited for Sam. He was running late, and I was in the process of stubbing out my third cigarette when I saw her.

Laura was smoking a cigarette too, and she was wearing a leather jacket over the burgundy velvet minidress that I had also considered. Pausing in front of the hat shop next door, she checked her reflection in the dark window and tugged at the hem of her dress. It felt like I had picked it for her, and for a moment I watched her as she smoothed the velvet over her stomach, studying—or admiring?—the curve of her hips, her breasts, inspecting herself as though she were preparing to walk onstage. She wants to sleep with someone tonight, I thought.

Incongruously, she had Converse on her feet, and the casual trainers made her look oddly unfinished and less put together than me. I wished I could strike up a normal conversation with her, say something casual and chatty like, "Shouldn't you wear heels with a dress like that?," but when she finally turned and caught my eye, she did a double take. Her eyes skipped from my blonde hair to my necklace, and then to my dress, and then back to the necklace. She looked alarmed. I fingered the rock protectively, rubbed its craggy edges between my fingertips.

"You changed your hair," she said, an accusatory edge to her voice. She had turned pale; a visible sheen of sweat stippled her forehead.

"Purple fades really fast," I said, reaching with self-conscious fingers to touch the split, dried ends. "I got sick of dying it all the time."

She took another drag on her cigarette, and she looked shaken, almost unwell. I wondered if something had happened. A fight with Eli, perhaps, or a scrap of bad news.

"Nice necklace," she said, and I instinctively dropped my hand to cover it.

"My boyfriend gave it to me," I replied, pinning it to my heart.

"I have one just like it." She narrowed her eyes.

"Yeah?"

"Yeah."

I swallowed, kept my fingers clasped around the crystal to keep her from seeing it properly. I coughed, cleared my throat. "Are you waiting for someone?"

"Just finishing this." She held up the rollie, burned almost to the filter, and then turned away to take a final drag. I pretended to riffle through my bag while she dropped her dog-end and stamped the ember into the pavement.

"See you in there," I said, and she left without looking back.

LAURA

Inside, the white marble atrium glows like the wax of a burning candle. My hands shake as I take a glass of Prosecco from a table shrouded in white and glance around for an escape route. I need to get away from Roach as quickly as possible; I need to disappear into the party before she can latch on to me. Her appearance has knocked the breath from my lungs. Her terrible dye job, hair fried to a crisp blonde. The amethyst around her throat. Even her outfit looks familiar, like the dress I wore on Halloween. It can't be, though, it can't be the same dress. She's just fucking with me, doing it on purpose to ruffle my feathers.

"Is there anywhere I can smoke?" I ask the server, a bored redhead in a white shirt who looks indifferent to the festive glamour around her.

"Roof terrace," she says, popping a bottle of Prosecco with a well-practiced twist.

The shop is labyrinthine with winding staircases and unexpected nooks and crannies. Electric candles jump and flicker in jam jars balanced on bookshelves, tucked into displays. The air smells like spiced wine and new paper, dust and vanilla, sweat and expensive perfume. Booksellers in cocktail dresses and suits loom from the shadows with exaggerated laughter, alcohol warming their blood. I swallow a mouthful of my drink, which is on the cusp of room temperature and tastes foul.

The laughter rolls over me, taunts me, and although the occasional bookseller reaches out, touches my arm, taps me on the shoulder, grabs me for a hug, I keep on roaming, anxious and untethered, half avoiding Eli, half looking for Sharona, and dreading the thought of facing them, of dealing with their kind disappointment.

ROACH

I stood exactly where Laura had stood, and admired my reflection just as she had admired hers. My body didn't curve the way Laura's did, and my breasts didn't fill the dress in the same way hers would, but I liked what I saw regardless. In the reflection of the glass, the Christmas lights could almost be gas lanterns, and beneath my feet, the wet paving stones were printed with boot prints that could almost be those of Jack the Ripper or Sweeney Todd. There was a dark frisson in the air.

"All right? You look fit." Sam appeared behind me, snaking his arms around my waist. He was wearing the same clothes he always wore—leather jacket, death metal T-shirt, black jeans ripped at the knee, scuffed-up boots. "Almost didn't recognise you," he says, tugging on a tendril of blonde hair.

"Do you like it?"

"You look like Nancy Spungen," he said. "Never seen you all dolled up before."

"It's a big night," I replied with a little Brodie shrug.

We walked into the shop and were greeted by a bookseller who was hovering by the door with a clipboard. He was the kind of posh goof who wore chinos, stood behind the till all day, and recommended *Moby Dick* to every customer. A normie with a private education, bookselling just a pit stop before a job in publishing.

"Hello, darling, what's your name?"

Fuck. "Roach," I said through gritted teeth. "It's um. It's Brodie Roach."

His easy smile faded into a frown of concentration as he scanned the list of names. "Brodie, Brodie . . . I'm so sorry, are you a Spines bookseller? Which branch?"

"Walthamstow," I said.

"Ah, they've let you out for the night, have they?" he quipped, running a blunt finger down the page, flipping over to the next with a flourish.

"Ha," I said, in lieu of laughter. Sweat prickled across my brow and I glanced at Sam. Hands deep in the pockets of his jeans, he had wandered deeper into the atrium, his face turned towards the grand marble staircase with a look of polite curiosity as he studied a ten-foot fir tree that twinkled with gold fairy lights, branches tied with red velvet bows.

"Look for Brogan," I hissed. "I go by Brodie, but it's Brogan."

"Aha!" he said, an empty performance of triumph. "Well, that will be it, then." He flipped back to the first page and starting the whole process again. Behind me, a queue had formed. "Brogan . . . Brogan . . . Brogan . . ."

Sam was walking towards us, confusion etched across his face. I willed the posh freak to stop repeating my name.

"What's the problem?" Sam asked.

"Bro—aha! There you are. Plus one." He ticked my name, my real name, off his list. "In you go, do feel free to have a wonder and enjoy yourselves. Cocktails on the rooftop terrace, canapés in the gallery, and the café has wine, beer, and soft drinks."

"Fabulous," I said, in clipped, cool voice, in Laura's voice, and I snatched the lapel of Sam's leather jacket and dragged him towards the marble staircase.

"Ah, they've let you out for the night, have they?" I heard the bookseller croon to the girl in line behind me.

LAURA

I feel calmer as I put some distance between myself and Roach. The rooftop terrace is bathed in a honey glow from strings of market lights. One of London's best-kept secrets, it hums with booksellers and the vibe is decadent, boozy, and relaxed. Over the years, I've attended many Christmas parties here, smoked many cigarettes, swallowed many free cocktails. Kissed more than one bookseller, cloaked in the anonymity of the shadows.

I weave my way between guests and spiky yuccas in square planters towards the bar. Space heaters warm the chilly evening air, and women in evening dresses wear men's jackets draped over their bare shoulders. Familiar faces bloom from the crowd, and while I exchange sporadic greetings with the odd bookseller I recognise from other shops, I don't let anyone slow me down.

The bar is lined with rows of pre-poured Prosecco and bottles of beer, but there's a chalkboard of cocktails on offer too. I scan the menu, can't decide what I want. Something strong.

"What's that?" I ask the stranger beside me, a dark-haired man with the rosy cheeks of an overgrown schoolboy. He holds a tumbler of amber whiskey up to the light. It glows like a lantern, punctuated with a curl of orange peel, and there's a silt of un-mixed sugar at the bottom of the glass.

"Old Fashioned," he says, in a rich baritone. His eyes dart to my décolletage as he turns away.

I order an Old Fashioned from the bartender, and the glass feels solid and heavy in my hand. Prim little champagne flutes are for girls, I think. I'm drinking whiskey tonight.

The sound of my name slices through the ambient noise of the party and floods me with a rush of nerves, but it's only Noor. She pushes through the crowd towards me, in a little black dress and too much gold highlighter, a long piece of black leather cord wrapped several times around her throat.

"Laura!" She throws her arms around my neck in a loose hug that suggests more than one visit to the open bar already. "I didn't think you were coming! What happened to you today?"

"Oh, yeah—there was a mix-up." I swallow a mouthful of my drink with a wince.

"Oh no," she says, covering her mouth with both hands. She looks mortified on my behalf. "Yeah, Sharona was *really* pissed. We've been calling you all day."

"My phone's broken," I say. The lie comes naturally. "Don't worry, it was an innocent mistake. Everything's fine, she knows I'm here."

Noor grabs a Prosecco from the bar, and then takes my hand and leads me through the crowd to find the rest of our team. Anxious butterflies flutter in my belly, and I kill them with a sweet swallow of whiskey.

"Look at you, you look gorgeous," Sharona says to Noor, and then she catches my eye and the warmth behind her eyes chills, just a little. "Laura—well, you look lovely too." I must look terrified, because she reaches over and squeezes my arm. "Don't look at me like that. I'm just glad you're okay."

"Roach!" Noor squeals. "Your *hair*!"

We turn around and the little rat is right behind me. A blaze of rage burns in my belly. She's clutching an empty champagne flute and holding hands with a rough-looking man in a leather biker jacket. The amethyst around her neck catches the light, and I blink at the familiar crags and cracks. It looks so much like mine, like my mother's. Had I taken it into work? Had I worn it one day, and lost it? No. I'd never wear it to work. On the other hand, you can buy raw amethyst like that anywhere. Every crystal shop sells necklaces just like it. Sharona has one in citrine.

It's uncanny, though, uncanny. I want to ask her about it again, see if she sticks to the same story in front of her boyfriend, but the look of disappointment on Sharona's face when she first saw me is enough to keep me meek, and I can't bear the thought of causing a scene. I'm too tipsy to let it go entirely, though.

"This your boyfriend, then?" I say, cocking my head at the stranger beside her.

"Yeah, this is Sam," she says, and he says hello and they all say hello back and I narrow my eyes.

"You have good taste," I say to him, and I'm referring to the necklace, but he grins and Roach glows and that's my mother's fucking necklace, I'm sure of it. A chilling image of Roach in my space, Roach going through my things, my books, my clothes, helping herself to my necklace. Impossible, but I feel like the party is closing in on me and a sense of panic rising in my chest.

"Have you guys met Charlie?" Sharona asks, and I realise the woman beside her with black-framed glasses and a blue-black pixie cut is not a bookseller from another shop but her girlfriend, and the man with the gun-metal-grey handlebar moustache laughing with Martin must be his husband, and that means—I crane my neck, and yes, there they are, Eli and Lydia.

Red alert.

She is small and pretty, with an upturned nose and a face that breaks into an easy genuine smile. She's wearing an expensive-looking leather

314

jacket, a bohemian maxi-dress and chunky boots. A delicate gold chain twinkles around her neck. Elegant and cool, with a tumble of beachy brunette curls, she accepts a glass of Prosecco from Eli's outstretched hand. It's strange to finally see her in the flesh, and I flinch at the memory of my drunken fumbling thumbs pressing the like button one of her old Instagram photos. I wonder if she even noticed. She pops on to tiptoes to deliver a thank-you kiss, and I see the angry bubble of a blister on Eli's pale white cheek. A fresh wave of shame creeps over me.

"I'll go to the bar, shall I?" Sharona says to Charlie.

I knock back my drink in one sharp sweet swallow, steeling myself. Eli turns as Sharona squeezes past him and catches my eye. He looks like he's going to ignore me, but then thinks better of it. Instead, he steers Lydia towards me.

"Lydia, this is Laura," he says, wrapping a comfortable—protective? possessive?—arm around her waist. "Laura, this is—"

"Lydia," I say.

"Nice to meet you." She raises her glass in my direction, a quick and elegant greeting teamed with a polite smile, like she has no idea who I am. She smells clean and citrussy, and her makeup is barely there and perfect. I can't breathe.

Sharona and Charlie reappear with a bunch of drinks gripped precariously in their hands. Sharona passes two glasses of Prosecco to Roach and Sam, and I hold my hand out expectantly, but she turns to ask Lydia about her short-story collection. They chat with ease, like old friends, and I stand there feeling foolish with my empty glass, the coarse grit of sugar catching between my teeth. Eli studiously avoids catching my eye.

"You all right?" I say to him, but the words sound stiff, pointed and mean.

"Yep," he replies, jaw tight. "You good?"

Roach and her creepy boyfriend just stand there, emanating a heavy, awkward silence, listening but never saying anything, never contributing.

Her presence is like a stone around my neck, like the fucking amethyst around hers, and I resent her more and more the longer she stands there, until finally I can't bear it any longer.

"Come with me to the bar," I say to Eli. It isn't a question and I don't wait for his response, just carve a path through the party and find a quiet spot on the other side of the terrace. I'm riffling through my clutch bag for a cigarette when he appears behind me.

"Can we talk?"

"What's there left to say?" he replies with a forced nonchalance, accepting one of my cigarettes. He picks up a candle from a nearby table to light it, and his hair falls over his eyes as he bows his head to dip the tip into the flame.

"Look, I'm not really sure what happened last night," I begin.

"Makes a change," he says, with a cold expression on his face, placing the candle back onto the table without offering me a light.

"But you kissed me," I say, blinking back tears.

"*You* kissed *me*," he says, and it comes out like a hiss, like he's unable to contain a sudden rush of anger. "I just kissed you back. And then you attacked me—do you at least remember that?"

I do remember that. The violence of it overwhelms me. I raise my hand as though to reach for his cheek, think better of it. I wish we weren't here. I wish we were anywhere but here.

"I'm sorry."

"I don't fucking get it, mate," he says.

"*Mate*. Don't call me *mate*."

He exhales a long stream of smoke into the sky and runs his free hand through his hair, tousling his curls.

"Look, let's just draw a line under the whole thing," he says, eyes sweeping over the party, at the faces in the crowd, as though he's afraid we're being watched. "We both regret it, we're both sorry. Let's just leave it there."

"I don't want to *leave it there*, I want to talk about it."

"What, like we did last time?" he says with a hollow laugh, stubbing his cigarette out into the soil of a nearby yucca.

He's referring to that first, awful kiss, the way I ghosted him afterwards, ignored his texts, moved shops to avoid him. Shame blooms within me, and I touch the corners of my eyes with my fingertips to stop myself from crying.

"I don't really remember much about that either," I admit.

A pained expression crosses his face, and his Adam's apple bobs as he swallows.

"Right," he says. "Well. It's *old news*, right? *Yesterday's weather.*"

I remembered saying that to him, all bullshit and bravado back in October, as we'd walked home from the Nib. That feels like a lifetime ago. I blink back tears.

"I didn't mean that," I say, and my voice cracks.

"I'm with Lydia, and I love her. I really love her. I think me and you—we just need to take a step back, cool off. Okay?" Something softens in his face. "The drinking doesn't help," he says, with the lightness of someone who knows they're delivering a message of significant weight.

"I'm just really sorry, okay?" Hot tears spill down my cheeks, and I cover my face with my hands. "I don't know what I'm doing."

"Laura—" he says, and he reaches for me.

"I need a minute," I gasp, and I stagger a little as I push through the crowd of booksellers and publicists, editors, and writers, all toothsome laughter and greasy fingers clutching black napkins of miso aubergine vol-au-vents and truffle arancini.

I grab another drink and swallow it, then slip through the crowd, eyes averted, to the bathroom. Locked in a stall, I press loo roll into the corners of my eyes to blot away my tears, stop them from falling in earnest. Head pressed against the cool metro-tiled wall, I think about how many times

I've found myself here on a night out, alone in a bathroom stall either crying or vomiting or both.

Is it too early for a French exit to be chic? I've made an appearance, had a row, and cried in public. Isn't that enough? I check the price of an Uber from here—too much, way too much—and think about getting another drink instead, or finding someone else to talk to, but everyone here hates me, and I'm already too tipsy to make a sensible choice, so I flush the loo and wash my hands and head straight back into the hell of my own making.

Back on the terrace, the cold air slaps me and alcohol burns in my blood. Roach is standing in my place, next to Eli, and he's smiling down at her, his face a mask of tender encouragement as she talks. Her dress really does remind me of the old scoop-necked Elvira dress I wore on Halloween, although she doesn't have the curves to fill hers the way I filled mine. Is it my dress? I know it can't be, but an irrational hatred is bubbling through my veins. My vision blurs, and her image fans into a monstrous tryptic, three faces, like the three-headed hound that guards the entrance to Hades.

As I rejoin the group, I catch a look of concern flash across Sharona's face. Lydia is talking and everyone has turned towards her, their petalled faces orientated to the sun.

"I've been doing so much grim research for my novel," she says. "I'm the girl at the party that everyone's, like, oh my God, don't talk to her, all she wants to talk about is cold cases and autopsies." She laughs a pretty laugh, and Roach beams with rapt attention and Eli smiles, his face radiating love.

"Oh, for God's sake," I say, and it comes out too loud and too belligerent to be anything other than a sneer.

Lydia blinks. She looks up at Eli through perfect lashes, her jawline sharp and lips plump, her skin shining with a natural pearly glow. She looks fresh and sweet and so untroubled, so untouched, so unbothered by the weight of the world that a spiteful streak of anger bolstered by booze flares in me and I have to ruin her.

"My mother was murdered by a serial killer," I say in a rush of blurred words. "How do you think it makes me feel to see you stand there and joke about autopsies? She was strangled to death and she pissed herself as she died. Is that the kind of thing you like to hear? How does that make you feel, you stupid fucking bitch?"

A shell-shocked silence from the surrounding partygoers. A ringing in my ears.

"Laura—" says Sharona, eyes wide.

"Fuck the lotta you," I say, and my tongue is thick and my words curdle in my mouth as I turn and push my way through the crowd, and my heart thumps and sweat trickles down my back, and then another drink appears in my hand. I swallow it and the world is off-kilter, spinning, spinning, spinning and the whole evening is one massive fucking cock-up.

I drift in and out of the moment as things come into sharp focus and then decline. Eli sneers, his arm around Lydia, hot breath against her cheek, the smell of his sweat and her perfume mingling in the air. Fade to black, lights up, and Sharona, scowling as she tries to give me water that I refuse, lips pursed against her insistent glass. A man with thick, wiry eyebrows talks to me about Proust, and I burp abruptly in his face, slopping Prosecco down myself, surprised to see I'm not wearing the dress I thought I was wearing—didn't I put on the long black one, the tight Elvira one, the one with the slit? Is my lipstick okay? The print on the glass is the wrong colour, a muted dark red instead of bold scarlet. I reach for my throat, and my amethyst necklace is missing.

Someone asks me to repeat myself, reassurance that I'm okay, meandering into the night, still clutching my Prosecco glass. Someone flagging a cab and we get inside together, and I keep babbling about a half bottle of

Prosecco in my fridge, and then I'm falling asleep in the back, the lights of London gliding over my face while I sit outside of myself, watching this girl, asleep with her mouth open, her face plain, and ugly, and she's utterly alone, alone, alone, and beside her there is

there is

there is

Roach.

ROACH

Sam and I watched Laura stagger around the party, getting increasingly wasted and making a fool of herself, spilling drinks, snapping and being unpleasant to people, sharing strange and intimate details about her mother's death, details that I hadn't seen anywhere else. Details that I could use. It was like she'd twisted a kaleidoscope, and the fragments of our shared experience had morphed and separated. I was no longer thinking about what we had in common, but instead what separated us. What I could learn from her, if only she'd let me in.

"She's smashed," Sam muttered under his breath, amused by the whole spectacle.

Sharona was watching too, but her expression was forlorn. She had already tried to coax her into sitting down, into drinking some water, into calling a cab, but Little Miss Laura Bunting wasn't in the mood to follow instructions.

"I'm going to have to take her home," Sharona said at last, knocking back the last of her Prosecco.

"Doesn't she live near the shop, though?" Charlie said, face pinched into a grimace. "That's bloody miles away, Shaz. Isn't there anyone who lives a bit closer that can take her?"

Eli glanced at Lydia with the reproachful eyes of a kicked dog, and she returned his look with a hard, glassy glare. He dropped his face and said nothing.

"Just stick her in a cab, then," Charlie said. "She's an adult, she'll be fine."

Charlie and Lydia both seemed to see through Laura's Pollyanna veneer, which I found curious. Her true nature—her insincerity, her alcoholism, her vanity, her attention-seeking—was really shining through. In fact, Laura's true self was shining so brightly, Kofi and Noor had vanished into the crowd, washed their hands clean of her, and Martin and Barry and their respective partners had disappeared too.

"Nah," Sharona said, brows knitted together in a frown. "Someone needs to make sure she gets home okay."

"I can take her," I said. "I live in Walthamstow. It isn't a big deal."

Sharona looked unsure, but the silence of her indecision was broken by the jarring crash of smashing glass. Laura had bumped into a server and sent an entire tray of champagne flutes hurtling on to the concrete floor. Broken glass and bubbles fizzed around her feet.

"Whoops," she said, with a belligerent sneer, swaying on the spot.

⁓

Sam sat in the front and plugged in his headphones, glad for an excuse to leave the party early. Laura plonked herself in the backseat behind the driver, took off her beret, and fluffed her dishevelled hair. Eyeliner bruised her eye sockets. She unlaced her wet, Prosecco-soaked Converse and kicked them off, and I was greeted by a brief, sharp smell of feet before she opened her window and closed her eyes.

As we drove through London, Christmas lights illuminated her face in gold and green and pink as she slipped in and out of consciousness.

"Fee if she's sick," the driver said, eyeing her in the rearview mirror.

"She's not going to be sick," I said, churlish. I knew the situation called for me to distract him from the state she was in but unfortunately charisma had never really been my strong point.

"If she's sick, I can't work. If she's sick, I have to drive all the way home to clean up."

"She's fine," I snapped.

I felt less confident about that as we headed north. Laura's face had turned a sour, pale colour, her mouth a slash of feathered lipstick that leaked a thin trail of drool on to her velvet dress. She looked like shit. She looked half-dead.

The driver hit the brakes at an unexpected red light, and she jerked awake. "Where'm I?" she croaked, wiping her mouth with the back of her hand and gazing around the interior of the car in a daze.

"Nearly home," I said in a sing-song voice.

"Where?"

"Nearly home," I said again. Even though I had been tipping my Prosecco out all evening, I felt a giddy pleasure, a second-hand tipsiness. Lydia's talk of autopsies at the party was the perfect social lubricant for a situation like this. Laura would surely let her guard down and jump at the chance to really speak her mind, her inhibitions obliterated by whiskey cocktails. I'd say something like "Lydia's just one of those fair-weather true crime fans. It's all just a fantasy to her, isn't it? She can't handle it when it's real," and Laura would look at me, wide-eyed, and say, "My God, you're so right."

I thought perhaps I'd get the chance to tell her about my project. I was convinced I'd be able to win her over with the right pitch. There was an insatiable hunger for fresh true crime content, and someone was bound to cover the Stow Strangler in more detail eventually. Wouldn't she rather be part of the narrative?

As we pulled up in front of Laura's flat, I realised I'd been so focused on getting her here in one piece that I'd completely forgotten to deal with Sam. He opened the passenger-side door, oblivious as he shrugged off his unclipped seatbelt.

"No, no, you should take the cab home," I said in a panic, shooing him back into the car.

"What? Why?"

"This is my chance," I said in a rushed, whispered whine. "Please, I need to get her alone, ask her about you-know-what. She won't open up with you there."

"But—she's barely conscious," he said, eyes flicking to where Laura stood, leaning against her garden wall with her head bowed. "And I thought I was meant to be coming back to yours—meeting your mum and all that?"

"I'll text you later," I said, kissing him on the chin and then pushing the car door closed, forcing him to slide back into the passenger seat. The expression on his face was clouded with confusion, but I didn't have time to feel guilty. I'd been excited to show him off to the other booksellers, but the purpose of the night had changed, my focus shifted. I didn't give him a second glance as I slammed the cab door and bustled up to Laura's front door.

I put an arm around her shoulders and guided her up the cracked garden path as the car drove away. As we approached the front step, a fox darted from the shadows and, in one fluid motion, streaked over the wall and into the neighbour's front garden. I gasped in surprise and, mind still reeling from the shock of it, reached for the key to let us in.

It was only when the key was in the lock and the door had swung open that I realised my mistake. Laura was frowning at her feet—we had left her Converse and beret in the back of the cab—and then, slowly, she raised her hand and opened it to reveal a set of keys looped onto a tiger's eye keychain.

"How'd you do that?" she said, blinking, confused, her drunken brain struggling to piece together what had just happened.

"With—with your key," I stammered, pointing at her keys. "You did it."

She lifted her head as though it were a great weight attached to her neck, and squinted at me. She was slack-jawed and perplexed, fighting to stay present in the moment.

"Do you . . ." she said, and there was a rising note of panic in her voice. "Do you have a key? Do you have a key to my house?"

"Laura—"

"Do you have *your own fucking key*?"

I felt like my entire body had been plunged into cold water.

"You're just drunk," I said, mind racing. It couldn't end here, like this, over one silly mistake. This was meant to be our happy ending, our reconciliation. She was unsteady on her feet, swaying on the spot, tuning in and out of the moment. This situation was salvageable, I was sure of it.

"You're just drunk," I said. "And you're seeing things and you're blaming me—as usual."

"What's in your hand, then?" Livid tears glossed her bloodshot eyes, and a slug of snot crawled towards her top lip.

"Nothing," I said again, squeezing the spare keys until the metal pinched my skin. "Just my keys, they're mine."

"You're lying," she said through clenched teeth, and something seemed to break inside her then. Her cheeks were growing red and her fearful expression boiled over into a look of rage. "It's always *you*, isn't it, Roach? Always *you*, crawling around, listening in—why is that? What is it about me that you find so fucking fascinating? Huh?"

A soft breeze gathered momentum, and then a strong gust of wind whipped first her hair and then mine and for a brief second all I could see was blonde. A bitterness welled within me, and I thought of all the care I had taken in my research, all the kindness I'd shown her. Buying her a cherry seltzer, offering to stay out for one more drink, returning her keys on their rose quartz keyring. She was selfish and ungrateful. Unsalvageable.

"I've only ever been good to you," I said. "But you're so stuck-up, so fucking full of yourself. This is the second time I've taken you home after you've had too much to drink, but has it ever occurred to you to say *thank you?*"

"Fuck you," she said. She was crying now, thick mascara-flecked tears streaking through the foundation on her cheeks. "Fuck you. You have no idea—*no idea*. And you're not a victim—you're not a victim, Roach! You're not a victim, and I don't owe you *anything*."

"I don't want anything," I snapped back. "I don't need you, I've got everything I need—I've got a boyfriend and I've got a job and I've got Lee, I don't need *anything* from you."

I pushed past her. It was over, it was done, but she wasn't ready for our connection to break. She snatched at my arm with sharp, mean fingers.

"What did you say?" she said, and her voice was low and dangerous. "Who's Lee? What do you mean, *you've got Lee?*"

"It doesn't matter," I said quickly, trying to brush her off. "I'm leaving. Fuck this."

"*What do you mean, you've got Lee*," she hissed, tightening her grip on my bicep.

"That hurts," I said, twisting my arm in a futile attempt to loosen her hold. "I don't need your permission. I can write to whoever I like. I don't need your permission, I don't need your blessing and I don't need your help. It's not just *your* story to tell."

The shock of it seemed to have smacked a moment of sobriety into her. Her mouth dropped open and she blinked, almost too stunned to speak.

"Are you . . . are you writing to Lee Frost?" Her face contorted with disgust, with horror. "Are you . . . *in touch* with him?"

"What do you care?" I said. She reared her hand back and slapped me as hard as she could. Her palm connected with my cheek with a sharp crack, and the unexpected sting of it made me gasp and I dropped the spare set of keys in surprise.

She didn't miss a beat. Laura lunged for the keys that were splayed on the doorstep and grabbed them, and then dashed into the flat, quick as a fox. She slammed the door in my face. The sound of metal scraping against metal followed as she slid a chain into place, and then she opened the door a crack to deliver one final blow.

"I'm calling the police," she said. "And I'm calling Sharona, and I'm getting you arrested and I'm getting you fired, you fucking *freak*."

"It's not a crime to have a spare key," I called to her through the narrow gap, a protective hand held against my flaming cheek. "You can't prove anything."

She slammed the door for a second time, and I slapped it once, hard, with the flat of my hand, then I turned away to face the dark street. A light switched on over the road, and the silhouette of a curious neighbour filled the window frame. Let them watch, I thought. What did it matter.

The whole exchange had left me winded, out of breath. I needed to gather my thoughts and think things through. I was on the precipice of something great, that much was certain. It was too late to salvage the siutation with Laura, but perhaps she had served her purpose. She was the bridge that connected me to Lee—perhaps that was all she was ever destined to do for me. I couldn't walk away now, though. I had to reset the narrative before I could move on with the story.

Face still raw from her vicious and unprovoked attack, I took off towards the park.

LAURA

Roach rifling through my past, Roach reaching out to Lee Frost. Had they spoken? Were they friends? Did she know him, had he told her things? I feel sick to my stomach. Roach, writing to Lee Frost, Roach, touching my things, my books, my clothes, my jewellery, my makeup. I can change the locks, I can change the locks but there is no exorcism strong enough, no exorcism strong enough to bleach Roach from the walls the floor the furniture the soul of this space.

She's infiltrated it. Infiltrated it, infested it, infected it, tainted it with her unwelcome touch. Everything that means anything to me has been tainted by Roach, by her greasy hair and stink of sweat, her dirty clothes and broken fingernails, her unbrushed teeth and sallow skin. My writing, my words, my work, my memories, my mother, and now even my home.

I call Sharona but she doesn't answer and I call Eli but he doesn't answer and they're ignoring me, I suppose, because of all the drama. I call the police, but I'm too drunk and I can't get the story straight, and the woman on the other end of the line is patient and she is patient until she is not.

"A cockroach has a key to your front door? Are you intoxicated, miss? Do you usually take medication?"

I hang up and try Eli again, and he doesn't answer, of course he doesn't answer. The adrenaline of the fight already feels diluted, the details slipping away. I pour myself a glass of bourbon, a large one that stings my lips, and collapse on to the sofa. Questions thrum through my head: has he written back? are they in regular contact? has he opened up to her? have they discussed my mother?

Does Roach know more than I do about my mother's death?

I close my eyes, smashed and exhausted, and dial Eli again, and again it goes to voicemail and I just

I cannot go on like this

I cannot go on

I cannot

ROACH

The crisp air smelled like woodsmoke, and I could almost believe it was the smell of my own hair burning, singeing under the flame of my pent-up rage. Apart from anything else, there was too much incriminating evidence of my creepy-crawling for me to leave things as they were—she had my set of keys, and I'd stashed my clothes under her bed earlier that night. There was incriminating evidence on me too—the amethyst necklace, the lipstick, the dress. If I could just return her things and reclaim mine, there would be no evidence. It would be her word against mine, and who was going to believe her after the way she had behaved?

I jumped the fence and walked briskly through the liquid dark of Lloyd Park. Bare branches swayed in a blustery wind, and I had to pull my hood up to stop the breeze from dragging my hair into my eyes. The park was empty—there were no fitness freaks on the kinetic gym, no teens drinking on the skate ramps, no pensioners playing bowls on the pavilion, no dogs wriggling across the grass.

When I reached the pond, a shallow moat that ringed a small duck island in the middle of the park, I used my phone as a torch. The light shivered in my shaking hands as I scanned the lip of gravel that hemmed the water until I found what I was looking for. A large stone, the size of half a house brick. I picked it up and weighed it in my hands. It was smooth on one side, and jagged on the other, with a craggy peak that reminded me of the chunk of amethyst tied around my neck. It was heavy enough to smash a window, to crack a skull.

With a deep breath, I counted to three. The sound of the rock as it smashed into my brow bone was the sound of an apple smacking concrete. I gasped an expletive and pain bloomed from the point of impact. When I touched my brow, my fingertips were coated in a dark slick of blood. I smeared as much of it as I could down my face, but blood dries quickly and it wasn't enough. I inhaled and struck myself again and again, until finally the blood flowed freely.

⁓

There was a light on, a gold glow bleeding through Venetian blinds. The house looked just like Laura's, the same garden path, the same bay windows. As I rang the bell, I imagined a group of carefree students up late getting wasted, or a bleary-eyed bartender just home from work, but when the door opened a crack, a tired-looking redhead peeped through the gap.

"Jesus wept," she whispered, clocking the blood. She pulled the door open all the way to reveal a tiny grub of a baby cradled in one arm. The child was asleep, gurning against a slobbery fist crammed into its mouth, lashes wet with recently fallen tears.

"I'm sorry to disturb you," I said, and she pressed a finger to her lips as she rocked the sleeping baby. I dropped my voice to a whisper. "I'm Laura—I live next door."

She took in my blonde hair, my bloody face. "Sure, I think I've seen you around," she said. "Are you okay? What *happened*?"

"I've been mugged, and I'm locked out," I said, in my best Laura voice—a panicked Pollyanna. "They took my phone, my keys—everything."

A cold wind stirred the loose frizzy hair that framed the woman's face. She shivered, and the baby in her arms emitted a thin whimper, a crest of sorrow rising in its tiny throat.

"Shh, shh, shh," she whispered, gently jigging the baby on her hip. "Look, do you need to go to A&E? I could call you a cab?"

"No, no—actually, I think I left my bedroom window open. I was thinking I might be able to climb over your garden fence and get in that way."

With a look of mild concern, she fished her mobile phone from the pocket of her cardigan. "Well, at least let me call the police?"

"No, honestly—"

"But you don't have a phone," she said, with a concerned frown. "If we call them right now, they might still be able to catch whoever did this to you."

The wind was blowing and the baby was grizzling, but she was standing strong, blocking my path like a bouncer. I had already wasted so much time. Laura could already have called the police, or Sharona, or Eli, and a sense of urgency was overtaking my rationality. This bitch wasn't going to let me into her home unless she had somehow interfered with my situation, that much was clear. A hands-on-hips busybody. A mugging wasn't an emergency, though, and a rowdy Saturday night in December would be keeping the police busy. I took a calculated risk.

"You're right," I said, forcing a customer service smile on to my stinging face. "Could I please borrow your phone?"

She unlocked an iPhone with a cracked screen and handed it to me and then, to my great relief, she stepped aside to let me in. The house was warm, the lights low. I dialled six-six-six. The phone clicked and I was connected to an automatic message.

"*The number you have dialled has not been recognised.*"

"Police, please," I said.

"Please hang up and try again."

I followed the woman through to a galley kitchen that mirrored Laura's. A small table was spread with an unfinished meal—a plate of buttered toast, a cold-looking cup of coffee with a milky film floating on the surface—and the detritus associated with a small baby: a packet of baby wipes, a thin white blanket, and a little fidgety chew toy, like something you'd give a dog.

"I just wanted to report a mugging," I said into the phone. "Two guys jumped me on Cazenove Road."

The smell of other people's houses always turns my stomach. Unfamiliar cooking, a different brand of detergent, a stranger's skin and hair. I swallowed.

"The number you have dialled has not been recognised."

"Do you want a cup of tea?" she whispered. I shook my head no.

I supplied the robotic voice with Laura's information, and a brief and generic description of my phantom muggers—jeans, hoodies, baseball caps pulled low, no, I couldn't see their faces.

"Please hang up and try again."

"That's great, thank you," I said, and then I disconnected the call.

The neighbour was walking in small figures of eight, rocking the baby in her arms with an almost mechanical rhythm. The rest of the kitchen was a mess of plates scabbed with dried food, and the bins were stacked with excess recycling.

"All he does is cry," she said, patting him on the back. "If I put him down, even for a second, he cries. If I fall asleep, he cries. Does he ever wake you up?"

"The police are on their way," I said.

She looked at me, studying my face. This was a bad idea, I thought.

"There's baby wipes there—do you want to clean up a little?"

"I just want to get home," I said, and it came out as a whine.

"Stay for a minute. Catch your breath."

My mouth was dry, and I swallowed. She kissed the baby's peach-fuzzed skull. "Do you want to be a mother, Laura?"

"No," I said. "I've never wanted children. My mother was murdered when I was a teenager. I can't stand the thought of bringing a child into a world this cruel. You don't recover from something like that."

A shadow crossed her face, and she paused her mechanical rocking, eyes fixed on mine. She tightened her grip on the baby in her arms. "No," she said softly, taking a small step backwards. "I guess you don't."

"I'd like to go now," I said.

The garden consisted of a dirty deck that stank of fox piss and gave way to a jungle of overgrown weeds. I dragged a wooden garden table to the fence, and gathered the hem of my dress in one hand.

"Will you be okay?" she asked, backlit by the bright light of the kitchen.

I gave her a thumbs up, terrified of my voice reaching Laura's delicate ears and alerting her to my presence. I hoisted myself up on to the wall and scrambled over to the other side, landing heavily on Laura's patio. As my eyes adjusted to the darkness, I was faced with rotten leaves, a pile of bricks, a broken barbecue, and several empty terra-cotta plant pots that were green with algae.

I had to sit for a minute and wait for some of the adrenaline to leave my system before I could trust my legs to support my weight. I imagined this whole situation being retold on a podcast. The *Murder Girls* would find the story both chilling and amusing in equal measure. That thought gave me the strength to continue.

The curtains were open in the bedroom, and I could see through the glass that the bed was empty. The window was stiff and snagged against its frame as I jimmied it open inch by inch, straining for sounds of movement from the dark flat. When it was open halfway, I slipped into her room and stood in the darkness, listening to the heavy silence, my heart beating, beating, beating.

The flat had all the stillness and silence of the shop after hours. No clattering in the kitchen, no music, no podcast, no television to keep her company. Had she gone out? I had the panicked mental image of her hailing an Uber and speeding through the night to a friend's house, some place of safety, where she'd tell her garbled story and I wouldn't be there to reset the narrative. On the other hand, if she was out, I'd be able to complete my clean-up in peace. But this felt unlikely. She was too drunk, too messy, too much. Where would she even go? The bedroom door was shut, but underneath it, a faint light glowed. She must be in the living room, I thought.

I creepy-crawled towards the door, opened it a crack and peeped into the hallway. My focus felt scattered. I'd feared an immediate clash, but now that I was here, the silence and the darkness was unnerving. Violent images flashed through my head. I saw her sprawled, empty pill packets scattered across the carpet. I saw her naked, floating in the bath, the rapidly cooling water marbled with blood, her wrists opened by the bite of a razor blade. I saw her hanging, a rope tied like a ribbon around her neck. I saw her falling, I saw her drowning, I saw her dying a thousand times, each more gruesome than the last, but she would leave such a lovely corpse. Blonde, hazel eyes, the perfect picture of tragedy.

Moving as quickly and as quietly as I could, I retrieved my clothes from their hiding place under the bed and stepped out of the ballet flats and tugged on my jeans. As I hauled the dress over my head, careful to avoid my bloody face, it smelled of my sharp sweat and sweet perfume. Was this incriminating, or would Laura recognise the scent of the whiskey-coloured eau de toilette as her own? There was no time to decide—I dropped the dress on to the swirl of fabric on the floor and pulled on my T-shirt and hoodie.

The amethyst necklace was tied tightly, and my fingers were clumsy and numb as I struggled to work the knot loose. I strained to hear signs of life beyond the bedroom door, my heart hammering. When the knot finally came loose, I tossed the necklace into a stray leather boot and tucked the boot under the bed. Let her find it on some snowy day, when she needed the perfect brown boot to match her Cambridge satchel. I returned the lipstick to its rightful place among her hoarded cache of tubes and slimes.

It was time to go, but with a sinking feeling I realised I was trapped. I couldn't go back the way I came—how could I possibly explain an encore appearance to the neighbour? There was only one way out. I tiptoed to the bedroom door and listened to the silence for clues, which were not forthcoming. I opened the door and slipped into the hallway. On my right, between me and the front door, there was a soft flickering glow from the living room. A candle, or a muted television perhaps. Even if I managed to sneak past the living room door without Laura hearing me, she would certainly hear the sound of the chain scraping against its metal track, hear the crack of the latch, hear the door peel open and click shut. It was too risky, I couldn't do it. I dithered.

On my left, the kitchen and bathroom beyond were both shrouded in shadow, so I creeped towards the darkness. The moonlight was thick and bright across the kitchen floor, and it illuminated the twisted trail of a skinny yellow slug as it crawled across the lino. A fellow interloper. A good omen.

In the dark hallway, I heard the alarming sound of Laura's slurred voice coming down the corridor. She sounded like she was on the phone. I had a split second to decide my next move. Like a cockroach scuttling away from the light, I followed the trail of slug mucus into the bathroom and stepped into the bathtub. There was a shower curtain, but it was only half drawn, and I didn't dare touch it in case the curtain rings rattled against the rod. It was a terrible hiding place, the move of a rookie.

Lady Luck smiled upon me, though: as Laura pushed the bathroom door open, it swung inwards and obscured me entirely. She snapped on the light.

"I dunno why you aren't anshering," she was saying, her words thick with alcohol. "But fuck you too."

She ended the call, and I held my breath as I listened to her piss. She flushed the loo, then blew her nose and washed her hands. I thought I was going to get away with it, would simply be able to wait until she was asleep and walk out the front door like I'd never been there in the first place, but then as I listened to the scrubbing sound of her brushing her teeth, she gently pushed the bathroom door closed and my hiding place was exposed.

We locked eyes in the mirror, and I saw her expression tilt as she recognised my blood-streaked face, not as a shadow or a trick of the light, but as a human presence in her bathtub. I imagined myself appearing from the darkness like a photograph developing. A look of dawning horror, a strangled gasp, and her phone clattered from her hand into the sink.

"Don't scream," I said.

She opened her lipstick-stained mouth, frothed with toothpaste foam, and filled her lungs with air, a deep breath ready to break. With no choice, I leaped out of the tub and grabbed her by the throat.

"You can't scream," I hissed, squeezing. "Someone will hear you."

She smacked me in the face, and the plastic toothbrush in her hand sunk into the bloody wound on my brow. An involuntary, guttural squeal escaped my lips, and I snatched at her thin wrist and banged it against the sink once, twice, three times until she dropped the toothbrush and it rattled across the floor.

With a clever little jerk of her hips, learned in some feminist self-defence class, no doubt, she twisted away from me and staggered into the kitchen. Unsure of what she was heading towards—the front door, to escape? a kitchen knife, to attack?—I lunged towards her and the momentum tipped us over. There was a dull crack as her temple connected with the corner of the kitchen counter, and then she slumped against the lino and then she was quite still.

"Laura?" I spoke her name, softly, an incantation.

I rolled her on to her back, and she was heavy but compliant. A dead weight. Her jaw was loose, her mouth slack, and her pale forehead sported a deep, bloody gash. A thick trickle of blood rolled down her temple and into her blonde hair. She was white and motionless, carved from marble. I reached towards her neck to feel for a pulse, but the thought of touching her again revolted me and I pulled my hand back.

This was a waste of time. I stepped over her and walked to the bathroom.

In the mirror, the whites of my eyes popped against the bloody patina streaked over my face. Everything felt hyperreal, like I'd just stepped out of a dark cinema and was experiencing three-dimensional reality for the first time in a while. Laura's phone was still sitting in the sink and I decided to take it, with half a mind to check if she had called the police, and to see whether or not she had sent any incriminating texts about our argument on the doorstep.

My hands trembled as I washed away the blood. Pink water circled the drain. My wound was still raw and bleeding, but at least I no longer looked like I'd just been murdered. Murdered. I switched off the bathroom light, and then stepped over Laura's supine body. She hadn't moved.

In the living room, I found a tableau of her final hours: a blanket cast aside, a glass of whiskey, and two bunches of door keys. The keys I'd had cut were looped on to a plain stainless-steel ring, but hers were hooked on to a tiger's eye key ring that I hadn't seen before. Tiger's eye. Something occurred to me then, and I pushed my hand between the sofa cushions. My fingers closed around the rough edge of a raw piece of rose quartz, and I extracted the keys I'd stolen, copied, and returned to her all those weeks ago. She'd never found them, but that didn't matter now.

I placed the rose quartz keys and the tiger's eye keys side by side on the table, swallowed a sip of the whiskey and pocketed the third set of keys. My set. Now, if she'd blabbed to anyone—Sharona, Eli, the police—about spare keys, they would indeed find two sets, both belonging to her.

It was over. I walked back to the kitchen and paused in the doorway, my hand on the light switch, and looked down at her once more. Until that moment, I don't think I'd ever understood the depth that velvet brought to colour. Just how dark midnight blue, or amethyst, or forest green, or burgundy, can appear in the folds of a velvet dress. Almost impenetrable, with a hint, the slightest trace, of colour. I switched off the kitchen light, and the velvet of her dress faded to black.

∽

It was gone midnight, and the pub was winding down. A barmaid—I think her name was Helena, but they came and went—was on the other side of the bar, talking to a customer with an intimacy that indicated they were friends or lovers. No one turned to look at me, no one noticed me at all. I was a ghost, a shadow. Head down to obscure the gash on my forehead, I darted straight upstairs.

Jackie was in her room, the gentle buzz of television drifting beneath her closed door. Her night had been ordinary. She hadn't met Sam, and she hadn't seen Brodie, Brogan, and Roach merge into one under Laura's influence. Her unremarkable world remained unchanged, for now. Would she still love me, as a killer? Would she believe me, if I said I didn't do it? Would she stand by me, if I was found guilty?

In the kitchen, I picked up a bottle of honey-coloured spiced rum, but the pin-up girl on the Sailor Jerry's label made me think of Laura's faded tattoos, and then I thought of the dark syrupy blood oozing from her broken skin. My mouth flooded with saliva, and I swallowed the need to vomit. I picked a bottle of Jack Daniel's instead.

Safe behind my bedroom door, I cracked the bourbon and took a warm, sweet swallow to mute the creeping sense of panic. If Laura was dead, if she was really dead, would that make me a murderer, or would it be classed as manslaughter? Manslaughter was so much less glamorous.

My lips were numb, my teeth chattering like I'd been out all night in the cold, like I'd seen a ghost. I'd always imagined myself as having a stronger constitution. All those hours spent listening to harrowing accounts of violence, reading about brutal murders, and looking at photos of graphic crime scenes, had not prepared me for the simple reality of spilled blood, of a body.

Bleep was unfurling against the glass of his tank, and I picked him up and placed him on my collarbone. The strong, almost tongue-like muscle of his body calmed my beating heart as he slid towards my left shoulder.

I sent Sam a text. *Can't sleep.*

He replied straight away. *Yeah well.*

Laura's fault, I said.

Shoulda killed her when we had the chance, he said.

The room slipped out of focus. Was that incriminating? I deleted the message. I knocked back a slug of bourbon, wiped the alcohol from my chin before any could drip on to Bleep.

I'm sorry, I said, but he didn't reply.

∽

My alarm sliced open the guts of the morning. A splitting pain emanated from my forehead, and I touched it gingerly. The wound felt like raw meat. *Laura.* Fractured memories spilled into my sleep, and I squirmed under the weight of them as I blinked myself awake. *Laura.* I reached for my phone and silenced the pounding alarm, then rolled on to my back. *Laura.* An ocean of nausea sloshed against my internal shore, a rising tide of acid. *Laura.*

The covers were tangled around my sweaty limbs, and they stank of Laura's sweet floral perfume. Alcohol, stale sweat, and the sickly smell of roses. I sat up, caught sight of my reflection in the mirror: an apparition of a blonde with a bloody injury on her forehead. *Laura.* A sudden bite of sick at the back of my throat. I twisted onto my front as hot vomit spattered over the books and plates on the floor by my bed. A rope of bitter phlegm dangled from my lips as I tried to catch my breath, then I fell back into the depths of a dark sleep.

⁓

A repetitive buzzing, like the drone of a bluebottle circling a corpse. Laura, in her wine-coloured dress. Laura, swirling an Old Fashioned, her third or fourth. Laura, a chiffon ribbon of cigarette smoke rising from her lips. Laura, her wine lipstick smudged.

Laura, her mouth agape, a trickle of blood rolling down her temple.

⁓

When I came to, the light was grey and my room stank of rotten sick. I groped around the bed until I found my phone. It was gone nine, and I had four missed calls from Spines Walthamstow. I called the shop, shaking with the adrenaline of a misstep.

"Hello, Spines." It was Kofi's flat Mancunian drawl.

"Hullo, it's Roach," I said.

"All right?" he said, indifferent to the sound of my voice.

"Did someone call me?"

"Oh, aye. Laura didn't show up for work again today. Sharona's raging."

Laura was dead. The truth of it rolled over me like a tide. I searched for the words a normie might say in this situation. The important thing was to remember to refer to her in the present tense.

"She didn't show up?" I squeaked.

"Missing, presumed hanging," he replied.

"*What?*"

"Hanging. Missing, presumed sleeping off a massive fucking hangover. Sharona wanted you in early to cover her, but no point now."

"I'm fine," I lied. "I'm coming."

I dragged myself out of bed, and Laura was dead. The acrid bourbon vomit would have to wait. I pulled on an AC/DC T-shirt and a pair of leggings over yesterday's knickers, pushed my bare feet into dank trainers and zipped up my System of a Down hoodie. An iPhone fell out of the pocket and clattered on to my bedroom floor. Laura's phone. Her lock screen was a picture of Taylor Swift, bright red lips and loose, wavy blonde hair. I didn't know the passcode. Why did I take this? It was useless, a brick. Could they trace the phone, find it here? I meant to toss it somewhere, but I hadn't been thinking clearly. I covered my face with my hands.

Laura. It had been around eight hours since I'd left Laura's flat. By now, her body would have cooled to an ambient room temperature, and a mauve blush would be bruising the places where her lifeless blood had settled.

My instinct was to rush to her place and see for myself, but a criminal always returns to the scene of the crime. Panic flared in the pit of my stomach, and I couldn't catch my breath. I should have called in sick, should have called in dead—dead, dead, Laura was dead—but I knew enough to know that I had to hold my nerve, act like everything was normal, nothing had changed. I'd had a late night, I'd taken a drunk colleague home from a party, I'd slipped on the ice and bumped my head, got a bad graze. That was all. I was hungover and looked like I'd been in a car accident, but everything was as it should be. Everything in my world was fine. Nothing had changed.

It was cold outside, and the clouded sky was dark and swollen with the threat of snow. I tried to jog, but I skidded and slipped on a pavement that sparkled with morning frost and I had to slow my pace to keep myself steady. My trainers rubbed against my bare feet, and my fingers turned peppermint pink.

∽

The shop was busy, crawling with customers who pawed at the stock, grabbed and snatched and got in each other's way. I pushed my way through the throng of Christmas shoppers to the quiet sanctity of the lift.

In the staffroom, someone had put out a plate of gingerbread men. I dropped my hoodie and tote into my locker and pulled on my uniform Aertex over my AC/DC T-shirt. Under the sink, I found the green first aid kit and took it into the bathroom with me. Locked safely behind the bathroom door, I turned on both taps as high as they would go. A fresh spasm of nausea passed through me, and I regurgitated a gush of biting yellow bile into the sink. As I watched it swirl down the drain, I wondered if Laura had ever vomited into this sink. I wrapped Laura's phone and the jammy red lipstick in loo roll, and then shoved them both into the sanitary towel bin. I washed my hands, wiped my face, and opened the first aid kit. I stuck a large square plaster over the mess of my forehead, then flushed the toilet for good measure.

In the staffroom, Eli was standing by the kitchen sink, throat constricting as he downed a glass of water. He looked rough, with an unshaven face, unwashed hair. As he finished the last of his drink, he lowered the glass and saw me standing there.

"Christ, are you okay?" He touched his brow and nodded at mine. "What happened?"

His eyes were piggy and bloodshot, and that curious circular scab on his cheek looked raw, as though he'd picked at it.

"Nothing," I said, mirroring his movements and touching the plaster on my brow. I turned my head away as I spoke, wondered if he could smell the sweet bourbon sick on my breath. "I slipped over last night. On the ice. It's not as bad as it looks."

"It looks pretty bad. Are you sure you're okay to work?"

"I'm fine," I said, pushing past him towards the door.

He reached out and touched my arm to stop me in my tracks. "Hey . . . I wanted to ask you . . . did you get Laura home okay last night?"

"Yes," I said, feeling the blood drain from my face.

"Did she seem okay to you? She wasn't upset or anything?"

"She was fine. She invited me in for a drink."

He blinked at me for several seconds, taken aback. "She did?"

"We sat in her living room and had a glass of bourbon, and she told me about her mother. She wasn't sad, though; she seemed happy. Happy to be sharing a memory."

Eli ran his hands through his hair, frowning and thinking, thinking and frowning. I needed to reel it in, but I couldn't help myself. Panic had taken the wheel.

"She wanted to go out and get another bottle," I said. "But I said we should leave it. I'd had enough to drink—clearly!" I touched the plaster again and forced a laugh that was shrill and inhuman. It echoed around the empty room and he winced at the sound.

"Okay, thanks," he said, although he looked doubtful, and I wondered if I'd said too much.

✍

At lunchtime, I caught Noor and Kofi refilling empty sparkling water bottles with supermarket gin and tonics. Not that I gave a shit. They spent the rest of the afternoon smirking and joking about having an unquenchable thirst as they stole sips between customers. Their breath smelled like acetone and lime and every time they passed me by, I felt a fresh swell of queasiness hit the back of my throat.

I stood behind the first floor till and battled nauseating contractions of anxiety. It wasn't as busy there, and I was free to let my mind drift down dark paths. I imagined what Laura would do if she was working today. She would strut through the crowd, probably in an attention-seeking outfit, like her forest-green minidress and red and white striped elf tights, cracking jokes and making customers laugh.

With Laura gone though, there was a chance I might get my True Crime section back. I stood a little taller after that, and when a red-faced woman with a list written on the back of an envelope approached the till, a plastic smile came easily.

"Hi," I said, in a bright, brittle voice. "How may I help?"

✍

Eli was in the stockroom, filling a trolley with armfuls of hardbacks to replenish the tables front of store.

"Has Laura called yet?" I asked.

"Nope," he said, his jaw set. He used the back of his forearm to wipe his brow, then reached for a plastic water bottle and drained it, his Adam's apple bobbing with each swallow. I wondered if he was on the gin, too.

"Sharona said today's shift was nonnegotiable," I needled.

"I don't know what you want me to say, Roach."

345

"Will she come in for the staff meeting?"

"I honestly don't know," he said. "I don't know where she is. I'm going to walk round to her place in a minute and give her a knock."

If she didn't answer the door, would he leave or would he try to force his way in? Would his mind flicker to the worst possible scenario—an accident, a suicide—or was that just me? Would he have a set of keys? How many spares did she have? Would he call the police if she didn't answer the door? Would they question me? Would they search my things?

"But it's Christmas Eve," I said, and my voice cracked. "Won't she be with her family?"

"We are her family," he replied, heading towards the stockroom door.

∽

As the last customers weaved their way from the till to the high street, I felt light-headed, like I'd just smoked my first cigarette. The day wasn't finished though. The doors still had to be locked, the bins emptied, reports printed, till trays taken up to the safe. I couldn't face it. I slipped into the lift with half a mind to hide in the bathroom and let the others do the close without me.

On the second floor, Eli was standing in the doorway of the manager's office, talking to Sharona. I wasn't particularly interested in eavesdropping until I heard my name.

"And Roach?" said Sharona.

I creepy-crawled towards the open doorway to listen.

"She said they hung out for a bit, had a drink," Eli said.

"That . . . surprises me."

"I'm really worried, Shaz. She left me some pretty wild voice notes and she sounded . . . not good."

"Look, Jim's just arrived. Let's get this over with, and then we'll walk round to her flat together, okay?"

"Yeah, okay," he said, running his hands through his curls. He turned towards the corridor then and saw me standing there, too out of it to hide my frank surveillance. "You all right there, Roach?"

"I feel really sick," I said, which was the truth. The thought of Sharona and Eli walking to Laura's flat sent a wave of blind panic crashing through me. "I need to leave. Can I leave?"

"One minute," said Sharona, leaving the office with a grim expression, like an executioner approaching the gallows. "I just need everyone in the staffroom. Right now."

∽

Jim, the area manager, had a fashionable haircut and an unruly ginger beard. He walked straight to Eli and gave him a hard slap of camaraderie on the shoulder.

"All right, mate?" he said.

A breath of expensive aftershave burned the back of my throat. I wondered if someone had died. Someone else, I mean. Our old manager Barbara, perhaps. Perhaps Christmas in Loughton had killed her. I swallowed a manic desire to laugh. I needed to calm down, take a few deep breaths. I was losing my mind, behaving strangely.

Martin and Barry took seats at separate canteen tables. I sank into my armchair and picked up *The Stranger Beside Me* out of habit. I held it in my lap like a talisman, running my thumb over the soft, buttery pages.

"Look, thanks for staying late everyone. I'm not gonna beat around the bush," Jim said, perching on one of the cafeteria tables. "I'm afraid I've got some bad news to share with you guys today."

The mood in the room shifted, like the sun disappearing behind a cloud.

"Despite our best efforts, we're facing an incredibly difficult time as a company. The high street's struggling, and this branch is stranded at the end of a long row of shuttered shops. Conversion has been incredible this Christmas, thanks to all your hard work, but the footfall simply isn't there. It's not enough for a shop of this size to survive, and we've failed to meet our annual targets by quite a stretch."

"But it's been so busy," Martin said, forlorn. "We've been rushed off our feet."

"It's not enough to make up for the rest of the year," Sharona said with a gentle note of regret.

"And look," said Jim. "I just want to reassure everyone here today that we're not talking redundancies yet."

"Yet?" said Barry, eyes glossed with a sheen of anger.

"Wait, are you saying the shop's *closing down*?" said Martin.

"I'm afraid Boxing Day will be our last day of trade," Sharona said, and Jim nodded, and Eli bowed his head, and I felt nothing.

"And you're telling us this on Christmas Eve?" asked Barry. His face was turning a deep red and he looked incredulous.

"It wasn't an easy decision for the board to make, and they've done everything in their power—"

"It's Christmas, for fuck's sake!" said Martin.

"I know this is disappointing news," said Sharona in a calm, kind voice. "And I know the shop's been home to many of you for a number of years. You're an asset to Spines, you really are. Shop closures are always the very last thing we want to see happen. Not just for our booksellers, but for the communities we serve as well."

I'd heard enough. I closed my eyes, embraced darkness.

⚘

Noor and Kofi headed towards one of the pubs on the high street, a motley twosome off to celebrate the end of the season and commiserate the end of the shop. They were young. They would simply move on. Kofi was a student temp anyway, and Noor had her sights set on a one-way ticket to Thailand. It didn't really matter to them. Martin and Barry walked in the opposite direction, perhaps for a consolatory drink of their own. Misery loves company, after all.

I stood outside the shop, staring into the middle distance, at the deserted high street, at the empty market stalls, at the shuttered shops, the absent signs, the peeling clearance-sale posters, the soaped-up windows.

"Aren't you off to the pub, Roach?" Eli asked, dragging doors open a crack to peep out.

"No," I said.

"Well—you don't have to wait for us. Head home, if you like?"

I wished for a way to freeze time, to prevent him from walking over to Laura's flat. I wished there was some urgent errand I could send him on, some goose chase that would buy me an hour, prevent the inevitable. Panic fluttered in my chest, but there was nothing I could say or do to change his plans. He and Sharona were going to lock up the shop, and they were going to walk to Laura's, and she wouldn't be opening her front door. It was as inevitable as time ticking on. There was nothing I could do.

"I know it must be a bit of a shock," he said, misreading the expression on my face. "But you aren't going to lose your job, okay? Sharona'll take care of you guys, find you somewhere new—maybe somewhere with a big True Crime section, yeah?"

A snowflake fell between us, and we both looked up to the sky. Another flake landed on my cheek, and Eli tilted his head to watch the erratic static of falling snow. He looked so ordinary in that moment. I couldn't see what Laura saw in him.

If this was a romance novel, and if I was Laura, he'd reach forward and brush a snowflake away with his fingertips, run his hands through my blonde hair. I had a wild, ridiculous image of us melting into each other's arms. Our lips could meet; we could leave the shop together.

But this wasn't romance, and I wasn't Laura. It was true crime, and I was Brogan Roach.

"See ya," I said, turning away from the shop and walking towards the Mother Black Cap.

"Merry Christmas," he called after me. "See you on Boxing Day for the last hurrah!"

As I walked through the market, I realised I had no intention of returning to the shop. I was done. There would be no new True Crime section, no new staffroom, no new door codes, no new regulars, no new colleagues for me. I was done with bookselling. Let them close the doors for good, let them scatter the booksellers across the other London branches. What did any of it matter.

I pulled out my phone, and sent a text.

⁂

In the Rose and Crown, an old man with long greasy hair and an unkempt imperial moustache was propping up the bar with a pint of bitter. He had that searching look of a customer trying catch someone's eye and I willed him to leave me alone, to find someone else to bother with his normie small talk about the weather, or Christmas, or the Queen's infernal speech. I kept my head down and ignored him as I ordered two pints of Dark Fruits and two shots of sambuca, and then I turned to find seats by the window.

Outside, it was snowing properly, a thick shroud obscuring the cars as they crawled along the main road, weak headlights battling against the blizzard. The warmth was sucked from the room every time the doors opened, and each time I glanced up and saw a stranger entering the pub, all pink cheeks and smiles, I tasted bitter disappointment. Perhaps it was too late. Perhaps he wasn't coming.

Intrusive thoughts of Laura waxed and waned. I pictured Sharona's tentative knock, the way Eli might wait at the end of the garden path with his hands in his pockets, breath fogging in the cold. They might both turn at the sound of a drunk singing a Christmas carol in the distance, might think of whatever warmth was waiting for them at home. They might leave without knocking again, satisfied they had done enough to quell their anxiety.

Or would their minds go straight to panic mode? Would they sound the alarm, cause a scene? Would Eli want to kick the door in, would Sharona call the police?

Perhaps Laura already had, last night. Perhaps the police were on their way during our final encounter. Perhaps her flat—the crime scene—was already swarming with coppers and forensics. Perhaps Eli and Sharona would be faced with blue and white police tape tied to her door like a ribbon. A grave-looking constable on the doorstep would refuse to give them any information, but they would know the news was bad.

Either way, no one would think to call me. No one would care to let me know.

"You owe me more than a fucking shot," Sam joked, taking his seat at the table. A light dusting of snow was already melting into his hair, dappling the shoulders of his battered leather jacket. His eyes bugged with surprise when he clocked the plaster on my forehead. "Jesus fucking Christ, what happened to your face?"

"I slipped over on my way to work this morning," I said, touching it with tentative fingers.

"But—Christ, Brodie, it looks fucking awful. Why didn't you tell me?"

"I dunno," I said, and something inside me finally unfastened and tears spilled down my cheeks. "I thought you were mad at me."

"Heyyyy . . . don't be like that." He moved to the seat next to me, took my face in the palm of his hands and kissed the tip of my nose. He was freshly showered, and his long hair smelled clean, like eucalyptus dandruff shampoo.

"I think I've really fucked up," I said.

"Nah," he said, tucking my hair behind my ear. "Nah, you're all right. I was pretty pissed off, but we were all smashed. Don't worry about it."

I realised then that I loved him, I really loved him, and that I wasn't going to tell him the truth. Some fantasies are best kept within the realm of imagination. I knew that now. I took a big mouthful of my drink. The glass was almost empty.

"Was everything all right with whatshername?" he asked. "Did you get what you wanted?"

"Nah," I said. "She was too wasted."

"Sucks."

He took a long swallow of cider, a third of the pint downed in one.

"I'm sorry," I said, turning my glass in my hands.

"Never make me go to one of them shit parties again, all right?"

"I don't think that's likely," I said, and I told him about the shop closing.

"Fuck it," he said, leaning over and handing me one of the sambuca shots. "Fuck the shop, fuck books, fuck all of it. It doesn't matter. And fuck that bitch, whatever her name is."

"Laura," I said.

"Fuck Laura. It doesn't matter. She's dead to us, babe. Dead." He lifted his shot glass and I lifted mine in a toast. We swallowed sambuca and he kissed away my tears with soft wet lips that smelled of sweet aniseed.

"Fuck Laura," I whispered, and finally I felt like I could breathe.

By the time the evening bled into the night, we were drunk and diabolical, feeding coins into the digital jukebox and blasting the otherwise calm pub with the raw and frantic energy of early AC/DC.

When the landlord called last orders, we spilled out into the night.

"I know a pub that's open late," I said, and we wound our way to the Mother Black Cap, sang "St. Anger" at the top of our lungs as we tripped past the normies eating kebabs on Hoe Street.

The bar was busy, and Jackie was in the thick of it, cracking jokes and telling stories in a sparkly top and her best jeans while "Fairytale of New York" pounded from the speakers. She almost didn't recognise me when she saw me, but her eyes went straight from my blonde hair to the plaster.

"What's this—what *happened*?"

"Slipped," I said. "On the ice."

"And when did you do this?" she said, reaching for a tendril of my hair and admiring the butter-yellow blonde.

"The other night," I said, letting her feel the texture of it between her fingers. Jackie had too much perfume on, too much hairspray, too much lipstick, but this cocktail of Obsession and Smirnoff, Elnett and Revlon, smelled like home. I felt a strange rush of affection towards her.

"You look like a young Debbie Harry," she said, and then she paused as she seemed to realise that Sam, who was standing by my side, wasn't just a customer squeezing past. He was with me.

"So, who's this, then?" she said, lifting her straw to her mouth as she nodded up at him.

"This is my boyfriend," I said, and he grinned. "Sam, this is my mum, Jackie."

"So, she turns up at midnight with a banged-up face, new hair, and a new man—is she even my daughter?"

No, I thought. I was no longer the daughter she knew. I was a different person—no longer a bookseller, no longer a virgin, no longer just a true crime fan. I was an active participant. I was a murderer, a criminal. I was diabolical.

Jackie was rolling her eyes with the slightest hint of a smile, and then she was prattling on again, her mouth moving faster than I could follow.

"Sam, you look like a roadie I used to know called Pringle. Matty Pringle. Toured with Maiden. No, Zeppelin. Zeppelin, and then Sabbath. He was a right laugh, Pringle. Dead now. I tell you what, he could get you backstage anywhere, from Liverpool to London for a bottle of Bacardi and a—"

"We're gonna get drinks," I said, slicing into her story before it had the chance to take root. Sam held my hand as we squeezed through the crowd towards the bar, but not before I leaned forward and touched my mother on the shoulder. She glanced my way and we locked eyes for a moment, and then someone called her name and she was gone.

Sam and I found ourselves a table in the corner of the pub. At last orders, my mother locked the doors and drew the curtains and we carried on, just us and the regulars. Sam and I cracked into a bottle of Jack Daniel's and he took over the jukebox, impressing my mother with his penchant for '80s metal. As night faded into morning, we screamed along to "Shout at the Devil" with sweet, sour mash breath, but I felt like the devil was right there with me, standing by my side.

∽

On New Year's Day, Laura's street still looked like a Christmas card: golden glowing windows, front doors sporting holly wreaths, each one decorated with pine cones, dried orange slices, and red velvet ribbons. Bits of foraged shit, because foraged shit was trendier than the tacky plastic garbage you could buy in the supermarket. Christmas trees filled the bay windows, their twinkling lights the jewel tones of Quality Street wrappers.

Returning to the scene of the crime was a rookie move, but it had been a week—a week of waiting, a week of scanning the news and searching social media and listening for the sound of approaching sirens. I was a killer, and it was inevitable that I would be caught.

There was something almost supernatural about serial killers when they were on the loose: their eerie ability to go unnoticed, to hide in plain sight, to disappear without a trace. And yet, it was so often ordinary humdrum things that led to their capture. A parking ticket. An ancestry DNA test. A blocked drain. Monogrammed stationery. A floppy disc.

I'd removed the most incriminating pieces of evidence from Laura's flat that night—the spare set of keys, my clothes—but I was only thinking about concealing my creepy-crawling. Laura's flat was going to be infested with my DNA—strands of my hair, traces of my saliva on the whiskey glass and on bottle necks and beer cans in her recycling bin, fibres from my clothes, fingerprints like confetti, scattered over everything. There would even be traces of urine, faecal matter, and blood in the bathroom. I hadn't been careful, because I had no intention of committing murder, and this was killing me. I had to at least check on the body. I had to know for sure.

There were no lights on in Laura's flat. The curtains were half closed and the living room beyond them looked grey. There was no crime scene tape ribboned around her front door, no police officer standing guard. It looked ordinary. I walked up the garden path and knocked on the door. I rattled the letter box, and then turned away so if someone opened the door, they'd be greeted by my cool indifference. My breath puffed against the blanket of night.

I tried to picture Laura alive, somewhere warm, somewhere cosy, surrounded by family, drinking mulled wine and eating mince pies, laughing, squabbling, a big thatch of March sisters sharing jokes and gently ribbing one another. But no—of course not. She had no siblings, no parents that I knew of. She was alone, inside the flat. The five stages of decomposition rolled through my head, a rosary. Putrefaction would have given her skin a light green tinge, like the flesh of a Granny Smith, or lime granita. Microorganisms in the gut would eat away at the soft tissue, secreting liquids which are molecularly similar to the chemicals that give raspberries their sharp, sweet scent. During active decay, blowflies would lay eggs in her mouth, nostrils, earholes, and eye sockets, which would burst into writhing pits of maggots.

The flat remained silent. No one was coming. Braced for the sweet stench of a body left to rot, I let myself in, but it seemed normal. A little mildewy, a little like stale cigarettes. I called her name as I edged down the dark corridor towards the kitchen, towards her final resting place. It was empty and clean, the surfaces gleaming. The mess around the sink had gone, the cupboards were bare. The fridge was switched off, the door ajar. Her bedroom door was open, her bed stripped. The floor was clear of clothing: the mess of dresses and discarded high heels, the stray lipsticks, the tangle of floaty scarves, the haphazard stacks of books and wine glasses, the postcards, the notebooks, the poetry—it was all gone.

I peeped into the living room. The dusty tea lights, piles of paperbacks, old coffee cups, empty wine bottles. Gone. Just the sagging sofa and neat, empty bookshelves. There was a strange pink, lilac, and white confetti spread over the couch. I ran my hand through the petals of paper, picked up a scoop and let them drop back on to the cushions, a soft paper blizzard.

It was several copies of her chapbook, the book that had meant so much to me, that I had loved so much, torn into tiny pieces, reduced to recycling. *their inconsequential moments were beautiful.* No one else would have done something like this.

It was a message. She was alive, and she was gone.

༄

When I got back to the Mother Black Cap, the bar was dark and quiet, the lights dimmed to a soft glow. Jackie was watching *EastEnders* with the subtitles on, as usual. She wore her hangover with a quiet dignity, but the liquid in the glass in front of her was the telltale electric orange colour of Lucozade.

"Oh, a letter came for you," she said, handing me an envelope. "I think it came a while ago. I found it behind the bar."

The address was scrawled in rough biro. I tore into the envelope and pulled out several handwritten pages. *Dear Brogan*, it began. *Thanks for your letter. You can call me Lee.*

EPILOGUE: PART 1

AUGUST 2022

A summer breeze carries the rich, smoky smell of a barbecue, stirring the leaves overhead. The shop shutters squeal as I slide them closed, and the key sticks in the lock as I stoop to lock up.

A quiet one tonight, I think. Last night, we'd only meant to have one, but old habits die hard I guess. We started with a sweet bottle of blush-pink rosé in a beer garden. Afternoon soon melted into evening, evening into night, and Gemma convinced me to go with her to Jessie's place. We sat around the firepit in Jessie's garden, drinking more rosé. Good friends and cold wine, a guitar, and the gentle crackle of flames. Warmth and love and laughter, with nowhere better to be.

It took me a long time to find my way here, to a place of safety. I'd felt fractured, paranoid, and out of control for such a long time.

I think of the night of the Spines Christmas party as "the missing night." The fragments that I've managed to piece together still don't make a whole picture. I have nothing, no lasting memory of the party, just a vague sense of feeling untethered, threatened. With a sick burn of shame, I remember snapping at Lydia, saying something awful to shock and embarrass her. Eli's wounded eyes, all that softness and hurt laid bare.

Sharona's obvious anger. And then Roach. Roach, in her cheap dress and badly dyed hair and messy makeup, Roach always there, always watching. Roach, wearing a necklace so like my mother's—but no, I had found that in the mess of my room. She hadn't stolen it from me. She didn't even know it existed. She'd taken me home when no one else would, and . . . well, the rest is a missing scene, a blank canvas, a black hole.

Eli helped me to fill in some of the gaps when I was released from hospital, but his version of events didn't make much sense either. I brewed us a pot of coffee and we sat at the powder-blue bistro table in my kitchen, like we had done so many times before.

"When you didn't show up for work again, Sharona was fuming," he said, cradling his mug in both hands. "But I knew something wasn't right. I just knew it. You'd sent me all these voice notes, like crying and mad at me for not answering the phone, but I hadn't seen them until morning. We went to your flat after work to check you were okay, and that's when we met your neighbour—Amber? The one with the baby?"

I shook my head. "I don't think I've ever met her."

"Well, she knew you. She said you'd been attacked the night before. You came knocking on her door for help, covered in blood."

"What?" I'd said, stunned. "Attacked?"

My mind went straight to Roach. I had this vague, jarring memory of a fight. A fight on the doorstep—or were we still in the cab? Or was I confused, was I thinking of the fight I'd had with—I could hardly bring myself to think of it. I forced myself to look the memory in the eye. Lydia, I'd said something awful to Lydia. Was I thinking of that? Uncomfortable, unpleasant memories swarmed like flies, buzzing in and out of focus.

"She said you didn't seem particularly drunk, just that you were . . ." He searched for the right word. ". . . on edge."

"On edge?"

"You climbed over her garden fence, and got into your flat through your bedroom window. You really don't remember that?"

I shook my head, trying not to cry. It was like someone else had taken control of me, made me do things I'd never do. I felt sick.

"She was really worried when we said you hadn't turned up to work. Like, *really* worried. She said you'd had a head injury, and we all agreed it was a potential medical emergency."

I touched the wound on my forehead, the crags of a freshly formed scab. "I have no memory of that at all."

"We called the police and asked for a welfare check. And . . ." His eyes shone with tears, and he ran a hand over his face. "When I saw you lying on the kitchen floor, I thought you were dead, Lau. If you hadn't knocked on your neighbour's door the night before, we might never have found you in time. It was a miracle."

A miracle. It didn't feel like a miracle. It felt like a nightmare. I tried to imagine the version of myself that would make these absurd, illogical choices: knocking on a stranger's door with a mask of sobriety plastered over my face, climbing over a garden fence . . . but it just didn't marry up. I would *never* leave my bedroom window unlocked. Although my phone was missing, my keys and purse were all on the sofa. I'd poured myself a drink, turned on a lamp. What on earth had happened? What had changed between Roach leaving and me knocking on my neighbour's door? It didn't make sense.

I felt haunted by what might have been, haunted by my missing memories and the elaborate possibilities that loomed in my mind's eye late at night. The space felt tainted, and my ability to know peace in Walthamstow had turned sour, rancid. It was time for me to leave. I had to move out of my flat anyway—my landlord had seen to that. But it was more than that. I had to leave Walthamstow, and I had to leave Spines. I had to get away from Roach.

Roach, the missing piece of the puzzle. I'd thought about sending her a message, asking her if she knew what had happened to me that night, but something held me back. When I thought of Roach, I felt out of breath, felt the rising panic of an anxiety attack tightening my chest. In the end, my desire to distance myself from her overwhelmed my desire to find out what happened, and deep down, I knew I'd never trust a word that came out of her mouth anyway.

Eli swallowed the last of his coffee and stood up.

"Sorry about your face," I said, nodding to the neat round scab that marked his cheek. He replied with a wry smile, and drew me into a hug. A warm hand found my shoulder blade, right where the wing would be if I were an angel, and with a vertiginous rush, he said: "I'm sorry, I'm really truly sorry that things ended the way they did."

"Me too," I'd said, thinking of both now, and then that first drunken kiss, that first scene missing.

"Let's hang out soon," he'd said, and I said sure. I began packing that night.

I handed in my notice. Sharona pushed HR into letting me take garden leave so I didn't have to work my notice period, and that was it. I was free. I started looking for work outside of London, and that's how I found myself here: working in a beautiful indie bookshop in a charming seaside town.

Sharona visited last year. She'd buzzed the curls from one side of her head, left the others to grow wild, streaked with grey. She liked the gentle vibe of the place, admired the little bookshop I called home.

"It suits you," she said, taking it all in. I knew exactly what she meant: the pink and white striped paper bags, the colourful sticks of rock by the till, the smell of doughnuts frying in hot oil drifting from the pier, the view of the endless glittering sea.

"It's much quainter than Brighton," she added. "We moved there, did I tell you? Fell in love with the shop, fell in love with the vibe."

"How was the refit?" I asked her lightly, and we both knew what I was really asking.

"Fine," she said, her eyes crinkling into a kind smile. "He asked Lydia to marry him."

"Gross," I said, looking away. She laughed.

We walked to a pub on the seafront for pints of lager in plastic cups. Gulls circled above our heads, their broad white wings taut against the wind.

"You're happy, though, aren't you?" she said, touching my hand.

"I'm happy," I said. "I just wish I could have found my way here without throwing petrol over my entire life and setting it on fire."

"You had to rest at rock bottom," she replied, "to gather the strength to swim back up to the surface."

I liked that. I had to rest at rock bottom to gather the strength to swim back to the surface of my life. I hadn't realised how long I'd been holding my breath, drowning under the weight of my pain. There's no resolution to grief, no happy ending. It's a clock that never stops ticking, a day that never ends. My mother is gone. It's just one of those things, and then it's everything at once. And while I ache for her—I always will—I needed space to breathe, space to heal.

Once I left Walthamstow, I found I could write again. I wrote about my mother, and I honoured the four other women who lost their lives that summer: Elsie, Agata, Safa, Lana.

I rediscovered joy in the simple things. Seeing old friends and making new ones. Feeling the sun on my face, sand underfoot. Finding sea glass on the beach, the sharp edges rubbed smooth by the tumbling waves. Joy in sharing my home again, joy in hearing the wind chimes play their melodious music, joy in finding a fresh bowl of fragrant tomatoes left by a kind neighbour.

Joy in coming home, and knowing I am safe.

EPILOGUE PART 2
AUGUST 2022

A distant church bell knells for eleven. I take a final drag on my rollie and flick the spent filter on to the cobblestones, where it catches on the briny sea air and tumbles into the gutter. Lazy waves lap against the shingled shore as I follow the gentle curve of the lane and stop in front of a small house with a front path like stepping-stones. Overhead, a seagull cries out, and the melodic notes of a wooden wind chime hanging from the rafters of the porch answer.

A still, quiet morning. It's beautiful here, peaceful.

There's a basket of misshapen tomatoes on the window ledge by the front door, pinning down a note that flutters in the breeze. I pick up a sun-warm tomato, feel the weight of it in my hand, and read the note, scrawled in quick pencil:

> *L & G,*
> *came knocking to see if you guys wanted some of these toms. We have loads. Pop in for a drink soon?*

The neighbours all know one another. A real community. They share what they have when there's a glut: rhubarb, courgettes, tomatoes. They drink in each other's gardens, walk each other's dogs. They even leave their doors unlocked from time to time.

I let myself in, and it's effortless and welcoming, nothing like the double-locked doors, frosted windows, and impenetrable blinds of London. The house smells fresh and clean, a floral hit under the pervasive scent of furniture polish. A shoe rack holds a neatly polished pair of Doc Martens with yellow stitches, several pairs of battered Converse, and a collection of ballet flats in forest green, cranberry, midnight blue.

The living room is lined with bookshelves, a framed *Frances Ha* poster on the chimney breast above a fireplace. The sofa is a rich green velvet. I run my hand over it like I'm stroking a cat, and the colour changes from sage to the deep green of winter foliage. The depth that velvet brings to color.

I walk to the bookshelves and scan the spines until I find what I'm looking for: a sombre literary memoir called *Their Inconsequential Moments Were Beautiful*. I smile at the familiarity of the title, turn the book over in my hands, feel the weight of it, stroke the hard matte cover, flip the pages, and take in the smell of freshly printed ink on paper.

Laura.

Laura, with her poetry.

Laura, with her tragedy.

Not Laura Bunting, but Laura Cordovan. Not the name of her father but the name of her mother. Of course she hadn't published under the name Bunting. Bunting was garden parties, Wimbledon, royal weddings. Cordovan was blood. Trauma and darkness. It was lonely London streets shrouded with rain, a killer, a murderer of women, on the loose for one miserable summer.

I hadn't been wrong: Laura Bunting had died on that kitchen floor. I had killed her, but there was no corpse, no autopsy, no funeral, no grave. Laura Bunting had died, but Laura Cordovan had risen from the ashes and taken her place.

When I realised I wasn't a murderer in the traditional sense, I'd spent a long time looking for Laura Bunting, but I never found her because she didn't exist. I went to poetry readings at the Nib, scanned the crowd for her bottle-blonde hair. I looked for her in the local bars and pubs, half expected to see her with a drink in hand, a bright crimson smile plastered over her face. I looked for her camel-coloured raincoat down the market. I looked for her in bookshops, peered through the windows of trendy indies and big branches of Spines, but she was never there.

I imagined her moving to Brighton, I imagined her leaving bookselling, I imagined her running her own shop. I imagined her and Eli falling in love; I imagined them falling out, never speaking again. All the possibilities spread out like a tarot deck, and there was no way to know which cards were correct. Her social media accounts were gone, and there was no digital trail connecting our shared past to her present.

Eventually Sam was the one who spotted it—a new hardback, a memoir of murder by a debut writer called Laura Cordovan.

Cordovan.

I knew this story. I knew it well. I looked her up, and there she was. She had been there all along, hiding in plain sight: her social media accounts, her website, her agent, a long read for the *Guardian*, an article in the *Bookseller*. It was all there, the last three years of her life falling open, one page at a time.

Her life online is sunshine and strawberry splits, seagulls and shingle beaches, sun-bleached huts painted in marshmallow colours. She looks happy. She buys herself flowers and secondhand books and coffees in paper cups, and she reads poetry and writes every day. I look for traces of who she shares her life with, a boyfriend or a lover lingering on the edge of the frame, but there are no clues. Perhaps just a flatmate, perhaps she's finally acquiesced and let someone else in.

I skim-read the blurb again. *Deeply personal memoir . . . mother murdered at the hands of . . . poetic examination of trauma . . . critique of contemporary true crime . . . lyrical, raw, and unflinching . . .*

Typical, so typical of Laura to give me so little. It doesn't matter though. Things are different now. I am no longer the night to her day. I am no longer a killer—if I could ever lay claim to such an auspicious title.

No. We're equals, peers. I slide her book back on to the shelf and from my tote bag, I pull out a proof copy of my own. In careful Sharpie—no scrawled biro for Ms. Laura Cordovan—I write a personalised dedication on the front page of my book, the project that I began on those lonely December night shifts, later bolstered by my correspondence with Lee Frost.

> *Dear Laura,*
> *I hope you're as excited to read mine as I am to read yours.*
> *Your friend and fan,*
> *BROGAN ROACH xox*

I hold it to my heart for a moment. When Laura reads my book, she will see the care and the love that I put into telling our story, the time I spent getting to know Lee Frost, the letters we exchanged, the friendship that blossomed, the details only he could give me. She will understand that we are not so different after all. We each have our story to tell.

I shelve the copy of *Summer of Frost: Walking in the Shadow of the Stow Strangler* by Brogan Roach next to *Their Inconsequential Moments Were Beautiful* by Laura Cordovan. Our books look good together, side by side.

For the first time in years, our dark connection sparks. The sea air stirs the wind chimes, and the front door opens. As she steps into the hall, I take a deep breath and smell roses.